Dor Slinkard is an unstoppable storyteller. Be it through writing or voice, her stories will enthral. Inspired by life, especially as a jillaroo in outback Australia and later as a race horse trainer, her imagination thrives. In her lasting marriage to Wade, a jackaroo now horse trainer, they have produced two children and they, in turn, five grandchildren.

ISBN **978-0-6452425-8-4** (Paperback)
ISBN **978-0-6452425-7-7** (E-Book)

First Published (2025)

ACKNOWLEDGEMENTS

All stories begin with inspiration, and although mine was a sad tale about Violet Murrell and her horse Garryowen. The tragedy of their death has touched me throughout my life. I hope I have paid tribute to Violet by creating a similar character in Davina, a strong, talented, and much-loved horsewoman.

I am deeply indebted to my friends who have edited, proofread, and provided valuable feedback. Without you, I would not have endured.

Sandy Gray, you are always my first go-to. I value your opinion greatly. Your honesty is paramount.

Carolyn Broadfield once said. "I do not read without holding a pen." Thank you, my dear friend. Your contribution was invaluable.

Sarah Howitt, your knowledge of dressage helped provide a believable journey through the horse competitions and depiction from Davina, my main character.

Toni Mathews, thank you for your advice and expertise on riding dressage and the primary breed of horses that first performed the art.

My LinkedIn friend Lee Rodgers, I value your information about Helsinki, particularly the Hartwall Long Drink, which was made there mainly for the patrons of the 1952 Summer Olympics. I am now a fan of the beverage.

Margaret Mooney, you are my guiding light in all things literary. I would not strive to improve if it were not for you sitting invisibly on my shoulder, beginning with my first novel, where I needed to amend nearly every sentence.

Deb Jones, my I.T. Angel and dear friend. I could not publish my books without you. You are a genius.

Finally, after meeting the delightful and avid reader, Jenni Bischkopf, who offered to proofread and help edit my near-final draft, I extend my utmost appreciation.

AUTHOR'S NOTE
EVIE AND ME

Researching historical facts gives me almost as much pleasure as writing stories.

At twenty-one, Davina Buchanan, after proving herself to be one of Australia's most prominent equestrians, was selected to represent Australia in the Olympic Dressage Competition in Stockholm 1956. FICTION.

Equestrian events were to be included in the Melbourne Olympic Games in November 1956. However, foreign horses had to be quarantined in Australia for 6 months before the games, making it impossible for their riders to compete. Therefore, the Australian Olympic Equestrian Games were transferred to Stockholm.

Australian dressage riders did not compete in Stockholm. However, the Australian Three-Day Event Team did. FACT.

Dressage was practiced unofficially in Australia during the 1900s. The Victorian Mounted Police were the first to give a dressage exhibition at the Royal Melbourne Show in 1872.

From then on, dressage enthusiasts around Australia held unofficial events, mainly in Victoria, until the Equestrian Federation, established in 1951, finally recognised the need for professional competitions.

Novice dressage competitions began at the Royal Melbourne Show in 1950. And after that, dressage thrived Australia-wide. FACT.

The art of dressage was first introduced in Europe in the 16th century, training war horses to avoid injury by moving fluently and evasively from their enemy. FACT.

By the same author

Bugger of a Kid
Wrong Side of the Fence
Henri-etta

***For the Love of* Trilogy**
Book 1 – For the Love of Patrick
Book 2 – For the Love of Freedom
Book 3 – For the Love of Justice

Dor Slinkard

EVIE AND ME

Come, howling wind,
Booming thunder
Beating rain.
Nature's orchestra,
Drown my fear.
For in your wake,
A new day is here.

Dor Slinkard

PROLOGUE

The sounds of laughter in empty hallways, the chill of absence settling in the marrow of her bones. The pain of loss weighs against letting anyone in again. These memories circled, as she tried to forget.

Then, as predicted, the storm unleashed its fury, extinguishing the lights.

Unable to see the final pages of her writing, the woman leaned back in her chair and let go of those old feelings. As quickly as they faded, an unearthly message arrived. *Love and Light will never fail.*

Smiling at the positive affirmation, she wondered how it would help the memoirs she'd almost completed.

She could still feel the loss lingering in the corners of the room, smell the faint wood smoke clinging to the faded armchair, and hear the brittle crackle of old photographs tucked away out of sight. As she listened to the sound of rain beating against the window, she recalled nights spent waiting for voices that never returned.

The storm lessened throughout the night, and the cottage quietened with the heavy residue of old grief.

Morning came, and the woman moved with practiced care, her gestures gentle yet uncertain. Each one shaped by recollections she rarely allowed to surface. She struggled over boggy ground to reach the open shelter and watched the child, Evie, sleeping at the horse's side, feeling a familiar ache—a warning she could neither name nor ignore.

Evie was drawn to the comfort of horses, especially the gentle protection of Polly, as she sought refuge from the world. The nearby 'big house,' once a part of the family estate, now served as a sanctuary for those with nowhere else to go. Wary of forming attachments, the woman resolved to help rather than to embrace, knowing the hurt of inevitable loss. She felt her compassion pressing against caution, given her current feelings.

She told herself she was only offering shelter, nothing more.

Yet, as she saw the child's silent plea for security, something shifted: a sense of kindness —or was it love ?—stirred, but was overshadowed by apprehension. The boundaries between longing and duty blurred in the hush of dawn. The cottage, *her* refuge, now felt exposed. As if the arrival of this child had disturbed something she had kept hidden even from herself.

Here in the aftermath of the storm, two lives, one marked by loss, the other by abandonment, would intersect in a quiet cottage on the edge of a charity estate. The woman, shaped by old grief and hesitant hope, compelled by her psychotherapist to confront her past, found herself unexpectantly linked to Evie, a child whose silence and resilience spoke of hardship.

The bright morning rekindled the estate's legacy, providing shelter to the vulnerable, as its benefactor wrestled with the possibility of finally healing.

The woman continued to watch the child embrace the old pony, Polly, who waited unmoving, as if guarding her foal. The woman weighed her every gesture, uncertain whether she was opening a door or building another wall.

In the ambiguity of morning, her resolve wavered, and the question lingered.

Was she saving the child, or was the child saving her?

The hush of the morning offered no answers.

Two lives drawn together by nameless forces, in a place where the past refused to sleep.

CHAPTER 1
DAVINA BUCHANAN'S MEMOIRS
EARLY CHILDHOOD

My Father, Jock Buchanan, owned one of Australia's most successful engineering companies, which afforded our family wealth and privilege. As a child, I rarely saw unfamiliar faces, and I was too young to be aware of other families struggling to make ends meet. I led a carefree and, what most would say, a pampered childhood. To others, my early years must have seemed like a fairy-tale existence - mostly, they were.

I'm sorry to anyone else who might read this. My psychotherapist said that writing my memoirs would aid in my healing. At this stage, I can only write facts without any emotional attachment. Feelings are my sleeping enemy, not to be disturbed lest they burn me to death, which is what I'm trying to avoid.

Or am I?

I was born on the first of August 1935, *the horse's birthday*, less than one year after my brother Joseph. Mother swore she'd never give birth again. I remember when I was old enough to understand the reason why. I'd often overhear her discussing the subject with her friends. "The children were born far too close. Not even one year apart. I almost lost my life giving birth to Davina," Mother would say. "It was such a terrible time for me. I hate to admit it, but I suffered dreadfully." At this point, she would sniffle into her embroidered handkerchief and then wipe away tears of self-pity.

Despite Mother's indifference to me, I was a happy and contented child. How could I not be? I had everything I wished for.

My parents were deeply involved in thoroughbred horse racing, and I recall on many occasions standing beside my Father, smiling up at him as he held a gilded cup aloft, or the trophy for that particular race. Later celebrations were held at our stately home, where our servants catered to us; most of them lived in cottages within the grounds of our three-thousand-acre property, Carlina.

Our staff consisted of Frederick - or *Freddy* - the chauffeur; Mary and Sarah, the maids; and my favourite - Betty, our cook. Oh yes, and the gardeners, Clive and James. They lived together in the same cottage. (I remember adults muttering about it being *very inappropriate* - I didn't have a clue why). And then came the jackaroos - Laurie and Jim. They resided on the far edge of Carlina, nearer the cattle yards and the river. From time to time, Father also hired mechanics and tradespeople from a nearby small village.

I think it's time to explain how our property's name, Carlina, came about. It originated from the first Jock Buchanan, who arrived in Australia in 1857. He was a Scotsman who believed in natural remedies derived from the Carlina thistle. Hence, he brought an enormous supply with him, and for want of a better name, he called the property Carlina. Although the plant survived in the harsh Australian landscape, it did not flourish as he wished. Therefore, Jock the Second, my great-great-grandfather, could only nurture the plants well enough for personal use.

The mansion we lived in had been home to the past four generations of the Buchanan dynasty, each of whom had added a wing or two, totaling twenty rooms. The ballroom is the largest of all. When our parents were preoccupied and the weather inclement, Joseph and I skidded fearlessly around the polished floor, our woollen socks providing a thrilling, slippery ride. When we were slightly older, around six or seven, we added roller skates to the occasion; it was the ultimate feeling of freedom. Even though our ballroom was small compared to the outside areas, I didn't mind – it was the speed and danger I loved.

At age ten, I was given my first pony, Polly, and from then on, I spent every waking hour with my adorable dapple-grey filly. If I wasn't brushing Polly, I was riding her, including lessons from Jacques Attal, 'the best riding instructor money can buy.' Father had claimed before introducing me to Jacques, who I later learned could not refuse Father's enormous monetary offer.

Initially, Jacques schooled me in dressage – a safe and elegant riding discipline, according to my father. But many years later, after Father died, I pursued the dream he had declared *far too dangerous for a girl*. I became a three-day event competitor, rode in point-to-point races, and became an amateur jockey around country race meetings in Victoria

- but more of that later.

Jacques Attal, my riding instructor, was a young German Jew whom Father not only hired as my personal riding instructor but also offered a cottage for Jacques to live in on Carlina. From the moment I met Jacques, I listened intently to what he told me and did my best to follow his instructions. Over the following six years, apart from riding, Jacques taught me to speak German.

He had escaped the Nazi terror campaign in Europe before the war had begun. His uncle Aaron had helped plan his nephew's escape. Aaron had migrated to Australia in 1935, the year I was born, and before devastation fell heavily upon the Jews in Germany. *My Jacques*, as I called him, would have died if not for his uncle Aaron.

Jacques told me, "I miss my little sister. Her name is Enid. For all I know, she is dead, along with my parents. You, Davina, remind me of Enid," he said wistfully, though I'd notice his sadness almost disappear when he smiled at me.

Once the war had ended, Jacques tried to locate his family but found no trace of them. They had refused to leave their home and business in Cologne, despite the presence of unmistakable warning signs. Uncle Aaron had offered his entire family the chance to come to Australia and make a new life. Finally, in 1938, after many arguments with his father, Jacques accepted his uncle Aaron's offer.

Aaron was a brilliant horseman and had played a significant part in training German warhorses, mainly Warmbloods, for the German Army. He'd trained Holsteiners to the highest level of dressage, including the prestigious Olympic Games. He had detested his involvement in the military, knowing his beloved horses would be among the inevitable fatalities on the war front.

Mr. Meyer owned the stables where Uncle Aaron worked. He was a tenth-generation German with political connections, so he knew about the coming danger for Jewish people. However, he was sympathetic to Uncle Aaron's precarious position as a Jew and held great regard for him as a man and an outstanding horseman.

Before the real trouble began in Germany, Mr. Meyer arranged for Aaron to travel to Australia, taking several of his Holsteiner horses with him. It was a clever ploy to save both Aaron's life and the finest of Mr. Meyers' warmblood breeding stock. Uncle Aaron would be safe in Australia, and he remained so, even when the internment of all German nationals became mandatory during the war. Fortunately, Aaron obtained special dispensation to continue training and breeding his Holsteiners. He also took on the role of Chief Instructor to the Victorian Police Cadets and their horses. I'm sure this endeared him to the many who had chosen to look the other way.

Although I was still young, I had no trouble understanding the situation and feeling pain for those unfortunate, innocent families who perished because they wore the Star of David.

Before and after school, I received demanding riding instruction from 'my Jacques,' whom I affectionately called, and we attended horse shows most weekends. If Father were not at the races or entertaining at home on a Sunday, he'd accompany us to whatever show we were competing in, no matter how many miles we needed to travel.

And we won every event.

After my hundredth ribbon, I felt guilty about winning all the time because, at each show, I'd take note of other children riding their often undernourished, dull-coated ponies who showed little energy after being ridden many miles to the show, usually the day before. Those particular families camped overnight in make-do tents, and I'd hear their laughter echo through the night while I lay alone, snug and comfortable in a caravan-come-horse truck. The families who made these sacrifices for their children appeared the happiest.

Of course, wealthy families like mine competed, but no other children had a personal instructor. They ostracized me because they thought I had an unfair advantage. I had to agree. Though I hated to be shunned.

At the same time, I felt sad for the families who had no money to buy top show horses for their children or even purchase good feed for their ordinary ponies. I thought seriously about the fairness of my situation compared to those who had far less yet seemed happy and content. It perplexed me until I felt I had the answer. If those needy children would not accept my help or my Father's charity, which I sometimes offered, I'd avoid the situation by simply not seeing those families again. I eventually realised I could not change their circumstances or mine.

The day came when I said to Jacques, "I'm almost twelve. I want to ride in dressage competitions like they do in Europe, and I want to do show jumping and cross-country." I added petulantly, "I'm bored with horse shows, riding around and around in silly circles."

Jacques smiled. "Of course, little one. You are indeed ready for dressage. However, it is a new equestrian mode in Australia with few competitions. We will talk about jumping later." He gave a conspirative wink. "But, I am sorry to say, Polly must be retired. You will need a bigger horse. And I should no longer call you 'little one.' You are so tall that I think you need a horse that stands around fifteen-two hands."

"But why?" I demanded. "Polly's well-trained, Jacques. She could compete in dressage; she'd be outstanding. I know she would."

"Yes, but she is too small for you now. And you are too tall for her." He chuckled. "I was about to tell you this, Davina, but you have now suggested we proceed to the next level, and I agree that is what we should do. Let me speak with your Father. I'm sure he will approve. And then, we can begin searching for a dressage horse." Jacques placed his chin in his hand before saying, "Yes, of course! My uncle Aaron! He has bred horses by crossing his Holsteiner stallions with thoroughbred mares. I will telephone him tonight. Perfect!"

Within a week, Jacques had selected a magnificent, fifteen-three-hand burgundy-bay mare. She was presented to me with a pink bow tied around her neck. I watched as she strutted elegantly out of our truck with her head held high. "My rise to equestrian fame has just begun!" I declared before reaching up to wrap my arms around her sleek neck. My wish, it seemed, was also my command.

A young, talented rider, Charlotte Simms, who worked for Uncle Aaron, had been schooling this stunning, kind-natured mare to the Intermediate Dressage level. Jacques shook his head in dismay when he heard the massive amount my Father had paid for the horse, which I named 'Miss Carlina Molly.'

It was in that moment that I became acutely aware of how privileged I was; whatever I wanted was given to me without question. I remember accepting this fact humbly because something within me always reminded me to be grateful for my good fortune. And the best way to show this was to become the finest rider possible, for my Father and Jacques, whom I knew, had told Father he wished to leave his employ to broaden his prospects. Father's comeback was to offer Jacques more money. He would have been foolish to refuse, and thus, Jaques remained my trainer on the condition that he could have every Monday and Tuesday off to work for his Uncle, Aaron. I've learned there is always room for compromise in everything we try to do.

In November 1949, Mr. Meyer, *Aaron's saviour*, died in Germany and bequeathed his Australian property to Uncle Aaron. Their Holsteiner Stud sat twenty miles north of Riddles Creek, where our property lay.

Jacques' change in routine allowed him to meet and mix with different people, in particular the lovely Charlotte Simms, who, as I mentioned, trained horses for Uncle Aaron. Their attraction was instantaneous, as Jacques later told me, much to my horror. I felt cheated and heartbroken! *My Jacques* belonged to me! I intended to marry him when I grew up!

I'm now able to call Charlotte lovely. Back then, I hated her. Jealousy and hate are two feelings that, many years later, I learned brought only destruction! It was the first time in my young life that I suffered the pain of jealousy.

What made it even worse was that Betty, our cook, would remind me of Jacques's love affair most days. I must say, she was as pleased as any surrogate mother could be. "I'm *so* happy for them. They make *such* a lovely young couple," said Betty. *Constantly.* After hearing this for the twentieth time, I swiped a bowl of cake mix off the kitchen bench during a fit of jealous rage. Betty cried, "Oh no! I had terrible trouble with that new recipe!"

I ran to the stables, sobbing uncontrollably, and threw myself on a pile of straw, which made me sneeze and sneeze. Polly whinnied before nuzzling me; *she felt my pain, I knew she did.* Who else could I turn to but Polly, *my first pony*?

I rolled onto my back, the straw crackly beneath, and lamented. I had no one to turn to. No one cared or understood. Not even my brother, Joseph, who most of the time had his head stuck in a book or was trying out a science experiment. My father frequently went overseas on business trips, and my mother didn't seem to care about my problems. I swore to hide the hurt in a corner of my heart. But then my inner voice said, 'Love, be generous, and never hate.' It was as if I were two people.

Later, I crossed my fingers behind my back and apologised to Betty.

"It was an accident, Betty."

"It's all right, pet," Betty said, embracing me. "But it would be best if you slowed down, Davina. You're always rushing about." She smiled, clasped my head, and tenderly kissed my forehead.

CHAPTER 2
EVIE'S STORY

On fine days, Evie's mother, Cathy, lined their rickety wheelbarrow with a woollen blanket, cushioning her daughter for the long, bumpy journey to her old pa's farm. The air shimmered with birdsong, their wings slicing through the sky above, and she listened to the brook's laughter entwined with the wind and cows' lowing.

These sounds and sights etched themselves into Evie's soul over the years, shaping her longing for a life in the country. Where nature ruled and hardship was part of the landscape. She knew instinctively that sharing the environment meant nurturing it, enduring the cruelest snow-filled winters, droughts that cracked the earth, and floods that swallowed the ground. Yet, her soul belonged there, and hardship was unimportant to one so young. Evie became more determined as the years passed, *"It's where I'm meant t'be, with Old Pa on his farm and wid Daisy, d'horse."*

However, back in their small cottage, nearer the village, which Ma kept clean and polished, Evie knew something wasn't right when Ma offered Evie's da, Sean, little to eat. He'd glare at his meagre portion as if it were Ma's fault. Ma would say accusingly, "Well, dere be plenty t'eat on m'Pa's farm."

Da would bang his fist on the table. "I'll never take food from dat old turd! We'll not be takin' anytin' from him ever again! And dat's dat!"

How many times had Evie heard this conversation? Yet whenever her da was away searching for work, Ma would lift Evie into the rickety old wheelbarrow and laboriously push her the three miles to Old Pa's farm, even when Evie was old enough to walk.

Once there, Ma would sink into Old Pa's armchair and sleep while he took Evie to milk Prudence, the cow. Next, they'd gather vegetables from the garden, and later, Old Pa would sit Evie on Daisy, and Evie would feel like she was on top of the world and there was no better place to be.

Evie loved Pa's gentleness with animals; it made her smile, and his magic tricks had her laughing. But Evie knew living on Pa's farm would never happen because Sean didn't like Old Pa, so Ma never told him about their visits.

When Sean went job hunting, he'd often come home stinking of whiskey and knocking things about in anger. "Y'like a bear with a sore tooth," Ma would say. Thankfully, he'd never be angry enough to lay a hand on Ma or Evie. Later, when in bed, Evie would hear Da snoring or Ma giggling.

One day, when Evie was six, Da came home as happy as a clown, waving a piece of paper like he'd won the lottery.

"Dis's our escape, Cathy. Finally! We're goin t'Australia. Assisted migrants, we'll be. Dere's more work dere than a man can handle. I'm tellin' y'm'beauty. Dis'll be d'makin of us." Sean grabbed Cathy's waist and twirled her around the kitchen until she laughed out loud.

"Let me be takin' a look at dat." Cathy grabbed the paper, her eyes twinkling with each encouraging word. She looked up from the document and, with a tone of bewilderment, asked, "Well, can y'be tellin' me, Sean, where are we gonna get d'ten pounds t'board d'ship to Australia?"

Sean lowered his head, shuffling his feet.

"Don't y'be worryin about dat, Cathy, m'love." He looked up with a cunning grin. "It's all been organised. I've got a special job dat's gonna pay big money - enough for our passage and t'set us up real fine in Australia. The man I'll be workin' for has contacts over dere. So don't y'be fussin', m'darlin. Just pack y'bags and be ready. We'll be leavin' on Mondee!" It was Friday.

Cathy had little time to let Pa know, but found the chance when Sean said the following day, "I have t'go out f'a wee while, Cathy. I'll be home later. After I've done d'job." He winked before his lips met hers in a passionate kiss. Cathy felt her head spin, and her heart sing - as it always did when Sean kissed her like there was no tomorrow.

Once Sean had gone, Cathy seized her opportunity, leaving Evie behind after handing her a pencil and paper. "That'll keep y'busy, m'darlin. I need t'be quick t'say goodbye t'Pa and be puttin' flowers on me ma's grave. Y'be a good girl now, Evie, and don't be movin', y'hear me?"

Evie nodded, making her own plans.

**

Old Pa's eyes filled with tears, and his fists clenched as Cathy told him her news. "How could y'be so cruel, Cathy? First, me only son was killed in d'war, and then m'beloved Maisie not long after. She died of a broken heart, she did. And now you and Evie are leavin' me!"

Pa's silent anger rose, focusing on Sean, whom he'd never trusted.

After marrying Cathy, Old Pa had given Sean a fair go when he offered him a job on the farm. But Sean was lazy, always finding the easy way to do things. Pa had told Cathy the truth. "That husband o'your'n has no common sense, and he's as lazy as an old cow lyin about chewin' her cud," Old Pa had declared after sacking Sean. "He's not only useless but downright dangerous t'have around, and he holds no kindness to d'animals. Sean might look pretty, Cathy, but he's good for nuttin'. Except drinkin' in d'pub with the money dat coulda put food on d'table for you and d'littlin. And where does he get d'cash anyway? I ask you? Maybe he's good at somtin, and dat'd be thievin! He's a cunnin bugga dat's f'sure!"

Eventually, Old Pa gave up trying to warn Cathy about Sean. She'd never listen. But now, he was about to lose his only daughter and granddaughter due to Sean's belligerence, so he gave Cathy another heartfelt plea.

"When she's grown, Evie'll be d'makin of dis family. You mark me' words, Cathy. She's smart. And she's willin t'learn about everytin in life. Please, Cathy, let dat bludger go. See what he can make of himself. And if he makes good in Australia, he can send f'yer. Yer has t'listen to me, Cathy. I'm talkin sense. There'll always be a warm bed and plenty t'eat here." Old Pa hung his head in shame. "Until I'd have t'be sellin the farm if things don't pick up." He then looked up, his eyes bright. "It should bring enough to clear me' debts and pay d'rent f'a few years. Maybe even buy a small cottage where we could live. Please, don't go. It would be breakin me' heart. It would."

Cathy sighed in recognition of all she'd heard before. And Old Pa knew his plea had failed. He flopped into his armchair, and Cathy kissed his forehead.

"I'm sorry, Pa. I have t'go."

Tears blurred Cathy's vision as she hurried to gather wildflowers for her mother's grave. She placed them reverently and sat on the ground, declaring, "I'm sorry, t'be leavin yer Ma. We'll be goin t'Australia. I tink it's f'da best."

Cathy kissed the earth covering her mother's corpse, crossed her chest, and hurried home.

When bursting into her cottage kitchen, she called, "Evie! Where is yer? Evie." Not a sound. "Oh, Dear Jesus, Mother Mary, and Joseph."

Searching each room, Cathy noted that Evie had packed her bag with everything she owned, including the pencil and paper. She sat, trying to fathom, "Of course! Dat's where she'd be. Pa's farm. But what will I tell Sean if I can't find her?"

Sean had forbidden Cathy to go to the farm since the almighty row he'd had with the old man. Cathy had never believed it, but Pa did. Sean walked a tightrope with the law. There were only minor skirmishes with the gang Sean was a member of. They stole saleable objects around their small Irish village and offloaded them miles away.

Pa and his friends could never prove what they suspected about the gang, especially since the handsome young men had every girl in the village singing their praises. Many of them, including Sean, had charmed the pants off the local girls and were now married with children.

Most families shrugged off the thefts with their hands in the air. Who wants to break up families and see their daughters unhappy and alone? Not old Pa or his mates. The entire scenario had caught in Pa's throat like a fishhook.

I only bear it because I'll lose me, daughter and granddaughter if I'd said too much t'Cathy. But I have notin t'lose now. They'll be gone anyway.

I'll go over der and have one last try to talk Cathy int'stayin.

He was about to grab his hat off the hook when he heard Cathy's call, "Pa, Pa, where are yer? I've lost Evie. Help me find 'er."

Pa shuffled from the hallway into the kitchen, where Cathy stood heaving for air. "Hold yer horses, Cathy. Now tell me what's happened?"

"I left Evie behind. She would've slowed me down." Cathy paused, taking deep breaths. But when I got home, I found Evie's bags packed. She's gone!"

His lips curled into a smile, and he raised an eyebrow. "She's a clever one, dat Evie." Pa's focus suddenly changed as if the Almighty had struck him. He held Cathy at arm's length, gently shaking her. "Can't yer see what yer doin, Cathy? It's all wrong. Australia's too far away. Evie knows she'll never be seein me or d'farm again. You know how much she loves d'animals, especially Daisy. And I'm tellin' yer d'truth, Cathy. Sean's mixed up in a thieving gang, always has been. So he'll be gettin in t'trouble wherever he goes!"

Cathy sighed. *Is Pa right? Should I stay until Sean makes good in*

Australia? She shook her head and walked away, searching for Evie.

A massive bag of potatoes rested on an angle in the corner of the pantry, giving Evie the perfect hiding place. She'd listened to old Pa trying to talk sense to her ma. *Maybe Ma'll change her mind, and we'll stay with Pa. And Da can go widout us.* Evie waited.

Old Pa followed Cathy, then held her against his chest.

"Please, me only child, don't do dis t'Evie or me. It'll be breakin our hearts."

Steeling herself, Cathy delivered her final proclamation.

"I'm sorry, Pa, but it's f'the best. We need t'be makin a new start in anuda country. Dere's notin f'us here. And dis may be our only opportunity t'find a better life." She kissed Pa on the cheek. "And when we're settled, I'll send for yer.' Maybe y'can sell d'farm, and we'll buy anuda in Australia. How'd y'like dat, Pa?" She smiled hopefully.

Pa shook his head.

"No, me' lass, dis's where I'll be stayin. I'd never be leavin Maisie. But you go, if y'tink it's f'da' best. I won't be standin in y'way. But as y'father, I had t'be warnin yer.' I tink it's d'wrong ting t'be doin."

"I'm sorry, Pa. Believe me, I am sorry." Cathy sighed. "Now we have t'be findin Evie."

"No! Pa said." *You'll* have t'be findin Evie. I'll take no part in sendin me' wee darlin across the world to a strange land where I'll never be seein her again."

Pa walked outside, seeking comfort at Maisie's grave. Sitting on the rock he'd positioned for such moments, he spilled his heart out.

At the same time, Cathy searched Pa's house, in every corner, under beds, behind every piece of furniture, until she heard the cat, Fluffy, purring loudly. She followed the sound into the pantry, where she spotted its ginger body rubbing against a large sack of potatoes. Cathy crept in and pulled the bag back to see Evie cringing against the wall.

With a sigh of relief, Cathy gathered Evie in her arms. "Me' darling girl, your Da and me can't be leavin y'behind, now, can we? I promise yer. Pa'll be changin his mind when we're dere and doin well." Her voice rose an octave. "Why, I'll send him a boat ticket. He'd love dat. Pa's always loved boats and d'sea." Cathy laughed, sniffing back tears. "Shoulda been a fisherman or a sailor. He shoulda. Now come on, Evie, let's be gettin home and pack our bags. It's gonna be a great adventure, me' wee lass."

CHAPTER 3
DAVINA GROWING UP

After months of rejection, Charlotte stopped trying to befriend me. Instead, whenever she came to Carlina, I'd receive her cold shoulder, which speared me like a knife. Then I'd hear that inner voice: *'Love, never hate.'*

At first, I'd looked upon Jacques as my handsome young Prince. He'd captured my heart, and I thought he felt the same about me. Then it hit like poison when he embraced Charlotte and kissed her. I'd gather my strength, huff past, and throw orders at Jacques like he was the horse groom, not the champion equestrian that he was. I'd storm off, lock myself in my room, and cry with shame at how I'd behaved.

I told myself I had to end my fantasies about marrying Jacques, although letting go of the man I loved was the most painful experience of my life thus far. Many months later, I understood it was my first crush. And so, after shedding a million tears and having no more to give, I felt mature enough to accept the ongoing love between Jacques and Charlotte.

The truth was, I didn't want to lose either.

I think I also fell in love with Charlotte. It wasn't difficult. Her eyes were like a stormy ocean sprinkled with golden highlights. Her nose was straight and small. Not like mine; long and Roman. Plus, Charlotte's blonde hair smelled like flowers. *How did she achieve that when working with horses?* I remember wondering if she applied lipstick to her perfect lips or if they were a natural pink. She was what adults called '*a natural beauty*.' No wonder I was jealous. I was plain to look at—mousy brown hair, a nose too long, and skinny as a rake.

My dislike for Charlotte waned slowly, as did my jealousy. When struggling with my juvenile behaviour, which, *in my opinion*, is a war between hormones rushing like a torrent through your body, and your brain is busy building dams to stop the flow. God knows I tried hard to be more like Charlotte.

I then discovered we shared many interests, including wildlife and art. Most of all, Charlotte cared for and loved horses passionately, like me.

Accordingly, after a few months of no conflict, our friendship gradually blossomed into something special, and we often took time off to relax and swim in the river.

While lying on our towels in the shade on a furiously hot day, I coughed, hesitating to ask a personal question, "Charlotte…" She looked at me from under her hand, protecting her eyes from the sun.

"Yes, Davina."

I sat up and bit my tongue, a diversion maybe, to a stupid question, "Ah… Does your passion for horses outdo your love for Jacques?" She laughed—a beautiful laugh like nobody else's.

"Horses come first, before any man, Davina!" Charlotte said before her eyes became dreamy. "I'd always say that to my mum. And she'd say, "No, my girl, when you meet the right man, nothing else will compare to your love for him." Charlotte gazed into the distance, "And you know what, Davina, my mother was right." She lay back on her towel and said, with a wan smile. "I love Jacques with all my heart. But I will never stop loving horses."

She then leaned on her elbow and looked deeply into my eyes, as if searching for something. At first, I met her stare, then, feeling uncomfortable, I shuffled about on my towel, took a sip of water, and turned my reflection toward the river. Trying to lighten her reverie, I said, "Well, when I marry, I hope it's to a man who loves horses as much as I do."

"You will, Davina…but be careful," Charlotte said, her brow furrowed.

"Oh, that won't be for a very long time. Let's go swimming!"

Charlotte's words, 'be careful,' stuck. Why would she say such a thing? I didn't want my future prophesied. I intended to be in charge of my destiny. Or at least I thought I did. *That was another constant battle.*

Later, floating on the river, I focused on the swaying gum leaves and listened to the various bird songs filtering through the silence, creating a beautiful harmony. It reassured me I would find my mate one day, as they had. I made a vow to love my children equally and unconditionally. How could I blame my baby for almost costing me my life simply by being born? To her shame, my mother had. I thought I would never forgive her. Instinctively, I knew it wasn't my fault. It wasn't anybody's fault. And so, I promised myself never to blame anyone for anything. It would be a waste of time and happiness for me and others. But, of course, I know now that's easier said than done.

**

At that time, I attended the local primary school with twenty-five other pupils. Joseph had just entered sixth grade, one year ahead of me. He soon became bored with the simple curriculum, as his intellect surpassed that of all the other students and rivaled that of the teacher, Mr. Fuller.

"Under no circumstances will I put up with a show-off," Was Mr. Fuller's mantra.

Frustratingly, Joseph received no praise or encouragement. Instead, Mr. Fuller caned him harshly for giving the correct answer on every occasion. Joseph would later show me the welts on his legs and laugh, but I'd cry. The injustice troubled me, and I began to see the real world beyond my almost-perfect bubble.

Father eventually learned about Joseph's dilemma - from me, because I had nightmares about Joseph being flogged. I'd wake up frightened, feeling the pain inflicted on my brother. Therefore, Father decided it was time for Joseph to attend boarding school, which had always been Father's plan, but not until Joseph had reached the age to participate in high school. Nevertheless, Geelong Grammar welcomed Joseph sooner due to his extreme intelligence.

I was happy for Joseph, and he was delighted.

"Thanks for your concern, Davvy. I should have complained about that idiot teacher, but the kids would have called me a sissy. Now, I'll have nothing to do but study and learn science. I'm going to be the most famous scientist ever!"

Father had mounted his soapbox before this, delivering his speech like a true politician. "The best teachers in Australia tutor at Geelong Grammar, Joseph. Hopefully, by sending you to a school that caters to advances in farming and animal husbandry, it will inspire you to take a greater interest in Carlina. In particular, our Angus cattle, which our family has been proud to breed and show for the past four generations, I might add."

I had to giggle at Father's righteous proclamation, but I hoped so, too. However, I knew Joseph would suffer terribly if he were made to stay at Carlina, completing only agricultural chores. Not when he was totally engrossed with scientific stuff, especially explosives. It worried me when Joseph created things that went off with a bang and filled the air with suffocating smoke.

When the day came, I waved a reflective goodbye to Joseph and wished him happiness, to which he answered, "I cannot tell you how excited I am, Davvy. I know I'll love boarding school. I just know it."

And Joseph did. He told me so in every letter he wrote me.

On the other hand, I dreaded the thought of going to boarding school. It would mean I'd have to leave my beloved horses behind. Dressage competitions would be out of the question, *few as they were*. Jacques was right. Australian riders were slow to take on the more demanding sphere of training horses to dance, as I called dressage.

I began praying that instead of being wealthy, we could be poor. I dreamt of being a part of those ordinary, happy families I'd see around the horse shows, laughing, cooking sausages over an open fire, and brushing scruffy ponies.

Still, I watched in reverence as those scruffy ponies did their best for the children who rode them, wishing simultaneously to be part of those families. They seemed to have fun without wanting anything more.

On the contrary, I believed I needed to win because I had a private riding instructor and the best horses in Victoria. It seemed to me that the less pressure other children had, the more pleasure they had.

My wins, I'm sure, never triumphed over the happiness those children enjoyed. Instead, I felt left out and saddened. Then, when I returned home to my reality, I'd blow my feelings to the wind as I rode alone, I'd smile, knowing I owned a magnificent mare perfectly schooled by Charlotte, 'Miss Carlina Molly,' in line with Miss Polly. They were happy names, and I'd never be more joyous than in my own world with my horses. I woke every morning anxious to be with them, to snuggle into their warm bodies and brush their coats while confiding in them about my problems. They'd whinny and wave their heads about, their long manes swishing. It made me laugh to think they understood everything I was saying.

Later, when competing with 'Miss Carlina Molly,' I found it challenging to make friends with the senior dressage riders. Most glared at me with envy, and some with spite. Didn't they know it wasn't my fault that we had a lot of money? Loneliness became my second name. Father, my go-to companion, was mainly away on business, and Mother stayed active with charity fundraisers, not that I ever sought her company, or she'd accompany Father on his overseas trips.

I began to think that attending boarding school was a good idea. Surely, there would be girls who'd experienced the same upbringing, with wealthy parents who had little time for their daughters, perhaps?

Still, I had Jacques and Charlotte, who had become my chosen family, especially in the final year before I left to board at Melbourne Girls Grammar. In that year, my riding became paramount. I thought of and did nothing but try to achieve what no girl of thirteen had ever accomplished in the horse world. I felt hungry for knowledge and was determined to earn the highest dressage points. While not over-demanding, Molly, I did expect the best from her, which she provided!

Poor Jacques, I believe he certainly earned his money that year.

Molly and I began our competitions as the Dressage Federation demanded, with rhythm and regular pace in a plain snaffle bit, with only moderate movements, such as extended trot, hand gallops, and side passes, to name a few. Molly, in private, was trained for higher, more complex movements. But first, we entered the novice class, trying not to appear too arrogant. And as I knew we would, we rocketed through the next level of dressage.

I heard undercurrents of gossip. Some opponents spoke with jealousy, while others spoke with respect. Unfortunately, dressage competitions were few and far between; they only became accredited in Australia in 1950, when I turned fifteen.

I believed no one knew the real me. I felt an oddity. I didn't even know who I truly was. But to be the best, I knew I needed to be untouchable, and if I were to be shunned in return, I'd pretend I didn't care anymore. I weighed up the hurt of my loneliness against the feeling of superiority. Yes, I would remain proud of my achievements and not care what anyone else thought of me.

I'd armour myself against outside contempt and inner loneliness.

I know now. That's impossible.

Hurt has a way of seeping into your soul like a slow poison.

CHAPTER 4
EVIE'S DEPARTURE

Evie trembled, feeling trapped, as if anchored to the monstrous ship. In contrast, the gleaming white giant sent her ma, Cathy, spiralling into delight. But no words could console Evie on this *'grand sea adventure'* as her da had put it. Cathy assumed that Evie's refusal to board the ship was her fear of sailing, but Evie's heart remained with Old Pa and Daisy. How could she leave them, even with Sean promising a wonderful life in this strange, faraway land called Australia?

"Look up, Evie," said Cathy, "The ship's name is 'Fairsea', it means we'll have fair sailin'. It'll be fun. I promise." She hugged Evie just before Sean snatched Evie away and dragged her along the gangplank. Each step felt like a tooth extraction. Standing above deck, the ship's Captain noticed Evie's unwillingness and felt deeply sorry for the little girl whose Father kept yanking her arm.

"Come on, Evie, y'gettin in d'way! Hurry up!" Sean felt the Captain's stare and looked up, shaking his head in frustration.

Captain Teddy was an empathetic man, well-liked and respected by his crew, although a deep sadness weighed heavily on his heart and reflected in his eyes. His daughter would have been about Evie's age had she lived. Tragically, she and her mother were killed in an automobile accident while he was at sea.

The memory of his daughter Rose came in a flash. *This little girl would be the same age as Rose. She has the same colour hair and dimples that show even when she isn't smiling.*

To avoid another wrench on his heart, the Captain hurried down the gangway and scooped Evie into his arms, taking Cathy and Sean by surprise. He smiled like someone who had just won a prize.

"If you don't mind, I'll show your daughter where we serve ice cream. If that is alright, Mr. and Mrs...."

Cathy blinked into the sun. "Calan. Our name's Calan," she said, as the Captain whisked Evie away before Cathy could say another word.

Evie relaxed at the mention of ice cream. It was her favourite. *The Captain smells so nice, just like Ma when she goes out. And he likes me even doh I don't want t'sail on his ship.*

Comfortable in the Captain's arms, Evie glided between people moving in all directions, including men in uniform directing guests to their cabins. Their animation kept Evie's mind in the present, and before too long, the Captain pushed through swinging doors into the central kitchen.

"I'm sorry to bother you, Chef," said the Captain, "but I was hoping you'd have a bowl of ice cream for this young lady. She was quite hesitant to come on board. So I'm trying to persuade her that this is a great ship." He grinned at Evie, "I do apologise, miss. I don't even know your name."

Evie smiled as the chef scooped ice cream into a bowl.

"Me name's Evie."

"Well then, Evie, I will leave you here with your permission, for I need to continue my duties." The Captain gave a salute, "Enjoy your ice cream. I shall return with your mother shortly."

"I will, Mr. Captain. I won't be movin," Evie said, her eyes glued to the bowl of ice cream.

And so it was for the remainder of the voyage that Captain Teddy found comfort in the little girl who, most days, kept him company, almost to the point where Cathy became a little suspicious of his interest until the First Mate, Mr. Keen, explained. "The Captain lost his only daughter in an accident, Mrs Calan. I've seen the Captain's family photo, and Evie strongly resembles his deceased daughter Rose."

While Sean was happy to be free of Evie, especially with her complaining about wanting to go home, Cathy had to agree that the journey would have been a nightmare without the Captain's constant care. Cathy chuckled whenever Evie returned with animated tales about steering the ship, learning the starboard from the bow, and the helm. The Captain gave Evie a sailor's hat, and she had lunch with him most days and ice cream daily. He taught her how to count the many lifeboats secured on enormous iron frames.

The Captain's close attention to Evie had passengers talking until they heard Mr. Keen's explanation. Then sadness linked the scene, and all on board felt immediate sympathy for the kind Captain, offering condolences about his daughter and brightening his day with humorous tales about all the happenings on board.

Usually, third-class passengers receiving a dinner invitation from the Captain was unheard of. However, Evie had stolen the Captain's heart, and while sensing a fractured relationship within the small family, the Captain sent them an invitation. He'd deduced from his rounds that Evie's Father, Sean, spent most of his time playing card games for money. Sometimes, he lost. Mostly, he won. That in itself was questionable. Cathy often seemed tense and unhappy, and rarely engaged in entertainment or contests with other passengers.

Yet, apart from confiding her heartbreak at leaving her Old Pa and Daisy, the horse, Evie appreciated the attention and friendship she'd gained with *Captain Teddy*, as she called him.

His crew members had never known the Captain to delve into other people's business. However, Evie's future had become his concern for reasons they could not fathom. He'd tried to separate himself from the family, particularly Evie. But a voice kept telling him he needed to help them. While he hadn't been able to prevent the accident that stole his wife and daughter, maybe he could assist this young family to find their bearings in a new country.

Wearing her new pink organza dress, Cathy walked arm in arm with Sean toward the Captain's table, where he stood handsomely in his uniform. Evie poked her head out from behind her mother's back and smiled. Cathy giggled like a young girl and curtsied awkwardly toward the Captain while Sean proffered his hand. "Thanks for invitin us, Captain. I must say we're d'talk of d'third-class passengers," Sean said, proudly, nodding to all the unapproving faces. He then glanced down at Evie. "I suppose d'littlin has somfin t'do with it. Y'can keep her if you'd like, Captain." Sean's words rang through his laughter. "Only jokin, of course! Christ, d'missus, 'd kill me; she would."

Again, Cathy giggled, wringing her hands together before smoothing her dress down. Sean pushed past the Captain to take his seat, and Cathy noticed him lean away, no doubt getting a whiff of Sean's whisky breath; she gave a wry grin as the Captain escorted her to her seat. He then studied Evie, who hadn't reacted to her da's rebuff about giving her away. *Fancy wanting to give his child away.* The Captain stood rigid, trying to remain calm; he smiled and said, "So, Mr. Cal… Or, perhaps we should be on a first-name basis if you will allow it?"

"Yes, no worries, mate. They say dat in d'Colonies." Sean grinned. "Me name's Sean, and dis's Cathy; of course, yer know our daughter Evie. You bein friends and all." He gave the Captain a sleazy wink, making him shudder.

Why do I think I can discuss anything with this self-obsessed paragon? And to offer help to a man devoid of humility? Although I can see that Sean is cunning and handsome, his intellect and sensibility seem to be nonexistent. Cathy seems to be Sean's puppet, no doubt. And what a shame for a pretty young woman to be taken away from her home and her adoring Father, being torn between him and her love and duty to her husband.

The Captain gave Sean a reluctant grin before gazing at Cathy.

"Well, I must say, Cathy, you do look lovely. I'm pleased you could all join me for dinner. I booked an earlier time, especially for Evie, knowing her bedtime would come soon. And I hope you don't mind me stealing your daughter occasionally." He smiled at Evie. "It appears Evie has grown fond of sailing on big ships. Especially after her fear was paramount when boarding. I couldn't help but put her mind at rest."

The Captain ran his hand over Evie's blond curls. She beamed up at him, and the thought struck. *I may be pushing the mark a tad too close, but she's a tough little cookie. Not even a flinch to her da wanting to give her away.*

"Well, as I said, Captain, she's all yours." Sean felt Cathy's kick. "Ouch!" He scowled. "I meant for d'rest of d'journey, dat is." Sean looked a little uncomfortable, which pleased the Captain. He coughed to stifle his amusement. "Shall we order? The fish is delectable. Or if you prefer meat, I can recommend the steak," said the Captain with a smile.

Their meal was primarily eaten in silence until the Captain asked, "Why did you decide to migrate to Australia, Sean?"

"I was headhunted," Sean answered proudly, "Der's an important man in Australia after men like me who have d'nouse and d'guts to pull off big jobs."

"And what sort of jobs do you mean, Sean?" asked Captain Teddy, assuming he knew.

Sean laughed, "Well, let's just say shiftin' tings around."

"Oh, like furniture and the like?" The Captain almost laughed at his own pun.

"Only if it's worth a cracker." Sean winked, and Captain Teddy coughed.

From what he could gather, Sean was headed toward risky ventures with shaky characters, but it was not for him to comment, only to silently sum up their situation. *Sean might take it the wrong way if I offer them support. Or, on the other hand, take it up with zeal. And I'd be forever handing out money to this man, whom I don't trust. The more I hear, the more I feel sorry for Evie. Cathy isn't the brightest flower in the bunch. But surely she'll wake up eventually and realise her life may end unpleasantly. Plus, she has Evie to consider, and I hope she does so.*

The Captain's planned evening of good intentions had ended in a stalemate. However, he'd not give up trying to help Evie and Cathy, so he handed Cathy and Evie a piece of paper with his home address and telephone number before disembarking the ship in Port Phillip Bay.

"Keep this information a secret, Cathy, and here's one for you, Evie. If you ever need me, I'll be there. Please keep it safe."

That was all he could do apart from praying.

**

Evie squeezed Cathy's hand tightly, breathing in the oddity of this new land, and thought, what would their life be like now, especially living on the outskirts of a big city? Evie had never seen further than her Pa's farm or the tiny village, which sat not far from their cottage. She closed her eyes, picturing the green ivy climbing over the white-washed walls. Ma had planted geraniums in pots, "t'pretty d'place up," Cathy had said, and Evie agreed. Flowers of all kinds had pleased her eye for as long as she could remember. But would they have a garden here where the sun shone so bright and hot? It was so hot that Evie's hand became a slippery eel in Cathy's.

"Hold on tight now, love. I don't want t'lose yer in d'crowd." Cathy kissed Evie's head.

Sean went ahead, struggling with their cases, and Evie turned to wave one last goodbye to Captain Teddy, hoping it would not be the last time she'd see him.

She felt a connection with Captain Teddy, almost as strong as the one she had with her old pa. Evie had placed the paper Teddy gave her in her pocket, although she couldn't read it yet. But he'd told her what he'd written. '*Keep it safe*' were the Captain's last words. A feeling of unease churned her senses. *Maybe I'm like my Great Gran —she could see into d'future? A Soothsayer, everyone called her. Or is it Captain Teddy who knows tings might not go well in dis land called Australia?*

A mass of people hurried toward the enclosed terminal, where they'd be asked to show their passports. The air became even more oppressive as they crammed together, fighting for a closer spot in the queue.

It seemed hours before they were finally free to breathe fresh air and head to their new home in Carlton. Unfamiliar sounds and strange voices rattled in Evie's head until she felt faint from the strain of trying to understand and take in the clatter of trams and pushbikes, their riders ducking and weaving through traffic, and pedestrians who appeared to be rushing for their lives.

Evie sighed and closed her eyes when they found a seat on a bus. Finally, a place to rest and dream about Pa and Daisy: Evie soon fell asleep and dreamed of Ireland. She woke up when Cathy nudged her,

"Come on, me' wee lass. We're here."

With the bus driver's help, Sean managed to land the three cases on the footpath. They walked a block until they stopped in front of what appeared to be a dumping ground. Rubbish of all sorts lay scattered in the small front yard. The stink was almost unbearable. Cathy crept slowly past towards the front door, with Evie following, their eyes darting here and there until Evie tugged at Cathy's sleeve, "We don't have t'live here, do we, Ma?"

"I hope not," Cathy said as Sean called out. "Come on, Cathy. I've opened d'door, love." His calmness had her confused and dumbfounded.

Maybe d'house will be better inside.

Not so. Soot from the old chimney laced the walls. A tattered couch and a sturdy armchair rested in front of the fireplace. Severely scuffed linoleum covered the floorboards. They continued to the room on the left of a narrow hallway, which held an iron-posted bed. The bare mattress showed stains from the previous owner's lovemaking. Or a testament to a sinister time. It smelled of decay; Cathy pinched her nose and pointed, "You'll have t'get rid of dat mattress, Sean! I'm not sleeping on dat!" Just as the words left her mouth, a fat, shiny rat scurried across Cathy's feet, and she screamed. "Oh, m'God. We can't be livin here, Sean."

Evie scampered after the rat.

"Come back, Evie!" called Cathy.

"Let her go. It'll keep her busy while we sort this mess out." Sean scratched his head, "I can only tell y'Cathy, it wasn't meant to be like dis.

Dat bastard promised we'd have a lovely home t'live in." Sean threw his cap on the ground, then took Cathy in his arms. "I promise y'love, as soon as he shows his face, I'll be sortin this deal out. Y'can count on dat!"

They looked to the right of the hallway and noticed another room with a pink quilt covering a brand-new child's bed and a teddy bear leaning against the frilly pillow. It was as if he'd been waiting forever and had fallen asleep. Puzzled, Cathy walked over and impulsively hugged the teddy.

"Who put you dere, little one?" she said, light-heartedly. Cathy felt a paper note attached to Teddy's back. It read, *This room is a taste of the finer things to come, Sean. So, follow orders and keep a close eye on your little girl.*

Cathy dropped the threatening note, threw the teddy on the floor, and ran through the kitchen to the backyard. "Evie, Evie, where are yer?" Come back now!"

"I'm here, Ma. Over here!"

Cathy ran to their tiny backyard. In the middle ran a long rope attached to two poles at either end; she almost choked as she ran straight into the rope. Bouncing back, she ducked underneath and hurried into the lane to see Evie bent over a drain.

"He went down dere, Ma. I'm waitin' f'him t'come back out." She smiled at Cathy, proud that she'd hopefully found a pet.

"NO Evie! He's a dirty rat. Y'can't be playin' with rats; dey give y'germs, and you'll get sick!"

The sorrow on Evie's face broke Cathy's heart. It framed the disappointment of coming here under Sean's promise of a better life, forcing Evie to give up everything she'd held dear. Cathy sobbed tears into Evie's hair. "I'm sorry, Evie, I'm truly sorry. I believed y'da. He said we'd have a grand home and loads of money." Cathy sniffled, holding Evie's face in her hands. "I promise ya, Evie, if tings don't get better in a month or two, we'll go back t'Ireland."

CHAPTER 5
DAVINA
LAYERS OF FRIENDSHIP

After three years of dressage competition, showing horses, and unbeknownst to Father, winning the occasional three-day event, I skyrocketed to be the most prominent junior female rider in Victoria, perhaps Australia. I pondered the pain of disappointment I felt when, finally, I packed my bags to attend boarding school, which came like a hammer to my soul. Then, with a sigh of acceptance, I stepped into my academic future with as much determination as I'd shown when competing on horseback.

I'd be the best I could be.

My first impression of the girls who attended Melbourne Grammar was that most tried to outdo each other with meaningless trivia, such as whose Father had the most expensive car, how often they'd travelled overseas, and where their parents had taken them. How could they travel when the war was raging?

I questioned them about the timing and was told, 'Oh well, I travelled before the war and now again after.' They were only babies during the war. And I suspect they made up stories about travelling later.

I'd noticed one girl who always sat by herself. She was tall and willowy like me, with the same mousy brown hair. We could have been sisters; we looked so much alike. Her name was Irene, and she'd won a sporting scholarship to board at Melbourne Grammar. I found her interesting from afar. Underneath my façade, I was shy - perhaps more scared than shy, afraid of being shunned—*my permanent tag*. I was curious about Irene, so one morning during our break, I asked, "May I sit with you?"

"Yes, of course. Please sit," said Irene, shuffling aside.

"I know your name is Irene," I said. "And I know you're here because you received a sports scholarship. Do you want to tell me anything else?"

I hesitated, fearing rejection. "Then, maybe we could be friends. My name's Davina."

Irene beamed a smile so bright I almost hugged her.

"I would like that very much, Davina. I feel so out of it here. Nobody talks to me. I'm only happy when I'm running in races. My coach says I could run in the Olympics if I keep improving." Irene hung her head, obviously not wanting to boast. I laughed.

"Oh, I am sorry. I didn't mean to laugh. It's just that you sound like me. I'm only happy when I'm riding horses."

"Really? I'd love to ride a horse. But I'm a bit scared."

"Well, maybe you could come and stay at my place and…'

The school bell rang, so we hurried to class, determined not to be late, as the consequences were too harsh.

Relief and happiness consumed me for the rest of the day, and I'd smile for no apparent reason. I'd made a friend!

Lunchtime came, and we sat together, catching up from where we'd left off. Irene told me how her father had fought in the war and returned with 'shell shock.'

"He's usually okay, but sometimes we hear him screaming at night. It's awful."

I held her hand, feeling my tears well up. "I'm so sorry, Irene." I dipped my head lest she see my emotion. "I know it sounds shallow, but I'm glad my dad was too old to go to war. However, he held a significant position as an engineer. He helped design and build aircraft and ships for the war effort." It seemed this information did little to help Irene's anguish. She gave a shy smile.

"That's just as important, Davina. I wish my dad could heal mentally and not have nightmares. Poor Mum, she's tired and worn out. I worry about her. And now I'm here at boarding school. I can't be there to help her with housework and cooking. She'll have no time to rest."

"Don't you have help? Like a cook and a housekeeper?" I asked, surprised.

Irene laughed. "I wish! No, we don't, Davina. We're not wealthy. I really shouldn't be here. My parents said that if I excelled at school and performed well in my running, it would all be worthwhile. That is, if I qualify for the Olympics. But I feel guilty." Irene had a habit of hanging her head.

"Look at me, Irene." Slowly, her eyes met mine. "My dad's rich. If I ask him, he'll give me anything. What do your parents need most?"

Irene's expression turned to shock and anger; she almost yelled, "I couldn't take money from your dad. And my parents definitely would not! We might be poor, but we're proud."

"I'm sorry, Irene. I just want to help." I felt heat rising to my cheeks. Why did I feel embarrassed about wanting to give what I could afford to give freely? I put it down to that voice again, and I sighed. "It's just from when I was a little girl; I'd see other children who looked poor. And all I wanted to do was give them money, thinking it would help. Although I rarely said anything. It was just how I felt." I went on to tell Irene about my family and how, sometimes, it saddened me to be rich. Then the bell rang again. "Before we go into class, do you want me to ask our house teacher if you could share my room, Irene?" She smiled.

"I'd like that. Thank you, Davina. And I'm sorry for yelling at you."

"It's okay. We're friends now, Irene."

Fortunately, Father, a generous benefactor to the school, had the power to grant my wish. My then-roommate, Louise, was one of the worst offenders of the up-yours, stakes. When informed of her upheaval, Louise threw her belongings into her cases with rage, before noticeably struggling to carry them out, accompanied by the parting words sprouting from a smug look upon her ungenerous face, "You think you're smart, Davina! Well, you're not. My family is wealthier than yours. We go back to the first 'free settlers.' So there!"

It appeared that not even Louise liked being shunned.

'*Good riddance,*' I muttered before tidying the room, ready *for my friend* Irene. Oh, that sounded so good, *my friend Irene.*

The years I spent at Melbourne Grammar with Irene will always bring a smile to my face. (There we go, my happy memories are awakening.) Once Irene had moved into my room, we became like sisters, even though her chatter rarely ceased. I didn't mind. I was happy to have her there.

I sometimes watched Irene's training runs and admired her determination to improve. Whenever Irene *did* shut up, we'd study well together. I'm not boasting, but schoolwork came easily to me, and I helped Irene pass every exam. In return, she made me laugh, and together, we found the strength to stand up to the *terror mob*—the snobs who thought themselves better than anyone else.

One day, when Phillipa, one of the most ardent offenders, walked past with her nose sniffing the air and her bum grossly protruding, *her way of walking*, and her group trailing behind, she said, "Say hello to our two ugly ducklings, girls."

Her followers giggled out, "Hello, ugly ducklings."

Quick on the uptake, Irene asked, "Will you loan me that stick, Phillipa?"

'What stick!" Phillipa replied indignantly.

"The one stuck up your bum!"

My sides ached with laughter as Phillipa yelled. "Uncouth, ugly trollop!"

Snide remarks were forever thrown at Irene about being '*the poor little poor girl*.' Finally, I'd had enough and so squashed their rant.

"Do you know, Phillipa, Irene's Mother has come into an enormous inheritance? Therefore, saying that no longer sways Irene. I'd give it a rest if I were you. Irene's parents could buy and sell your parents now."

Later, we choked with laughter. I'd never laughed so much since meeting Irene. And I never thought I had enough confidence to stand up to the condorsensors. (If there is such a word) Irene taught me both. Eventually, we, the two ugly ducklings, were left alone. The old saying is, if the fish don't bite, don't go fishing.

Irene was delighted that her mother had said 'yes' to her staying at Carlina during the school holidays. "Only the final week, though, Mum said. But then I felt guilty, Davina, when she said, 'I'm sorry, Irene, but I could use some help in the first week, especially since I work part-time.' The money helps, particularly when your Father isn't up to scratch. The boss has been sending him home more often." Irene hung her head before looking me in the eye, "I still feel guilty. But Mum insists that we have fun. She said, "You're only young once, and you deserve some fun." I think she's chuffed at how well I was doing at school. Mum said, I know Davina helps you tremendously; therefore, I cannot say no. And I'm looking forward to meeting this young lady. I'm happy you've found a lovely friend, Irene." She smiled.

"Thank goodness," I said, "but please don't feel guilty, Irene. Your mother's right. We're only young once, and we need to have fun!"

With the weather unusually warm for May, I sat cross-legged on the grass at the end of our mile-long driveway without noticing the postman's little red truck until the horn blew, and I jumped. After handing me the mail, he smiled and waved goodbye. I sat back on the ground, looking through the letters, until I heard a car and saw Irene hanging out the window. An uncontrollable scream escaped. Irene's Father wound the window down, grinning.

"You're here!" I yelled. "Did you find it easy enough?"

"Yes, thank you, Davina, and thank you for having Irene stay."

"It's our pleasure, Mr. Gibbs. I'm so excited. And, of course, Father will drive us back to school, so you won't have to pick her up." I pointed, "Just follow the driveway to the house, Mr. Gibbs."

Irene jumped from the car, and together we ran, legs brown and lean, our faces glowing, hair flying.

I remember Mother being gracious in her superior manner, and Betty had excelled with morning tea. However, I sat gazing at Mr. and Mrs. Gibbs, looking like fish out of water, their eyes wide with admiration for our antique furniture and original paintings.

Mother accepted the prompt, "Some of our paintings have adorned our walls for generations, transported from Scotland when more riches came the way of Richard's ancestors," she said, smiling proudly. I had to giggle silently. It rarely occurred to me how our home appeared to others. " It's one of Australia's most valued mansions," Mother continued. "The furniture and artwork alone would bring millions if sold at auction."

I don't know why this information had never affected me. My mother appeared so different from me. Sometimes, I thought perhaps I was not her child. Though I felt sure about Father, "I love you unconditionally, Davina," is what he'd always say, and he'd show it in so many ways. How could I ever feel unloved by the most generous, compassionate man I'd known?

That week, having Irene stay is among my happiest memories. How could I forget teaching Irene, an already supreme athlete, to ride horses? We stayed up late talking and laughing about everything and anything.

On our final day, Irene felt confident enough to ride her horse to the river, where we let them graze while tethered. The weather had remained warm, so, unashamedly, we stripped down to our undies and were about to swim when we heard a whimper. We hurried along the riverbank and found a tiny, sodden puppy battling to climb out.

"Oh, poor baby. How on earth did you get here?" I said, hugging him. I dried him off and forgot about swimming. Instead, I smothered the puppy with cuddles and kisses. I assumed he would be about six weeks old, not quite old enough to wean. Irene stroked his head, saying," Someone must have dumped him upstream. Do you think?"

"I can't think of anything else, Irene. He's too small to swim this far on his own." I said, hugging the crying pup.

Suddenly, Irene jumped up and sprinted to the river before I could stand. I then noticed a hessian sack floating past.

"What is it?" I called.

"You don't want to know. Bastards!"

We dug a shallow grave with a stirrup iron for the dead puppies and named the surviving pup 'Lucky.'

I felt sad about leaving my six-week-old Lucky when I returned to school. It was one of the hardest things I had to do when I was young.

Betty promised to look after Lucky. I didn't trust Mother, who said, "I will not have a dog in the house! I'll have Frederick take him to the pound!"

So I phoned Father at his office and told him my fears.

"Don't worry, Davina. Put your Mother on the phone, and I'll talk to her."

Mother's unnatural attitude toward me remained like an open wound until Father explained that Mother had many problems stemming from her childhood. I tried hard to understand, especially as he would never tell me the entire story. Years later, I softened and understood when Father finally described Mother's depression. Although growing up being the brunt of her agony was debilitating and hurtful. I could go on about it, but I'm sure anyone who reads this will get the picture.

Lucky grew to be my loyal companion. He was an intelligent, intuitive dog. He'd never leave my side when I was home, and I'd take him to all the horse shows. I can still see Lucky's nose sniffing and his jowls flapping as he hung his head out the truck window, his ears waving in the breeze. Occasionally, he'd bark at our cattle, wanting to herd them, but he knew never to chase horses. However, he'd never fail to spot a rabbit and go for the hunt.

Irene and I were driven back to School by our chauffeur *and friend*, Freddy. Again, Father promised I could keep Lucky before we left, which made me deliriously happy. Plus, the week before Irene's visit, I'd competed with Molly in an advanced dressage test and received the highest points. So, yes, I felt fortunate once again. Although I can still see my first pony, Polly, trotting beside the horse float, whinnying, 'Take me too!' Following that, I insisted Polly come with us to keep Molly company.

After her stay at Carlina, Irene told me about her parents' attitude toward the difference in our upbringings. I was a child of wealth, with everything. In contrast, Irene had to work hard for everything. Our mansion and my mother had stamped the difference. And as much as Mrs. Gibbs tried not to, she'd felt an overwhelming sense of inadequacy, as did Mr. Gibbs when they were compelled to sit straight-backed and smile while my mother prattled on about everything money could buy.

"Do you think being so close to Davina is a good idea?" Mrs. Gibbs had asked Irene, "After all, she may not want to know you once you leave school. The difference in our wealth and social class is so vast, Irene. Therefore, I cannot see how you could retain a true friendship." Irene had told me what her mother had said the morning after we'd returned to school.

"And what do you think, Irene?" I asked, confused and hurt.

"I hope we can be friends forever, Davina. Do you think you're better than me because you're rich and have everything you want?" I sighed in relief,

"No! I don't. And that's my point. I have never *wanted* to be rich. Just happy. And loved."

"That's what I told Mum. I can't understand why people think the rich and the poor should never meet. It's bloody stupid. You are who you are, regardless of where you live or how much money you have. And you know what? You are the best friend I've ever had. I don't care how much money you have. I'd like you, rich or poor."

We hugged, then pushed each other away, giggling.

"We'd better go, or the *terror* mob will eat our dinner. Come on, Davina. Beat you down the stairs."

"Well, of course you will, Irene," I said dryly. "But I'll break your leg one day, so you can't!"

Her laughter warmed my heart—such a wonderful sound.

CHAPTER 6
EVIE FINDS A MATE

Cathy wiped the sweat from her brow and groaned as she rose from scrubbing the floor, taking a moment to breathe before she called, "Evie, where are ya, Evie!" Under her breath, Cathy cursed, shuffling stiffly towards the open kitchen door and into the tiny backyard filled with fluttering sheets. She avoided the one about to slap her in the face and looked up. "*Another cloudy day. Still, it's hot and windy. I hope dey dry before d'rain comes.*" Cathy muttered, then called down the laneway, "Evie, come here!" *I'm sick and tired of yer traipsing off t'find stray dogs and cats.*

"Not another mouth t'be feedin Evie. No, I said! We can't afford to feed ourselves, let alone an animal." They were the words Cathy preached almost twice a week when Evie found a stray animal.

However, Cathy never considered the money she'd hidden for their return to Ireland; she'd squirreled away a load of cash as their lifesaver.

Every day, Cathy worked hard to restore the cottage to its former glory, leaving her with no spare time to enroll Evie in school, which Evie refused to attend.

"I'll even walk ya to the school," Cathy had said, smiling to encourage Evie. "I'll talk to da Principal. It's called 'Pidgeon Street Primary School. Isn't dat a funny name?"

But, no matter what Cathy said about the school, contempt appeared on Evie's face, and she'd plant her feet and fold her arms.

Thankfully, the school sat within walking distance, on the same road as the shops where Cathy intended to ask for a job.

"*I can cook and clean, and I'm friendly, so I'd like t'meet people and serve them in y'lovely shop.*" Cathy planned to tell the Butcher, the Baker, and the Milkbar owner after she'd taken Evie to school.

Sean went out every morning and didn't return until after dark.

Cathy thought it was as if he didn't want to be seen. Whatever job he did, he never earned a weekly wage. Coins and sometimes pound notes appeared sporadically from his pockets and were thrown on the kitchen table.

"Dat should keep us goin until d'big jobs come in, Cathy."

So he'd say before kissing her neck, making Cathy giggle and forget about their grim situation. Evie watched with a smile that never reached her heart.

"Evie!" Cathy called after returning to the moment; she called again. "I'm warnin you! Come home now!" A faint whisper came from behind the neighbour's fence.

"I'm comin, Ma."

Evie appeared, climbing through a gap in the fence, carrying an undernourished mongrel pup. Her eyes pleaded. And for once, Cathy softened at the sight of the helpless creature, his patchy coat crawling with fleas, his skin raw and bloody. Cathy stroked his tiny head and noticed his tail wagging.

"Bring him into the wash house, Evie. He needs a bath." Cathy smiled lovingly at her daughter, giving Evie faith that all was good and just in the world.

"Didn't d'Priest say we should be kind and help others, includin God's creatures, Ma?" Cathy kept smiling down at her daughter as she guided her into the washhouse.

Together, they gently washed the pup in soap suds until dead fleas floated to the surface. Cathy then warmed a saucer of milk and added a slice of stale bread, which the pup ate before collapsing on an old towel that Cathy was about to use as a duster.

"Does dis mean I can keep him, Ma?" Evie clasped her hands in prayer.

"I suppose so, Evie. He doesn't look like he's gonna grow too big. So he shouldn't cost too much t'feed."

Evie's hands trembled as she held the pup to her breast, rocking him gently. "I'll love yer forever, *mate*. Dat's what all d'kids here call der' friends. I'll call yer Matey," Evie sat on the floor, tears of happiness clouding her blue eyes.

Later that evening, Sean arrived home grunting after Evie rushed to the door and showed him the pup, "I saved him from a sure death, Da."

"Cathy me' love. Come here!" Sean called over Evie's head.

As usual, he'd come home after dark and sat in the only comfortable armchair beside the fireside. It was summer, so Cathy had decorated the fireplace with a large jar full of gum leaves she'd gathered from the almost treeless neighborhood. The eucalyptus leaves extended their fragrance, and Sean inhaled while ignoring Evie's plea, "Pat d'puppy, Da!"

Instead, he kicked his shoes off, straightened his legs, and stretched his arms out as Cathy entered. "Come sit on me' lap, darlin. I've got good news. "

Cathy sat, wrapping her arms around his neck.

"So tell me, Sean. What is it?"

"I've pleased d'boss, Cathy. He says he trusts me now. Now I've done all d'little jobs; he's gonna give me some big payin' jobs. He said if I do d'right ting, we'd soon be rollin in money. " He swung Cathy around and planted a kiss on her full lips.

Evie sighed, wondering if they'd ever leave this place and maybe buy the farm Ma had promised. Cathy pushed Sean away and rose to face him. "Does dis mean we'll be movin out soon, Sean? It is not a nice place t'be bringin Evie up. Now, is it?"

Evie looked at Cathy in amazement. *She's readin me' mind.*

"Of course it does, Cathy. Though not straight away. We have t'save our money."

"Why can't we just rent a nice home in a better suburb, Sean? I'm not too fond of livin here. And Evie hasn't made any friends," Cathy said with a whimper.

Sean sprang to his feet. His temper erupted whenever Cathy questioned him.

"I'm tellin' ya', Cathy. We need t'be keepin a low profile in case d'cops get suspicious!"

Cathy clamped her mouth shut. *He'll lose his senses if I go on about Evie's needs, and he'll start punching d'walls—tank heavens he never hits Evie or me.*"Alright, den. But do yer promise t'give me all d'money yer earn, Sean? And as soon as I've saved enough, we'll be buyin a home in d'country where Evie can have a pony." Cathy smiled at Evie, hugging the pup. "And her wee dog."

Sean glared at Evie, "About that flamin dog…"

"No, Sean! It bothers me when you don't tink about Evie or her wishes. She needs dis puppy, and dat's final!" It wasn't often Cathy stood up for Evie, but when she did, Sean listened.

Later that evening, while Cathy slept soundly, Evie lay smiling in her sleep with Matey wrapped in her arms. Meanwhile, Sean removed his black clothes from the bag he'd stashed and pulled them on over his pyjamas. He couldn't help but grin, thinking Cathy hadn't found where he'd hidden the bag. She was so meticulous about cleaning.

He crept from the house and walked briskly one block, where he found Frankie, his partner in crime, tapping his fingers on the steering wheel of the pickup truck. The big boss had ordered them to meet other gang members at the Carlton United Breweries in Lygon Street near Sean's home. Guards were bribed, and all plans were set to steal an enormous amount of beer to sell on the black market. Escape boats awaited at Port Phillip Bay to ship the haul to Sydney and Queensland.

They'd chosen the night carefully. With no moon and the street lamps dimmed, the robbers had an ideal backdrop for the act. Sean went through the motions, tactfully discharging the brewery of a sizeable load. Much more than anticipated. The gang's responsibility was to deliver the stolen goods to the waiting boats. Sean did so with courage and excitement, the two natural elements that ignited his spirit. He smiled and breathed a sigh of relief after unloading the final case of beer onto the boat, then jumped into Frankie's pickup truck, heading for home. Five trucks had waited with their drivers and accomplices, who'd stolen their share. Job achieved!

The following afternoon, Sean arrived home just as Evie and Cathy walked through the gate before him. Cathy turned, with worry etched on her pretty face. "Where was yer last night, Sean?"

He shoved Cathy inside. "Never say dat when we're outside." He whispered. "Not where people can hear ya."

Once inside, Cathy flung her hands to her hips.

"I don't like it, Sean. What if y'get caught? What's gonna happen t'Evie and me?"

"Notin'll happen. We're too smart, f'dat! So don't be worryin y'pretty head me' darlin."

Sean led Cathy by the arm into the bedroom, where he threw a wad of pound notes on the bed. "There now, y'see! It's our first instalment on a farm. Is dat what y'wanted? A farm f'Evie?"

Cathy's eyes bulged; she'd never seen so much cash. She counted the money and envisioned a pony galloping around an open paddock, a cow grazing, chickens in a large pen, and a white cottage surrounded by rose bushes. She quickly wrapped the bundle in a pillow slip and slid it under the new mattress, then thought a moment before taking a pound note to buy quality food for a change.

Meanwhile, Sean, anxious to enjoy a relaxing soak in the tub, struck a match to light the boiler. He'd thrown the bag of *night clothes*, as he called them, in the corner of the wash house where the bathtub sat. Cathy later walked in to see Sean lying back, luxuriating. Her eyes went to the bag in the corner. She plucked it up and shoved it abruptly under his nose.

"What's in here, Sean? Dirty clothes t'match yer dirty deeds?"

He laughed, throwing his head back. "Well. If yer tink it's dirty, Cathy, den give me back d'money.'"

She threw him a scowl before departing with her fists clenched.

Evie watched her mother storm into the kitchen and clued in to what was happening. She'd grown accustomed to her father's cloak-and-dagger antics and the worried expressions on her mother's face. But Evie felt there was nothing she could do to change things. Especially today, as it had been her first day at school, and she'd found it hard to concentrate when the teacher kept yelling, "The new girl. Pay attention!" Evie had thought of nothing else but living on a farm with Matey. Her daydreams were enhanced by gazing out the window at a vivid blue sky. *Dere's no boundaries in d'sky, just like in d'country.*

Later, when home, Evie sat on her bed, cuddling the pup, "Don't worry, Matey, we'll soon be leavin here. Far away from everyone. Just you and me and me pony." She held his tiny face in her hands, looking him in the eye. "And I won't have t'be puttin up with dose bully kids at school!"

That evening, the newspaper headlines told about the robbery of Carlton United Brewery. No clue was found as to who had committed the crime. Sean had a sneaky suspicion the cops were in on it, along with many more shenanigans happening around the area. He didn't know for sure and didn't want to know. So Sean pulled his head in and stuck to whatever job came his way. He'd heard the *Top Boss Man* was above reproach and, therefore, well away from being implicated. And Sean knew if he were to learn the man's identity, he'd soon be dead.

******

Over the following year, the money kept rolling in as the jobs came Sean's way. He'd matured into a smooth operator, with nerves of steel and enough confidence "*t'sell ice t'Eskimos!*" He'd once boasted to Cathy.

After months of successful heists and never under any suspicion, Sean declared one morning. "We're sittin pretty, Cathy! What did I tell yer? We'll soon be buyin dat little farm."

Sean's words played like a Brahms lullaby to Evie. At last, her dreams would become a reality. *Maybe Old Pa'll come, too?*

CHAPTER 7
DAVINA
LIFE'S LESSONS

My years at boarding school were a mix of highs and lows. Firstly, I was unable to ride and compete with my horses as often as I liked—a real downer. Then, I felt proud of my academic achievements, as well as helping Irene pass her exams. Therefore, winning important running races and excelling academically cleared Irene's guilt. All systems led to her competing in the next Olympic Games, held in Helsinki, Finland, in 1952.

We would be seventeen years old.

Irene pinned a photo of Marjorie Jackson on the wall and said, "Goodnight, M.J."

I had nobody famous whom I admired enough to hang a picture of and to say goodnight. Although I missed Charlotte and Jacques. Jacques now worked for Uncle Aaron, educating his Holsteiner horses. Jacques also gave riding tuition to wealthy and passionate equestrians. *At a high price!*

Jacques told me he and his Uncle planned to enter the Helsinki Equestrian Games. He said that three of Uncle Aaron's horses had already been sent to Finland. And, of course, Charlotte would accompany Jacques, leaving me behind—feeling rejected.

I would be seventeen on August 1, 1952, having completed ten years of schooling. I assumed I'd had enough education, but Father argued.

He insisted I remain until I'd completed twelve years of schooling and then go on to University for a degree.

I debated, "But why? When all I want to do is spend my life with horses!"

He threw his hands in the air, "We'll talk about this later, Davina."

Determined to get my way, I refused to return to school after the term holidays. Father, who usually gave in to my wishes, held firm against my leaving school. So I faked illness at home, moaning in agony until I laughed at Betty after I'd placed a hot water bottle on my forehead, "I'm burning up, Cookie." (I'd nicknamed Betty) Please take my temperature." She almost fainted when the gauge reached 102 degrees.

"Oh, dear God! Somebody call an ambulance!" She yelled until I told her what I'd done. Betty understood - *eventually.*

I was single-minded about going to Helsinki, where Irene had secured her spot on the Australian Athletics team. And Jacques had made it into the Australian Equestrian team.

However, after much discussion and numerous meetings with the leading bodies, it was ultimately decided that an Australian Equestrian team would not compete in Helsinki. Instead, an offer came for Jacques to join the German team, but he and his Uncle, Aaron, refused. Uncle Aaron had previously shipped his three dressage horses to Helsinki, a costly endeavor.

After the Australian officials' disappointing announcement, Aaron sold them to a Swedish millionaire whose daughter was to compete in the 1952 Equestrian Olympics in Helsinki.

Then came talk about Australia hosting the 1956 Olympics, restoring Uncle Aaron's enthusiasm, especially when he became one of the primary Selectors of the Australian Equestrian team. He soon accumulated a talented group of riders, *including me,* who might participate in the home games. To top Uncle Aaron's happiness, Jacques and Charlotte had announced their engagement. They would be married in late December 1952, and Charlotte asked me to be her bridesmaid. I accepted.

Thankfully, after Jacques informed Father that I was a candidate to compete in the 1956 Equestrian Games, he permitted me to leave school.

"Although it's such a shame, Davina," said Father, "Your academic skill is to be congratulated. And, of course, as you know, nothing is impossible for women to achieve these days. You could be anything you wished. A doctor, an engineer, a scientist!"

I laughed.

"Father, are you not aware that women already hold those professions? I believe we should follow our passion. Surely, it will lead us to where we should be in life. And horses are and always will be my absolute passion. You told me from a young boy that you wanted to be an Engineer. And so, I'm telling you, I want to ride horses for a living."

"You're a hard nut to crack, Davina. However, I must say that I admire your conviction and talent. Let us hope your dreams come true. Except for riding in point-to-point races. And those terribly high jumps. No! I say no! It's far too dangerous. Yes, far too dangerous!" His tone softened, and I could see tiredness and perhaps something else in his eyes. "I'm not feeling well, Davina. I think I'll take a rest before dinner."

That was the beginning of Father's long-suffering cancer. It's a terrifying word. We may as well declare it a death sentence.

Irene told me her parents would love to be in Helsinki to see her compete. But, of course, money was the brunt of their disappointment. They scarcely had enough to pay rent and feed themselves.

I sat, head in hand, twirling scenarios around until I said. "I know, Irene. Why not say you purchased a lottery ticket and won? That way, I can give you the money. And then you give it to them!" I felt proud of my brilliant idea.

"It's full of loopholes, Davina," Irene said, shaking her head. "I'm not old enough to buy a lottery ticket. And my parents would tell me to put the money in the bank, saying I'd bought the ticket; therefore, the money was mine."

"If you don't mind me saying so, Irene, your parents sound stubborn."

"No. Davina. They are proud." Irene said, rubbing her eyes. "But, yes, I suppose you could say stubborn."

"Then why don't you say you found a bag of money sitting on a seat in the park? You noticed it when you were out for a run. Ask your mother to place an ad in the newspaper, saying, '*Parcel found on a bench.*' Name the park and ask the recipient to describe the bag's appearance and its contents. If nobody comes up with the right answer, then legally, it's yours. How about that?"

Irene laughed. "Will you ever stop trying to give me money, Davina? My parents would never take charity. Well, maybe if we were destitute and had no food. Anyway, they can listen to the games on the radio. So it's not all that bad." Irene Bear hugged me. "I love you, Davina, but please stop. Maybe I'll marry a rich man or I'll earn big money.' She dipped her head, contemplating. "Well, maybe not. I want to be a physical education teacher when this is all over. Not in a private school, though. I want to go bush and teach kids who have fewer opportunities. Besides, most kids from rural areas are great runners. Probably because they have to walk or run miles to school, what do you think, Davina, would I make a good P.E teacher?" she asked, lifting her head, presenting an enthusiastic sparkle.

"Of course you will, Irene. You'll be the best. Plus, you're the fastest female runner in Australia." I thought about what I'd just said. "Well, maybe Marjorie Jackson has it on you at the moment. But I reckon you'll win gold in the future. No doubt about it!"

"Oh, and what about you, Miss Horse Rider Extraordinaire! I can't wait for the next Olympics, Davina. We can both compete. I reckon they'll be in Melbourne."

"That's what they're saying. But nothing's certain until Helsinki is over."

Father, noticeably ill, spent most of his time visiting specialists.

I weighed up the excitement of going to Helsinki to see Irene compete against staying home with Father and accompanying him to his doctor's appointment.

My father had recently bought a three-bedroom unit overlooking the Yarra River, to be his base while having treatment for his life-threatening illness. Mother, in true character, fluttered about like a caged butterfly, showing off her interior designs to the who's who of the social set in Toorak and South Yarra. All attended her self-proclaimed famous cocktail parties, and sometimes, I would join them, but only to support Father.

Before, I lost control and had a screaming match with Mother about her insensitivity to Father's suffering when holding her flamboyant and noise-filled parties. Father told her, "No more parties, dear. I don't think you realise how ill I am. I need peace." I stood beside Father when he said this, and he looked up at me with misty eyes. "Plus, I need to see my children as much as possible. Will you phone Geelong Grammar in the morning, Davina, and ask Joseph to come home? Just for a while. I'm sure he'll not fall too far behind in his studies." Father smiled, squeezing my hand. And with that, Mother stormed to her room, a crying mess.

Father sighed, taking a moment, I'm sure, to decide if I was old enough to learn about Mother's mental illness. He patted my hand and asked me to sit beside him before he proceeded to go into great detail about her being shunned by her parents and never feeling truly loved by either, among other terrible things that had happened to her. I could finally comprehend! And in the end, Father's plea for my understanding woke me up like a cold shower.

"So you see, Davina. It would be helpful now that you're mature enough to appreciate your mother. No matter how hard it must be. None of us truly understands mental illness. A physical illness like mine is easy to recognise." He rubbed his chin, contemplating, "I'm sure there will be a cure for cancer in time. I'm not so sure about mental illness. Sad, as it is. Please promise me to be patient and treat your mother respectfully when I'm gone, Davina. She is, after all, a sick woman. It breaks my heart to see her crying and defaming herself. You and Joseph never see that part of her. She realises she needs help. I've tried my best. And so, too, has her psychiatrist. Your Mother refuses to take the tablets the doctor prescribed. It's a shame because they help, although they make her sleepy. She prefers to drink alcohol in excess. She says it dulls the voices in her head." Father swept his hands as if trying to brush away Mother's problem. "I don't know what's worse, Davina, drugs or alcohol. Maybe both are better than putting up with mental torment. Constantly.'

He gave a brave smile, if there is such a thing. 'I'm sorry I haven't told you all this before, Davina. It may have given you a better understanding of why your Mother blamed you for her shortcomings. She knows the problem lies within herself. It's her monster. Some say I should have committed her to a mental institution. I could not. No, I couldn't put her in one of those homes where patients sit all day, to be fed on sedatives, staring into space." He took a deep breath, seeming to contemplate his following words. "She does try, Davina. I know how hard she tries." Father squeezed my hand before dropping it like hot coal to rub his forehead. "My only regret is how you've had to suffer. And I'm sure what added fuel to her fire was that she understood how much I loved and idolized you. My beautiful Daughter." Father reached out and held my hand again, his eyes showing the love I will never forget.

I kissed his cheek. "I'm sorry, Father, but I'm not beautiful. You know that. But thank you for telling me about Mother." I moved silently around the room, thinking about my childhood with my unstable Mother, until I turned to look him in the eye, "I promise you, Father, now I truly understand. I will take care of Mother and try never to place her in one of those homes."

"Thank you, Davina. I know you will do your best."

"What do the doctors say? Is she likely to get worse with age?"

"Yes, most definitely. However, there will always be sufficient funds for a personal nurse. And when that happens, Mother will be unable to refuse medicine. Maybe then she will find some peace."

"Perhaps you should have told me a lot sooner, Father."

It struck me then how, from a very young age, I'd always tried to see and feel things from another person's point of view. I remembered studying those less fortunate families at the horse shows and putting myself in their place. I thought about our staff and how Father treated them as equals while still being their boss. Different relationships would always intrigue me.

"Without being too smug, Father, I have always held enough empathy to understand Mother's pain. I only wish you'd told me sooner." I stood at my full height. "Let's not worry about it now. You need your sleep. And I can only hope Mother has cried herself to sleep by now. I don't mean that badly. It's just that sleep is far better than being awake and tormented, I assume." I gave him a warm cuddle. "Call me if you need me, Father."

"I will, Davina. And you're right, sleep is good." He grinned in an almost condescending way, then refrained. "Please don't forget to phone Geelong Grammar first thing in the morning. Good night, Daughter of mine. And you are beautiful. Never forget it."

I felt suddenly grown up in that moment of clarity. My father thought I was mature enough to hear the sad truth about my mother and to hold me responsible for her care when he was gone. Oh, how I hated even thinking about my world without him.

The following morning, I phoned Geelong Grammar, as Father wished. Joseph packed his bags, and although he seemed to be in his own world most of the time, I knew he cared deeply for Father, a man of integrity and compassion, in everyone's opinion. I was proud to call him my father. And I loved Joseph dearly. It would be good to have him around for a change.

The following day, I tried talking to Mother, hinting that I understood her problem, whereas I hadn't before. I suggested we go for a walk along the banks of the Yarra River and talk. At first, she declined until I pointed out that we needed to face the reality of Father's illness. It took the focus off her problems, and she agreed. After many silent pauses, we finally sat on the riverbank to admire and feed the magnificent Black Swans. We talked at length and opened up to each other. I could feel my mother's torment and believed she did try hard to be '*normal*,' as she'd often referred to on that memorable day. We genuinely hugged each other for the first time I could remember.

I thought this was our turning point. I hoped so.

CHAPTER 8
DAVINA IN HELSINKI

I rarely visited Father's office, but I needed to give my trip to Helsinki one last try. Under constant persuasion, he said, "Yes, alright, Davina. I know it's a chance of a lifetime for you to support your friend." He kissed my forehead and smiled, then frowned, "Are you sure Irene's parents won't accept my offer to pay for their airfares? I would be more than happy to help them. I'd hate to miss my daughter competing in one of the most prestigious sporting events in the world," he said, shaking his head.

"I've tried, but Irene's parents are extremely proud."

"I rarely judge people, Davina. But I'd say a little foolish into the bargain! And now I insist you go. Especially since Irene's parents won't be there to support her. So you go with my blessing, and a chaperone." He winked, "Charlotte has already told me she would love to go with you."

I don't know how many times I hugged and kissed Father; it seemed a million or more. Then, Frederick, or Freddy, as I chose to call him, drove me home. I ran inside, adrenaline pumping as I packed my bags, including a stuffed kangaroo and a small flag of Australia. Irene later cried with joy when I phoned and told her the news.

"I will be there with you all the way, Irene." I said, "I know you'll stay in the athletes' village. And we may not see each other as often as we'd like. But remember, I'll be right there cheering you on. Oh yes, and so will Charlotte. She's my chaperone. Father would not allow me to travel alone, and he greatly respects Charlotte, so I'm chuffed. We'll have a great time and do some sightseeing in the bargain. I can't wait. Can you?"

"I'm as nervous as a pregnant nun! *I suppose it's natural.* My coach says it is." She laughed. "I don't mean the pregnant nun! *That's not natural.*"

"Oh, Irene, you are a card. I'm so happy you run like a rocket. Otherwise, we would never have met. I hope Father's secretary has secured a ticket for me on the same flight as you. I'll check and let you know. Goodbye, for now, my dearest friend."

Although Charlotte and I were not on the same flight as Irene, we arrived at Helsinki airport the day after. Weary but excited. We hurried through the crowd to grab our bags when I noticed a silver-haired, ruddy-cheeked man holding a sign with our names on it. He was our chauffeur, Hanns, whom Father had arranged for us. Hanns welcomed us and carried our cases to his car before driving us to the Grand Hotel, located near the athletes' village.

I felt overwhelmed by being in a city so removed from Australian-English architecture, with its sleek lines and modernistic style; I thought it must be one of the most avant-garde cities in the world. I needed to taste, smell, and experience everyting.

Excitedly, Charlotte and I showered, dressed smartly, and then ventured downstairs to meet our tour guide, a young chauffeur whom Hanns had recommended and organised after explaining his inability to drive us beyond the hotel. A tall, fair-headed, handsome young man with dreamy but piercing sky-blue eyes entered the foyer. *Ten minutes late.*

"Please forgive me, ladies. I am so sorry. I was delayed with a last-minute assignment." He smiled, revealing his perfect, white teeth. "I do not normally drive around. Sorry, I mean chauffeur. I am a university student studying Architecture. I am sorry. I am what you say - rambling. I am so sorry. I am pleased to meet you both. My name is Felix." He bowed, proffering his hand. Charlotte and I giggled like schoolgirls.

Charlotte whispered, "Perhaps we should call him sorry, not Felix."

I immediately liked Felix; we seemed to share an energy I couldn't fathom then.

Father had selected our hotel perfectly. It sat within walking distance of the Olympic stadium, which Felix drove slowly past. It was an architectural masterpiece that fitted my description of a *space-age* city.

Helsinki's *historic* buildings sat on the City's outskirts, and I asked Felix to drive us there. Excitedly, he went on to explain what we were about to see with profound animation. I had to giggle.

After Felix parked the car, we strolled around these time-marked buildings. It had me in awe of their design, artistry, and history. My favourite was the Helsinki Cathedral, and we stood motionless, allowing Felix to inform us about the massive white structure that sported an enormous dome at its center.

"From 1830 to 1852, this building was built in honour of Tsar Nicholas 1 of Russia, and designed by world-renowned architect Carl Ludwig," said Felix. I admired him even more when he whispered. "My relative, Ernst Lohmann, later altered some of the Cathedral's structure. He, too, was a great architect. But that was two centuries ago." Felix smiled, dipping his head, sending a truss of blond hair over his eyes.

Suddenly, I knew I'd witness that for years to come. It stole my breath. Then, and just as quickly, I gathered my senses and listened studiously to Felix's structure analysis. There was no mistaking his passion for architecture.

After we'd toured most of the City and its surroundings, I, too, was hooked. Not so, Charlotte. She'd nodded off to sleep in the back seat. I'd chosen to sit beside Felix.

"So," I asked, "is your surname Lohmann?"

"Yes, I am Felix Lohmann." He turned with a smile and barely missed a cyclist. "Watch out!" I screamed.

"Oh, I am sorry, Davina. I keep my eyes riding on the road." I laughed at his terminology.

Sadly, it came time to return to the hotel. I would have liked to see Felix again, but I thought there was little chance unless I asked him to show us more sights.

Felix appeared innocent but enthusiastic about everything, especially when he questioned me about Australia. I had to bring him back on track, as I was there to see Helsinki and learn as much as possible about the place. It was such an incredible and vastly different country. I hadn't travelled out of Australia, so I wanted to see more.

After shaking Charlotte awake, I thanked Felix and, although nervous, asked, "Will you be watching any Olympic events, Felix?"

"Yes. I have tickets to the running races and swimming events," Felix lowered his voice, "I nearly made the Olympic swimming team."

"Really? That's fantastic!" I shouted, and he laughed.

"I would like to talk with you more, Davina. Maybe share a cup of coffee?" He smiled coyly, "I mean, we could have our coffee in different cups." I watched his cheeks pinken, and my heart reached out to him, "That is, if you have free time."

"I'd love to, Felix. Are you available tomorrow? It doesn't matter what time. We can meet here if you like. There's a coffee lounge on the ground floor."

"Yes, I would like that very much. I do not have lectures until tomorrow afternoon. Would ten o'clock in the morning suit you, Davina?"

"Yes, I look forward to us talking more, Felix. And drinking our coffee in separate cups." He laughed.

Charlotte stood beside me, rubbing her sleepy eyes. "Goodbye, Felix, thank you," she said with a yawn and a wave.

Felix arrived before me the following morning, and he threw me a beaming smile as I walked toward him into the hotel coffee shop. We sat facing each other across the table and spoke freely about many things, including our ambitions. Although we were traveling different paths, we were genuinely interested in each other's stories. Felix's fascination with architecture consumed him, and my love of riding and competing at the highest level left no room for anything else.

I became melancholy after admitting my passion for horses. Maybe my mood prompted the following statement. "But who knows, perhaps I'll fall in love and marry. Then, my obsession with horses may cool a little. I'd have other things to worry about." I said, trying to lighten my stupidity, with a giggle.

Fancy mentioning marriage to Felix. He must think I'm hinting at a relationship. Then, gratefully, Felix admitted, "I, too, would like to marry and have children."

Oh no, I hope he doesn't think I'm suggesting… We quickly changed the subject, a knee-jerk reaction, I'm sure.

While sitting opposite this young, handsome man, I suddenly realised I'd forgotten how plain I was. He didn't make me feel ugly. Not once did his blue eyes leave mine. In fact, his admiring looks sent my heart racing. But I dared not believe he had anything other than friendship in mind. We were comfortable in each other's company, we laughed at the same things, and Felix seemed genuinely interested in my horses. So, I squashed any romantic notions and stayed true to who I was and why I was in Helsinki. Later, Felix surprised me by handing me a ticket to the swimming finals.

"You have so many great Australian swimmers. I thought you might like to join me and cheer them on. Unfortunately, I cannot see Finland being in the finals," he said with a shrug and a cheeky grin. I accepted the ticket, delighted that we would stay in contact.

Charlotte and I spent the rest of the day shopping for gifts and were thrilled to try on some of the latest European fashions. Intermittently, she'd questioned me about Felix. *Was she suggesting something lay between us?* I scoffed at her implication.

"He's a nice young man, Charlotte. And we're interested in the same things, even though Felix has never ridden a horse. He said his adopted sister, Hilda, rides well. She owns a Holsteiner and competes in dressage. Not to Grand Prix standard, because she doesn't have time. Hilda's studying to be a doctor. We just talked a lot and shared each other's stories. I like Felix as a friend."

"I saw how he looked at you, Davina, I'm telling you……"

The glare I gave Charlotte prevented any further discussion about romance. Secretly, I didn't want to be hurt or shunned by Felix. And then it struck me, at no time did I feel nervous or self-conscious with Felix. It was as if we were friends from a past life—soul mates. I didn't want to ruin that.

Sadly, only a one-time slot allowed Irene and me to meet. It was the day before the Grand Opening. We hugged, cried, and laughed until I discovered nerves were almost devouring her. I'd never seen Irene in such a state. Usually, she focused so intently that nothing penetrated her barrier.

"Hasn't your coach helped you control your nerves, Irene?" I asked, a little surprised.

"He's wonderful, but it's all so overwhelming." Irene sniffled back tears and wiped her eyes. "Even Marjorie Jackson pulled me aside and told me to focus on the things I love. *Other than running.* It was to relax me and take my mind away to other places. However, I find it impossible when I'm away from home, competing against the world. My parents' efforts and sacrifices will be for nothing if I fail. And I know everyone will be watching me! I'll be ashamed to go home if I'm no good. I can't stop thinking about it. I can't!"

I hugged her until she finally stopped sobbing, then I held her apart and looked into her eyes, remembering the words I'd often hear our Jackaroo say.

"That's bullshit! Now you listen to me, Irene. To be here at seventeen is a triumph in itself. Whatever you do in Helsinki, you will improve in Melbourne. I guarantee it. Use this opportunity as a practice run. Don't think about the pressure. Have fun and run like a bloody tiger is after you! Yes, that's it! Run for your life, Irene. And remember, as you mature, you will learn to control your emotions. So don't let your demons beat you before you even run!"

She held me tight, "I'll try, Davvy."

We spent the rest of the day relaxing by the sea, laughing, and eating the best ice cream I'd ever tasted. Perhaps my sisterly advice had taken effect, as Irene settled into her old, funny self by the day's end.

The following evening, Charlotte and I enjoyed the spectacular opening of the Olympics. The highlight. I believe in my eyes was the torchbearer, 'The Flying Finn.' He entered the Stadium to booming applause, and my heart skipped a beat.

I knew little about Paavo Narmi —his real name —beyond that he was a champion marathon runner and his country's hero. The atmosphere was electric, and I felt a deep connection. The urgency to compete in dressage at the Melbourne Olympics became monumental. It was a passion I thought would fill me for the rest of my life; I could taste it in those thrilling moments.

The first heat of the 200 metre women's running race came the following day. Charlotte and I took our seats and tried hard to send positive vibes to Irene. I'd brought Father's binoculars, so I had a close view of Irene walking behind her starting position, shaking her hands and feet, limbering up. She took deep breaths and blew them out slowly through her mouth.

I prayed.

The runners crouched in the starting position for what seemed an eternity before the gun fired. Then, Irene sprang like a gazelle to quickly settle third on the inside track. I prayed she'd stay there and be within the time needed for the next heat. And she did. Irene ran a close third. Charlotte and I stood and hugged each other while Irene ran around the track until she spotted us and blew kisses. At the same time, I heard, 'Davina! Davina!' I turned to see Felix above us. He excused himself to all, hurrying towards me with arms outstretched as if we'd known each other forever. I fell into them.

"You must be so excited, Davina. That means your friend Irene will be in the next heat tomorrow. I will be here. My seat is five rows above you. I saw you, but did not want to take away your concentration." He smiled into my eyes. It sent a delightful frisson of excitement through me. "I need to return to my studies at the University now. I will see you here tomorrow, Davina."

He walked away, and with a backward wave, he said, "Goodbye,

Charlotte."

We watched Felix make his way out of the Stadium, saying 'sorry' to everyone. We laughed. "I told you we should call him, *sorry*," said Charlotte, winking.

We needed to walk past Felix to take our seats the following day. He stood as we approached and bowed to us. *So charming*, I thought. I could not imagine meeting a more courteous man.

"Good day to you, Felix. Are you able to join us for refreshments after Irene's trial? Charlotte asked, and my heart skipped a beat.

"Yes, only for a short while. Then I must leave. Let us pray it will be a celebration drink. If Irene wins this heat, she will be in the first semi-final. Am I correct?"

"Yes, you are correct, Felix. See you later," I said as I walked down the aisle to our front-row seats.

As expected, Irene won her next heat in almost record time, putting her against her idol, Marjorie Jackson, in the semis. I was beyond myself with excitement and nerves, and wondered how Irene felt. I could only pray she would follow Marjorie's advice and not let nerves destroy her natural ability.

Later, as Felix suggested, we found a bar within the Olympic complex to enjoy a celebratory drink. I was too young to drink alcohol in public. Still, Felix and Charlotte enjoyed the Hartwall Long drink, a mix of Grapefruit juice laced with a generous amount of Gin, specially concocted for the Helsinki Olympics. I chose lemonade. We then saluted Irene and her future gold medal win. The more Felix and I conversed, sharing many laughs, the more my heart argued with my mind. Will our friendship go further? Will Felix stay in contact when I leave?

Our night ended with those questions unanswered, but I was warmed by the tiny flame he'd ignited in my heart. I'd never lacked courage when riding horses, but it vanished within my personal belief. I smiled, feeling the heat rise in my cheeks when we shared a promise to celebrate after Irene's predicted victory, leading to the women's 200-metre race finals.

Later, walking to our hotel room, Charlotte surprised me, "Felix really likes you, Davina. Will you keep in touch after you return home?"

"We'll see." I hung my head lest she notice the colour rising in my cheeks.

"There's no harm in having a pen pal, Davina. I think it's lovely that you've found another friend. He doesn't have to be your boyfriend."

"I know that, Charlotte. We'll see," I said through gritted teeth.

That was the end of our conversation about Felix. Never again did I allow the what-ifs after I told Charlotte bluntly, "Besides, I'm keen to return home and prepare for the 1956 Olympics. And I won't have time for anything else."

My overseas trip, combined with experiencing the Olympic Games for the first time, had inspired me beyond all imagination. Plus, I was only seventeen, far too young for a boyfriend, *I told myself.* And I needed to be convinced that Felix truly liked or, better still, was attracted to me. I always felt my life would be filled with one-way romances. Never in my wildest dreams could I imagine a handsome, intelligent young man genuinely loving *me, the ugly duckling.*

**

Irene's nervous energy radiated as she lined up for the final of the two hundred metres. I could feel her nerves and see her aura. Yes, she'd made it after running another excellent time the day before. With my binoculars, I got a close view, and I noticed Marjorie throw Irene a Mona Lisa smile. 'God bless her,' I whispered.

The sun, shining brightly, sent a golden glow over Irene. It had to be an omen. Charlotte and I had rushed to our allocated seat seconds before the starting gun fired, and I focused on Irene's every stride, knowing she'd have her race planned. So I didn't panic when I saw her running second-to-last.

Then, over the final fifty metres, Irene gave her all to pass most runners and produce the fastest time of her short career. However, her brilliant effort was insufficient to win a medal and beat the all-conquering Marjorie Jackson. Charlotte and I were not *too* disappointed. Whichever way we looked at the race, Marjorie had won gold for Australia, and Irene had done her personal best.

Later, a philosophical Irene said, "I'll do better in Melbourne. I only need to improve a tenth of a second." Then she laughed. "And hope Marjorie doesn't."

I was later shocked to hear that Irene had qualified for the Final 800-meter hurdles. "Oh my God, I didn't know you hurdled, Irene."

"Well, it's not my specialty, Davvy. But I'll give it my best shot!"

I watched, horrified, as Irene knocked most hurdles over and struggled into the last position. I cringed with her every mistake until, to our delight, Australian Shirley Strickland-de-la-Hunty won the race. So, again, we had reason to cheer. Later, Irene came in with a clanger.

"I won't be hurdling anymore, Davvy. I think I've split my difference."

Charlotte and I cried, laughing.

We watched many fabulous events over the following days, including Lis Hartel from Denmark winning a silver medal in dressage. A remarkable feat, as Lis is paralysed from her knees down and needed to be lifted onto her horse.

Also, in his tenacious 200-metre breaststroke swim, Felix and I cheered John Davies to win another Gold Medal for Australia. John was Australian-American. What did that matter? He swam for Australia.

Sadly, the games had to end. Although my happiness outweighed the disappointment, especially knowing I'd found a friend in Felix and experienced the most fantastic, memorable time of my life.

Felix drove us to the airport and then helped carry our luggage to the boarding lounge. He placed the cases on the floor and smiled in his shy, boyish way.

"This is where I bid you farewell, Davina. I trust it is not goodbye. When my University degree finishes, I hope to come to Australia and see you again." He hung his head, but not before I could see moisture clouding his blue eyes. I hugged him tightly.

"I cannot wait, Felix. I'll write to you often. Until we meet again," I said, struggling to keep my emotions intact.

"Don't be sad, Davina," Felix spoke into my shoulder, his warmth infusing mine. "It has been a happy time. We are friends now, and we will spend more time together. I know we will, but I must leave you now."

He turned to kiss Charlotte on the cheek. "Goodbye, Charlotte. It was a pleasure to meet you. And all the best in your upcoming marriage with Jacques." He turned and kissed my lips in a lingering moment of bliss. He then stepped back and held my face. "Please write to me, Davina."

With those parting words and that kiss tingling my senses, I watched dreamily as Felix walked away, weaving his way against the oncoming passengers. "Sorry. I am so sorry," he said repeatedly, and Charlotte laughed while I floated on a cloud, unable to move until she grabbed my arm. And even then, I turned to see Felix, but he was gone.

CHAPTER 9
DAVINA'S HOMECOMING

Once home, I hurried to the stables and embraced Miss Molly, breathing in her scent. It was the best place to think about what had happened. *Does Felix genuinely have feelings for me? Yes, he does. No, it's only my imagination. I can't believe a man like Felix could ever love me.*

Molly nuzzled my neck, making me giggle, "I know, you know, what I'm feeling, Molly. Thank you." I stroked her pretty head, "I need to get back to work. So I best not dwell on Felix." Molly nodded. I assumed in agreement. I walked away feeling sad that Molly was neither good enough nor tall enough to compete in Grand Prix Dressage.

When Father first agreed to my leaving school to pursue a riding career, he'd asked Jacques, "What horses in particular would Davina need to compete at the highest level? Money is of no consequence, Jacques."

And while I was in Helsinki, four magnificent Holsteiner horses arrived. One at a time, thanks to Jacques and Father. I had no sooner walked away from Molly that day when Jacques and Charlotte arrived.

"Fancy seeing you here, Charlotte." I said, "It's been such a long time." She laughed.

"Wasn't it fabulous, Davina? I still can't believe how generous your father is."

With Charlotte's words, the contrast between Father's fading health and his generosity hit like a sledgehammer. He'd become so frail in the past month that I barely recognised him. His hair had turned white, and his frame skeletal. It was apparent he'd come home to die, and I would not encourage him to return to Melbourne for further treatment. Instead, I hoped he'd take comfort in sharing happy memories with his family.

Instinctively, I knew then to step back and ask Jacques and Charlotte to train my new horses and choose which ones they thought were the best Olympic dressage prospects, so I looked Jacques in the eye.

"I need to spend all my time with Father." Tears welled, and I sniffed, "I…I don't think he has long."

Jacques hugged me and whispered, "Of course, little one, we will train your horses." He then included Charlotte in his embrace, "We will always be here for you. And your family."

I immediately summoned Joseph home from university, where he was becoming a well-respected young scientist. Unfortunately for Father, Joseph had already expressed that he would not follow his forefather's ambition to breed the best Angus cattle on the planet. Joseph's mind, it seemed, was beyond our earthly realm; he was a genius, and I wished he'd never matured because we had such fun as children. I suppose I felt sorry for Joseph, leading an insular life, not interested in anything beyond what makes something work and what will happen if you do this to that. I know it's basic terminology, especially as I follow my heart. I believe I'm a realist who admires the pioneering work of dreamers and artists.

At this time, Mother was visiting a new doctor, recommended by a friend or acquaintance, *as most were*. And on my return, she even hugged *me*.

"I've missed you, Davina." Mother said sincerely.

"I've missed you, too, Mother. Do you want to talk about Father?" I asked kindly, hoping we could have a normal conversation. Instead, she lowered her head and began weeping into her handkerchief. What could I do but hug her again?

"It's alright, Mother. We can talk later. When you're ready."

I learned later from Father that Mother had finally accepted her prescribed medicine and took it religiously. Plus, she refused alcohol. For the first time, I felt proud of my mother.

Dear Cookie had also guided Mother into *her* world.

"I'll keep Mrs. Buchanan occupied. She won't have time to be thinking about anything else." She confided.

Much to everyone's amazement, Mother excelled at producing culinary delights that we enjoyed daily. Mother even suggested that Betty and she donate their brandy-infused fruit cakes to the less fortunate in our district. We couldn't agree more, so the conveyor belt began, and the distribution went forth, keeping Mother extremely busy and happy for a change.

What do you know, our family was living a simple life and enjoyed it.

I knew that Father enduring pain and accepting his finality must be difficult, but I'd never seen him so happy or content. It seemed Mother had shed her self-indulgent personality and rallied brilliantly to the call of our family and the wider community.

Joseph spent most of his time reading books to Father, albeit science books, until I'd surreptitiously slip a Charles Dickens under his nose—Father's favourite author. And then, Joseph would smile, enticing me to shuffle my memory back to the adventures we shared as children while I sat in Mother's feathered armchair, half-listening to Joseph reading aloud.

I found it fascinating how vividly I could reproduce our past experiences. I'd close my eyes and see movies of us building tree houses, racing each other on roller skates, galloping ponies into the bush, picnic lunches bouncing in our saddlebags. We were warned never to swim in the river unless accompanied by an adult, but Joseph and I, being strong swimmers, took no caution. However, we stayed relatively safe by swimming close to the bank. Then we'd enjoy our picnic lunch. Be it summer or winter, we'd ride to the river and eat lunch in the same spot under the enormous peppercorn tree our great-great-grandfather had planted. And later, we'd run our fingers over all the initials carved into its massive trunk.

It makes me happy now to shut my eyes and gather those memories. My psychologist was right about returning to happier times. It does help.

I began spending time in Father's office, reading about our family history while Joseph gave Father his attention and Mother occupied herself in the kitchen.

Our entire family history was recorded in several large, leather-bound books spanning the past ten generations — their births, deaths, and lives, including their significant achievements. Plus, the downfall of some whose entire story appeared clouded — incomplete. I thought, well, at least they were mentioned. I suppose that's what you'd call owning the truth but not admitting it.

No family is perfect, they say.

One thing that struck me was our family's knowledge of the benefits of Carlina thistle and its proven value in treating a wide range of ailments. As I read the intricate transcript, the distant voice I often heard, which had led me to do things better and see everything more clearly, came again to confirm that this information was accurate.

Carlina Thistle is one of God's gifts, my great-great-grandfather had written. *The Lord God created these healing shrubs to cure our ailments.* A revelation, most definitely! I wanted to use a loudspeaker and voice the conclusions of many who have discovered the secrets that grow under our noses. The Chinese have employed natural therapy for over a thousand years, demonstrating its effectiveness in treating various diseases.

Later, I asked Father if he'd stopped taking the 'Carlina Remedy' because I knew he'd begun taking it when his cancer first appeared.

"Yes, I stopped taking it, Davina. My doctor said it would do no harm but presumed it would not help."

"Why on earth would you even tell him? I suspect you stopped taking it when I left for Helsinki. Before then, you looked fine. A little tired, maybe, but not ill. You had colour in your cheeks, and your hair was only specked with grey. Now, you're…"

"Now, now, Davina. I have a terminal illness. So, of course, I will disintegrate before your eyes. I'm sorry. But if it makes *you* feel better, I will retake it." He stood, I assumed, to get the Carlina medicine. "Oh yes," He said, "And an old school friend gave me some other liquid from the ocean. He says it works wonders with cancer. Or anything else that ails us." Father lifted my chin, "I'll go and fetch the so-called natural cures right now, my darling girl. And you make sure I take them every day. My new nurse, Davina." He said, chuckling as he shuffled away.

Whatever hope there was, I needed to cling to it. I didn't know how I'd cope without Father. It was a time of deep reflection, and I tried not to dwell on his eventual passing, but instead to show him my love and respect, and to share his knowledge and compassion for all living creatures. I suspected I'd inherited his love of nature. Even though he'd designed and built significant objects from steel in the past, which were complex and almost indestructible, he loved and appreciated nature's delicate yet essential phenomena, so easily destroyed if we allowed it.

Father returned with a glass of water and both concoctions, then handed them to me. "I keep the herbal medicine in the cabinet above my bathroom basin, Davina. Now that you know, you can give it to me twice a day. That's what the labels state. Is that alright with you, my dear?"

I laughed, "Yes, I will take charge. Starting now!"

I read the instructions and the benefits of both, thinking that if they did what they claimed, it would give us more precious time to share before the inevitable. And I can honestly say it wasn't long before Father lifted miraculously like parched earth after rain, all within a month of swallowing his alternative medicine.

Our days continued in harmony, and by the time Mother and Betty baked one hundred fruit cakes, Father felt well enough to venture outside to inspect his cattle. Finally, and most importantly, to watch me ride my horses through their paces. It seemed to raise his spirits endlessly, and his enthusiasm inspired me. I prayed he would live long enough to watch me compete in the next Olympics.

**

Two years of hard work and training had passed, filtered with tender letters and photographs from Felix; I could not help but adore this amazing young man. My heart filled with joy, and my hands shook with excitement as I wrote back. Finally, after his constant writings, I decided that Felix cared for me deeply, even knowing his passion for architecture almost outshone my love for horses, and we might be heading in opposite directions. I suppose I created a moving picture when riding dressage. Although it would not stand the annals of time, only the art form would. Felix possessed the gift of creating timeless structures that would last for centuries. Everything is relevant, I know. But I understand that whatever we achieve doesn't matter as long as we keep building it and not destroying it.

The most significant part of our relationship was that Felix did not judge me. His affection was genuine, I knew, because he'd finished his letters *to the girl I love, Davina.* My heart soared with those words, and I knew we'd eventually be together. How could we not? After two years apart, our friendship and then our love had somehow grown. It was almost a miracle!

Meanwhile, my dearest friend Irene remained steadfast in her pursuit of winning gold at the Melbourne Olympics. And so, under pressure to train and succeed, we spent little time together, though I looked forward to our long, informative phone chats and our shared laughter. It was better than any vitamin tonic. However, my concern was that Irene had found a boyfriend. A young man named Billy Peterson from Ballarat, whose family owned a sheep station twenty miles north of the township. It was where Billy did most of his training to make the Olympic track and field team.

I should have felt happy for Irene, but something bothered me whenever she spoke of Billy. Was it jealousy about their relationship or worry for Irene's safety because Billy, Irene boasted, drove his car at breakneck speed? Billy was gifted a car for his eighteenth birthday, making it easier for him to travel to his main training sessions in Melbourne.

Along with Billy, Irene seemed to relish the velocity they reached on the open country roads. He loved speed and declared to Irene that he'd be a racing car driver when he finished running in races. My enthusiasm for meeting Billy and driving in his car always ended with a reluctant pause after listening to Irene's banter about my hero, Billy. I prayed for their safety every night.

December 1954 seemed to arrive in a blaze of heat. Fortunately, the weather cooled down on the day of Jacques and Charlotte's outdoor wedding, which they'd postponed from 1952 for one reason or another. I was the only bridesmaid, and Uncle Aaron looked most distinguished as the best man. Charlotte's father gave her away under a trellis of climbing apricot roses. We enjoyed an intimate, joyous wedding on Uncle Aaron's property. The food was delicious, the champagne flowed, and we danced the night away. The following day, the happy couple departed on their two-week honeymoon to Brisbane, a city neither had visited. I felt only happiness for them.

They were my dear friends.

CHAPTER 10
EVIE'S FARM

After twelve months of living in Carlton, feeling unwelcome in a tight-knit, suspicious community, Sean came home late one evening yelling, "Pack y'bags, Cathy! Be quick. We're leavin!"

Evie woke to Sean yelling and her parents hurrying about, knocking things over. "Why Sean? What happened?" asked a shocked Cathy.

"I've no time t'be talkin, Cathy. Get d'money yer stashed. Pack yer things. We're goin bush. We have t'lay low f'awhile."

Cathy soon hurried into Evie's room, filled a bag with Evie's clothes, and wrapped her in the eiderdown. All the while, Evie clung to the whimpering pup. "Shoosh, Matey, we're goin bush; Da's found a farm."

Evie snuggled with Matey in her arms on the back seat of the car Sean had bought that day and drifted off to sleep. She didn't wake until the sun shone through the window. Evie sat up, rubbing her eyes to focus on cows grazing and sheep with lambs chasing each other. It made Evie smile. It was like a painting with no one in sight, unlike the city, where the noise and rush of crowds unnerved her.

Ma's pleading broke Evie's pondering. "How far is it, Sean? Y'have t'stop? I need a pee."

"Okay, Cathy. I'll pull over, and yer can squat over dere."

"I need t'pee too, Ma!" Evie scrambled out of the car with Matey.

Thankfully, Matey's bladder held until he flooded the dry grass, which made them laugh.

"How on earth did he hold onta dat lot!" said Cathy.

"Come on, girls, we're almost dere!" Sean called.

"Is it our farm, Da?" Evie said.

"Yep. Yer got y'wish. We'll soon be dere."

Sean slammed on the brakes when he saw a misshapen barrel

sitting precariously on top of an iron pole with the number 559. The old, rickety gate looked as if it'd topple over if Cathy opened it too quickly, so she carefully lifted it aside for Sean to drive through. They sat silently as he drove up the long track leading to a weatherboard home surrounded by an overgrown garden. The front door, painted brown, sat in the centre, flanked by two large windows. Three wide steps led to the generous veranda, and two well-worn wicker chairs sat on either side of a round wooden table. Cathy laughed.

"I can just see us sittin dere on a hot day sippin a cold lager."

"Yep, looks like a good spot f'a beer, Cathy. Now, let's take a look inside. Where'd I put dat key?"

"In d'glove box, Love. Remember?"

Evie hurried out of the car and placed Matey on the ground, where he did another long widdle. "Good boy, Matey," Evie said, before she remembered, "Ma, where's me teddy bear?"

"I'm sorry, Evie, I couldn't carry everything!"

They stood together, listening to the occasional bird song breaking the silence. Evie's face lit up as she gazed at the acres of land and the vast blue sky, filled only with gum trees, so tall they seemed part of the sky. Once inside, they inspected the spacious lounge room. Hands on hips, Cathy declared, "Well, at least it's clean, just a little dusty. Notin I can't fix. I'll have it gleamin in no time."

Sean landed a peck on her cheek.

"Dats m' girl. I reckon I'll be likin' dis place. For a while. Dat's, until the boss finds me jobs in d'city." He held Cathy to his side, "You'll be alright out here on yer own, won't yer, Cathy?"

"I'll never be alone. I'll always have *Evie*." *He's forgotten about Evie. Again!*

"Evie and I'll grow vegetables and get d'garden lookin pretty. And we'll ask the neighbours if they know of a pony for sale for Evie."

"Dat's good," Sean said, taking no heed, "'cause I'll have t'be travellin back and forth t'oder states. But I'll make sure yer have plenty of money."

Cathy reluctantly accepted another squeeze and a kiss before taking a deep, calming breath. "So y'hasn't told me who the farm belongs to, Sean."

"It belongs to d'Boss. But not on paper. He's got a dummy owner. D'boss said if I keep doin good in d'business, we can have d'farm for real.

In place of payment, dat is."

"What payment? Does he owe yer money, Sean?"

"No, he means instead of paying me cash in d'future, alright?"

Cathy sighed, shaking her head. "Me worry is Sean. You'll be caught and jailed." He laughed,

"I told yer before, Cathy, I'm too smart, f'dat. Y'can do what yer like wid d'money, I don't care. I'm only interested in d'challenges and havin adventures wid me mates."

Cathy turned to gaze out the window with her thoughts: *Ireland, dats where Evie and I'll be goin wid d'money. Dough I'd hate t'be leavin Sean, I love him. Silly bugger dat he is. I know he can't be changin his Devil May Care* attitude. *Me only consolation in writing to Da, and whether he was telling d'truth or not, I can't say. But he wrote,* 'I'm feelin well, Cathy— the farm's doin fine. Though I'm missin' you and Evie somtin terrible. Yer wouldn't consider coming home, Cathy?' *Yes, I will, Pa, if Sean ever gets thrown in jail.* Cathy didn't write that. Instead, she wrote. I'm savin' money, Pa—Sean's doin well at work. We'll come home t'Ireland when I've enough money.

**

After weeks of hard work, Cathy and Evie had manicured the front garden. They'd dug deep into the rich soil and spread cow manure before planting petunias and daisies. A rainwater tank supplied only their personal needs. Therefore, a good rainstorm would be a blessing for the garden. Lately, there'd been very little. Whenever they worked, the windmills pumped bore water for the garden and the livestock. It frustrated Cathy as she would love to wash the house down with rainwater. At the moment, the house looked grey. It was supposed to be white.

D'rain water'll bring it back t'life. I hope it fills d'tank. D'bore water's filthy.

She and Evie worked tirelessly planting vegetables in raised garden beds they'd fenced behind chook wire. And each day, they'd walk the boundary of their one hundred acres. After three weeks, Cathy and Evie were familiar with every shrub, tree, wildflower, and most birds and creatures that lived on what Cathy had named 'Evie's Farm.' Cathy had asked Sean to paint the sign. Aversely, he found a piece of wood, painted the name on it, and nailed it above the front gate, which he'd also fixed to swing. They were the only chores Sean had accomplished in the past four weeks.

Sean spent most of his time travelling to the village, using the public telephone booth to call his boss. He'd then frequent the pub, acting like the rookie farmer, wanting to learn all he could about sheep and cattle. Until Jock, the oldest grazier who lived on the farm next to Sean, looked up from his frothy beer and said, "You'll never make a living out of a hundred acres here, mate. You're best to sell up while you're ahead. That's if you own the place," Jock lifted his beer with a smile.

Sean laughed, "If d'truth be known, Jock, I only bought d'place for me' daughter, so she could have a pony. I was just tryin t'be friendly. Do any of you fellas have a pony for sale?" He patted old Jock on the back. "So yer got me, Jock. Still, I tink we could be runnin a few head of cattle and maybe some sheep t'kill for d' table. The land don't look *too* bad."

Their discussion then hit an honest note, especially when Sean told the men he had a job doing *shift* work in the city. (That was correct. He shifted a hell of a lot.) "Dat's how I earn me money. I only bought d'farm f'me daughter." Sean's admission brought a lenient attitude from the men around the bar.

The following day, Jock towed a small trailer behind his ute, loaded with one ram and four young ewes, to 'Evie's Farm.' Sean peered suspiciously through the window. Satisfied, Jock was no threat; he hurried outside to meet him.

"Good mornin t'yer Jock. And where might yer be goin with dat lot?" Sean said, scratching his head.

"I thought I'd save you the trouble of going to the sales, Sean. This mob is as good as any you'll get there. You can have them for half the auction price if you're interested. Ten bob a piece."

Cathy appeared on the front verandah, wiping her hands on her apron.

"Sean, aren't yer gonna ask yer friend t'come in for a cuppa tea and d'scones I just baked?"

Jock tipped his well-worn Akubra hat, "Thanks, Mrs... I'll take you up on that offer when Sean tells me what to do with the sheep." He gave Sean a quizzical look.

"Okay, Jock, I'll buy 'em." Sean turned to Cathy, "Have we got a decent paddock?"

Evie ran from behind the house with Matey chasing, and before Cathy could open her mouth, Evie called, "I know a paddock, Da. Follow me, Mr...."

Evie ran ahead while Jock drove slowly, following Evie to the paddock where she and Cathy had mended the fence. Evie opened the gate for Jock to move the trailer through, then watched as he unloaded the sheep. They closed the gate and leaned on the fence posts together, eyeing the sheep before Evie looked up into Jock's faded blue eyes, "I reckon dis is a real farm now, Mr."

Jock proffered his hand, and Evie shook it.

"I reckon it's a start, young lass."

"Me name's Evie. What's yours?"

"My name is Arthur Smith, but you can call me Jock. Everyone else does."

Between conversation, mouthfuls of tea, and cream scones, Jock sat back, studying Sean. *He's hiding something. That's why they've ended up in this small town. And with a little more investigating, I'll learn how he came to know about this mostly deserted farmhouse.*

Living on the adjoining property, Jock knew when strangers camped in the house. Not for long, though. Before meeting Sean in the Pub, nobody had stayed for more than a week or two. Drifters, Jock called them, but wondered why they all seemed to know about the place. He wouldn't push that question today. Instead, Jock thanked Cathy for the best scones he'd eaten, including those of his dear departed Bessie.

Before leaving, he noticed a telephone attached to the wall.

"I see you have a telephone, Sean, so I'm wondering why you use the public phone in town?"

"I can't get it to work, Jock," Sean said, a little uneasy.

"I'll take a look." Jock dialed Martha at the exchange, "Hello Martha, it's Jock. I'm just checking on Sean and Cathy Calan's phone." He smiled, "Yes, they're the new people. Yes, they live next door to me."

Their chat continued while Sean looked on, anxious, but then decided Jock hadn't given too much away.

The three stood on the verandah and waved goodbye to Jock.

Sean turned to Cathy, "He's a good old bloke, Cathy. Best yer invite him for dinner when I'm gone. But don't tell him anything. Okay?"

The sudden clarity of Sean's words hit her like a piece of four by two.

"Gone! What do y'mean gone!"

"I only mean from time t'time. You know, Cathy, I told yer. Interstate travel." He lay Cathy back in his arms and kissed her passionately, knowing it would melt the tension. He then turned to tell Evie to nick off. But she'd gone, and he didn't care where.

Evie had run with her heart pounding, excited about owning sheep.

"Now we have a real farm, and Ma can send f'Pa," she said to Matey, who tilted his head before their attention turned to a ram mounting a ewe. They observed with interest until he'd done his job. "She'll be havin a baby soon, Matey," he barked, seeming to understand. "Now, all I need is a pony t'round-up d'sheep. They have t'be sheared, yer know. Then we can sell the wool. Maybe we'll be rich!" Evie laughed, ruffling Matey's head, "Come on, boy, we'd better make sure dey have water. The old windmill don't look too good. Maybe Jock'll fix it. *I know Da won't.*"

They eased through the fence and checked the water. It was only dripping into the trough, but there was enough until the windmill worked.

Evie trekked home with a large stick to protect them from the snakes her ma had warned her about, singing the Irish ballad '*Danny Boy.*' Cathy said she had a sweet voice and wondered how she remembered all the words.

"Old Pa taught me dat song, so I'll never forget." Evie smiled down at Matey.

"Ma, Ma," Evie called, shaking her boots off at the back door.

"I'm here, Evie, in d'lounge room."

Cathy looked up from writing a letter and smiled at Evie, who never ceased to amaze her. Though Evie was seven, she behaved more like a ten-year-old; admittedly, she'd seen and heard more than she should. But it seemed to Cathy that Evie was born with a knowing, and while not agreeing with everything she heard, Evie remained silent, making her own plans. Cathy knew Evie would cope with whatever happened. The thought put her fears at bay.

I'm feelin safe for a change, and Evie's happy. Dis farm is just d'place. I'll go t' d'local school tomorrow and ask about Evie attendin'. I'm worried, though, after her terrible time at d'Carlton School. I know she doesn't want t'leave d'farm. Jock said, d'bus stops out d'front to pick Evie up, and then it drops her home. Now dat'd be easy!

Cathy stirred from her thoughts, "Yes, Evie. What is it?"

"We'd better ask Jock t'fix the windmill, Ma. It's leanin' somtin' bad. And the water's just dribblin in. So d'sheep won't have notin t'drink soon."

Cathy placed the pen down and opened her arms. "I love you, Evie. You're such a good girl." Cathy brushed a tear away and happily announced, "I've been writing t'Pa. I told him we live on a farm now, and maybe he'd like t'come t'Australia and live wid us."

Sitting in the kitchen, Sean heard their conversation and rose quickly, sending the chair crashing to the floor, before he stormed into the lounge room.

"Yer won't be sendin dat letter, Cathy! I'll not have dat old bastard livin here. So yer can forget about it." He reached over, grabbed the letter, and tore it to pieces. "And you!" He pointed his finger at Evie. "I'll be fixin d'damn windmill. What d'yer tink I am, useless!" Cathy held Evie close.

They watched as Sean clenched his fists, stormed from the room, and slammed the back door. Cathy held Evie's shoulders and looked her in the eye. "Don't take any notice of yer Da. I'll be talkin to him t'night when you're asleep." Cathy kissed Evie's forehead. "Don't be worryin now. Go, play with Matey."

CHAPTER 11
FELIX IN AUSTRALIA

After almost three years of taking alternative medicine, Father was still alive and looking much better than he had when I returned from Helsinki. Was it the Carlina therapy? Or the love and support he'd received from everyone who knew him, including his Business Manager, Jamie Suitor, a young man who'd worked his way up in Father's Engineering firm. Jamie began as a junior runner for all things needed. Later, he studied to be an engineer. And finally, after ten years, Jamie proved to be hard-working, trustworthy, and fair when dealing with other workers. 'Young Jamie is the perfect choice to become CEO,' Father had said about the business he wished us to continue after he was gone. While Joseph and I had no interest in running the company, we agreed to attend board meetings—a necessity, given that we would eventually own it.

I began thinking about my future. If I had to run a business that I had no interest in, would I truly be happy? I concluded I would be glad to sell if Joseph and Mother agreed. None of us held a passion for engineering, *sad as it was.*

With those pressing matters discussed with Joseph about 'Buchanan Engineering,' Joseph returned to the university where he studied for his Science Degree. It was only three months after I'd called him home to spend precious time with his father, I assumed. But, as I've said, miracles appeared to be happening.

Even though Father never regained the strength to run his business entirely, he kept a close eye on it. He felt confident in his assessor, Jamie Suitor, who offered his valued opinion while Father was incapacitated.

It allowed me to return to full-time training of my horses, and, of course, to continue my constant letter-writing and phone calls to Felix. From his letters, I learned everything about Felix and his family. He held nothing back. They sounded well-balanced, as I knew Felix was. Yes, I knew him better than if we met on weekends, at local dances, or at the movies.

In one letter, Felix revealed how his family had been active against the Nazis from the beginning of their evil doings, around 1937. The Lohmanns, along with most of their friends, shared the same mindset. From the tragic stories they'd heard about the constant bullying and later the inhuman slaughter of mainly Jews, to the tales of the young Aryan-type women used as breeding machines. Those women were matched with officers whom Adolf Hitler and Heinrich Himmler had mostly hand-picked to breed the Master Aryan Race. The babies born from those robotic matings had been left for dead when the war ended.

The pictures of neglected and abused orphans haunted Felix's mother until she discussed adopting a little girl with her husband. They agreed and were successful in their pursuit. They named their little girl Hilda. At the war's end, Hilda was three years old and a perfect specimen of her Aryan parents. Felix's family held enough love and intelligence to never think of Hilda's pedigree, only to love and care for her as their *special* child.

This was until one day when a recently formed society called for all the Nazi's experimental Aryan children to be identified and reunited with their mother if she so wished. Felix's parents spent months of anguish and heartbreak, waiting for the dreaded phone call to say they had found Hilda's mother, and she wanted her back. If it were to be, Felix's mother, Nina, threatened to take Hilda to the Swiss Alps and never return. Such was the love she held for her blond-haired, blue-eyed darling child.

Ever patient, even as a young boy, Felix stood by his mother, constantly consoling and comforting her.

The situation was challenging until goodness prevailed, and Hilda remained with the Lohmann family. The decision brought a flood of love and gifts to Hilda, the child they believed deserved everything. She was their symbol of freedom, democracy, and all things good and just in the world. Therefore, Hilda grew up thinking she was unique and superior to everyone.

I can still quote Felix's letters without rereading them.

I wonder why, later, I agreed to take the ill-tempered Hilda in to try to teach her the gentle method of training horses by winning their trust, not their fear. Whether dressage, jumping, or racing, horses must be respected. I find Hilda's story the most challenging. But I must write about it because my psychiatrist insists. It is the only way for me to heal enough to cope with my future. "Find your inner strength, Davina," she said. "Console and forgive. Only then will you be able to move forward."

Like bitter medicine, it's easier to swallow if sweetened, so I return to when my father was still alive, and the Melbourne Olympics loomed.

My days back then were fixed in learning different riding and training techniques, which I thrived on; perfection and winning became the drug to which I was addicted.

Each morning, I awoke to *my improved mother* calling, "Up you get, Davina. It's time to prepare your horses".

I'd smile, wondering what sort of pill her Doctor prescribed. Whatever it was, it had a positive impact, transforming her into a better person.

"Good morning, Davina," Mother would say, smiling when I appeared in the breakfast room with a plate full of bacon, eggs, and toast. Suzie, my darling dog, always sat at my heels, waiting for her treats. Lucky had recently died from a snake bite, and Suzie came to me from Lucky's first mating with a cattle dog bitch next door.

"Good morning, Mother. And what are you up to today?" I'd ask each morning. And she'd rattle off a list of charity meetings or good deeds in the village that she needed to attend. But, again, I found the flourishing shift in Mother's disposition challenging to comprehend. At first, I thought her behaviour was a flash in the pan, and I'd soon see her fall into the self-obsessed woman she'd been for as long as I could remember. But no, Mother had become a genuine crusader for the downtrodden. Her rise to empowerment initially overwhelmed my reasoning. Still, I felt totally at ease when I realised she was just as excited as I was about my progress toward the Olympics.

With just over one year to go until the Melbourne Olympics, I felt an all-encompassing desire to see Felix. I needed to face him and prove the words he'd written, '*to Davina, the girl I love.*'

Felix's absence from my *physical* life had produced what I could only describe as grief. It distracted me, and I made mistakes. The mental and physical effort required to maintain my intense training schedule left no room for error. So, I had to do something about Felix. Therefore, I made my decision and approached Father.

"I know this may not be an appropriate time, Father, but I hope you understand. It's been well over two years since I've seen Felix. In that time, we have grown to know each other better than if we lived nearby. Our letters are heartfelt and honest. I know all about his family, as well as Felix's likes and dislikes. Not that he has many dislikes." I took a whimsical breath. "Felix is such a kind and loving person, Father. He wouldn't hurt a fly." I smiled. "Now, that could be a problem in Australia." We laughed.

Father's eyes never failed; they told everything. He drew me into his embrace. "I shouldn't be selfish in taking up your time, Davina. I do understand how you're feeling. And I believe this young man, Felix, is worth the trip to Finland. From what I've heard." Father held me at arm's length—his smile contagious. "Yes, I know what you were about to say, Davina, though I may have a better suggestion. Why don't I send Felix an air ticket? Or do you feel you need a break from training? Maybe your horses would benefit from a rest? Would you like to fly to Felix?" I cried tears of joy and hugged him tight.

"Thank you, Father. I'll go to the post office right now and send a telegram to Felix. I'll tell him what you said and let him decide." I noticed the questioning look on Father's face and smiled. "I can't phone him, Father. He'd be asleep, and I don't want to wait."

He chuckled, "That's my girl, always a quick thinker."

Felix's telegraphic reply came at dusk. 'I will work it out.'

Within twenty-four hours, I received a telephone call.

"Hello, Davina, I am so excited." Felix continued before I had time to say, *"Hello, Felix."* I laughed as he talked on without taking a breath.

"I have spoken to my professor and parents, and both agree I should come and see you and meet your family. I can afford a two-week holiday from my studies and my new job. As you know, I have worked part-time for a prominent Architecture Firm in Helsinki. They are happy with my progress. I have a natural talent, they say. Of course, I should not be so proud, but it is hard not to be when I have worked so hard. I have topped the class in every subject, and my future looks set. But you are the only missing link in my life. It is like building a skyscraper without a solid foundation. You are my foundation, Davina. I will fly to you next week. My parents do not want your father to pay my way. He is very kind, but they are proud and can afford the airfare. I must go now. I have so much to organise. Goodbye, my love."

The line went dead. I held the receiver, dumbfounded, until I burst out laughing. I hadn't said a word.

I've gone over that conversation at least five hundred times and still remember the disbelief that a handsome young man with such a beautiful spirit could love me, the ugly duckling. I almost phoned back, saying, 'Please don't come, Felix. I'm not pretty enough. I'm not good enough for you. You are so beautiful and kind, and I'm just a spoilt girl who rides horses and is given everything she wants. I feel guilty. I don't deserve what I have. And now I have you, Felix. I could never have dreamed of a man like you liking me, let alone loving me.'

Instead of phoning him back and saying just that, I gathered a little chutzpah, called Irene, and asked her advice on looking my best for Felix. Her initial scream of delight turned to hysterical laughter.

"Bloody hell, Davina! I'm sorry for laughing, but where did you get the idea I could help you look good? What I'm saying is you do look good. You're thin, and clothes, especially the expensive ones, hang on you beautifully. *That only you can afford.*" After a pause, Irene almost yelled, "I know! Billy's sister, Florence. She's a model. She's eighteen and always looks stunning. How about I ask her to help us?"

"Whatever and whoever. Thanks, Irene," I said gratefully. "I didn't want to ask Mother; she still thinks I'm a ten-year-old. Could you please ask Florence if we could meet in Melbourne soon? Felix will be here at the end of next week."

"No worries, Davvy."

Irene then spoke about her boyfriend, Billy. I rolled my eyes and listened as she talked about nothing else lately. I worried her enthusiasm for running in races was squashed by her overriding passion for Billy.

What kept me focused was that my riding had significantly improved, as had my horse's performance. Therefore, I was on track and qualified to compete in the Equestrian Olympics in Melbourne in November 1956. I would have turned twenty-one that August. Plus, I'm sure it helped that Felix was not here to distract me physically.

Two days later, Florence, Irene, and I met at David Jones in Melbourne and were escorted up to the seventh floor by the department manager. *No doubt, Father had phoned beforehand to make that happen.* It was where all the top fashion labels hung like gems, but none could outshine Florence's classic beauty. Besides being mesmerized by her looks, I noticed that she turned heads wherever we went. I found it challenging not to keep staring and admiring her. Florence was not only beautiful but also spoke intelligently and appeared to have many depths, just like her eyes. *Eyes are the mirror of our souls*, I've heard. And I wondered then why Florence chose to be a model, given that it requires minimal academic achievement, only physical beauty. I wanted to befriend Florence, if only to understand why.

Trying on beautiful dresses designed by Christian Dior and Pierre Balmain, as well as suits by Coco Chanel, was an exciting experience. Irene and Florence complimented me as I modelled each outfit, but I hammed it up for a laugh.

After the parade, I felt Florence's gaze and read her thoughts. *How else could I make Davina more attractive?* Then, finally, she said. "Davina, would you trust me to offer more advice on improving your appearance?"

How could I refuse? We stood facing the full-length mirror; Florence gathered my hair to rest just above my shoulders.

"There you see. A shorter haircut will flatter your longish face, Davina. Your body is the perfect clothes hanger. Everything you put on looked amazing." She giggled, "I think you should be a model, Davina."

I felt a blush coming, so I turned away.

By lunchtime, two suits and three dresses were packed and ready for delivery to our property. After lunch, with some trepidation, I allowed Florence to guide me to the hairdresser. I need not have worried about her suggestion, not after the award-winning hairdresser created magic with her scissors. I smiled at my reflection. I loved the shorter bob cut, and it was still long enough to sit in a bun tied neatly below my Top Hat—a must-do when riding in dressage competitions. I sat slightly stunned and even more so after the cosmetician stepped up to add her unique artistry.

My hazel eyes appeared twice as big, although I reneged when she suggested false eyelashes. I wanted to look *better* —not fake— using only natural, soft makeup. On completion of my makeover, audible sighs came flooding my way. Many women, including Florence and Irene, had seen me walk in unenhanced to later witness the transformation of my plain face into what I can humbly say was a masterpiece. Yes, it was worthy of their gasps. And mine. What would Felix think? Would he like the new look? I would soon find out.

I purchased all the makeup the artist had used, along with her explicit instructions on how to apply it. I felt like a new person, much more confident, and I was grateful to Irene for suggesting Florence as my beauty mentor. I was amused at the thought that I would never introduce her to Felix. Florence was so stunning that he might transfer his love to her. Tut-tut. A little jealousy?

Springtime in Melbourne is mainly volatile, and the day Felix flew in was no exception. Thunder boomed, seeming to rock the ground before continuous shards of lightning pierced the dark cloud mass.

"Please, God, land Felix safely," I whispered over and over until I heard the voice over the loudspeaker. 'Flight Seven Fifty-Four from Finland has now landed.' I'd gone alone to meet Felix, except for Freddy, our chauffeur, who'd driven me and now waited outside by the Bentley.

Sweat ran between my breasts and down my face before I wiped it with a handkerchief. The threat of moisture ruining my delicate pink cotton dress worried me senseless. I'm sure the leakage was due to nerves, not the humidity. Then, when I spotted Felix through the window walking from the plane to the terminal, my heart skipped a beat, and my body flooded with excitement. I needed a beach towel to mop it up. I felt my makeup trailing down my chin. How could I face him looking like a washed-out doll?

I rushed to the bathroom and tried desperately to mend the storm damage with paper towels and more makeup. Once satisfied, I took a deep breath, gathered courage, and went forth, smiling into the open arms of the man I adored. We laughed and cried. *We did that a lot.* Felix then held me apart, studying me, "Davina, you have changed. You have grown into a beautiful young woman." I swooned to the point of almost fainting. "Not that you were not beautiful before, I simply mean…"

"I know what you meant, Felix," I said, trying to recover, "and I can tell you it took a lot of work and money to have me looking like this." I struck a pose, and we laughed. "I hope you like the new me?"

"Only if you have not changed inside, Davina. I loved the old you," Felix said sincerely, "Though I do like the new look. It is very becoming," he said with a wink. *Charming.*

Felix's charm on Mother and Father continued. They were noticeably impressed with his open style and genuine interest in everything related to our property, particularly our Angus cattle and, of course, the architecture of our home. His intellect glowed, as did his manners.

"He's been well brought up," Mother whispered.

She'd lost her manners, I thought. *'One should never whisper in front of our guests. It's bad manners.'* So I'd heard her say a thousand times.

The stormy weather persisted for the following two days, preventing us from thoroughly enjoying the outdoors. We mostly stayed inside and caught up on all the happenings since our last meeting. Not that there was much more to divulge after our constant letter-writing. However, I learned more about Hilda, Felix's adopted sister, who'd begged him to bring her with him.

"I refused," said Felix, "thinking it was inappropriate on first meeting with your parents." He then asked. "Would you mind if Hilda accompanied me next time, Mrs. Buchanan, Davina?" He bowed his head, and a truss of blond hair fell over one eye, and I remembered thinking in Helsinki that I would see this vision many times in the future. Then he looked up and smiled.

"Of course, Hilda would be more than welcome," Mother announced before I had the chance. I smiled and nodded.

"Of course, she will. We have horses in common," I said, "and it's not unusual for young people to want to travel overseas and experience different cultures."

Felix's *Next time'* echoed in my head a hundred times that day, meaning he would return.

We were all at breakfast the following morning when I suggested that Felix and I go to Melbourne and stay in our South Yarra apartment. "We'd be close to the city, Father, so it would be easy to show Felix around."

"I think that's a wonderful idea, Davina. I have an appointment with my specialist in Melbourne tomorrow," Father said, raising his hands. "Why don't we all go? Your mother could do with a bit of spoiling. She has been working extremely hard with her charity work. A few evenings out for dinner, shopping, and a live show. Perfect!" He smiled tenderly at Mother, and she returned the same.

I'd hoped Father might have allowed us to go alone. However, I suppose that, knowing how much I loved Felix, the situation of us being alone overnight might be asking for trouble, so I made no argument.

From the moment we arrived in Melbourne, I dragged Felix from Captain Cook's Cottage through the Botanical Gardens to the Melbourne Art Gallery, then to the Museum, where we stood and gazed at the magnificent taxidermy of Phar Lap.

"He's the best racehorse Australia has produced." I said, "But I shouldn't say that. Phar Lap was New Zealand-bred. Still, we claimed him as ours because he was trained here."

Felix nodded, saying, "Perhaps he would not have performed as well in New Zealand?"

"Perhaps you're right, Felix. Although I doubt it." I said, raising an eyebrow.

We walked from the bottom of Collins Street to the top end, crossed the road to Bourke Street, and then up again, then across to Spring Street, to see the magnificent Parliament House, boasting Roman-like pillars and fan-like steps running the width of the building. As many visitors do, we sat on the steps and caught our breath before strolling down to the Yarra River. Thankfully, park benches were plentiful, so we sat and discussed the architecture of Melbourne's prime buildings. Felix knew his business and rattled off most of the architects responsible for their design and structure. I was impressed, and it gave me an understanding and much more respect for those talented men. Although part of me wondered if Australian Architect Florence Taylor had been a man, would she have outclassed and improved on her rivals' influence on the buildings we had just seen?

I went on to tell Felix about Florence and her remarkable architectural talent. I finished my spiel: "Unfortunately, she was admired mainly for her choice of flamboyant hats!" He laughed.

"That is a wonderful story, Davina. Though not so wonderful for Florence. Many women are prevented from doing what is traditionally considered a man's job. Architecture is one profession, I think, where women should and could be superior, if they had the chance. It is, of course, art mixed with arithmetic. So why can't women be brilliant architects?"

He squeezed my hand and kissed me softly, supplying the same sensation as floating on a soft cloud.

Father seemed a little sedate that first evening when we dined at the Windsor Hotel. I hoped he hadn't received bad news from his doctor. He would not say. Mother seemed oblivious to his sombre mood, maybe because she'd been shopping for new dresses—one, a stylish indigo satin she'd chosen to wear to dinner. I observed how she humbled herself in response to our flattery. *Another turning point, perhaps?* She usually glowed with compliments.

The following evening, I was pleasantly stunned when Irene and Billy walked towards us just as we were about to order dinner.

"I thought I 'd surprise you both," Father said with a glint of conspiracy. "I didn't want to say anything until Irene confirmed that she and Billy were free to join us." Father stood, held the chair out for Irene, and then shook Billy's hand. "I'm pleased you could both make it. I've asked Frederick to drive you young people to whatever nightclub you wish." He smiled, "After dinner, of course!"

Irene smiled into Billy's eyes as he gently squeezed her shoulder. It pleased me that perhaps she'd found a mate for life -- like me. Hopefully.

When our entrees arrived, I noticed Irene eyeing Mother's oysters. Irene's nose twitched, and her mouth puckered before she said, "Mrs. Buchanan, I hope you don't mind me saying. But I don't know how you can stomach those," Irene pointed her fork as if she was about to kill the oyster.

Mother smiled sweetly, "Well, Irene, I happen to love oysters. So much so that I would like to die eating them!" Mother placed one in her mouth.

Irene shrugged, "You probably will, Mrs. Buchanan, if you eat a bad one, it'll kill you."

I thought Father was about to choke laughing; it took a moment longer for Mother to get Irene's humour.

After dinner and a farewell to my parents, we hurried outside, where Freddy was waiting for us. "Hello, Freddy," we said in unison and jumped into the car.

"Ciro's Night Club in Exhibition Street, please, Freddy. "

"Yes, Miss Davina. I've heard excellent reports about Ciro's, especially about their house band led by Bobby Limb. He's the talk of the town."

"Great! Well, then, let us dance the night away to Bobby's music, shall we?"

I was amazed at Felix's dancing skills. He had rhythm to spare and taught me a few new dance tricks, and when he gently laid me back in his arms at the end of each song, I swooned.

It is now one of my happiest memories.

After two joyful and exhaustive days and nights, we packed our bags and hit the road to Carlina. After a reflective time gazing out the window, Felix turned to me and said, "I refuse to return to Helsinki until I have seen you ride, Davina. I want to see you in the full regalia, a tail coat, top hat, and riding dressage to music."

I laughed. "*Why not?* I'll make it my Olympic dress rehearsal and farewell gift to you, Felix."

I phoned Charlotte and invited her and Jacques to lunch the following day. My surprise dressage performance could wait until they arrived, as I needed their help. I felt confident enough to perform at my very best, thanks to my dear friends and coaches. I must never forget that without Charlotte and Jacques, I would not have achieved my level of horsemanship.

Betty excelled in serving a perfect lunch of smoked trout, which she proudly announced, "I caught and smoked it myself." Then she laced her famous bread-and-butter pudding with a generous supply of sultanas soaked in sherry. I ate small portions only because riding on a full stomach is uncomfortable.

It was a perfect Spring day, with a cloudless blue sky and a slight north-easterly breeze. *Now, I sound like a weather forecaster.* After lunch, I left my guests to dress in proper riding attire: a top hat, a tailcoat, white breeches, and long black leather boots. I looked the part, especially with my new hairstyle neatly tied in a bun. Charlotte was kind enough to help saddle my number one horse, Carlina Forever Grace, whom I'd chosen after taking each of my six horses through their paces spanning the previous three years. Charlotte, Jacques, and I had agreed that Grace was the main event. She had everything needed to win Grand Prix events. Her movements were liquid gold; she was intelligent and willing to learn. Her perfect conformation stood out even more under her gleaming black coat. Two white front socks added pizzazz to her overall appearance. She was a stunner, and I'd received many offers to purchase her, though none were enough. Grace was priceless.

Jacques and I chose bouncy tunes for the movements of Passage and Piaffe, and a relaxing melody for the walk. I felt highly nervous riding in front of Felix, though I'd managed to stay focused enough to do my best. I hoped.

Our competition-sized dressage arena, which measured sixty metres by twenty metres, was kept in perfect order by our gardener, Clive, who stood with Jacques at the tape recorder. My parents, Felix, Betty, Charlotte, and Suzie, my dog came to watch in the sheltered seats near the arena while I imagined this was my Olympic Dressage Final.

Jacques started the music, and I rode Carlina Forever Grace into the arena at a regular canter. Halfway, she formed the perfect halt, all four hooves in line. I gave the invisible judges a nod before I gave Grace the aid to passage to the corner of the arena, next, a half pass across, or traversal to the other side, and a full pirouette at the end of the arena, then an extended canter on the diagonal. The performance continued for ten minutes and was almost flawless. My feeling of being at one with Grace was mesmerizing. Perhaps I could liken it to an out-of-body experience, where such fluency and elegance imbue all things with a spirit of sheer beauty. The only thing that brought me back to earth was the sound of applause. Even my most ardent critic, Charlotte, gave a standing ovation.

It was the pièce de résistance, having Felix there. I felt no pride, just simple gratitude for all I had been given and the accomplishments I had made. I felt blessed beyond all expectations because I could never have achieved my dreams without the finest horses and the immense satisfaction that arose from always doing my best with whatever came my way. I concluded I was not spoiled. Simply fortunate.

Felix stayed another seven days, enjoying all Carlina had to offer, including our natural parkland, which Father had resurrected from one hundred acres of pasture. It bordered the river at one end and our North garden at the opposite end. The park contained gum trees of every variety, including my favourite, the Paperbark, with its intricate bark that sheds itself to reveal a ghostly white trunk, the complex and delicate blush-red fingers of the Grevillea, and Hairpin Banksias. From a distance, they appeared like cobs of yellow corn. The Hickory Wattle has sage-green leaves and wispy, light-yellow flowers. My father had planted hundreds of different shrubs, including the Silver Holly Saltbush with its holly-shaped leaves, which offered a substitute for our Australian Christmas wreath. They were all entwined, scattered throughout the area. Father had created a natural environment for bees, wombats, kangaroos, and pesky rabbits. All creatures, great and small, thrived there. Carlina Parkland was as near to perfect as Father could make it.

Felix called it "nature's architectural masterpiece."

"With a little help from Father and his gardeners," I'd said, resting my head upon Felix's shoulder on our final day together.

Within that dense natural habitat, we'd finally found seclusion. Felix smiled into my eyes and held my gaze, his blue eyes showing desire as his fingers softly explored my body, sending shivers like a thousand tiny shocks. I, in return, slowly undid his shirt and ran my fingers over his chest, lowering my touch until, with a quivering breath, I touched him...

he moaned and lowered his head to nestle on my shoulder. Breathlessly, Felix whispered, "I think it best we don't go any further. We should honour the trust your Father has given us, Davina."

I felt cheated. Although I knew Felix was right.

"But when will I see you again, Felix? I want to show you how much I love you." He rocked me back and forth in a lingering embrace.

"When the Olympics are over, and I finish my degree."

"Another year? How can I possibly wait that long?" He kissed my head.

"We will have to wait, Davina. And we will be on neutral ground when we make love."

The following morning, Felix left. I chose not to accompany him to the airport. It would sadden me, and I needed to stay happy and be grateful for our time together. Felix's visit was like a tonic for the soul, a feeling that would have to last until we met again.

CHAPTER 12
CHANGES TO THE EQUESTRIAN OLYMPICS
1956

The latest news delivered to the Australian Equestrian Committee came as a shock. We assumed that the six-month quarantine for horses coming to Australia for the 1956 Melbourne Olympics would be lifted for the duration of the games. It was not. Instead, Australian riders and their horses would be transported to a training facility in Stockholm, Sweden.

Did they say Sweden? Overwhelming joy flooded me like a cool shower on a hot day. Finally, I'd be close to Felix. I'd only have to travel by train and ferry to see him in Helsinki. Or he could reach me the same way.

I was the lone Australian woman chosen to compete in the Olympic Dressage. Probably because I was the only one who could afford the process, my joy was soon replaced with guilt when I thought that, if Father had not lived longer than expected, I might have made the three-day event team, which was all male. Instead, I'd managed to compete in the odd show jumping and cross-country events without Father knowing. *It was not easy.*

I'd struck up a friendship with Olympic team member John Winchester, with his cheeky smile. And the tallest man on the team, Bunty Thompson, who's a real character. They supported me in my endeavors to ride the jumps, and we often competed against each other in point-to-point races around Victoria.

When the Australian Three Day Event team was finally announced, I became aware that some men had never been schooled in dressage. So I set to work with Charlotte and Jacques to help instruct them before the Badminton Equestrian trials in England, which would be their first time competing in all three disciplines.

And I'm delighted to say that the Aussie men excelled and earned their place amongst the world's top elite riders. Finally, they were destined for Stockholm. I'm sure I was as excited as they were.

I couldn't complain; I had the money to go to Sweden and train my horses. However, that meant I would be away for over a year. Could I cope with that? What about Father? Could I leave him? No, I should stay home and go to Stockholm three months before the games. Or would I? I had to rethink my priorities, and I soon realised Father was more important than anything and anyone.

So I remained home.

**

After months of not seeing Felix —unable to be close to, touch, or kiss him —my frustration undermined my training regimen. Like a puppeteer, the rider pulls invisible strings from their legs, seat, and hands. Suppose the puppeteer's rhythm breaks due to a lack of concentration; the puppet then fails to produce the required movements. All is lost. That is precisely what was happening. Grace became confused, and I became impatient.

Father remained nobody's fool, and his observations were rarely wrong, as they were on that memorable day, when the sun shone brightly, the scent of blossom permeated the air, and the birds sang merrily, *unlike me.*

Subsequently, I tried to breathe in that perfect day and feel happy. But the constant thought of being so far away from Felix, after wanting to be near him, *selfishly*, would not leave me.

Day and night, I juggled the feeling. Should I be in Stockholm? No, I should be here with Father. He needs me. No, I want to be with Felix.

While trying to summon peace in my turmoil, I rode Grace into the arena and saw Father leaning on a nearby fence. His presence gave me every reason to concentrate. However, despite my efforts, I was unable to connect with Grace. I knew what was about to ensue after hearing Father cough at the end of my performance.

"Davina, would you mind giving me a moment of your time?"

"Of course, Father."

I jumped off Grace, handed her to Peter, my new stable boy, and smiled. He was doing a great job.

"You know I come here occasionally and watch you ride, Davina. And I think I've learned enough to realise something is not working between you and your horse."

Father waited, his head tilted like Suzie's when she looked for an answer.

"I know, Father, and I'm trying hard, but the magic seems to have left."

"Could the magic be Felix?" Father asked, his smile curious.

"You never miss a trick, Father."

"I try not to, my beautiful Daughter."

I scoffed.

"You are beautiful, Davina. Never believe anything else. I am so proud of you. I could burst."

I climbed through the fence into his arms; my words muffled into his shoulder. "Thank you, Father. I don't know what I'd do without you."

"Yes, you would. And you will. Davina, look at me."

His eyes relayed what I needed to hear.

"I want you to go to Stockholm and train your horses. You're missing Felix terribly, I know. Please don't worry about me. I intend to sit in the front row and see you win a medal."

I stood speechless before I cried blissful tears.

**

With everything set in place for the transportation of Carlina Forever Grace and Carlina River, a burgundy bay Warmblood gelding, my reserve horse. I packed my bags and left behind many tears, singing my new mantra. *I am a woman, and the world is mine.* Was it false confidence?

I look back now and can honestly say – yes, it was.

When Felix met me at the Stockholm airport, my inhibitions dissolved with his embrace. Standing behind Felix, I noticed a tall, attractive young woman.

I studied her unfathomable expression for a moment before I realised she must be Hilda, his adopted sister. I smiled, broke our grip, and proffered my hand. "You must be Hilda."

I'm sure I heard her heels click, as is the way of the German Army. Did it amuse or frighten me?

"Yes, I am Hilda."

"It's a pleasure to meet you, Hilda."

She nodded once. No expression.

From that moment on, we found it impossible to lose Hilda. She stuck like glue, though I felt grateful for her translation whenever I needed it. Hilda became our Captain, organizing our restaurants, museum tours, and theatre tickets. She also sat between Felix and me everywhere we went until I managed to take him aside one evening at the theatre when Hilda needed the bathroom.

"I have to tell you, Felix, Hilda, sitting between us all the time is a little weird. Couldn't you ask her to leave us alone for at least one day?" My final word had no longer floated away when Hilda returned with an accusing look, first at Felix and then at me.

"Well, are we going back for the second half?" she said accusingly. "I find it boring. But if you insist, Davina, we will stay."

"If it's so boring, Hilda, why don't you return to the Hotel?" I said with authority and meant it.

"On my own? Are you joking? I came here with Felix and will not leave without him!"

Felix remained silent, looking down, shuffling his feet.

"As you say, Hilda. If you and Felix want to leave, please go!"

I marched off, hearing Felix gently reprimand Hilda.

I flopped in my seat, frustrated, but soon felt his hand on mine and his sweet breath on my neck. "I am sorry, Davina. I did not want Hilda to come to Stockholm. It's just my mother insisted. I am so sorry."

I turned to take advantage of his soft lips before I laughed.

"Charlotte was right. We should call you. *Sorry.*"

And we laughed together.

Fortunately, Hilda had obeyed Felix and returned to the Hotel.

We managed to be free from Hilda on our final day together. Felix assured me Hilda would be fine. I didn't care if she was or wasn't.

A flood of relief washed over us the following day, when we were alone. We held hands as we wandered around Stockholm's significant sights, including Djurgården. We then strolled through a lush forest in the medieval town of Gamla Stan, with its ancient cobblestone streets. But I needed more than just seeing new and interesting sights; I needed to seal our relationship with passion. Only then would I know if Felix truly loved me.

When our feet were too tired to walk further, we returned to the Nobis Hotel. Its grandeur and historical value had captivated me, as it had Felix. I stood transfixed at its beauty, thinking about making love in one of the most romantic places on earth. Finally, I returned to reality enough to find my room, which was three doors up from Felix.

"Give me fifteen minutes, Felix," I said, before I kissed him.

"Are you sure, Davina?"

"Yes. I've never been surer." I gave him a cheeky wink.

I quickly showered before unwrapping the satin nightgown I'd bought for the occasion. After slipping it on, I admired its beauty in the full-length mirror. The doorbell sounded, and I glided like a movie star to open it. I coaxed Felix in with all the allure I possessed, *which wasn't much*. Nevertheless, he held me tight and whispered. "I have never done this before, Davina. I am sorry."

I laughed, "Okay, '*Sorry*,' we're in the same boat."

From that moment, we shared our first love, gradually at first, until our passion overrode all our inhibitions. I cannot speak for Felix, but the sensation of losing oneself in sublime euphoria surpassed any feeling I had ever known. The experience was pure, unadulterated joy and love, and I knew then I adored him with all my being. And more importantly, Felix loved and adored me.

Saddened as I was to say farewell to Felix, the following day, *not Hilda*, I felt enriched and more confident as a woman. So, naturally, I'd happily resume the training of my horses when they arrived in Stockholm, which was only a few days away. And with Felix's promise, "We will spend every weekend together at the end of each month, Davina." I felt blessed.

I moved into a lovely apartment in Stockholm, close to the Olympic Training Complex. Most nights, I'd spend hours on the phone talking to Irene, then Father, and occasionally Mother, who assured me she was taking good care of Father and also taking her medicine. That particular news pleased me more than Irene's announcement that she and Billy were engaged. My father also promised to attend the June Equestrian Games in Stockholm.

Life was good.

CHAPTER 13
DAVINA'S CHALLENGE

My months in Stockholm became increasingly pressured. Every day, training for hours. And nights, dealing with officials discussing what was permitted and what was not regarding the horse competitions. The rules in Sweden were far more rigid than in Australia. I suppose we were a young nation of students, not experts, unlike those in one of the oldest Equestrian countries in the world. Most Australians had never heard of Dressage. I learned something new every day to the point where I felt utterly unprepared. How could I compete with European riders who had already mastered the art before I could even walk?

Fortunately, I found a genuine friend, Phyllis Crowe, a jewel among riders. She was an Englishwoman with the grace and poise of royalty, though Phyllis reminded me of Irene. Her sense of humour and honesty came to the fore on most occasions, especially when I became tongue-tied in front of my superiors.

"They're only trying to defeat you, Davina. You're a much better rider than you give yourself credit for. Don't let them upset you," said Phyllis.

A few intense months passed before Phyllis persuaded me that competing with her in a Grand Prix event in a country village near Ahus, renowned for its horse population and Equestrian events, would lift my spirits.

Seven days later, we loaded our horses and gear onto a borrowed truck.

The night before, I'd spoken to Felix over the phone and told him how excited I was to compete and to see more of the Swedish countryside. He assured me I would find it most picturesque. "Good luck, my love," were his final words.

We headed south, and once away from the suburbs, the

magnificent crops of gold, lime, and yellow, set against a vivid blue sky, floated by in a masterpiece of tranquility. It lifted me to another sphere where the nearing competition faded into nothingness, and all things lived in harmony. I know it was a poetic dream, but it was how I felt at the time. The scenic trip had set a precedent for me to perform at my best. I only hoped Grace was in the right mood. She'd been in season for the past three days, with her temperament suffering. It was Spring, April the tenth to be exact, only two months before the opening of the summer Equestrian Olympics.

Phyllis and I were fortunate to have employed two talented young dressage riders who seemed honoured to assist us as our grooms. My groom, Norman Hyett, was always one step ahead, keeping my nerves and anxious moments at bay with his quirky humour. Plus, his blond hair and dreamy blue eyes were most appealing.

When unloaded safely, Norman saddled up Grace while I dressed appropriately. I warmed Grace up and felt relieved; she was okay. No temper tantrums, her movements were fluent, and all seemed perfect for a good showing. Phyllis had taken time away from her commitments to watch us in the practice arena. "You'll be hard to beat, Davina. Grace looks great. She's moving freely, and she seems happy," said Phyllis.

Her confidence gave me the catapult I needed.

I was about to move Grace into the main arena when the marshal called my number. I heard a familiar voice: "Good luck, Davina." I turned to see Hilda grinning like a Cheshire cat, and I asked myself. *What is it about that woman that sends shivers down my spine?* I smiled back. Nothing or nobody was going to spoil my day. I'd worked hard for years, and I needed this event to prove to myself and my contemporaries that I was among the best riders in the world.

Nothing, including Hilda, could distract me.

There are strict rules for spectators. First, and most importantly, they are not to talk or applaud until the Equestrian competitors have completely finished.

I'm sure Hilda knew this. However, during my second movement, a perfect passage along the centre line, Hilda's applause came suddenly and extremely loud. It caused Grace to falter and miss her step. I remained calm, coaxing her forward to complete the action. To our credit, we continued to perform flawlessly after that mishap.

I was beyond nervous waiting for the judge's score, and I was also angry listening to Hilda apologise at least fifty times for clapping inappropriately. *Strange behaviour, I thought.* It was even more bizarre when the judges awarded me the second-highest score, and Hilda didn't clap. Instead, she threw me a snide grin. I turned to congratulate Phyllis on winning.

My genuine happiness for her surpassed every other feeling.

Phyllis and I later joined the committee for a glass of champagne. We purposely avoided Hilda, who we saw talking to Norman as he walked Grace to hose her down. I thought, *poor Norman.* Plus, I observed a large tote bag attached to Hilda. *Where on earth was she going? Not with me, I hope.*

After our celebration drink, I scrambled into the truck quickly - away from Hilda. I hadn't asked how she'd travelled to the show. I didn't care. She could find her own way home. Was I being mean and judgmental? *After all, Hilda had travelled a long way to see and wish me well. She didn't realise she wasn't supposed to applaud. Did she?*

I returned home around six in the evening, still angry at Hilda's behaviour but concurrently joyful with Grace's performance. Phyllis had taken the win in her stride. She was such a professional, humble to the core. I felt grateful for Norman doing all the work when we arrived back at the stables. I could barely drag my feet to open my apartment door. Then the phone rang.

I almost didn't answer. *It could be news about Father.*

"Hello, Davina speaking."

"Hello. It is Hilda. I missed the last ferry back to Helsinki. May I stay with you tonight?"

It was the first time I'd whispered, *fuck!*

"Yes. Okay, but you'll have to sleep on the couch. I'm going to bed. I'll leave the key under the doormat." I hung up.

The following morning, I was only just awake when I heard the kettle whistling and Hilda singing in the kitchen. I was rubbing my eyes when Hilda appeared in my bedroom, carrying a tray laden with Limpa toast —my favourite spiced bread —cheese, fruit, and a pot of tea. My jaw dropped.

"I have made you breakfast, Davina," Hilda announced - no smile.

"Thank you, Hilda, but if you don't mind, I'd rather eat in the kitchen."

"Of course." And *with* that, she turned and marched away. She always seemed to march rather than walk.

I sat opposite, feeling uncomfortable as Hilda stared at every mouthful I took. I smiled in between sips of tea, "Have you not eaten, Hilda?"

"No. I do not eat breakfast."

I didn't want to discuss why she did or didn't, so I simply said, "Oh."

I'd tried hard to like Hilda, and maybe she grew on me a little when she then admitted, "It was wrong of me to intrude on your time with Felix when you first arrived."

Ah! A softening of sorts. However, her ice-blue eyes didn't convey the same.

I was relieved later when Norman finally offered to drive Hilda to the ferry, particularly after she'd followed me to the stables and constantly questioned my training methods with Carlina River. Grace was enjoying a day in a nearby paddock, as a reward after her brilliant work the day before.

Again, I was glad to be rid of Hilda, and again I scolded myself. *I should be more patient. After all, patience is my finest quality, especially with horses. 'Your patience is to be admired, Davina.'* Jacques would say, and I'd feel proud.

I vowed to be kinder to Hilda in the future.

Later that afternoon, Phyllis watched me ride. She waited until I'd dismounted and passed Carlina River over to Norman.

"Thank you, Norman. Could you please walk River until he's dry after hosing him down?"

"I will, Miss Davina." He said, bowing his head. Norman was so formal. Even his neat attire and college-boy look enhanced his persona.

"That was great work, Davina," Phyllis clapped. "How about we go out for a drink tonight?" Phyllis threw her arm around my shoulders.

"I think we could do with more than *one drink*. Let's make it two!" I turned spontaneously and kissed her cheek. "Actually, Phyllis, I think three drinks may be in order." I shook my head, "Oh dear, I hope I'm not becoming an alcoholic like my mother!"

"Is that true, Davina?"

"What, me turning into an alcoholic? Or my mother being one?" I laughed, "Come on, I'll tell you all about it over a drink."

Hartwall Long drinks remained a fashion staple after their creation for the 1952 Helsinki Olympic Games. Unfortunately, I was not old enough to enjoy the pleasure back then, but I vowed to make up for it that night.

After showering and applying my Helena Rubinstein makeup, I put on a slinky black dress. Phyllis soon arrived, and we strutted our stuff to the famous Compagniet Night Club, where we drank and danced when invited to do so by young gentlemen. Then we drank and danced some more until, reluctantly, the bewitching hour arrived. We thanked our handsome dance partners and left, much to their disapproval.

I walked home lighthearted, thinking how I'd attracted men, and my confidence soared to a level I had never experienced. At last, I knew the power of beauty, plain Davina. Well, what do you know, those men hadn't known how much money I had. *Boy, what a bit of makeup can do!*

One charming young man had asked for my phone number, which I didn't give. The other complimented me, "*You have a noble nose and beautiful eyes, Davina.*" I almost swooned. No man has ever sweet-talked my appearance. Perhaps my riding ability. I'm leaving Father out, of course. And Felix's praise is genuine, not flattery.

Phyllis lived in an apartment three doors down, and I said goodnight with a promise, "We'll exchange our life stories another time, Phyllis. Perhaps over a quiet dinner. Not drinks and dancing."

She laughed and agreed.

Thankfully, my overindulgence the night before had done me no harm. I jogged happily to the stables the following morning. As I entered the enormous barn, never suspecting a problem, Norman hurried to meet me. His worried expression hit me before he stammered, "Miss…

"Tell me what's wrong, Norman," I said, holding my heart.

"It's Grace. I was about to phone you, but I called the vet first. He's on his way."

I took deep breaths, trying to calm myself, "Okay. What are Grace's symptoms?"

"She's acting like she has colic. Biting her stomach, trying to lie down and roll. I've walked her constantly. Now John's walking her."

"Good. You've done everything right, Norman."

I turned when I heard a car door slam and saw Dr. Duckworth, the veterinarian. I greeted him, and together, we hurried to inspect Grace.

In an organised manner, Dr. Duckworth addressed the problem.

I was even more impressed when he refused to leave Grace.

By mid-morning, Grace was still not out of trouble. Neither Norman, the vet, nor I had an explanation for why she suffered colic. Her feed and straw bedding had remained the same. Perhaps the stress of competing two days prior may have caused Grace's colic.

"I need to take a blood test, Davina," said Dr. Duckworth. "There may be something more than meets the eye. I'll need to operate if Grace does not show significant improvement. She might have an obstruction in her bowel."

How could I be lifted to the stars one minute and dropped on rocks the next?

I hated seeing Grace distressed. The painkillers helped, but her defeated look nearly killed me. Finally, our despair triggered empathy from everyone; even our most ardent rivals rallied to support Grace, and some gave her soothing massages. Their care was a tremendous source of positivity in a time of anguish. Dr. Duckworth, Ian, as he insisted I call him, finally decided he had to operate.

"What are Grace's chances, Ian?"

"I cannot say until I open her up."

We loaded Grace on a truck to travel ten miles to the operating clinic. Norman held Grace upright the entire journey. Phyllis, a tower of strength, drove behind the horse truck and sat with me throughout Grace's operation, sharing stories about the horses she'd owned, including those who had undergone the same procedure, and how they'd recovered. I had never dealt with a sick horse before—especially one who needed an operation. I wish Jacques and Charlotte were there to hold my hand. 'New friends are silver. Old friends are golden.' Father always said.

Finally, after two hours, Ian walked toward us from the operating room, smiling. "I have good news, Davina; Grace will be fine. Although the cause of her colic was strange." Ian scratched his head and wrinkled his brow, "Does Grace have a liking for rubber gloves?"

"What are you saying? Did she have a rubber glove inside her gut?"

"Yes, she did. Well, it was a finger from a surgical glove, sealed at both ends but with pinholes throughout, and it contained a chemical substance. We're having it checked in the lab. Whoever did this must have used a mouth gag, similar to what horse dentists use, and they shoved it down Grace's throat." Ian squeezed my shoulder, "I'm sorry, Davina, but it was foul play."

"How could anyone do that to my beautiful horse?"

"I don't know, and I cannot understand why she didn't pass it in her manure. Unlucky, I suppose. Instead, it got lodged in her intestine." He shrugged his shoulders. "The substance that caused her pain was released slowly through the pinholes. The good news is her bowel had not completely twisted." Ian smiled reassuringly, "I'm certain Grace will recover to her normal self."

"How long will it take, Doctor? Will she be ready to compete here?"

"Well," he said, hand under chin, "It's only seven weeks until the Olympics. You would not have enough time. I'm sorry, Davina. I must be honest. Grace will not compete in these Olympics."

At that moment, I knew how it felt *not* to have everything handed to me. I'd never dealt with such intense disappointment, and I didn't know how to cope. So I sat dumbfounded until I crumbled into a heap, sobbing, "No! I must ride Grace! River is nowhere near as good as her."

Ian kept repeating, "I'm sorry, Davina. I am truly sorry."

Where were Jacques and Charlotte when I needed them? I ran from the building crying until I found a public phone box and rang the overseas operator. I didn't care if it was the early hours of the morning in Australia. "Collect call to Australia, please. The number is MW-7406. Thank you."

I waited for what seemed an eternity before hearing Charlotte's sleepy voice, and then, through a flood of tears, I told her the entire story, yelling, sobbing, and begging, "What can I do, Charlotte?"

"Firstly, Davina, try to take control of yourself," Charlotte said calmly. "Secondly, think of Poor Grace; imagine the agony she must be going through. You're fortunate she's still alive. Go straight to the police. It was a criminal act. They call it nobbling when some bastard tries to stop a horse by giving it drugs. They didn't want her dead, obviously. Or they would have given her the entire dose at once. Instead, they aimed for a slow release. I feel the same way the vet does, Davina. Why on earth didn't Grace pass it through her manure? It's all a puzzle. I'll tell Jacques we're hopping on the next plane to Stockholm. We should have gone with you in the first place instead of waiting until the competition started. And at the risk of sounding like Felix, I am genuinely *sorry* to have left you alone in a strange country." There was a noticeable pause, "and perhaps I shouldn't tell you, Davina, but your father suggested we let you go alone to learn about life and to solve your own problems. I suppose he meant for you to grow up a little. But I'm sure he didn't mean for anything like this to happen. Poor darling Grace. She will be okay, won't she, Davina?"

I tried hard to find the strength to answer, mainly to stop crying. I took a deep breath before saying, "Yes, the vet, Ian, is confident. Grace will recover."

I heard a knock on the telephone booth and turned to see Phyllis. "I have to go, Charlotte. Ring me when you're at the airport. Goodbye, and thank you. I love you."

Phyllis opened the door, and I fell into her arms, weeping. Then, I remembered what Charlotte had just said and wiped my eyes. "I need to see the police, Phyllis. Somebody has sabotaged us. The bastard should be shot."

"I agree, Davina. I'll help you in any way I can." Phyllis held me again and whispered, "We'll find out who did it and string them up by their balls!"

I chuckled, "Okay, let's go!"

We went directly to the police station, where I wrote my statement. I told the officer that he'd have the vet's report in the morning. He thanked me with a smile.

It was getting late, and I was emotionally and physically exhausted, though ravenous. Phyllis and I found a little café serving the best cheese fondue in town. In between mouthfuls, we discussed who would be so cruel as to drug Grace. As far as we knew, nothing like this had happened in the Equestrian Olympics. We knew all competitors would be scrutinised, which only added to our confusion about who and why. Grace and I were no threat to them. Well, at least I didn't think we were. The dressage event Phyllis and I entered last weekend was not significant. Although it was a Grand Prix event, only young riders learning their trade, riding semi-retired horses borrowed from older masters, competed there. The Olympic riders thought it was a joke that we even went.

Still in a quandary about who had done the dirty deed and why, we agreed to sleep on the mystery after we visited Grace at the Veterinary Hospital, and my heart lifted when I saw her nibbling on her dinner. She whinnied when she saw me, and I sniffed back tears.

Then, Norman appeared like a sentinel, "I will sleep outside Grace's stable, Miss Davina. Please do not worry anymore."

I kissed him and held him tight. "Thank you, Norman. You are a blessing." And with that, Phyllis and I left to find sleep, hopefully.

CHAPTER 14
EVIE'S DREAM

Months of everyday living on the farm had passed until one morning, Evie heard her ma saying goodbye to Da and telling him to be careful. Then the back door closed, and the car engine hummed down the driveway.

Evie sprang from her bed, grabbed her dressing gown, and eased on her slippers. Matey stretched, yawned, and followed.

"Mornin, Ma. Has Da gone to d'city?"

"He's goin t'Sydney, Evie. Dere's a big job dere. So you best be gettin ready f' school. The bus'll pick yer up out front." Cathy looked at her watch, "In half an hour. So y'best be quick. I'll make y'porridge while y'get dressed." She smiled at Evie, who stood rigid. "Y'look like a stunned Mullet." Cathy giggled. "Dat's what Old Pa would say." Cathy's expression turned serious: "Now go on, get dressed, Evie. You know I've been warned by d'education department t'take yer t'school. No more *home* schoolin!"

Evie dragged her feet down the driveway while Cathy assured her, "You'll be fine, me wee girl. The kids in d'bush are much friendlier dan d'city kids." Evie threw her a questioning look. "Please don't ask me why. They just are."

They waited five minutes before they saw dust rising from the road and heard the rumble of the school bus approach, its brakes creaking to a halt. Joe, the bus driver, tipped his hat at Cathy, and she smiled at Joe's warm, friendly eyes, almost hidden among voluminous lines on his face. *They'd outdo Flinders Street Station. He looks too old t'be drivin d'school bus.*

"Have a good day, Evie," Cathy said, holding back emotion.

Evie climbed the steps to see all the kids on the bus smiling.

"My name's Jill." Said the older girl, patting the seat next to her. "Is your name Evie?"

"Yes," Evie said with a sigh of relief. She remembered the first girl she'd met at the Carlton school, who'd shoved Evie into the brick wall and warned her, '*I'm the boss. You do what I say, or else!*'

"I heard your mother say your name. Do you come from Ireland, Evie?"

"Yes, we're Irish. And I'm goin home soon as Ma saves d'money." Jill reached for Evie's hand, "We'll be friends until she does. Okay?"

At that moment, Evie thought, *if I had a pony and a good friend, I'd be happy t' stay for d'rest of me life.* She smiled at Jilly, "Okay, den."

Their teacher, Miss Marie Mitchell, was all Evie could have hoped for. She was kind, patient, and understanding. Everything about the small country school and its people appeared to be the opposite of the Carlton school, and Evie's heart danced, thinking she would return every day until Saturday.

At three o'clock, Cathy stood at the end of their driveway, waiting for the school bus. The balmy afternoon drifted in, bringing storm clouds. She looked up, '*Good. I'll be able t'wash d'house if dose clouds burst.*'

Earlier in the day, Cathy had brushed the cobwebs down and, beyond her better judgment, scrubbed the weatherboards with a soft broom dipped in soapy bore water. But the white paint still looked grey. She'd always been the same as her ma, fussy with housework. '*Cleanliness is near to Godliness.*' So her ma used to say—those thoughts, plus praying for Sean's safety and Evie's happiness at school, had crowded her thinking all day. Cathy wrung her hands together, which helped relieve her stress. She kept it up until the school bus stopped, and she saw Evie jump down the steps, flashing a smile before waving to Jill, who called, "I'll see you tomorrow, Evie!"

"T'be sure yer will, Jilly."

Oh, tank d'Lord, Evie's happy. Dis is all I could wish for.

As they walked up the driveway with Evie, prattling on about all the wonderful things at school, Jock arrived in his ute, driving slowly behind them. Cathy stopped and waved.

"Hello, Jock. If yer here t'see Sean, he's away at work."

"I don't need to see Sean, Cathy. It's about a pony for Evie. I may have found her one. Plus, I thought you might need a Jersey cow. She gives plenty of milk. I've got two, and I only need one."

"Okay, den, come up to d'house. It's gonna rain any minute. We'll talk about it over a cuppa."

Jock heard raindrops on his car roof, "Hop in then, or you'll both get wet."

Matey sat on the verandah, barking, his neck straining at the lead. Cathy had tied him up just in case he chased the bus. Unfortunately, he'd gotten into the habit of chasing Sean's car. Evie ran and snuggled her face into his coat.

"I missed yer somthin terrible, Matey."

Meanwhile, Jock noticed how clean and homely the cottage looked, which prompted him to use the boot scrape and hang his hat on the hook outside.

Cathy noticed and smiled fondly at Jock. *Sean was right, 'he's a good bloke to have around when I'm alone.'*

"I'll be puttin d'kettle on, Jock. Make y'self at home." She turned to Evie, "And you go wash yer hands if yer wants cake."

Cathy busied herself, placing cups and the fruit cake she'd baked earlier on the kitchen table and then filling the kettle. "So, Jock, tell me about d'cow. How much y'want f'her?" Cathy said with her back to him.

"I'll wait till you sit down, Cathy. I like to look people in the eye when doing business." *And I'd like to know how much money you've stashed away from Sean's dodgy shift work, as he put it.* He kept his thoughts to himself, as he did his suspicions.

Evie hurried back into the kitchen and sat next to Jock. "So, Jock, can y'be tellin me about d'pony and d'wee cow," Evie said, business-like. He laughed.

"I'll be tellin' yer about d'pony and d'wee cow, Evie, when yer ma sits down and looks me in d'eye. Dats d'way, I do business."

Evie giggled, "Awh be off wid yer Jock, yer no Irishman."

"No, I'm not, but my granny was an Irish lass. She came here on a steamboat, chasing the young lad who'd escaped her attentions in their small village near County Clare." He winked at Evie, "Granny got him in the end. And they had ten children. My mother was her first child. So there you go, Evie. Most Australians have a little touch of Irish in em."

Evie winked, "And a wee bit of d'malarkey, too…!"

Cathy huffed. "Pour milk in d'cups, Evie, instead of goin on with all *your* malarkey."

After *wetting their whistle,* as Jock put it, he told them about a quiet-tempered pony he knew of. "I think it's a good price."

"And what would dat be, Jock. Not too much, I hope," asked Cathy.

He gave a cheeky grin. "How about nothing, Cathy? Well, maybe a bunch of that spinach you're growing. The pony belongs to a mate, and his daughter's outgrown it. They only want a good home. So I told him Evie would look after him very well." He looked at Evie, "Was I right in saying so?"

Evie sprang from her chair and danced around the room, "YES! YES! Me very own pony! I can't believe it! All me live long life, I've dreamed of ownin a pony." Suddenly, she stopped and glared at Jock, "Does he have a name, Jock?"

"All your wee live long life, Evie?" He chuckled. "Aren't you only seven? That's hardly a long life." Jock said, laughing.

"Well, y'd be knowin' what I mean, Jock." Evie placed her hands on her hips. "So, does d'pony have a name?"

"Yes, his name's Bobby. But we'll wait for Saturday before we pick him up, so you'll have time to get acquainted before you return to school."

"Now about d'cow, Jock. How much d' y'want?" Cathy asked seriously.

Evie winked at Jock before she sat down, smiling at her visions.

"One pound will do, Cathy. She's getting a bit old but should see you out for another year or two."

Cathy shook Jock's hand, "It's a deal, Jock. Can y'deliver her, or should we climb d'fence and walk her here?"

"No. She'll travel on my trailer with no trouble. The dear old cow that she is. Her name's Dora."

Cathy nodded, "I'll go and fetch d'money, Jock."

When she'd gone, Evie held Jock's hand, her eyes pleading, "Can I go with y'Jock t'get d'cow?"

"Of course, Evie, if your mother doesn't mind."

Jock struggled to stand, and Evie helped him to his feet. "You okay, Jock?"

"Yes, just a bit of arthritis. Old age, Evie, that's all." He smiled with a grimace,

"Tell me, Evie. Does your mother keep a lot of cash at home? It's not safe. Someone could rob her, especially out here on her own."

"I don't know how much Ma has. Da gives her all his money, and Ma stashes it away. She hides it real well; she does. She told me when we had enough money, we'd be goin back t'Ireland. Me old pa has a wee farm dere. But it's bigger dan dis one."

Jock sighed reflectively, plopped his hat on, but turned when Cathy came and handed him the money. "Thanks, Cathy. I just told Evie that having a lot of cash around is unsafe. I don't want to scare you, but I've seen a few drifters camp in this house. They don't stay long, a couple of days. A week at the most. So make sure you lock the doors."

A wry smile creased Cathy's lips. She was aware of the men and the cottage being used as a safe house for criminals. She also knew they wouldn't hurt her or Evie. They were part of the gang that worked for the same bossman as Sean.

"I'll be lockin' d'doors and d'windows, Jock. So don't yer be worryin about us. We'll be fine."

"I'm goin wid Jock, Ma. We'll be back, f'dinner." Evie gave Jock a wink, "Isn't dat right, Jock?"

"If you say so, Evie."

Cathy waved her hands, "Oh, be off wid yer now. Tea'll be ready at six."

Luckily, they made it to Jock's before the downpour. With Matey hugged to her chest, Evie gazed in wonder at the rambling homestead and its wide verandahs. The white window panes and white doors contrasted nicely with the grey stone. Pink Azaleas bloomed on manicured bushes lining the front entrance. "Wow," she said, hesitating to walk inside.

"Does *wow* mean you like my home, Evie?"

"It's a mansion, Jock."

Evie's eyes widened even more when Jock opened the door and ushered her into the sitting room. She paused, studying the paintings of Stud rams, Thoroughbred racehorses, and family portraits covering the walls.

"I never tought yer had a grand home like dis, Jock," Evie said, then heard a high-pitched voice.

"Is that you, Mr. Smith?"

Jock raised an eyebrow and sighed, "That's my housekeeper. Yes, Mrs. Faulding. I'm home." He called, then whispered to Evie, "Mrs. Faulding is even older than I am. She suffers from memory loss. Flossy has been the housekeeper since I was a young boy. I don't have the heart to put her in a nursing home. She has no one else to care for her, so I told her she can stay for as long as she needs."

Evie smiled, seeing Arthur Smith's – *Jock's* kindness exposed.

They walked into the kitchen, where Mrs. Faulding stooped over the bench, struggling to cut a pumpkin with a large knife. Jock hurried over.

"Here, let me do that, Flossy." She turned slowly to see Evie. "Oh dear, you shouldn't call me Flossy in front of the little girl, Mr. Smith."

After introductions and with the pumpkin cut, Jock told Mrs. Faulding, "I need to deliver Dora the cow to Evie's Farm. So I won't be home for dinner. I'm sure you can boil an egg. It's your favourite. "

She nodded, "I'll do that then. And we'll have pumpkin soup tomorrow night, shall we?"

Their chat continued and lasted long enough for Evie to take in the cupboards, countertops, and kitchen utensils hanging with copper pots off a wooden structure attached to the ceiling before she said, "Y'could feed a hundred people outa dis kitchen, Mrs. Faulding."

Jock and Flossy laughed, "And we certainly have in the past, young lady," said Flossy with an emphatic nod.

With the cow loaded and delivered safely to Evie's Farm, they sat down to a simple dinner of lamb chops, mashed potatoes, carrots, and peas, all picked from Cathy's veggie patch, followed by golden syrup dumplings. Jock rubbed his belly, "Well, that was the best meal I've had in a long time. Thank you, Cathy. And now I must bid you goodnight. I don't like leaving Flossy on her own for too long."

Jock drove home, assuring himself. *Cathy has accepted me as a friend, so I'll keep an eye out. But at the same time, I'm worried that I might not be there when and if they need me. I'm getting older, eighty-two next month. I feel the strain of running this property, although I don't have much stock, and I'm always concerned about Mrs. Faulding. I don't have the heart to place her in a care home. But I'll have to if she keeps wandering off, leaving the stove on, and forgetting who I am. Life's been difficult after Masie died, especially with my son marrying an English girl and living in London after meeting her on his trip around the world. I wish I'd never financed him. Alice lives in Adelaide with her doctor husband and their five children. She's always too busy even to talk on the phone. But now I'm happy to have Evie and Cathy.*

He put his thoughts to rest and parked his work ute in the barn.

**

Sean had reached Sydney at eight a.m. after driving solidly through the night. He'd been told by the second in charge over the phone, 'It's a significant job, Sean. Meet me at the Cocharane's Hotel tomorrow night at five. The Pub closes at six. Don't be late.'

Before leaving home, Sean had grabbed a wad of cash from Cathy's hiding place and declared, '*I'm gonna spoil meself in Sydney!*'

Once in Sydney City, he found a parking lot and booked a room at the Lord Nelson Hotel in The Rocks. As weary as he was, Sean went in search of a men's clothing store. *After all, I'm t'meet d'second in charge. I don't want t'look like a common thief. More like a successful businessman now dat I'm comin up in d'world.*

After buying a new outfit, Sean whistled as he strolled through the Rocks, admiring the historic red brick buildings standing side by side, their pitched roofs covering four stories, still in use as wool stores. The harbour lay home to tug boats and ferries, all motoring about. *I'll jump on d'ferry t'Manly before I go home. Good fish'n' chips dere, I've heard.*

Finally, Sean stopped to read about the Sydney Harbour Bridge, completed in 1931, which begins at Dawes Point and ends at Milsons Point. He studied the coat-hanger frame designed to make a statement. '*A bloody masterpiece! Jesus, a man'd kill himself if he jumped off dat. It must be about five hundred feet high!*'

After returning to the hotel, Sean, weary and in urgent need of a nap, asked the desk clerk, "Could yer wake me at four pm, mate? I have an important meetin." He handed the older gentleman a quid, and his eyes lit up.

"Certainly I will, Mr… "

"Sean, just call me Sean."

CHAPTER 15
DAVINA'S PERIL

My bedside telephone rang, waking me from a disturbed sleep. However, I felt grateful; it was eight a.m. and I'd slept in. I picked up the receiver to hear Norman's greetings. "Good morning, Davina. I just wanted to let you know Grace had a comfortable night and ate most of her dinner. Though I'm not so good after a sleepless night. Could I have the remainder of the day off?"

"Of course, Norman. And again, I cannot thank you enough. But if you feel up to it, could you please return to the stables later this afternoon?"

"Yes, I'll only need four or five hours. I'll see you later, Davina."

I ate breakfast, got dressed, and was ready to ride Carlina River through his paces. However, first, it was essential to obtain the vet report and deliver it to the police station. Then, maybe find another groom to help Norman. It would be a hectic day with so much to do and think about; I'd never had to deal with anything as terrible, *catastrophic, really*. It jolted me into realising *again* how fortunate I'd always been. But then I smiled, thinking Charlotte and Jacques were on their way. They would arrive in forty-eight hours—*what a relief.*

I was about to leave home when a knock sounded. I opened the door to Phyllis.

"Hi, Davina. I hope you slept well?"

"Not much, how about you?"

"A little. Now, what do we do first? How can I help?"

We sat down to a discussion over coffee.

"Meanwhile, my groom, Joseph, will handle our horses," Phyllis assured me. "So don't worry. I'll drive you to the vet's surgery and then to the police station. That should start the ball rolling. And you can concentrate on training River." With a warm smile, Phyllis placed a reassuring hand on my shoulder, "River will do better than you give him credit for, Davina. I like him very much. But, of course, he does have an attitude. River is not as subservient as Grace, but sometimes that adds to his performance. A certain je ne sais quoi,' as they say."

I shrugged, but then, I began to see Phyllis's reasoning. *Maybe we aren't out of the running?*

All went to plan: Doctor Duckworth's report sat ready and waiting, and the young police officer, who'd greeted me the day before, was on the case when we arrived at the Station. "Good morning, Miss Buchanan. We are about to interview suspects. I assure you, we are deeply troubled that this could happen in our Olympic Equestrian Games. Please be assured we will do all we can to solve this mystery so you can concentrate on training your horses." He cast a beaming smile. "Good luck."

Feeling slightly relieved after his assurance, we left and grabbed a coffee from our favourite barista—another heart starter to a day in the saddle.

I was always lucky to have someone to help me through my problems—Jacques, then Charlotte, later my dearest friend Irene, and now Phyllis. The saying goes, we only need one good friend. And I had more than I'd ever counted on: a great comfort in this time of need. So, I put the past behind me and carried forward with the training of Carlina River. Hopefully, he'd prove me wrong and perform beyond my expectations.

After a positive day in the saddle, I phoned the police.

"I am sorry, Miss Buchanan. Unfortunately, we have no further news. But we will continue to make inquiries."

What could I do but accept they were doing all they could and go home for an early night? I made it home just before heavy rain fell. I breathed a sigh of relief when I leaned against my closed door. There, I continued to think about how frustrating it was not to know who or why anyone would drug Grace.

A shower, yes, a long hot shower, that's what I needed.

And I was right. I felt like a different person after washing away the day's grime. After making a toasted cheese sandwich and enjoying a camomile tea, I felt relaxed and ready for bed. That was until the phone rang. It was Hilda.

"How are you, Davina? I heard about the terrible thing that happened to Grace. Is she alright?"

"Yes, thank heavens. And it's more than I can say for the person who drugged her. If I get my hands on them, I will strangle them!"

"Have you heard from Felix, Davina?" Hilda said condescendingly.

"As a matter of fact, no. Not since I told him Grace had been drugged. But in the same sentence, I told him she would be okay."

"Oh, I suppose Felix has been busy studying. He has a new study partner. Her name is Dianna. She is very bright and beautiful. She helps Felix with *everything*."

"Is that so, Hilda? Well, I do hope they pass their final exam. And then maybe I will see more of Felix." I said impassively.

"I doubt it. Felix will be working as an architect in Helsinki. *With Dianna*."

"I have to go, Hilda. Goodbye." I slammed the receiver down so hard I felt the vibration through my hand.

I immediately phoned Felix. His voice rose an octave; *was it guilt or delight?* "Hello, Davina, my love. How are you, and how is Grace recovering?"

I tried hard to dismiss my jealousy.

'I'm fine. Although I wish I knew who drugged Grace. It just doesn't make sense." I then lightened my tone. "She loves being spoiled by everyone at the centre."

"That is good, but I agree, it is a terrible mystery. The main thing is that Grace is okay. And you are, too. Please try to rise above what happened, Davina. You have so much at stake. All the years of training and hard work have paid off. Look at where you are now. Please take care of yourself."

"I will. Jacques and Charlotte will be here the day after tomorrow."

"I am so happy they are on their way to be with you, Davina. It must be a dreadful ordeal for you."

"Oh, and by the way, how is your new study partner, Dianna?" He laughed.

"Dianna is not my study partner. We simply did a project together. It was to determine how we reacted to someone else's ideas. In other words, to see if we were team players. Anyway, who told you?"

"Hilda. Who else?"

He laughed again, but I noticed a nervous twinge.

"Felix, are you holding something back?"

"No. Not at all. It's just that you should not take any notice of

Hilda. She always wants to be the centre of attention. She knows my parents adore her. But she is unsure about me. So, she is a little jealous of anyone who comes between us."

"And why is that, Felix?" I didn't want his answer because I knew. So, instead, I rushed into my following statement. "I must say, I cannot warm to Hilda, and I'd prefer if she did not contact me."

"Oh, please do not say that, Davina. Hilda admires you. She would like to be as good a rider as you one day. So please forgive her childish ways. She means no harm. I love you and nobody else, Davina." Of course, I softened. How could I not? I loved Felix with all my heart and soul. I didn't want to lose him.

"When are you coming to stay with me, Felix? I miss you so much."

"And I miss you, Davina. I will be free next weekend and on the first ferry to Stockholm. I am also looking forward to seeing Jacques and Charlotte."

Our conversation turned to small talk, plus reminiscing about his time in Australia. It lasted almost an hour before I said with a yawn, "Goodnight, Felix."

Feeling much better in the morning after eight hours of sleep, I sprang out of bed, looking forward to riding River and spoiling Grace with her favourite brew – a bucket of molasses water.

Phyllis was already in the arena riding Benjamin the Great. I admired the pair's fluent beauty and wondered how I could possibly beat them. Then it struck me. This was my first Olympics, something thousands of riders could only dream of, so I pinched myself and simply admired Phyllis's riding prowess. River stood beside me, seeming to be as interested as I was, and I giggled, patting his shoulder.

When finished, Phyllis rode over, "Hi, Davina, what do you think?"

"I think you and Benjamin are amazing. You will be hard to beat."

"Don't say that too loud." Phyllis whispered, "We have nobblers in camp, remember?"

I didn't know whether to laugh or cry. Phyllis noticed, "I'm sorry, Davina, that was tactless. Have you heard any more from the police? Everyone here is genuinely upset and watching their horses closely." She leaned over and rubbed my shoulder, "The arena is all yours. And if you like, I'll give Benjamin to Joseph, and then I'll stay and watch you go through your paces. I may be able to help with small things you're not feeling." With Phyllis's warm smile, how could I refuse her offer?

After riding River and accepting Phyllis's advice, which helped tremendously, I wondered what I had to worry about. I felt confident with River; he knew the challenge and understood he needed to do his best. You don't spend nearly every day with horses, not to learn that they know and feel more than most people give them credit for. I thanked River later with a bag of carrots.

Phyllis and I freshened up and invited our grooms to lunch at a nearby café, where the coffee was sublime and the croissants superb! It was another thank-you for their above-and-beyond service.

As horse people do, we spoke of little else but how our horses were going toward the Olympics. Then, it struck me how little time I had left. Nerves drained my appetite. So I giggled when Norman eyed my second croissant. "Please take it, Norman. I'm just a little nervous. Time's running out, and I hope I don't make a fool of myself."

My statement brought scoffs, "Davina, you have River going brilliantly." Phyllis held my hand, her expression serious, "You should be proud of yourself. After all that has happened, you have lifted yourself and River to meet the challenge!"

The door opened, and I noticed the police officer in charge of my case enter the café. He looked around until he spotted me and then walked over.

"Miss Buchanan. I'm sorry to interrupt. But I first went to the stables to find you; one of the grooms said you were here." He removed his cap, twirling it in his fingers. "Could I ask you to accompany me to the station? When you have finished your meal, of course."

"Do you have news, Constable?"

"I am not at liberty to discuss it in public. I am sorry."

"In that case, Constable, I will go with you now."

I said my goodbyes, paid the cashier, and strolled with this charming young policeman.

"May I ask your Christen name, Constable ....? I'm sorry I forgot your surname."

He coughed, slightly amused, "My name is Christon Fiffer." He gave a quick grin, as did I.

"Well, Christon, do you have good or bad news? Have you found the culprit?"

He stopped and turned to face me. "I'm sorry to say this, but the only person who had the opportunity to administer the drug was your groom, Norman." The inquiring look on Christon's face told me he'd noticed my disbelief when my jaw dropped. "You couldn't possibly think it was Norman. He's been a perfect groom. He loves Grace. He would never..."

"We have information, Miss Buchanan. Norman has, in the past, kept company with disreputable people. He may have drugged your horse for money. We know money is the only thing holding him back from being a respected Grand Prix dressage rider. Norman has little money, and as you know, owning and competing on horses at such a high level takes a considerable amount of cash. We feel someone wanted you and your horse out of the running and used Norman to do the deed."

I stood deflated. But no matter what Christon said, I could not believe Norman had anything to do with hurting Grace. And why were Grace and I the target? Many other competitors had a significantly better chance of winning. Therefore, I could not and would not accept their findings.

"Have you interrogated all the competitors and their grooms?" I asked accusingly.

He sighed and guided me by the crook of my arm.

"I think it is best to talk about this at the Station, Miss Buchanan."

Once there, Christon pulled a chair. "Please sit, Miss Buchanan."

"Call me Davina, please."

"Okay, Davina. We cannot go any further with our suspicions about Norman without your help."

I sat back like I'd been shot. "Surely you cannot expect me to spy on Norman! I told you, I don't believe he's guilty. He had nothing to do with this...this nobbling!"

"I am sorry, Miss...Davina, but Norman is our only suspect. Your stables are locked at night. Only you and Norman have a key. We have questioned all other competitors and grooms. They have alibis, and as you say, they all think they are better than you. So they had no reason to drug your horse." Christon shrugged before jumping to attention when his superior officer entered the room.

A tall, distinguished man in his early fifties, I guessed, approached, smiling, with his hand proffered. "Miss Buchanan, I am Larsson, Chief of

Police. I must apologise for the distress this deceitful act has caused you. This type of thing has never happened in our Olympic Games. I cannot imagine who or why anyone would do such a terrible thing." The Chief Larsson bowed his head. "May I ask if you have any suspicions of your own?"

"No, I don't. Since being here, I've not met anyone I'd call underhanded or suspicious. So I cannot help you. But I know in my heart Norman would not have drugged Grace. He loves her."

"I understand," said the Chief, "Do you mind if we bring Norman in for questioning?"

"I don't mind as long as you don't accuse him. He may recall something or someone who had a chance. So yes, of course, he may be able to help."

I'd always felt as if I'd grown like a foal with long, shaky legs, unsure where to land her hooves. But when predators advance, the young filly, in this case me, senses danger and flees, surefooted in her escape. I'd been pressured and threatened in many ways lately. And so I knew in my heart Norman was not a predator. I would stand by him. He did not drug Grace. The mystery remained. Who did? And why?

CHAPTER 16
SEAN
ENTRENCHED IN CRIME

After drinking a few beers with whom Sean assumed to be *the second bossman*, Sean's ego rose with his compliments, peppered with warnings sent in whispers across the table. "I'm telling you, Sean. You'll do well if you continue to do the right thing," said the bossman with a wry smile.

Sean had learned to keep his mouth shut in Australia, even when he saw an opportunity to talk, unlike in Ireland, where he was involved with a gang of young, smart-arse boys who stole for fun. There was no doubt he'd met his superiors here. They were smooth operators, and he'd heard about people who'd gone missing after they'd squealed or done the wrong thing. So Sean sharpened his cunning and proved his bravery—*his two best attributes*. He listened and agreed with everything the bossman said.

"You understand, Sean, you have a massive job to do, and you'll be the main player. So I'm warning you. Don't talk to a soul. Do you understand what I'm saying? All will be explained two nights before we act. Now, go straight to your hotel room and lock the door. We'll meet once more in Manly. I'll leave a sealed envelope at your hotel desk the day after tomorrow." The boss man stood and shook Sean's hand. Anyone observing the men would never suspect them as criminals, assuming they were respectable business partners.

Sean walked briskly back to the hotel, anxious to phone Cathy and tell her he was okay and would be home in around two weeks. But he feared the warning: *do not talk to anyone*. Therefore, he locked the door, undressed, turned on the radio, and lay on his bed listening to Brian Crabbe's popular music on 2UW until he fell asleep holding a packet of half-eaten peanuts.

**

Cathy always sang when she tended to the simple pleasures of life. Walking to and from the bus stop with Evie, milking the cow, attending to her vegetables and the rose garden, then cleaning the house. She'd sigh, contentedly knowing she had enough money to keep her and Evie out of trouble for twelve months if necessary. Jock had been a constant friend and guide to anything they needed. Cathy, in return, offered to spend time with old Flossy to assess how badly her memory had failed. Jock said Cathy's opinion would help him decide whether to place Flossy in a home. *And maybe then I could help him wid d'housework for a small wage?*

With many chores to keep her busy, Cathy had little time to think about Sean. Plus, she'd always followed her instinct, warning her when he was in trouble. It had happened twice in Ireland, once when he'd run from the law and hid in an abandoned cottage nearby. Something told Cathy to go and see how the old stone house had fared in the recent storm. Plus, it held Cathy's imagination. She'd heard plenty of ghost stories about the place, and that night, she felt an urgent calling. Cathy was right. Sean sat huddled under a bundle of damp straw, shivering from the cold.

"How did yer know I was here, Cathy?" Sean said meekly as she pulled away the wet hay.

"I tink I've a callin, like me granny."

The police later found Sean at home, sitting by the fire. Cathy gave them an alibi before bidding them goodnight, feeling even more confident in her psychic callings.

Sean's safe. I can feel it. Evie and I can enjoy our simple life here on d'farm.

A week had passed since Sean left, and Cathy still hadn't heard from him. Then, finally, Saturday arrived. '*No school taday,*' Evie said as she rose out of bed. Matey tugged on her pyjama pants. Evie giggled as she hobbled into the kitchen. "Y'won't be gettin warm milk if yer keeps doin that, y'naughty rascal!" She shook her leg free from Matey, who flew across the polished floor before barking at the door. "Who is it, Matey?" Evie hesitated. *It can't be Jock; I'd hear his car.* The knock sounded faint, *someone's dere f'sure.* Evie hurried to wake Cathy, who'd warned her never to open the door to strangers.

"Ma, wake up, Ma. Somebody's at d'kitchen door." Cathy peered at the bedside clock. "It's not even six a.m., Evie. Who'd be here at dis time, I ask yer."

"I dunno. But dere's somebody dere, Ma."

Cathy sighed, shrugging on her dressing gown as she shuffled to the kitchen. Then, leaning on the door, she asked, "Who's dere? Who are yer?"

A whisper came back. "I'm a friend of Sean. The boss sent me."

Cathy grabbed the iron rod she kept handy. Gingerly, she opened the door to find a young man slumped against the wall. He looked as if he was about to faint, so she helped him in and sat him at the table, where he hung his head and moaned with pain.

"Give me a look at dat wound yer hugging," Cathy ordered.

The man, *maybe in his early twenties*, Cathy assumed, sat up, exposing a blood stain on his shirt below his rib cage. She gently pulled the fabric apart to see a bullet hole.

"How did y'get here? Where's yer car?"

"They dropped me off out front. I'm in agony. Is there anything you can do, Mrs.?"

"I'll call a doctor. Y'needs the bullet t'be comin out, t'be sure!"

"Please! No doctors. Can you do it, Mrs…?"

"Well, I've never taken a bullet out. But I could have a go. It might hurt, but I've got plenty a' scotch whisky and a sharp knife." The young man looked at Cathy pleadingly. She laughed. "It's okay, I've done plenty of cuttin and stitchin in me' life. On animals, dat is. You'll be right." She turned to Evie, who stood intrigued. "Evie put d'kettle on. D'man needs a cup of sweet tea before I operate. And make sure y'put plenty of Da's whisky in it." Cathy said with a wink. "Now y'best be tellin' me y'name." Initially drawn to the wound, Cathy noticed his hesitation and raised an eyebrow, "Any name'll do, mista."

"Bob. My name's Bob."

"Same as me pony," said Evie happily.

Thirty minutes later, Cathy had removed the bullet, which had fortunately missed his vital organs. She'd stitched *alias Bob* with a cotton thread soaked in whisky, like everything else she used. She then helped him to the spare bed, where he fell asleep.

The radio played while Cathy scrubbed the kitchen, thinking, '*If the cops come, they won't be findin a spot of blood!*'

Meanwhile, sworn to secrecy, and after eating her breakfast, Evie went about her chores, feeding the chooks and watering the veggie patch. Only then would Cathy permit Evie to ride Bobby. But first, Cathy always needed to know where Evie intended to ride. "It's for y'safety, Evie. I need t'know how long you'll be gone and where you'll be. Do y'understand?"

When Evie returned from her chores to change into her riding gear, she sniffed the air. The kitchen smelled like disinfectant. With her back to Evie, Cathy sang along with the radio as she mopped the floor, so Evie crept past into her room, where she saw Jock's car coming up the driveway. *Oh no, I best be warnin Ma.*

Matey had waited outside for Evie, though when he heard Jock's car, he ran to chase it; Jock wound the window, yelling, "Git Matey, go on git!"

Matey chased harder until Jock stopped the car, and finally, the pair stood at the locked back door, with Jock reprimanding Matey. "Naughty boy! You shouldn't chase cars, Matey."

Bob woke to the commotion, confused and in pain. He struggled to stand before Cathy pushed him down and whispered, " Go back t'sleep, Bob. It's only our next-door neighbour, Jock. He don't need t' know yer here."

Cathy hurried to the kitchen, calling, "I've just mopped d'kitchen floor, Jock. Come around t' d'front door." She stood on the front verandah, flustered but smiling. "Dis is an early visit, Jock." Cathy peered at the rising sun, tucking strands of hair under a scarf.

"I know, and I'm sorry, Cathy, but I just heard on the radio about an armed robbery last night. The crims are still at large." He looked around as if he could detect something wrong.

Cathy scratched her head, looking baffled, "What does that have t'do wid me, Jock?"

"I'm just here to warn you, Cathy. Don't open your door to strangers, okay?"

"I won't, Jock. Now, if yer doesn't mind, I'm busy wid me' housework."

Evie stood beside Cathy, catching on to Jock's suspicions.

"I'm goin t'ride Bobby now, Jock," she said eagerly, "Can I ride over t'your place? Maybe Flossy would like t'pat him. And give him a carrot. She likes Bobby." Evie smiled, hiding her concern.

Jock chuckled, "Of course, Evie, you and Bobby are always welcome." He turned to Cathy and caught a glimpse of uncertainty. "It's alright, Cathy. I've put a gate on our boundary fence. Evie'll be safe riding through the paddocks and not down the road. But remember. Be on the lookout for suspicious individuals. And phone me if you have any problems. Goodbye for now."

Feeling relieved, Cathy returned to her patient.

"Bob, are y'awake?" He lay facing the wall, groaning.

"Yes, I am. Do you have any painkillers?"

"Of course, I should have given em to yer before. I'm sorry."

Cathy returned with four aspirin. *It might be overdoin it a little, but it shouldn't hurt him.*

"Dere y'go take dese, and you'll be feelin better in no time at all, t'be sure."

Bob smiled at her Irish brogue before swallowing the tablets. He then sighed as Cathy sat on a chair next to the bed.

"So, d'yer want to talk about y'problems, Bob? Tell me, what sort of trouble have ya be in?"

"You won't go ratting to the police, will you?"

"Now, why would I be doin dat when me' own husband works for d'same boss? Don't worry. I know all about y'shenanigans. All I want t'know is how long y'll be stayin. I can't be puttin me'self and Evie at risk."

"I should be gone in a couple of days, Mrs. Calan, if that's okay with you. And if you'd ring the boss and ask him to send someone to pick me up along the road to Melbourne, I'd appreciate it." He smiled, showing perfect teeth. "I wouldn't ask them to come here and put you in danger."

"I won't be ringin d'boss. I don't know the code words. Only Sean does."

Cathy took a moment to study this fine-looking lad. *He's got d'face of a choir boy, not a criminal. So why would he be out committing crimes for money instead of working a decent job?*

"Anyway, you've put us in danger already, Bob. But I knew dis place was a safe house. Dough, I tought it was our home, and we'd be left in peace. You're d'first to come here in twelve months since we moved in."

Bob looked around and managed a smile. "You have the house looking nice, Mrs. Calan, and your little girl, Evie, seems to be a happy, bright child."

"She is. And if anyone laid a finger on her, I'd kill'em!" said Cathy with her fist clenched.

Whenever Sean was out of the picture, Cathy realised how much she loved Evie. *I love her more than I love Sean.* Her memories went back to when he'd never shown Evie any interest, which baffled Cathy so much that she tried to understand why. *I tink he's jealous of Evie? When I told him I was pregnant, he acted like a spoiled child asked to share his toy. The more I tink about it, the more it rattles me.* Finally, she'd made a vow. *If Sean ever smacks or yells at Evie. I'll bash him senseless before I leave him!*

When seeing the anger in her eyes, Bob recoiled, "That won't be *me* hurting Evie. I like kids. I've got a little sister about Evie's age. Mum married twice. Not that I ever see them. My stepdad's a mongrel!" Bob turned away. "I need to rest now." And with that, Bob pulled the blanket over his head, and Cathy patted his shoulder.

Looking out of Bob's window, she thought how their substantial driveway was a blessing; it gave her a clear view of approaching cars from about two hundred metres away. So Cathy kept mainly on the front verandah where she'd have enough time to lead Bob to the dugout, which was hidden under bales of hay in the shed. Sean had shown it to her the day they arrived. But hopefully, hiding Bob wouldn't be necessary.

CHAPTER 17
DAVINA
WELCOMING FRIENDS

The continuous hubbub at Stockholm Airport suppressed my worry about Grace. All I could think of was seeing Charlotte and Jacques. It felt like years, not months, since we'd been together. I had to prevent myself from screaming when I saw Charlotte waving to me over a magnitude of tired, dishevelled heads. She made it into my arms first. Jacques looked on, smiling.

"Oh, Davina, I'm so glad we're here. I can't believe what's happened. You poor darling, all on your own. Never mind, we're here now, and we'll look after you," Charlotte turned to Jacques, "won't we, Jacques?"

"Yes, of course we will." He winked, "That's if Davina needs us. Let's get our bags. Then I need a stiff drink before anything else. Do they still make the Hartwall Longs, Davina?"

"Of course they do! They're as popular as ever!"

I'd asked Norman to exercise River and care for Grace while I went to the airport, thinking it was another way of showing him my loyalty. I'd told Norman I didn't want him to take the police interrogation personally, 'I know you could not have done such a thing, Norman.' When I said that, he hugged me tightly.

Now that Charlotte and Jacques were here, I wanted to dig a hole, throw all the nasty business in, and enjoy our special time together. And, of course, Felix would arrive tomorrow evening. Perfect! We'd eat, drink, and sleep on our first night. After that, our hectic schedule would begin, and we needed to be bright-eyed and bushy-tailed, as Betty, our cook, would say. So I offered Jacques and Charlotte my double bed. I'd sleep on the daybed in the sitting room.

Finally, after a chatty evening and early to bed, the sun came streaming in the morning, triggering my eyes to open. I rose to prepare our breakfast of fresh fruits, croissants, and cheese. The coffee in Stockholm, I'm sure, is the best in the world; I devoured two cups before my guests woke.

Over breakfast, we discussed a plan of tactics to find the nobbler! However, none of us knew where to start, as it seemed the police had covered all the bases. "Something may come to light after they question Norman later today," I said with a cup held to my lips.

Jacques then changed tack, "Come on, ladies, we have no time to waste before the games begin. Davina, let us concentrate on Carlina River, shall we?"

"Yes, of course. But I feel terrible. I haven't asked how Father is?"

Charlotte placed her arm around me, "Your father is fantastic, Davina. He's so well that he walks out every day, inspecting his cattle before he checks on what's happening with his engineering company. Nobody, including his doctors, can believe it."

"I'm so relieved because when I speak with him, I'm unsure if he's covering something up."

"Well, he's not. And he's booked a flight to watch you compete. So, let's get to work. Shall we?" Charlotte kissed my cheek before giving me a gentle shove. With the good news about Father lifting me, we left happy and ready to tackle anything.

Grace seemed to enjoy the pampering she'd received since her operation. Norman had found her a sunny grass-filled paddock near the stables, which she appreciated during the day. After seeing Grace happy and content, we left to work on River. Jacques saddled him up while I introduced Charlotte to Phyllis.

"I'm pleased to meet you, Phyllis," said Charlotte. "I've heard so many good things about you. I must thank you for helping Davina through this horrible time. We were shocked when we heard. And, of course, being so far away, we felt helpless. I'm pleased you've been here for her." Charlotte embraced Phyllis.

"It has been my pleasure, Charlotte. I liked Davina the moment I met her, and so I took her under my wing like a big sister."

Phyllis turned to me with a compassionate smile. I appreciated then how much she meant to me, and we have remained friends.

"Good!" And now I'm all in favour of the best horse and rider winning," said Charlotte, "So why don't we all get to work!"

The day continued with introductions to new acquaintances between our training sessions, which went flawlessly, especially after receiving valuable advice from Jacques. Then came the time to go home, shower, and be ready to meet Felix. Hopefully, he'd not be too tired, and we'd eat at our favourite café, the Gastabud. It was charming, cosy, and served the best food in town.

I was in the shower when the phone rang. I knew the police would be interviewing Norman around that time and wondered what the outcome would be.

Charlotte answered the phone and later called out. 'It was Constable Christon, Davina. I told him you were in the shower. He asked if you could phone him as soon as possible.'

I dressed and opened the door to find Charlotte sitting on the couch, clean clothes folded over her lap. She smiled, 'I hope your policeman friend has found out something.'

"Yes, I'll ring him back right now. He's a nice young man."

Christon answered, "Your feelings were correct, Miss Buchanan. Norman has convinced us he had nothing to do with drugging Grace. And he hasn't been in contact with the underhanded mob for over a year. I confirmed this after checking with a member of the gang with whom Norman was associated. So we are no further advanced as to who had reason to drug Grace."

I thanked him and hung up, thinking *the case may go down in Stockholm's almanac as one of their Great Mysteries*. I had to put it behind me, but at the same time, I had to be mindful of any suspects. Christon assured me that the police would not give up, which made me feel better.

Twenty minutes later, we opened the door to leave, and Felix stood with his hand up, ready to knock. I laughed while falling into his arms, "What great timing. We were about to go to the ferry and meet you."

"I couldn't wait. I caught an earlier ferry. I'm sorry."

Charlotte cracked up laughing, and Jacques threw her a warning look.

"It's alright, Jacques. Felix knows I nicknamed him *Sorry*."

It was a beautiful evening with a cloudless sky, allowing the stars to sparkle as we walked one mile to our chosen restaurant. We chatted, catching up on each other's news. Unfortunately, Hilda's name pierced the conversation, not because I chose it, but because Felix thought I'd like to know that Hilda had won a novice dressage test on the new horse his parents had purchased for her birthday.

"That's nice," I said with a sarcastic twinge.

"I'd like to meet Hilda one day," Charlotte said sweetly. "I'm sure we could help her." Charlotte smiled at my frown, and then lost her smile. "With her riding, I mean." She coughed, trying to swallow her words.

I couldn't believe Charlotte would encourage Hilda when I told her how much she annoyed me. I glared harder at Charlotte.

"Oh, she would be most grateful, Charlotte," said Felix, missing the exchange. "Hilda has dreams of riding as well as Davina does one day. And you will meet her. She is coming with my parents to watch the Equestrian Games."

I needed to change the subject. "So what do you feel like for dinner, Felix? I always choose their baked fish served with a delicious lemon sauce." I held him close and kissed his cheek. He kissed me back and said, "I think fish is an excellent choice, Davina."

With the intoxicating wine and flickering candles creating a romantic atmosphere, I wished Charlotte and Jacques weren't in my bed that night. Felix looked more handsome than ever. His blonde hair, slightly longer than usual, gave him a rakish flair. And his blue eyes sparkled whenever he laughed. I stared dreamily at Felix until I felt a gentle kick under the table. Charlotte coughed before looking at Jacques, "You know, Jacques, I'd like to stay in a hotel tonight. This restaurant has put me in a romantic mood. And I'm sure Davina would like to sleep in her own bed for at least one night."

Jacques winked conspiratorially, "Of course, my love. How could I refuse?"

And with that, we gulped our liqueurs down. Once outside, we headed in opposite directions. I smiled while throwing over my shoulder, "Won't you need your P.J.'s?"

Charlotte laughed, "I hope not!"

Later, Felix and I made love in a cloud of tenderness. It was one of the most romantic nights of my life. I can still feel his arms around me and his soft breath against my neck as we drifted to sleep.

Morning arrived, and I awoke with a rush of adrenaline, realising I had only six days to perfect my dressage tests. Then I remembered Charlotte and Jacques were there to help me perform well and avoid humiliation. Once again, I felt blessed.

CHAPTER 18
EVIE
MOVING ON

Bob recovered quicker than expected. In the three days he'd been living with Cathy and Evie, he'd proved to be a lovely young man with impeccable manners. It led Cathy to ask, "Where did yer come from, Bob? And why on earth would yer be joinin a group of thieves?" Bob hung his head, seeming to contemplate the answer, before he looked up.

"It was just how my life turned out, I suppose." He took a moment to reflect. "I did well at school until Dad died. He was a great dad. He always had time for me. I still feel angry that he died." Bob sighed, shaking his head, "It was an accident at work. He was a builder. He fell off a roof and broke his neck." Bob looked out the window, silent for a moment. "At least it was instant. He didn't suffer. Mum spent months just lying in bed, never talking. It was a hard time for me, plus I had to look after my little sister because Mum couldn't cope. Anyway, she got over it and met another man. They were married a year later. He was a bastard and still is. He's nothing like Mum thought he was. I knew the truth, but Mum wouldn't listen. She thought I was jealous. She became a bit strange after Dad died. I suppose I felt lost and didn't know where to turn. And that's when I joined what you'd call a *bad* group, but at least I felt I belonged to someone." Bob hung his head and whispered, "Once you're in, it's hard to get out." He sipped his tea while Cathy pondered.

"Do yer like it here, Bob? Could ya live in a small country town?"

"I suppose so. But there's not much to do."

"Dere's honest work if yer wants it. I know Jock, our neighbour, is findin his workload hard. Would y'consider workin with Jock?"

"I'd consider it. Though I'd have to front the boss and hope he trusts me to keep my mouth shut."

For the past four days, Cathy had sent Jock away, making excuses about painting the inside of the house, which she'd partly done, so it wasn't a lie.

Evie entered the kitchen, dressed and ready for school. She noticed Matey sitting at Bob's feet. "Ah, so dere y'are Matey, y've found anoder friend have y'me' wee pet!" Evie said, and Bob laughed,

"He knows I give him toast. That's all," Bob patted Matey on the head, "I'll keep him here while your mum walks you to the bus, Evie."

When they left, Bob sat, pondering. *I don't want to struggle anymore just to stay alive and out of jail. So far, I've been lucky, just like the bullet I copped; one inch to the right, and I'd be dead. It wouldn't hurt to meet this Jock and see what he's like. I've got a good feeling about this place. But I wouldn't want to put Evie and Cathy in danger!*

The day unfolded as Cathy invented a story to tell Jock about Bob, whom she later discovered was Russell *Hobbs*. The police sought Russel on suspicion of armed robbery. Cathy heard it on the radio later that morning. One of the gang members had squealed, implicating Bob, also known as Russell, in the robbery that went wrong.

Cathy had been tending to the back veggie garden and assumed Bob was reading a book and resting in his bedroom when she later went into the kitchen. "Bob!" Cathy called, "I've made a sandwich for y'lunch and just pulled a cake from d'oven. I'll put d' kettle on."

No answer, *that's strange.* Cathy searched the house before she went outside. Matey sat tied to the verandah post where Bob had left him. "*I didn't put you dere, Matey,*" Cathy then searched the barn to no avail. *Surely he wouldn't leave widout sayin goodbye. She shrugged. He'll come back. Probably just gone for a walk.*

An hour passed when Cathy heard a car engine backfire. She hurried to the front of the house and saw Jock driving his old ute with another person in the front seat. *Oh, no, it's Bob!*

Jock got out and helped Bob, who was having trouble getting out of the car. He then locked Bob's body against his and looked accusingly at Cathy, "I found this young man hitchhiking on the road to Melbourne. He's in a bad way. He says he fell on an iron dropper in your paddock, said he's been staying here with you, Cathy."

"Yes. Yes, of course, dat's true. I told Bob not t'leave yet. He fell while fixing a fence. So I stitched him up." Cathy wrung her hands together, a sign Jock knew that her nerves were frayed.

"Well, I suppose it's none of my business, but you should have called a doctor, Cathy. I was going to take Bob to the hospital, but he refused. I think his wound's infected. Best we take a look."

"Yes. Straight away, Jock. Come inside."

Cathy helped Bob onto his bed and took his temperature, "40 degrees, he's delusional." She looked pleadingly at Jock, "What should I do, Jock?"

"I think we'd better take him to the hospital. He's too sick to argue now."

"I don't understand. Bob seemed fine dis mornin. I made him a sandwich f'lunch, but when I called him, he'd gone," Jock sighed, placing his hand on Cathy's shoulder, "I hate to ask you, Cathy. But are you telling the truth about Bob falling on an iron dropper?"

She hesitated before feeling confident in Jock's friendship to confide the entire story, which she did.

"So yer see, if we take him to d'hospital, they'll wake up t'who he really is. And he's such a lovely young man. He's just made wrong choices."

Jock held Cathy by the shoulders, "I don't care what he did, Cathy. We need to drive Bob to the hospital. He has a raging temperature. He needs penicillin."

"I know dat Jock," Cathy said, tears welling.

"And as I've told you, Cathy, plenty of drifters have stayed here. So tell me, how do they know about this house?"

"I'll tell yer all about it, Jock. If y'promise not t'tell another livin soul. Okay?"

And so Cathy began the story after they laid Bob on a mattress in the back of the ute. She continued as they made their way to the hospital. They'd almost passed Evie's primary school when Cathy said, "I tink it's best if I pick Evie up now, Jock."

Jock pulled up, and Cathy hurried to the classroom, knocking on the door before entering. She then spoke with the teacher, who allowed Evie to leave. Evie saw the strained expression on her mother's face, so she sat silent until they arrived at the hospital.

"I'll go tell d'nurses t'bring a wheelchair, Jock." Cathy pointed her finger at Evie. "Evie, don't move without Jock. He'll tell y'what happened t'Bob."

Once inside the hospital, Bob was given a bed, and Cathy explained to the Doctor, "Bob came lookin f'work, so I gave him some fences t'fix in exchange f"food. Plus, a little money, and a place t'stay. I was about t'pay him when he fell on an iron dropper."

Bob was too incoherent to argue. His temperature had risen to 42 degrees.

There seemed to be no suspicious circumstances surrounding Cathy's story, so the doctor administered a tetanus shot to Bob's arm and then attached an intravenous drip filled with antibiotics. He inspected Bob's wound and concluded that perhaps an iron dropper could have done the job.

"But why would you sew it up, Mrs. Calan? Why didn't you bring him into the hospital?" He asked as Cathy hung her head.

"I shouldn't have, Doctor. I know. But I've sown up plenty of animals on our farm back in Ireland. And I put lots a alcohol on Bob's wound. So I tought he'd be okay." Cathy smiled coyly. "I'm a frustrated doctor, I suppose," she said, walking away, hoping to avoid answering more probing questions. The doctor's eyes followed Cathy's hurried steps. *Mmm, there's more to this.*

The small Woolumbindi Hospital, built in the early 1900s, appeared insignificant among the massive trees planted at the same time. Peppercorn trees, jacarandas, and manicured rose gardens distracted Cathy's worries about the what-ifs. Instead, she sat on a garden seat, admiring the beauty, waiting for Jock. Evie ran around the corner, breaking Cathy's trance.

"Here y'are, Ma. Jock bought ya ice cream." Cathy smiled.

"How long has it been since I've had an ice cream in a cone?" she said before looking into Jock's inquiring eyes. "Tank y', Jock. Now let's go home. I don't want t'hang around. If d'police come, I might be in trouble."

Jock patted her hand. "I understand," he said, his smile hiding his concern.

Evie couldn't wait to be home and ride her pony. Although mainly self-taught, she'd become a proficient little horsewoman. After Jock had told her one day, "Keep her hands and heels down, Evie, and plant your bum in the saddle!" Jock grinned down at Evie, "I can't tell you how much I look forward to our rides, Evie. It takes me back to when I rode with my children." He'd smiled into the distance and laughed, "Although my bones and muscles were much younger then."

"I feel d'same, Jock," Evie looked up with a cheeky grin, "Not me old bones, just bein happy ridin wid y'Jock. I reckon we're mates."

"Yes, we are Evie," Jock had said, wiping his eyes.

The following morning, Cathy answered the phone.

"Hello, Mrs. Calan; this is Matron Brown from the hospital. I rang to tell you that Bob ran off during the night. Is he with you, Mrs. Calan?"

"No, he's not. I hardly know him. As I told d'doctor, Bob just came here lookin f'work."

"Well, it seems strange, that's all," said the matron. "But, I'll have to inform the police. He may be in trouble, or worse still. He may relapse and die."

"Could I ask where y'got me' phone number, please, Matron Brown?"

" Martha at the exchange, of course!"

"Yes, of course. Thank ya, Matron. I hope Bob'll be alright."

Cathy hung up. *'Why did Bob take off? Especially after I suggested he work for Jock? He seemed interested. But what can I do now? Worrying won't help.'*

The same afternoon, Cathy stood at the bottom of the driveway, waiting to collect Evie from the school bus, when a police car arrived. Once out of the vehicle, Sergeant Smyth approached, and Cathy's heart sank. He tipped his hat."Good afternoon, Mrs..."

"It's Calan. " Cathy felt heat rising to her cheeks.

"Right, you are. Well, I've just come to talk to you about the young lad who worked for you. Do you know where he came from and where he may have been heading?"

"No, I don't. Bob came lookin for chores t'do. And out of d'kindness of me' heart, I gave him some. But den he had an accident. I told d'doctor everytin I know." The school bus came chugging along, "I'm sorry, Sergeant, I have t'be getting me wee girl from d'bus. Excuse me." Cathy smiled.

With her heart pounding, she hauled Evie off the bus and hurried her up the driveway. Sergeant Smyth looked on before deciding to let Cathy go. *If they find the lad, I'll ask her more questions.*

The following day, Bob's body was discovered face down in a local creek. The farmer who found him reported the incident to the police. They called the doctor from the Woolumbindi Hospital. He said that he suspected Bob's temperature had risen, making him delirious, and he'd fallen into the water.

The body would be transported to Melbourne Morgue for

identification. When the police notified Cathy, she knew it was not the end of that story. And now she felt doubly at risk, as that morning Cathy received a letter from Sean, the first in over four weeks. He couldn't risk the telephone exchange. *Martha always listens.* Sean wrote.

Go to the coast, Cathy, and book into the Rosebud Caravan Park under Sue Smith. Don't move, and don't talk to anyone. Ring me when you get there. The number is…. You've got enough money for a car. You know how to drive. Do it now! I got the bank money. Now rip this note up!

Cathy looked at the postage stamp. *Italy? He's got d'bank money. I'd better be quick!*

Cathy filled a bag with cash and ran down the driveway to catch the bus she knew would stop in ten minutes. One came by every three hours, and this would be the bus she'd take to do her shopping. *No one will be d'wiser, except I'll buy a car at d'second-hand dealer.*

While sitting on the bus, Cathy pondered, *instead of doing what Sean says, we'll go t'Melbourne on d'bus, and be on d'next ship t'Ireland. I have d'money. We'll leave Sean and all his troubles behind and live a normal life with Da. Dis is it. I have my chance t'escape. I heard on d'radio about a bank robbery in Sydney.* Three thieves escaped with an enormous amount of money before two of them were found shot dead. So far, the police have not found the third robber who they suspect of the shooting. *I know Sean shot em. Dis means he'll have t'stay in Italy, so Evie and me will go home t'Ireland?*

Cathy bought the bus tickets and strolled happily around the shops, saying hello and chatting to a few people she'd met over the past twelve months until it was time to collect Evie from school.

She stood at the school gate, feeling regretful of leaving this country town and Jock, whom Evie and she had come to love. *I'll tell Jock dat I needed t'see a Collin Street specialist. And we'll be away for a couple of days. What about Matey? Poor little dog. I'll ask Jock t'mind him and look after d'place until we return at d'end of the week. But dat won't happen.*

The school bell rang, and Cathy stood, waving at Evie until she ran into her arms.

"What are y'doin here, Ma?"

"I've got a surprise for ya, Evie. Come on. I'll tell y'when we get home."

CHAPTER 19
DAVINA
LET THE GAMES BEGIN!

My parents arrived in Stockholm on June 8, 1956, and stayed at the Hotel Miss Clara, a delightful Art Nouveau building designed by Architect Gert Wingardh. Felix had recommended the hotel; it was little wonder, as he adored Art Nouveau, a style my father also admired.

It's hard to put into words my immense joy at seeing Father, who looked well, although a little frail. Then I realised he'd kept his promise to stay alive and see me compete in the Olympics; it was beyond my dreams. I could only give thanks to God or the universe, *whoever rules our destiny.*

Another treat came when Father told me Mother had continued taking her happy pills. I was amazed from then on when she agreed to whatever I suggested and stayed by Father's side throughout their holiday without emphasising his frailty.

My respect and love for Mother skyrocketed.

We shared one day of sightseeing as a family before the games began, and I knew then how Irene had felt when competing for the first time in Helsinki, so I followed the same advice. *Be rid of your nerves, Davina. Enjoy the games. You'll be a better competitor with the experience.*

Felix's parents had booked into the same hotel, and Father invited them to dine with us the evening before the Opening ceremony. Our dinner guests included Charlotte and Jacques, *our extended family,* and, of course, Hilda.

I'd seen photos of Felix's parents, but they were even more attractive in the flesh. Hans stood at least six feet two, looking fit and distinguished with his greying sideburns and sparkling blue eyes, just like Felix. Nina could have been a top model; she was so elegant and beautifully groomed. Hilda looked divine in a pale mauve satin dress, her hair styled in a French roll, which made her appear older than her years. No matter how much Hilda annoyed me, I must admit she behaved remarkably well that night, paying attention to everyone and only speaking when asked questions. So I sat back, studying this enigma, and concluded I could never figure her out.

Not so my mother. Like Felix's parents, she became charmed by Hilda. My father's subdued attitude toward Hilda? Well, he'd tell me later. Felix kept asking if I was alright. Obviously, he was concerned about my quiet mood; therefore, he paid me more attention than I deserved.

After a delightful dinner mixed with happy chatter, I said, "I'm sorry, everyone, but I need to sleep," and all nodded their understanding. However, I hesitated to leave after Hilda shouted, "I cannot wait to come to Australia and stay with you, Charlotte." Hilda's smile encompassed the group before she continued, "Charlotte has agreed to instruct me in dressage. I hope to be as good as Davina one day." Hilda's tone had changed from sergeant major to sickly sweet. She reached out and grabbed my hand.

Inwardly, I fumed. *Not a good time to lose it,* so I threw a killer smile at Charlotte, who hurried to my side. After seizing my hand from Hilda, Charlotte and I walked a few steps away, with Charlotte whispering, "Honestly, Davina, I never told Hilda she could stay. She's twisted everything. Please let it go. We'll talk about it later. You need to focus on the competition."

I trusted my smile was convincing when I turned to say, "Good night, all."

I took a sleeping pill that night, something I rarely did. Thankfully, it helped because I woke refreshed for the official proceedings the following day.

The organisers had summoned all equestrians to finalise the routine for the opening ceremony. After all the hoo-hah, thankfully, the hour arrived for my parents and Felix's family to take their reserved seats, offering a perfect view over the entire arena for The Grand Opening.

I, of course, remained with the other competitors on the sidelines, where we watched the Swedish Folk Dancers twirl in traditional costumes until, with skill and vibrant colour, they formed perfect Olympic circles. Although I couldn't help but think amusingly, *hang on a minute, this is the Australian Olympic Equestrian Games. Where's the Boomerangs and the Didgeridoos?*

Then, finally, we equestrians from all countries entered the main arena on our horses. We rode a lap of honour before Swedish Hans Wikne entered, on his magnificent chestnut gelding. Hans went on to light the Olympic torch.

The evening went perfectly, and we prayed for a brilliant and safe Olympics.

Two days later, I was mounted on River and about to compete in my first attempt for a place in the dressage medals, when Norman gave me a nervous grin, reached up, and rubbed my arm until we both relaxed. A few moments afterward, we laughed when River farted continuously during the warm-up! I then heard my number called. *Thank heavens River got rid of that lot beforehand.*

The audience sat respectfully during the momentous occasion, appearing like figurines, allowing me to maintain my unperturbed concentration. I began by cantering River into the arena and bowing to the judges after a perfect halt. Our dressage test continued flawlessly, to the point where I had to keep a lid on my emotions to avoid losing control of my aids.

I was proud of River's performance and our partnership that day. I had grossly underestimated this horse. If the judge's total score did not reflect what I felt it should, I would walk away content, knowing that River and I could not have performed any better at this stage, as we were both young and relatively inexperienced. However, I reminded myself I was there only because my father had paid for my incredible journey. And I felt humbled.

It felt like we'd left the Arena in slow motion. Norman clapped slowly on the sidelines, tears smudging his eyes. Whether it was the euphoria of the moment or something I'd intended to do, I bent over, reaching for Norman's hand, and said, "When the games are over, River belongs to you. And I will sponsor you until River retires." I fell off the horse into Norman's arms. We laughed and cried.

Later, Norman squeezed my hand while we waited for the final scores. I screamed when I heard 'Davina Buchanan and Carlina River, 80.5,' I didn't care who heard. We were in the running for a medal.

Once again, I felt fortunate to have Norman take care of River, wash him down, walk and groom him, and give him a generous pick of grass before putting him to bed. Norman also looked after Grace, leaving me free to catch up with family and friends.

I should have been happier that evening at dinner, but I was not.

My nerves were still at play from the pressure of competing and reviewing my performance. I sat silent, ensuring I remembered every detail to help with future dressage tests—namely, the final. I'm sure Father, in particular, noticed my wafting off, so he suggested I leave for an early night. I took his advice and went home with Felix. Again, his gentle lovemaking soothed and convinced me of his devotion. *God, I loved that man.*

At daylight, the phone rang. I crawled out of bed, trying not to disturb Felix.

"Hello, Davina speaking."

"Hello, Davina, it's Norman. I thought it best, you know. Hilda visited your horses around midnight."

Norman had offered to sleep with Grace and River, saying, "We cannot allow another catastrophe, Davina."

"Why on earth would she do that, Norman? And how did she get into the barn?"

"I don't know. I tried asking Hilda, but she was drunk. She said she just wanted to say goodnight to Grace and River. I immediately escorted her outside and hailed a cab. I didn't want to phone you then, Davina. You needed your sleep."

"I appreciate it, Norman. I'm sure it's nothing to be concerned about." I lied. "I'll speak to Hilda later. I'll see you in about an hour. But first, could you give River a walk in the sunshine and some carrots? He deserves it."

I took a deep breath and promised myself I'd cover up my concerns in front of Felix. Instead, I attacked him when he walked sleepy-eyed into the kitchen. "Why would your sister get drunk and visit my horses at midnight?"

Felix stepped backward, hands in the air, "Davina, please, what is wrong?"

"What do you mean! What is wrong? How dare Hilda break into the horse barn at such an hour? Just as well, Norman sleeps there! He said Hilda was drunk!"

"I don't understand. I'm sorry, Davina. Please come here."

Reluctantly, I fell into his open arms, and when he hugged me, I felt terrible. I knew it was not Felix's fault. "You don't think Hilda is capable of harming my horses, do you, Felix?" I mumbled into his shoulder.

"No, I do not. Hilda loves horses, although she is a little tough when training them." Felix stood to one side and scratched his head. "I don't understand how Hilda could be drunk. She does not drink."

All I needed was another mystery.

"Okay," I said, shaking my head, "let's forget it. I should go to the stables so Norman has some time off. He's been incredible. Even when the police questioned him as a suspect, he understood."

I never thought jealousy would raise its head with Felix, but when he said indignantly, "I suppose you think Norman is very good-looking, too!"

I laughed. "Yes, as a matter of fact, I do." I kissed Felix tenderly, "But nowhere as handsome as you. You are the only man I will ever love." Then all was forgiven. The problem with Hilda could wait until later, when Felix and I would join her for coffee.

I first went to the stables and found time to relax with Phyllis, who was always great company. I then felt guilty, "I'm sorry I didn't invite you to join us for dinner last night, Phyllis."

"It's okay, Davina. You have little time to spend with your parents. And I think it's lovely that you've finally met Felix's parents. But I'll be disappointed if I'm not invited to have at least a drink. Unfortunately, my brother and his family can't make it. Not even to the finals." Phyllis appeared downhearted, "that's if I'm lucky enough to be in it." She then brightened, "And by the way, congratulations again on your fantastic score. Fancy beating me by half a point. Still, the top score is 86. Henri is almost unbeatable, not to forget Liz." Phyllis gently squeezed my arm, "Never mind, it's an excellent achievement just to be here at your age, Davina. You are the youngest competitor of all time. So that's another accomplishment." Phyllis kissed my cheek. "I'm so proud of you, especially after all that has happened to you and poor Grace."

"Thank you, Phyllis. Your friendship means a lot."

I was often tempted to ask why the attractive Phyllis had never married. Maybe it was none of my business. She would tell me in time, no doubt.

I was then about to tell her about Hilda coming into the barn at midnight. But before I could, Phyllis asked.

"What do you make of Hilda, Davina?"

I lowered my voice, "I never know what to think. I have an uneasy feeling about Hilda." Then I pulled myself up. "But I'm not usually like that, *judgmental.*"

"I don't think having a gut feeling about someone is judgmental."

Said Phyllis stiffly.

"I know. Still, Hilda's parents love her. And Felix always sticks up for Hilda. So I try to like her."

"I'm pleased it's not me in the middle of that sandwich, Davina," said Phyllis, patting my back.

We shrugged it off and continued training our horses until it came time to meet Felix, Hilda, and Charlotte for coffee. Unfortunately, Phyllis declined, declaring she had a headache. *I think Hilda was her headache.*

Of course, Hilda was apologetic after I questioned her about coming to the barn at midnight. "I am so sorry, Davina. I stayed behind in the bar last night when everyone left. A nice young man asked if I cared for a nightcap. I didn't know what that meant and didn't want to appear unsophisticated, so I said, Yes, I'll have whatever you have. I almost choked when the brandy slid down my throat, but the warmth and flavour tempted me to have another."

Hilda hung her head, sniffing back tears. I was unsure if it was embarrassment or if she didn't want to meet my accusing eyes. After listening to Hilda's snivel, Charlotte hugged her, "Don't worry, Hilda, we all do silly things when we're young." I cringed, wishing Charlotte would shut up.

"Just answer one more question, Hilda," I asked like a detective, "How did you get into the barn? It's always locked."

Hilda's eyes lit up like a pinball machine. "Oh, a nice young man was coming out, and he let me in. I cannot remember his name."

Then Felix, sounding like a schoolmaster, said, "Well, I'm sure, Hilda, that you will not drink with strangers again."

"No, I will not, Felix," said Hilda, smiling smugly.

No harm had come to my horses, so I dropped the subject and tried to enjoy the coffee while feeling outnumbered.

Our dressage competitions continued, with points from each test adding to our final score. I felt confident that we remained in the running, but I knew I could not win gold. Accepting my fate gave me time to enjoy watching the various three-day event teams compete. Our Australian team made us proud, and I cheered the loudest after their extraordinary dressage performance, knowing I had played a part. They finished a more than respectable fourth in the final tally.

I'd phoned Irene many times from Stockholm, but she never

mentioned Billy. Irene was only interested in my news from Stockholm, which I was excited to share—and then I asked, "How are your running times, Irene?

"I'm on track, and looking good for gold in November, Davvy."

I couldn't be happier for my dearest friend.

After five days of dressage competition, with all scores tallied, it was announced, as Phyllis had predicted. Henri Saint won a Gold Medal for Sweden. Liz Hartel gained Silver for Denmark. And although Liselott Lisenhoff won the Bronze for Germany, Phyllis thought she and Benjamin should have beaten them. I agreed, but Phyllis's horse, Benjamin the Great, faltered on the piaffe in their final test, which cost Phyllis the essential point. I left happy with my score, ranking sixth on the leader board. I felt confident that I would improve my craft and go for gold in the next Olympics.

After arranging Carlina Grace's return to Australia, I packed my bags, feeling a mix of sadness and satisfaction. Next, I said goodbye to Norman and River. I had no regrets about leaving River with Norman. After all, he'd done most of the work and taught River the fundamentals of a perfect 'half halt.' Something I'd failed to do. Plus, I felt for those talented riders who could not afford the best horses. It was a similar situation to the kids I saw at gymkhanas, with their lackluster ponies, when all I wanted to do was help them.

I was homeward-bound and couldn't wait to reach Australia. If only Felix could join me, my happiness would be complete.

CHAPTER 20
CATHY'S DEMISE

Once on the bus home, Evie asked, "Ma, what's d'surprise? Are we goin somewhere? Do y'have a present f'me?"

"Shoosh, Evie, I'll be tellin' yer when we're home." Cathy smiled, squeezing Evie's hand.

The driveway seemed doubly long as Cathy hurried, anxious to get packed and be on their way. Matey barked from his usual tie-up on the verandah, and Evie ran to untie him. "Oh, Matey me' boy," she said, accepting his face licks with a giggle. Cathy stood watching, remembering their past year on the farm and how happy Evie had been. She sighed and left to begin packing.

Cathy later phoned Jock, conscious that Martha would be listening at the exchange. "Hello Jock, I need t'be askin yer a favour. I have t'be goin t'Melbourne in d'mornin t'see a specialist doctor. Evie and I'll be away for a few days. Could y'take care of Matey and keep an eye on Bobby and d'sheep?"

"Of course, Cathy. But I have a better suggestion. Why don't you leave Evie with me? So I can take her to school."

"No. No, thank ya, Jock. I have other tings t'attend to. I need Evie wid me."

"I'll be straight over, Cathy. We can talk about it then."

"Okay, Jock, I was goin t'ask yer for a lift int' town t'catch d'bus. It leaves at ten tomorra mornin, but if yer wants t'come now and take Matey, dat'd be good."

Jock sat tapping his fingers on the desk, trying to fathom Cathy's sudden departure before he told Flossy where he was going, not that she'd remember, so he wrote it in her notebook. With his mind spinning, he trekked to his old work ute parked in the barn and heaved his arthritic leg over the mudguard. He refused to sell the old ute because his dear Massie loved to drive it into town to do her shopping, "I just throw everything in the back and put the tarp over."Massie would say, smiling. "It's so easy, Jock."

The vehicle started with its usual backfire, accompanied by smoke streaming from the exhaust pipe. "Good old girl," he said, patting the dashboard before looking in the rear-vision mirror to see a man wearing a pinstripe suit and a white Panama hat approaching the back door. Something told him to drive off quickly, grab Cathy and Evie, and get them out of sight. Jock watched the man, whom he suspected had knocked on the front door first. *That'd be right. Flossy can't hear the doorbell. Maybe I should stay and see what happens. No. I have a bad feeling about this.* Jock drove slowly down his driveway, '*Don't you go backfiring on me, old girl. We need to be quiet.*' He went two miles down the road before turning into Cathy's driveway and driving around the back of the house to be out of sight. "Cathy! Cathy, come quickly!" Jock yelled, and Cathy bolted outside.

"What on earth's wrong, Jock?"

"There's a stranger at my place. He looks like a gangster. He didn't notice me. I don't think. I have a bad feeling about him. You and Evie get in the car. We'll go for a drive. Come on, let's go, Cathy!"

"Oh, you've been readin too many crime stories, Jock." She laughed nervously.

"Maybe I have. But now I'm worried about Flossy. I shouldn't have left her." Jock rubbed his forehead, "I'd best phone home and see what's up." He struggled out of the car and stumbled inside. After going through the telephone exchange, Flossy answered, "Hello."

"Hello, Flossy. It's Jock. Are you alright? I saw a man knocking on the back door."

"Of course I'm alright. A lovely man came to ask if we needed a new vacuum cleaner. I said no, thank you. And he left after I gave him a cup of tea."

Jock hung his head and sighed, "Okay, Flossy, as long as everything is alright. I'll be home soon."

Cathy burst out laughing, putting Jock's suspicions at bay. *And hers.*

"I'm sorry, Cathy. With the Bob episode and all, I'm a little jumpy."

Cathy's joy came with knowing she was finally going home to Ireland, away from Sean and all his shenanigans. She'd weighed up the good with the bad in their marriage, and the bad now outweighed the good, so it was time to leave.

"I know, Jock, and I'm so sorry you had t'find out about Bob. But don't be worryin y'self. We'll be fine." Cathy hugged him.

"You will come back, won't you, Cathy?"

Cathy crossed her fingers and smiled. "Of course, Jock. How could we be movin away from yer?"

"Alright then. I'll take Matey with me now. And I'll pick you up at nine in the morning."

"That'd be much appreciated, Jock. Have yer time f'a cuppa now?"

"Yes, of course, Cathy. Thank you."

Cathy had ordered Evie outside once they were home, "Go feed d'cow and Bobby. And be quick. There'll be no time f'ridin t'day. We need t'pack and be ready f'Jock to pick us up in d'mornin." Evie had grumbled as she ran to do her chores. *What's d'flamin secret?*

Cathy offered Jock the last of her fruit cake and a cup of well-brewed tea. As Cathy was about to pour the tea, Evie burst in with Matey close behind.

"I've done me' chores, Ma. Will y'tell me d'secret?"

Jock looked from one to the other before resting on Cathy.

"So it's a secret, Cathy, about you going to a doctor, is it?"

"No, I just taught Evie would like d'bus trip to Melbourne. Dat's all, Jock."

Well, as I said, Evie can stay with me if she likes."

It was Evie's turn to look from Ma to Jock, "I'd rather stay with Jock, Ma."

"I'm sorry, Evie, but you y'can't. I have uda business in Melbourne dat involves you." Cathy glared at Jock, "You shouldna said anything until I told her, Jock!"

"I'm sorry. I was just trying to help."

Cathy softened, "I know y'are, but y'can't help us. Only t'care of Matey, Bobby, and d'otha animals ." She held the cup up to hide her lying eyes.

"As long as you come back, Cathy."

"We will. Of course, we will." Cathy said convincingly.

The following morning, Cathy and Evie waited on the front verandah with their suitcases packed to the brim. Finally, Jock arrived at ten past nine, with Matey barking in the back of the ute; Evie ran to him and whispered, "Jock'll look after yer, Matey." Then, with her face snuggled against his fur, she said her last teary goodbye.

Evie's tears had soaked her pillow the night before, even after Cathy had tried consoling her with promises, "We'll be livin with old Pa in Ireland, and you'll have a new pony." Cathy rocked Evie in her arms, "Shh, Evie. Just tink, Matey loves Jock and Flossy. She gives him treats. Please, Evie, y'have t'understand. We need t'go home. We're not safe here anymore. And don't tell Jock what we're doing or where we're goin. Please don't say anythin to anyone, or y'might put us in danger. Do' y'understand, Evie? Don't speak to anyone! Don't trust anyone!"

After saying goodbye to Jock and Matey at the bus stop, Evie promised Cathy, "*I'll never speak to a stranger ever again, Ma.*"

They climbed the steps into the bus, found a seat, and Evie lay her head on Cathy's shoulder. Time soon lapsed as Evie became mesmerized by the passing acres of brown grass, hemmed in by straggly gum trees. It was nothing like Ireland's clear, wind-swept green fields. *I wonder if Captain Teddy'll sail the Ship back t' Ireland*; with that thought, Evie drifted into a dream where she saw Old Pa again.

Finally, after five hours, the bus stopped at Flinders Street Station. Cathy paid the fare as they hopped onto another bus going to Station Pier, Port Melbourne. She assumed it would be as simple as buying a ticket at the port and boarding a ship to Ireland in no time. Cathy took Evie's hand to cross the road to the 'Booking Office.' She approached the glass door, framing a woman at her desk, head down, wearing black-framed glasses. With her hair tied neatly in a bun, the woman appeared dignified.

Cathy smiled, "Hello. I'm here t'buy two tickets t'Ireland. Is dere a ship ready t' go?"

The woman said without lifting her eyes. "The next ship to *England*! And then you must find your way across to Ireland. Leaves in seven days. You can purchase the tickets here." The woman studied her information sheet. "The Ship is called the M.V. Fairsea. Two tickets, Madam?" She said, looking up with a grin.

Evie's heart jumped. *That's Captain Teddy's ship.*

Noticeably disappointed with having to wait a week, Cathy paid the money, then asked, "Do yer know of any nice bed and breakfast houses nearby?"

"Try Mrs. Hopkins. She lives two blocks away. If you're lucky, she might have a room." The woman handed the tickets to Cathy and then wrote the address on a piece of paper.

Once outside, Cathy mumbled, '*Dese suitcases are bloody heavy.*' She smiled down at Evie, "I'll hail a cab, Evie."

"Am I allowed t'talk, Ma?"

Cathy laughed, "Of course, y'silly duffer. I only meant, don't talk t'anyone else but me!"

"Dat's good. Because d'case is as heavy as a pregnant pig!" Evie said, looking under her eyes at Cathy, who laughed. "Do yer remember d'Fairsea, Ma? It's Captain Teddy's Ship."

"Why, so it is, Evie. Dat's clever of yer t'remember."

"I still have d'paper wid Teddy's address, Ma."

"I doubt if we'll be needin his help. But y'never know. So y'best be keepin it, Evie."

A cab pulled up to the curb, and they hurried inside while the driver loaded their cases into the trunk. Cathy then gave him the address.

"Ya Irish! Same as me." He said happily. "Ya should be livin in St Kilda. Dat's where all d'Irish live."

"We're only here f'seven days. Den, we're catchin a ship back t'Ireland."

The cabby introduced himself as Paddy, and Cathy felt lucky they had only a few blocks to travel, as Paddy was determined to vacuum her life story—none of which Cathy divulged. Evie didn't speak, even when Paddy asked her name. So, Paddy gave up asking questions. "Here's d'house, Mrs…"

"Thank y' Paddy, and good luck t'ya!" Cathy called as Paddy drove away, shaking his head.

Cathy opened the gate to a substantial two-story brick house. She stood a moment to admire the well-manicured garden before she knocked on the door. Soon, a solid woman with a ruddy complexion opened it. "Can I help you?" she said, smiling. Cathy exhaled.

"Yes, I hope so. Me daughter and I'll be needin a room until our ship leaves f' Ireland in seven days. Me' name's Cathy, Ca… Brown."

"Well. You have the luck of the Irish, t'be sure, Mrs. Brown." Mrs. Hopkins chuckled. "I have a gentleman leaving this very moment. If you wouldn't mind waiting in the parlour, I'll see him off and have my cleaner refresh the room. I serve dinner in the dining room at six thirty. Breakfast is served buffet-style from 6:00 a.m. to 8:00 a.m. I don't do lunch. And it's four shillings per night."

"Thank y'vera much, Mrs. Hopkins. I'll be happy t'pay in advance."

Cathy gazed past the woman into the hallway to see a highly polished timber floor and dust-free ornaments on what appeared to be a solid antique sideboard. Cathy then proffered her hand with a grin, "The lady from d'bookin office said t'come here. And I'm happy I did, Mrs. Hopkins. Dis place is lovely. Here's a week's money in advance."

Mrs. Hopkins accepted the money with a glint in her eye.

No answer came from Evie when Mrs. Hopkins asked her name, Cathy's warning ringing in Evie's ears. '*What a strange child. She must be shy.*' Mrs. Hopkins smiled and stroked Evie's blond curls as she passed into the parlour, where they waited in silence.

Their room on the second floor appeared comfortable, with two single beds, a washbasin, armchairs, crochet doilies on the arms, and a small coffee table in the center. Then Evie noticed the white Formica radio on the mantle above a small fireplace.

"I like dis room, Ma. But why did you say our name was Brown?"

"I don't want anyone t'know we're here. And yes, I like dis room too, Evie, mainly because it's clean. I reckon we'll be safe here until d'ship leaves. Though we won't be goin anywhere until it does, okay?"

The entire first day, Evie sat on the armchair Cathy had positioned so Evie could watch two Willy Wagtails build their nest in an Elm tree not far from their window. Evie smiled, watching as the birds flitted in and out, carrying different grasses and small sticks in their beaks. With precision, they tucked and weaved their goods around and around on a sturdy branch until the sides were high enough for Evie's approval. *Clever little birdies, nobody'll see y' from d'ground, and y'too high f'cats t'climb. I wish I were a bird flyin free.*

Jock had shown Evie many native birds and their habitats on occasion. The black-and-white Willy Wagtail had intrigued her. With its white eyebrows, black body, and white belly, "it looks like a mini penguin," Evie had said. And Jock laughed, promising to show her the penguins who lived at Phillip Island. "It's a long way from the farm, but we can camp on the beach, Evie." Jock also said, "Aborigines say the Willy Wagtail is a bad omen. When they nest nearby, the birds listen to their private business. And before they can say boomerang, trouble begins within their tribe."

Of course, Evie didn't believe it, but she had a bad feeling in her gut when Cathy experienced cramping pains in the abdomen the following day. "*Damn periods,*" she cursed, holding her stomach.

"What's d'matter, Ma? Are y'sick?"

"I've got a pain in me' belly. But, it'll soon go."

Cathy swallowed her last two aspirin. And lie on the bed in a foetal position. Evie sat rubbing Cathy's back, singing '*Molly Malone,*' one of the Irish songs old Pa had taught her.

"Oh, dat's a beautiful song, Evie. And y'sing it so well."

Cathy then felt liquid running between her legs, so she sat up carefully and asked Evie to grab the hand towel. Cathy placed it between her legs. Unfortunately, the blood soon soaked the towel. And Evie noticed.

"What's wrong, Ma, y'not bleedin t'death?"

"No, Evie. And you're not quite old enough t'tell about d'facts of life. But I suppose I'll have t'explain it now."

And Cathy did, to a *not-surprised* Evie, who'd spent long enough around animals to figure it out.

"So, I need ya t'go see Mrs. Hopkin. Tell her I need menstrual pads and aspirin. Ask her if she could please give me some until I can go to d'shops. I'm bleedin' somethin' terrible."

"I will, Ma. You just rest." Evie stopped in her stride. "But y'said not t'speak t' anyone." Cathy smiled. "It's alright, Evie. Just dis once, okay?"

Mrs. Hopkins was delighted when Evie spoke, but also apologetic. "I'm sorry, Evie, I have no use for those pads. I'm too old, you see. And I'm out of aspirin. But I have an idea, why don't I give you money to go to the Chemist? It's not too far, and you can buy an ice cream on your way back. How about that?" she beamed. "Besides, I'm too busy to go. Your mother can pay me back later." She finished by patting Evie on the head.

I'd love an ice cream. And I know all about being a grown-up. So I can do dis.

"Alright, I'll be back quick, so Ma won't know."

"I'm sorry, Evie, but I must tell your mother. I'm sure she'll understand."

Evie accepted the paper money Mrs. Hopkins placed in her palm, her eyes wide. She'd never handled so much cash.

"Okay. But please tell Ma I won't talk t'strangers." Evie hesitated with a cheeky smile, "Only d'Chemist."

Mrs Hopkins shook her head, chuckling.

After running and then heaving for air, Evie opened the door to an empty shop except for the man wearing a white coat, whom she assumed was the Chemist. "Me ma needs some of dose pads f'when she's bleedin. And a big packet of aspirin!" Evie said proudly, looking up at the tall man, who laughed and shook his head. Evie's eyes narrowed. *Damn cheek. What's so funny about dat!*

Evie handed him the money, and he gave her the change, along with the menstrual pads and aspirin wrapped in brown paper. She then hurried two doors down to the ice cream shop. After looking at the prices, Evie studied the coins in her hand. *Should I be greedy and have a doubleheader? No. It'll be too hard t'run back t' Mrs. Hopkins and eat me' ice cream.* Even so, Evie took her time returning to the Guest House, enjoying the cold, creamy sweetness and clutching the parcel with the leftover coins jingling in her pocket.

Meanwhile, Mrs. Hopkins climbed the stairs to tell Cathy about Evie going to the shop. Returning downstairs, she heard a knock and opened the door to a good-looking gentleman who spoke English with an Italian accent, "Escusa me, Madam, but do you have a Cathy Calan staying here?"

"I have Cathy Brown, not Calan?" Mrs. Hopkins threw him a quizzical look.

"Sometimes she's a known asa Brown." He smiled knowingly.

He'd been to the ticket office at Port Phillip and, with the same story, received the information needed from the woman in charge.

He continued, "I'm a gooda friend of her husband. I'm a come to give Cathy some a sad news about him." He looked deep into Mrs. Hopkins' eyes. "I musta say, you are a beautifula woman." He said, smiling seductively.

Mrs. Hopkins's hands flew to her chest, heat rising in her cheeks, "Oh dear, thank you. But I'm afraid Mrs. Brown is not feeling her best. What a shame. However, I'll go and tell her. Please come in and wait in the parlour." She smiled demurely, pushing her hair in place.

Cathy had just folded another towel and placed it between her legs when she heard the knock. "Who is it?"

"It's Mrs. Hopkins, Mrs. Brown. I'm sorry to bother you again, but an Italian man is waiting downstairs in the parlour. I'm afraid he h…

The only thing Mrs. Hopkins remembered when questioned by the police later was, "I opened the door to a well-dressed man who asked to see Cathy Brown, and so I climbed the stairs to tell her. And when I was on the landing, he must have hit me over the head."

Unbeknownst to Mrs. Hopkins, the man had then barged into Cathy's room, knocked her out, tied a cloth around her mouth, and grabbed her handbag, which held her identification. He then dragged her from the room, downstairs, through the kitchen, and out to the back lane, where a vehicle with a driver awaited.

CHAPTER 21
DAVINA
THE WEDDING AND THE OLYMPICS

I'd missed my solitary walks by the river, something I'd longed for in Switzerland. *Silly as it sounds*, the river listens to my problems, and today, I needed to accept Father's inevitable death. His five years in remission were over. Yet, my belated birthday celebration was in preparation. And my only wish was to see Father smiling when I blew out my candles.

I'd often send challenges to the universe, so I threw a stick in the river and said aloud, *"If you float to shore, Father will live until I blow my candles out."*

It floated downstream.

What then? Would I be the head of our family? None of us could rely on Joseph. He lived in another world. And Mother? Well, who knows how she'd respond when Father died? All family matters and decisions, I knew, would be left to me. But was I ready for such an enormous responsibility? And would Felix ever ask me to marry him? If so, would he agree to live in Australia, or would he prefer me to live in Switzerland? With so many questions, my head spun, but I remembered Uncle Aaron telling me, "We should live in the moment, Davina. It's the only way to be happy and focus on what we must do." He'd grinned, nodding, "Believe me, I know from experience." Aaron then dipped his head, "The war, you see."

I now sit and reflect on that day by the river. It was the day I was awakened to being a woman. A woman who'd choose her own destiny, I vowed to live life to the fullest and accept whatever came my way with dignity. I, therefore, spent as much time with Father as possible. But at the same time, I was driven to do what I'd always wanted. And that was to ride in races and jump my horses as high as the moon, weaving and ducking through trees, flying over water jumps, competing in cross country. I asked myself, was my need for speed and danger a reflection of my anger that Father had to die? If I pursued my dream right now, would he live, if only to prevent me from perhaps breaking my neck?

Whatever the reason, I'd already asked Jacques to find me the best jumping horses money could buy. Why should I go through what most riders do? Spend years training second-rate horses because they can't afford the best?

I could buy anything I wanted. *Lucky me.*

I can't say I liked that part of me, which I no longer own. I am a woman who wants nothing material—only love and happiness—the two most difficult things to find. But then, I suppose, that's all I ever truly wanted.

Nevertheless, I went all out for what I thought I needed.

So, while Jacques journeyed around Victoria inspecting jumping horses, I kept Father company while he lay in bed, depleted of energy. Of course, he appreciated it, as Mother only had to look at him, and she'd cry.

Joseph was spending all his time working on a significant scientific breakthrough. He told us he could not spare the time to be with Father, *who forgave him.*

"I don't need Joseph by my side, Davina. He is, after all, a highly valued scientist, and the world needs him more than I do." Father coughed before lying his head on the pillow.

"May I ask a favour, Father?" He laughed as best he could.

"I'll try, Davina."

"My twenty-first birthday party is in five days. Could you please stay with me until then?"

The pain and disappointment in his eyes told me he couldn't, and that night, he passed away.

My only compensation was that Felix flew from Switzerland to attend Father's funeral *and my birthday party.* Unfortunately, Hilda came too.

I decided to hold Father's Memorial on the same day as my party. Most said it was '*bizarre*,' but to me, it meant a double celebration— firstly, Father's life that he'd lived with humility and compassion, and my twenty-one years of trying to be the best daughter possible, which wasn't difficult.

I felt his spirit there that evening.

Considering the diverse celebrations, sadness slowly gave way to joy on that evening, as I had hoped. My tears and laughter spilled into many champagne flutes, and Felix supported me in whatever I said or did. *Where on earth did he come from? Heaven? Who sent him, I wondered? Did I deserve his love and attention?*

As the night progressed, I became more inebriated. Some said disorderly.

No, that was Mother when she burst into my room the following morning, lecturing me on her version of events. My head ached with her every word, and my mouth tasted like a cocky cage.

"Oh, please, Mother, leave me alone. Let me wallow in self-pity. I've punished myself enough. Please go!"

And she did, but not without sniveling. "You should be here for me, Davina! Not behaving like you're happy you're father's dead!"

That's when I rose like a Goliath!

"How dare you!" I yelled despite the explosion in my head. "I have been a rock to Father. He wanted me to celebrate both his life and mine. I'm a woman, not a little girl! And I will follow his wishes!" *(Well, not quite. After all, I had two jumping horses arriving soon.)* Mother snorted and left, and I prayed it would be the last time she'd blame me for everything, the same as she'd done when I was a child.

I showered, dressed, and drank a gallon of water before hobbling to the morning room, where Betty had set out a buffet breakfast or brunch, depending on when our guests arrived. Felix immediately stood and withdrew my chair. "Good morning, Davina. Would you like me to serve you?" His double innuendo made me laugh, *oh my poor head.*

"Not now, Felix. I'll refrain for the moment."

Then Hilda, in her usual stiff German accent, said. "A hearty breakfast is good after drinking too much alcohol."

I glared with venom, "I'll be the judge of that, Hilda." *Oh no,* I'd promised to be kind. But it never proved easy with Hilda. Fortunately, Joseph strolled in.

"Good morning, everyone. I trust we are not suffering from overindulgence." He focused on me. At least it was less accusatory than if he'd come out and said, "Davina."

"I must admit, Joseph. I overindulged. *Slightly,*" which made everyone laugh, including Hilda. I'd never heard her laugh. But then I noticed her flashing Joseph the same smile I'm sure Cleopatra gave Mark Antony.

Over our morning chit-chat, I made a point of eavesdropping.

Mmm, did I miss something the night before? Hilda and Joseph seemed to be getting along well. Yes, very friendly indeed.

The calm weather remained until a cold, blustery wind hit at lunchtime. We stayed inside, relaxed, played board games, or read books. It suited me. I didn't want to admit that I was hungover with a mix of alcohol and sadness. However, the thought of my new horses arriving late that afternoon helped my equilibrium.

With the aid of our jackaroos, Jacques had almost finished a cross-country course, plus a sand-based jumping arena. Soon, I'd be all set, but not for two weeks, as I had other business to attend to—namely, Father's funeral, which would be a private cremation, his business, and his Will. As equal shareholders, Joseph and I needed to decide whether to sell Father's engineering company. *Or not.* Plus, I knew I had to give Mother more attention, even though it would be difficult while dealing with *my* heartbreak.

Felix asked if he and Hilda might be of help. If so, they would stay a little longer. Of course, I accepted with pleasure, especially as Joseph had taken a liking to Hilda after she'd followed him around like a puppy dog, wagging her tail and jumping on his lap. Moreover, Joseph appeared happy with her attention. And so Hilda transformed from a robotic personality to a cheerful young woman whenever Joseph was around. Their mutual interest in chemistry and science kept them engaged in conversation.

Well, what do you know?

Additionally, Hilda was about to study medicine the following year, and Joseph seemed impressed. The only thing that unnerved me was how Hilda continually glanced at Felix to see if he was paying her attention. Strange *behaviour.* Was she attempting to make him jealous?

Irene, her parents, and Bill had attended my birthday party, but left early because their training schedule took precedence. Mrs. Gibbs had taken me aside the moment they arrived and confessed how frightened she'd been of Bill's driving. "Although I must admit, Davina, Bill is extremely competent. He told us he's going to be a racing car driver when he's finished running. Mind you. His parents are upset because he isn't interested in their farm."

"I know how they feel. My brother Joseph hasn't the slightest interest in our cattle." She rubbed my arm. "That's a shame."

Our small talk continued until Mrs. Gibbs, after appearing

hesitant to admit it, said, "I'm sorry, Davina. I was wrong about your friendship with Irene. I thought it would end after High School." She squeezed my hand, "And I'm most grateful for your support. We knew Irene was a brilliant runner, but she lacked the academic skills and the confidence to grow into the lovely young woman she is today. So thank you, Davina."

"Don't worry, Mrs. Gibbs, that worked both ways." I laughed inside. The truth was, Irene had brought out the humour and courage in me.

Those two attributes proved essential for my survival later on.

We embraced for a long moment before Mrs. Gibbs continued, "Mr. Gibbs is feeling much better after seeing another doctor who prescribed a different medication. He also sent him to a psychotherapist, and now our life is much better."

We finished on that happy note, as I needed to spread myself around, talking to friends who were sad about losing Father but happy in their lives. It lessened the blow of Father's death. I knew life went on; Father had told me enough times. And I suppose my birthday celebration proved it.

Two days later, Felix and I made an excuse about going to South Yarra to ensure our flat was in order. Naturally, we received raised eyebrows, but I didn't care. I was twenty-one and nobody's child. Secretly, I hoped Felix would propose marriage. And my wish came true on the second night in our flat.

Over a candlelight dinner, Felix asked, "Will you marry me, Davina? I love you so much. I do not want us ever to part."
Of course, I said, "Yes, yes, yes!"

Felix had begged the owner of a local restaurant to deliver the food. To my surprise, he'd set the table with our best china and crystal glasses, complemented by a centerpiece of red roses amid two glowing candles.

I now sit, many years later, trying to recapture that perfect moment, and apart from thinking, *'perhaps Father has paid Felix to love me,'* I believed then that Felix did indeed love me - unconditionally. The feeling was sublime.

We set a wedding date for February 1957, thinking it might be a bit too hot. But I intended to hold the reception at home, where I'd have a swimming pool built in the garden. Father would never agree when

Joseph and I were children: "It's far too dangerous," he'd say, "A child left in our care could drown if we weren't paying attention."

But now I was the chief, with no contenders. Therefore, I would have a swimming pool built! And if the guests felt so inclined, they could swim after our nuptials, of course.

Like Charlotte and Jacques, Felix and I agreed to a casual garden wedding.

"I've chosen Irene as my bridesmaid and Charlotte as my matron of honour," I said, knowing he would approve. "I know you want Jacques as your best man and Joseph as the groomsman."

"But what about Hilda?" Felix asked.

"Well, I suppose I could have two Bridesmaids. Irene and Hilda will just have to share Joseph." I smiled, and Felix nodded in contemplation.

My actual thoughts? I'd hoped Hilda would *not return* after she and Felix flew back to Helsinki in two days. I drove them to the airport, said farewell, and went home to inform Mother of our wedding date.

"Oh, Davina, that's wonderful news!" Immediately, her imagination spiralled. However, our plans for the wedding differed. Mother's formal and mine casual. "Please, Mother, I know your ideas sound lovely, but it is my wedding, and I only want close friends and family here in a casual atmosphere."

So please, God, help me when I tell her about the swimming pool.

"But it's sweltering in February, Davina. The guests will melt in the garden. Why can't we at least hold the reception in the Ballroom? It's air-conditioned and has ceiling fans." Mother's sickly, sweet smile was the same as when she wanted Father to agree. I embraced her, "That's a good idea, Mother."

And so it was. I allowed Mother to choose the room, the menu, and the flowers, keeping her and Betty occupied and out of my space.

However, the Melbourne Olympics took precedence first. And November arrived. "*Faster than Phar Lap down the Flemington straight,*" Irene said.

Irene had forged a spot in the one-hundred-metre sprint and the two-hundred-metre race. I felt incredibly proud. She was my sister in every way except blood. And Billy had earned his place in the marathon. I couldn't imagine *walking* twenty-six miles, let alone running it. What a trooper.

Unfortunately, my darling Felix was unable to attend the Games.

Moving to Australia in January meant he needed time to tie up loose ends in Switzerland.

I remember my fears turning to delight when I asked Felix if he would consider living in Australia before he left.

"Yes. Of course. I love it here, Davina. And I'm sure I will find a position as an architect in Melbourne."

"That won't be a problem," I'd said, "My father has many contacts in the business. Although I have the money to set you up in your…"

"I will not hear of it," Felix said with one hand raised.

And I could only smile at this honourable young man I was about to marry.

**

And let the games begin!

Father had been a privileged member of the Melbourne Cricket Ground. Therefore, we, his family, gathered in the best seats.

Bill's father joined us in the stand most days, but he chose to be on the road when following his son's progress over the gruelling twenty-six miles. I'm sure Mr. Petersan covered more ground than Bill on that day. After all, Mr. Petersan walked for miles daily, herding his sheep with the help of his Border Collie. He preferred it that way. Obviously, Bill owned the same genes.

The grandstands hummed with excitement before each track and field event. Even though I was not competing, my excitement doubled since Stockholm. I suppose being in our hometown and soaking in the atmosphere of Australians cheering together for one goal created an unforgettable experience. So much so that I wanted to put on a pair of runners and feel the same buzz and pride as our athletes; the only problem was that I'd make a fool of myself. Simply because I have long legs doesn't mean I can run fast. Maybe the hurdles? Nope, not interested.

I could go on for hours about the 1956 Summer Olympics and the countries that boycotted the Australian Games for political reasons. Namely, Egypt, Iraq, Lebanon, etc., after the Western lands of Europe, including France, invaded the Suez Canal to free it up for their personal use.

It's upsetting when politics influence what should be a sporting event for the world's greatest athletes, not the world's political leaders. But enough about that.

We supported those brilliant athletes on our home soil, regardless of which nation they represented. And I don't feel the need to write about who won what event. I've tried not to turn my memoir into a travel diary or give my view on world events. But I will say that, in the end, Australia made us proud. We ran third among seventy-two nations, with thirteen gold medals, eight silver, and fourteen bronze medals - thirty-five medals in total. The Soviet Union won the medal count, followed closely by the United States. Their medals tripled ours. That's understandable, given the population density.

Irene missed a bronze medal by a fraction of a second in the two-hundred-metre race. Billy ran fifth in the marathon.

Irene, unfortunately, was disqualified in the one-hundred-metre sprint for jumping the gun twice. I never thought I'd be telling that sad tale. However, I will say that a great deal of consoling was given to Irene later, by *yours truly*, over a bottle or two of champagne. We talked at length about the outcome of her years of hard training and the sacrifices she'd made to compete against the world's best athletes in a ridiculously short time slot of 1 or so minutes. Perhaps Bill had it right; at least his race lasted two and a half hours. *More or less.*

Finally, after sixteen days of victories, disappointments, and camaraderie between athletes from seventy-two nations, everyone packed up and returned home. The Melbourne Cricket Ground reverted to its original role as a cricket ground. I drove back to Carlina, where I became immersed in training my horses and discovering more about riding over high jumps. It was the one equine pursuit I hadn't done.

The horses I'd purchased were professionals, and I didn't want to make mistakes and confuse them. Accordingly, Jacques suggested I learn from a former top jump rider, Tommy Law.

Tommy was in his late sixties and had broken more bones than a turkey on Christmas Day, which saw him walk like a bow-legged duck. But he was the best coach I could have wished for, and he made me laugh, which took the pressure off, and therefore, the horses responded brilliantly.

I aimed to be part of the Australian Three-Day Event Team at the upcoming Rome Olympics. I assumed women would surely be accepted into the team by then—if they were good enough—and I would be!
Of course, I became a little anxious about my wedding plans, although I shouldn't have because Mother and Betty had everything under control.

Plus, the swimming pool was under construction, much to

Mother's surprise. "Davina, there are bulldozers and diggers in the garden. What's going on?" When I told her, she screamed, "I always wanted a swimming pool, but your father never allowed it. Goody gumdrops!" She applauded childishly, and I realised I had become her mother.

At that moment, I had to think. Would I remain living at Carlina with Mother after I'd married? Would Felix be happy to reside in South Yarra during the week, only to be home on weekends? If so, I'd stay a night or two with him during the week. It would work. It had to, as I wasn't sure how Mother would cope alone. She'd relied more on me as the days and weeks progressed after Father's funeral. And, I'd promised Father I would care for her, and I was duty-bound to keep at least one promise. I considered myself lucky to have avoided making any guarantees concerning my horses.

Our wedding day arrived, and I'm sure most guests thought it a bit corny to be wed on Valentine's Day, the fourteenth of February, and I agreed. But there you are. Sometimes, being corny can also mean having fun and being light-hearted. And our wedding was just that.

As Mother predicted, the day was a scorcher. Thankfully, we gave our vows to cherish and love each other under the shade of an English Elm, the garden's oldest and most prominent tree. My mother had begged us to be married in a church. Naturally, we disagreed, although I was most grateful she'd set the wedding breakfast in the ballroom, which was deliciously cool.

Mother had produced a perfect vision with white roses arranged in gold vases on each table. The seats looked divine, covered in bleached calico bound with gold satin ribbons. With help from outside caterers, Betty had created a superb menu, featuring an entrée of smoked trout on a bed of pearl couscous, followed by Filet Mignon or Chicken Veronique, and then a dessert of Berry Pavlova or Apple Charlotte. Mother had perfected her brandy-infused fruit cake. And with Betty's help, they decorated a magnificent four-tiered wedding cake.

I had to keep pinching myself to see if it was all real. I know that's a well-used cliché, but it's the only way I can describe the feeling of being loved unreservedly by such a handsome and caring man. And to know I loved him with all my heart and soul, well, the whole scenario was surreal when, on that day, I became Mrs. Davina Lohmann.

CHAPTER 22
EVIE IS LEFT ALONE

Evie ran through the front doorway and into the kitchen, smiling, ready to give Mrs. Hopkins her change. But she wasn't there. Evie thought it strange that the front door had been left open. So she walked back to shut it, then climbed the stairs to give her ma the package.

On the landing outside their room, Evie saw a motionless body on the floor. She crept closer to see Mrs. Hopkins' blood-stained head, so she poked her body with her finger and then pushed her shoulder. No movement. Evie gazed at the half-open door and cried, "Ma, Ma! Mrs. Hopkins's hurt bad. I tink she's dead! Ma, come here, Ma!"

No answer. Evie entered gingerly, noticing the bedclothes askew, as was the floor rug. She straightened them, then sat in the armchair by the window, waiting for her ma to return. *Ma will know what t'do, tell the police or get a doctor.* Time went by, and Evie began to panic. *Ma's not comin back. I can feel it in me' bones. She's in trouble. I need t'do sometin.*

Evie remembered Jock's story about the Willy Wagtails and how they were said to bring bad luck. She picked up a pinecone from the fireplace, opened the window, and threw it at their nest. "Go away, y'buggers! Where's me ma? What did y'do t'her!"

Evie ran from the home sobbing, but her instincts told her to alert the next-door neighbour. Still frantic, Evie banged on their front door, and when it opened, she yelled, "Y'better go see Mrs. Hopkins. She's hurt bad. I need t'find me' ma!"

Mrs. Finn looked at Evie, whom she'd never seen before, and wondered what the child was on about as she watched her vanish around the corner. Mrs. Finn shook her head, then thought it best to see what all the fuss was about. When she finally found Mrs. Hopkins lying unconscious on the floor, she screamed, which revived the suspected dead woman.

Later, the police questioned Mrs. Hopkins in the hospital, where she told the entire story to a young constable who fancied himself a detective.

"I'll soon put two and two together, Mrs. Hopkins, don't you worry."

"But I am worried, Constable. Something terrible must have happened to Mrs. Brown and her little girl. *Such a sweet child.* Although she's shy and doesn't talk much."

"As I said, Mrs. Hopkins, don't worry. We'll find Mrs. Brown and her daughter. And whoever hit you. You just rest and get better."

Evie ran, stopping to peer inside shops, looking for Cathy. She dared not talk to anyone. It may bring more trouble. *Maybe Ma's gone back t'Carlton. She's probably forgotten sometin.* Evie knew that wasn't true, but where else should she look? She remembered the address because her ma had said, "If y'ever get lost, Evie, y'should know where y'lives."

I'll have t'talk t'someone. Dere's a bus stop across d'road from where we got off d'ship. Someone'll know which bus goes t'Carlton.

Evie felt the leftover coins jingling in her pocket, hoping they were enough for the bus fare. Weary, she strolled toward the shipping terminal, all the while looking out for Cathy. *I remember walking off d'ship onta a strange land with me heart still in Ireland. I was frightened, but I have to be brave now. I'll find me ma if it's d'last ting I do.*

Relief came when Evie found the bus stop. She sat on the bench beside an older man who turned and smiled. Evie thought he looked like Jock, with his blue eyes and kind face. "Hello, where's your mother, little one?"

"Ma said t'catch d'bus t'Carlton. Can you help me find d'right bus, Mr. ?" Evie said, holding back tears.

"Yes, I can, but a little girl shouldn't be catching a bus alone!" He noticed her tears welling. "Don't worry. I'll make sure you hop on the right bus." He gave her another smile and squeezed her hand. "I have a granddaughter about your age. How old are you, and what's your name?"

"I'm not supposed t'speak t'strangers."

"Well, we're not really strangers anymore. I'm going to help you get where you're going." He leaned closer. *He smells clean, so he must be a good person.* "Could you please tell me your name, little one? My name's Byron."

"Okay, me' name's Evie, and I'm nearly eight."

"Oh, that is a lovely name. And by the sound of it, you come from Ireland. My ma and da came from Ireland. It was soon after they were married. I was born in Melbourne. My da worked on the docks." Byron looked dreamily into space, "And now and then, I come here to feel close to him. He was the best da a boy could have. We'd go fishing in the boat we built together." Byron said proudly. "We'd go after he'd finished work. And, of course, after my schooling. I remember those days like they were yesterday." Byron closed his eyes and smiled. It was as if he were dreaming. After a moment, he turned to Evie. "So, do you want to tell me about yourself, Evie, especially why you're here alone?"

"Nope. I'm just going t'find me' ma. I mean, go home, t'Ma."

Byron sighed deeply, "If you say so, Evie." He glanced at his watch, "I'm going to St Kilda, but I'm pretty sure my bus goes near Carlton. I'll ask the bus driver when he comes. And that should be any moment." Byron smiled and tapped Evie's hand.

He seems nice. But Ma said don't speak t'anyone or trust em.

Therefore, Evie never spoke again, even when the bus driver asked, "Do you want to hop on board, little one? I'll drop you off at the next stop. You'll catch the bus to Carlton there." Evie showed him the money in her palm. The driver took one coin and said, "You'll need that tuppence for the next bus."

Evie clung to the cash and sat alone. Every so often, Byron turned to her with a smile, and as tempted as she was, Evie never spoke.
Soon, the Bus Driver called, "This is your stop, little girl. The next bus will take you to Carlton."

Byron watched as Evie hurried down the steps. He felt guilty for not taking her home, but he was eighty-three and tired as a kelpie after a hard day's work in the heat.

After waiting ten minutes among strangers, who kept smiling at Evie, the Carlton bus arrived. Evie handed the driver the correct money, proud that she could read the sign. He took it, saying, "This will get you to Lygon Street, Miss. Is that okay?" Evie nodded and sat in a seat nearest the window, keeping an eye out for Cathy.

She spotted ladies who looked like her ma twice and almost called out to them. But their faces disappeared as the bus moved on. Soon, Evie was off the bus and walking down the street she'd trodden over a year ago. She saw the same kids playing hopscotch and cricket, using rubbish bins for wickets and tennis balls instead of the hard cricket balls. They spotted her and called, 'Hey, watcha doin back here, Irish!"

"Where y'been? Hidin in a rabbit burrow!"

"Na in the potato patch," another cried, and they all laughed.

Then, Patricia, the only girl Evie liked, ran to her. "If you're going back to that house, Evie, nobody's there. It's empty. No one's lived there since you left. Only sometimes. My mum said bad men stay there for a few days, then leave. She told me never to go there because they're dangerous." Patricia placed her hand on Evie's shoulder, Evie pushed it off, "My ma's comin back soon. I gotta go." Patricia shrugged and skipped away.

Evie ran to the green picket fence, opened the gate, and lifted the particular garden rock that hid the key. Once inside, she searched the rooms. They remained almost the same as when they'd left in a hurry. By chance, the kitchen cupboards still held the tinned food Cathy had bought just before they left, including powdered milk. Luckily, the mice couldn't reach the height where Cathy had stored the perishables. Evie took a glass from the dresser and filled it from the tap. With her thirst satisfied, she strolled into her bedroom, feeling tiredness overpower her. She lay on her bed and fell asleep.

Evie woke when morning sunshine filtered through the curtains. She blinked, rubbed her eyes, and called, "Ma, Ma, are yer here?" Evie waited for a reply. Instead, she heard the sound of traffic, voices yelling, and people laughing. She wished she and Cathy were back at the farm, listening to the birds singing, Matey barking, and Dora the cow mooing. *"Ma would be cookin breakfast and packin me lunch, and I'd be doin me chores. We were happy dere. But what do I do now, Ma?"* Evie said aloud. Thinking she heard her ma say, "Wait, Evie."

I'll wait for y'Ma." But I'll go t' d'red telephone and phone Jock. He'll help me."

Evie opened a can of baked beans with a tin opener and scooped them up with a teaspoon. *Ma always heated 'em on d'stove, but I ain't got enough money for d'gas meter.* 'Cleanliness is next to Godliness.' So Cathy would say. Therefore, Evie placed a teatowel over the half-eaten beans and put them high on the shelf, out of reach of the mice. She then washed and dried the spoon before continuing with her daily routine: washing her face and hands, brushing her teeth, and getting dressed. Fortunately, Ma had left a few pieces of clothing behind. After all, they'd been in such a hurry the night they left.

It now seemed a long time ago.

Evie chose a clean but mended dress, undies, and socks while wondering why nobody else lived in the house. There were a few tell-tale signs, such as cigarette butts and empty brown beer bottles. Cathy's bed, Evie noticed, was unmade, and the sheets looked dirty. *Somebody's stayed, just like Patricia said. I hope dey' doesn't come back.* Evie also prayed. *I hope d'telephone works. Sometimes, d'kids smash it.* She looked at the wall clock; it read 9:30.

The kids will be in school, and der mothers will be doin housework or out at work, like der da's.

Evie was right. Luckily, she went unnoticed to the end of the street where the telephone booth sat, undamaged. After pulling open the heavy glass door, Evie studied her coins and then looked up at the sign that indicated which one to use. She placed a penny in the slot and rang the Wolumbindi exchange. Lowering her voice and pronouncing her words correctly, she asked, "Put me through to Jock."

"Yes, certainly. One moment, please." *Jock's phone keeps ringing,* "Nobody's answering. I'm sorry." *I know that Irish voice.* "Is that you, Evie?"

Evie hung up, and Martha sat puzzled. *She enjoyed* a mystery. "I'd better let Jock know about Evie calling him. He's probably out in the paddocks. But why didn't Flossy answer? I hope Evie's not in trouble," Martha said aloud to the peeling walls in her tiny exchange office, which sat aside from the Post Office, come general store. She regarded the damaged walls thoughtfully, "I'd better tell Bert for the tenth time to paint these bloody walls! Bert, Bert, where are you!"

With Evie's voice momentarily forgotten, Martha ordered Bert as he entered the room. "I need you to man the exchange, Bert. And I'm telling you for the last time! Paint these damn walls! I'm driving over to see Jock. I think Evie's in trouble."

"Who's Evie?" Bert asked, scratching his head.

"Oh, you know—the little girl who lives with her mum next door to Jock. God knows where her father is. And that's all you need to know! I'm off to solve a mystery. Paint the damned walls, Bert!"

CHAPTER 23
MRS LOHMANN

After our wedding, I assumed Hilda would return to Helsinki. Not so! Unbeknownst to me, Hilda had discussed immigrating to Australia not only with Felix but also with Joseph. They both agreed it would be a good idea. Oh well, I suppose I had to try harder to like Hilda. In my happy delirium, I'd accept anything. I'm sure Hilda wanted to like me, too. But her insincere adulation irritated me. I was not beautiful, as she said, and not the best rider in the world, as she claimed. Friends who I trusted told me I had lovely brown eyes, and after applying makeup and dyeing my mousy brown hair burgundy, they said I looked most attractive. I knew their comments to be sincere, but not Hilda's.

Yes, life was good in the first six months of our marriage. Hilda attended the University of Melbourne, near the building where Felix worked as an architect. They stayed in our South Yarra unit throughout the week, and on weekends, they'd return to Carlina, where I'd arrange a barbecue meal and invite our friends most Saturday nights. That's if I wasn't attending a three-day event or riding in amateur races.

After about eight months, Hilda began skipping Uni classes. She'd fake sickness most Monday mornings. However, she couldn't wait to ride my horses later in the day. I watched Hilda closely and noticed she had little patience or empathy with horses. Finally, I'd witnessed her hitting one of my horses over the head, so I threatened, "I will not let you within cooee of my horses if you ever do that again, Hilda!"

Hilda snivelled, apologising simultaneously, "I love you, Davina. I am so sorry. I was frustrated because I wanted to show you how good Star worked for me."

"There's no excuse for hitting a horse, Hilda. Never do it again!"

End of story, I hoped. But no, Sampson, my precious Warmblood, who'd jump the moon if you asked, received a flogging from Hilda after he'd refused to take a jump. I had not witnessed the incident, but my groom, Sandra, had; she took the reins from Hilda and inspected Sampson's legs and feet, discovering that he had slipped a shoe, and a nail had penetrated his foot. Sandra then led the confused and lame Sampson to his stable. After fronting Hilda with her anger, Sandra phoned me.

"Oh my God." I said, "How much more do I have to put up with before I order Hilda off my property?"

"It's your call, Davina. But I wouldn't let her near the horses!" I took note of Sandra's anger.

I confronted Hilda and received another crying apology. Against my better judgment, I sucked it up.

After a time, Hilda's unbridled devotion became creepy, and I wished my brother Joseph would come home more often; at least he held Hilda's attention. But this rarely happened, so Hilda followed *me* around like a lost puppy. Hilda, *the paradox* I called her, the one I failed to work out.

Unfortunately, Felix and I began quarrelling over whether Hilda should remain in Melbourne seven days a week.

"She could spend more time studying instead of riding horses all weekend. Besides, she could mix socially with other students in Melbourne," I said.

Felix's response was forthright and firm. "I would feel like I was shunning her, Davina. And I do not think it is right to ask Hilda to leave. After all, she is in a strange country and needs her family's support. *I am sorry*. Besides, you are the only person she wishes to learn from. Plus, I am sure Hilda will eventually learn to be patient with horses. Especially with you showing her. I am sorry, but I disagree with you, Davina."

For once, Felix's saying 'sorry' did not endear him to me. On the contrary, it was the only word that hit like a blow to the chin, and I fumed. "Eventually, she'll learn, you say! What do you mean, Felix? After she's mutilated one of my horses? And I'm sick of you saying *sorry*. You shouldn't need to *feel sorry*. If I'd spoken the truth about Hilda, I might have felt *sorry* for hurting you! Don't say *sorry ever again*. I hate the word!"

Was Hilda causing a breach in our marriage?

I knew then that I had to let the Hilda situation go, or perhaps I should talk to her privately and try to convince her gently that she needed to focus on her Medical degree. I'd say after she'd passed the final exam, she could ride horses all day, every day, and be the master of her destiny.

Ultimately, I found the right time when we were alone in the horse barn.

"But I do not understand, Davina." She said, her lips pouting like a codfish, "I am helping you with your horses. You said my riding has improved. I do not want to stay in Melbourne on weekends. I already live there five days a week."

"No, you don't, Hilda. It's only two or three days because you're faking sickness. You must admit you always recover after Felix leaves for work." She cried sunshower tears, *barely apparent*, but I was damned if I'd console her. So I walked away, throwing over my shoulder. "Think about it, Hilda, because I will not allow you to ride my horses from here on." I felt an ounce of guilt when I heard her sobbing, so I yelled over my shoulder, "It's for your own good!"

The same evening, Joseph arrived home unexpectedly. I watched Hilda fall into his arms like a child clinging to her only relative. I then realised she'd called for the cavalry. But, of course, what else did I expect? So I braced myself for the firing squad. Why couldn't anyone else see what I saw and felt? My gut told me never to trust Hilda. And then, to see how her sweet, caring performance passed muster with the boys —it sickened me. Even Mother refused to hear me out when we were out of earshot.

"I think you're overreacting, Davina. I don't mean to be nasty. But is it because Hilda's so pretty that you don't seem to like her?" Mother's voice then rose an octave as if speaking to a child. "You seem a little jealous, Davina."

"You say you don't mean to be nasty, Mother? Well, you bloody well are! Your passive-aggressive attacks insult my intelligence! And the one ounce of beauty I own!" I stormed away into a chasm of unreality.

Why did I ever think I could confide in Mother?

I decided to give up talking to *anyone* about Hilda. Then I thought of Irene. Yes, my closest friend. I could always confide in Irene. I thought about my preordained meeting with Irene at boarding school. I needed to believe now more than ever that there are angels sent to deliver us from hell on earth. Irene and Felix were my angels. Although, was Felix playing a double role? Could he be sent to help both Hilda and me? I sighed and placed the phone down; I'd talk to Irene in the morning. It was getting late, too late.

The sun shone brightly, sending a message opposite to the gloomy feeling I had when I entered the morning room and saw everyone smiling as they tucked into a hearty breakfast. I'd arrived late in a haze of uncertainty, especially after Felix only pecked my cheek when he said goodnight.

However, I rose above my shattered feelings and tried to appear happy but business-like, mainly to Joseph, "I have important business phone calls to make this morning, Joseph. I know you're not interested, so maybe you could take Hilda for a walk. The parkland is thriving. There's so much to see, and I'm sure Hilda would love it."

I didn't want her or anyone else eavesdropping on my telephone conversation.

Joseph agreed, and they left to explore straight after breakfast.

Once Felix and I were alone, he threw me an accusing look. I smiled, saying,

"Well, Felix, what do you plan on doing *outside* while I'm on the telephone?" I waited, but received only a cynical smile. "For one thing, you can take that smug look off your pretty face. In my opinion, you have every reason to believe what I tell you. And no reason to accuse me of anything!"

Felix stood over me. "Whatever you say, Davina. But I know your phone calls have nothing to do with business. I know you, Davina. You must air your feelings about Hilda to your friends."

"Fucking hell. Now you're a mind reader and a condescending one at that! So tell me, Felix, what should I do if you won't listen or care about my feelings?" I stood furious with him and myself, scraping my chair back – defiant, I said, "I'm warning you, Felix; sooner or later, you'll have to choose between Hilda and me!" Anger propelled me from the room.

Mother had remained in bed, declaring she had a headache; it was just as well, as she couldn't handle confrontations. Sadly, I was sure Betty heard everything from the kitchen. I'd not involve her in my problems, although she'd know after my outburst.

Holding back emotion, I hurried to Father's office and fell into his leather chair before my tears flowed. A minute later, I heard a gentle knock. I gathered strength, wiped my eyes, and called, "Come in."

Felix approached, looking sheepish, before cupping my head in his hands and kissing me so tenderly my heart did a free fall onto a cloud of love.

"I will not say *sorry*, Davina. Instead, I will speak with Hilda today and ask her to return to Helsinki as soon as possible. I can see she is causing you unease. And you are the most important person in my life. I will never stop loving you." He walked away, closing the door quietly behind him.

Felix had chosen *me* without a second thought. I then prayed he would never hold his decision against me. *And he never did*. What an angel of a man I'd married.

Feeling relieved and relaxed, I phoned Irene—my fountain of wisdom and understanding. After listening to the Hilda drama, Irene said, "I often think we were twins separated at birth, Davvy, because I feel your pain, joy, and apprehensions. I'm telling you, you're right in asking Hilda to leave. We both have a gut feeling; I reckon something's not quite right in Hilda's head. Please don't feel guilty. Let her go and rekindle your relationship with Felix. He loves you to the moon and back. And yes, I've seen Hilda trying her sexy charm on Felix, but it will never work! That's another thing I'm sure of. It's sickening."

Irene's words enveloped me like a shield.

I'd managed to avoid Hilda throughout that day. However, over dinner, she sat opposite, sending a visual message that needed no decoding. *Our battle is not over, Davina.* What made the situation worse was that Joseph appeared more attentive to Hilda, asking her benevolently, "Is your dinner too hot, Hilda? Betty makes the best curries, in my opinion. But if it's too spicy, I'll ask her to cook you something else."

Sporadically, he'd whisper in Hilda's ear, making her laugh.

Was I going insane, imagining everyone was taking Hilda's side? Did they think my asking Hilda to return to Helsinki was just another command because I always got what I wanted? And, did I imagine Joseph shunning me?

As far as I knew, he'd taken no interest in women. His career had always stood paramount. I firmly believed Hilda had him under her spell. The sooner she left for Helsinki, the better. I fervently hoped Joseph's infatuation with Hilda would then dissolve. Gratefully, Irene's support gave me the strength to prevent my leaving the dining table.

From the time Felix spoke with Hilda about going home, it took two long, arduous months for her to depart. She'd begged Felix to stay in Melbourne with her, to show her every major attraction before she left. Escort her to live shows and the latest movies. I thought, 'Oh well, keep her there as long as she's not at Carlina.'

I suspected Felix did whatever Hilda asked out of guilt, but I paid the price; he began to drift away. Was she trying to steal him from me? *Of course, she was.*

It felt as if Felix and I were on separate life rafts, tied together, fighting a ferocious sea until our rope eventually snapped and we floated apart.

No! I would not let that happen. Felix would come back to me. He had to, or I would die. I tried hard; God knows how hard I tried to rise above this mixmaster of dark thoughts, attempting to squelch who I truly was.

But who was I?

The only comeback to the real me was when I competed with my horses during those two problematic months. I entered every event, including amateur races around Victoria, three-day events, and show jumping competitions. Sometimes, Jacques and Charlotte joined me for support. Although I felt they were more like my guardian angels sent by Father. I needed to believe in angels or something similar to save me, given that the world seemed to have turned against me. Charlotte never mentioned the Hilda situation; she was smart enough to know it would upset me to the point of disrupting my concentration, which I needed 100% to win. Yes, winning was still my drug, and it was the most exhilarating experience I've ever had. To fly over five-foot jumps like a bird and gallop with the wind, riding against the clock to ensure we were the bravest and fastest competitors. The feeling is unbelievable! I will never fail to love and cherish horses. They are God's supreme athletes.

One bright light amongst the Hilda gloom came when Norman, my groom from Stockholm, phoned me, "Could you do with an in-house vet, Davina? My cousin, Sven, has just finished his degree and wants to come to Australia."

How could I refuse? We then chatted happily, going over the victories Norman and Carlina River had accomplished in Europe. To say I was thrilled would be an understatement. I was ecstatic!

When Grace came home after being quarantined for six months, I paid to have her covered by Duke, one of Uncle Aaron's Warmblood Stallions. Eleven months later, Grace gave birth to a magnificent filly, whom I named Carlina Supreme. I called her Sally, for short. Every day, I'd visit Grace and Sally in their lush paddock, where I'd sit for ages and watch their mother-and-daughter connection. It put a smile on my face and warmed my heart. One day, I hoped to be a mother, although I'd taken measures not to be for the time being because, unfortunately, the timing was not right. And I wondered if it would be when Felix returned from Melbourne without Hilda. *If he did?*

"Sven is not only a vet, but he's a master horseman, Davina," Norman continued. "He wants to see as much as possible in his twelve months in Australia, so he has applied for a three-month working visa. All Sven has to do is fly to New Zealand and stay for a week every three months, and then he is permitted to return to Australia; he has it all worked out." Norman laughed before he continued. "I cannot thank you enough, Davina."

And I couldn't thank Norman enough. He'd become a loyal friend and confidant who shared my feelings about Hilda. He confirmed I'd done the right thing by sending Hilda packing back to Finland.

After discussing Sven's visit with Norman, I needed to phone Phyllis in England. I refrained momentarily, not knowing whether to laugh or cry, thinking I was gathering my defence force. What a terrible state of being, with my family all seeming to go against me, yet my close friends supported me; if only my father were alive, things would be different. Father was a master judge of character, good, bad, or evil. He'd back me up.

After going through telephone exchanges, I finally heard Phyllis's familiar voice. With our initial chat about health, the weather in England, and our equine achievements, I led Phyllis into the main reason I'd phoned. Not to say I wasn't interested in her life, but I needed desperately to know I wasn't imagining things.

"Davina," Phyllis said in all seriousness, "I will tell you now, I have more than a strong suspicion that Hilda drugged Grace in Stockholm. She had the opportunity when we were at the dressage competition. Don't you remember Norman asking her to stand by Grace while he went to the bathroom and grabbed something to eat? And you came with me to meet the committee, who then popped a bottle of champagne. I've played that memory over repeatedly, and I feel as you do. I never liked or trusted Hilda. I think she is capable of doing something like that."

A chill ran down my spine before I thanked Phyllis for her opinion. However, I felt it best to keep Phyllis's *assumption* close to the mark. If it were true, I could have easily killed Hilda.

It was uncanny that on the same day Hilda flew out of Melbourne,

Sven flew in. I chose not to go to the Airport and say farewell to Hilda. Although I found time to write her a letter, *I'm sorry our relationship had to come to this, Hilda. I wish you well in your future.* That was all I could say, and then I prayed she'd find happiness *away from us.*

I'd asked Jacques to give my letter to Hilda and accompany Felix to the Airport for support, not to spy on him, *even though the thought had crossed my mind.*

When the men returned home, I didn't know if it was relief to finally be free of Hilda or the illusion I saw when Sven walked towards me. His snow-white hair looked radiant, contrasting with his olive complexion and dark eyebrows. I couldn't help but feel exhilarated by his beauty and the halo that I'm sure I saw hover over him.

"Mrs. Lohmann. I am so pleased to meet you." Sven smiled, his hand proffered, "It gave me great pleasure watching you compete in Stockholm. You were brilliant! And to know that you gifted Carlina River to my cousin, Norman. It was the most generous gift anyone could give him."

Sven bowed his head, took my hand, and kissed it, sending a flush of heat from my neck to my temples. I coughed, slightly embarrassed.

"Thank you, Sven. Norman told me you'd be a breath of fresh air, and I think he's right. But please call me Davina. I'm too young to be called Mrs."

I noticed Felix narrow his eyes at me from behind Sven.

CHAPTER 24
EVIE
RUNNING OUT OF BASES

Martha steered her car into Jock's property. She drove slowly to admire the London Plane Trees that Jock's great-grandfather had planted almost a hundred years ago. Sixteen one-hundred-foot masterpieces sat on either side of the private road: their leaves, a cool, lush green in Spring, fluttered gold and red in autumn, creating a spectacle that Sunday drivers came to see and appreciate.

'*Lucky bugger, being left all this. Still, he's a nice old fella, wouldn't harm anyone,*' Martha muttered, before she came to an abrupt halt when she spotted old Flossy wandering around talking to herself with Matey limping behind. Martha honked the horn, causing Flossy to jump before she hurried toward the house.

"Bloody hell, Jock should have put her in a care home by now."

Martha drove to the back of the homestead, where Flossy and Matey had disappeared. She lumbered out of the car, muttering about Flossy's condition until she reached the kitchen door and called, "Flossy. Flossy, it's me, Martha. Martha from the telephone exchange!" No answer. "Flossy, Flo! Where are you?"

Martha entered the kitchen, noticing a pile of dirty dishes in the sink. *Jeese, the house needs a good clean, that's for sure.* She twitched her nose. "It smells terrible." The ill odour became more pronounced as she walked down the hallway toward Jock's bedroom. Matey sat outside the door, whimpering, and Martha patted him. "It's alright, little one."

She'd been inside Jock's house only once before, along with Bert, when they'd attended his wife, Bessie's, funeral. Martha had never forgotten the luxury of the homestead. *But now, the stink!* It became evident when Martha opened the door to see Jock, unmoving, tied by a rope to his bed. Congealed blood covered his forehead, and faeces stained the bedspread. Martha flung her hands to her mouth, preventing a scream. Gingerly, she approached Jock, covering her nose with her free hand, and felt his pulse; it was faint. Martha untied him and then hurried to the bathroom to dampen a facecloth. Jock moved slightly, moaning after a minute of Martha sponging his face. She crossed her chest, "Thank you, Dear Lord." Matey looked up doe-eyed, seeming to understand.

She hurried to the phone and dialed the exchange. "Bert! Hurry, get the ambulance. Jock's almost dead. Quickly, get the ambulance!"

"Yes, dear, right away!"

Well, at least he answered the call. I wonder if he's painted the walls?

Martha continued her search to find Flossy. *Hopefully, she can tell me what's happened here.* Flossy was in her bedroom rocking a doll in her arms, repeating, '*Sleep, little baby, don't you cry.*' Martha smiled, nodding. "You've finally found peace in another world. Poor Darlin. Never mind, Flossy. We'll take care of you. Our community looks after its own." She patted Flossy's hand, "I should go back to Jock, but I'll stay with you, Flossy. It's too depressing seeing Jock like that. And I can tell you, he won't be runnin away anytime soon."

The ambulance arrived speedier than expected, and Martha sighed in relief when young Sam, the Ambo Officer, said, "Jock just needs some TLC, and he'll be alright. Don't worry, Martha, he's a tough old bugger. He survived Gallipoli, and he'll survive this." He gave Martha's back a gentle rub. "Can you wait until the police get here, Martha? They'll arrange everything for Flossy and find somebody to clean up the mess."

"Of course I'll stay. I wouldn't leave poor old Flossy. But someone should get in touch with Jock's children. I know his daughter's phone number. And what about the dog? He looks starved, and he's limping, poor little mite."

"I'll take him. I'll get the vet to look at that leg." Sam smiled, patting Matey's head.

**

It became tricky for Martha to remain her efficient self on the switchboard as everyone in the district wanted to know what had happened to Jock.

"Well, it's all because I got suspicious and…. " Martha told the same story to the entire Wolumbindi congregation.

Meanwhile, Jock drifted in and out of a coma, and as much as Martha didn't want Jock to go anywhere else, she said, "I think they should send Jock to a Melbourne Hospital, don't you, Bert? He doesn't seem to be getting better here."

"Yes, dear," replied Bert, "all I can say is thank heavens you had the good sense to go out there. If you hadn't found Jock, God knows what would have happened. I reckon it has somethin to do with those people livin next door. Cathy somethin or other. Remember, she said she was going to Melbourne for the day? Well, she hasn't come back, has she?" Bert nodded in thought.

"You're right, Bert. There was something about them that wasn't kosher. Not little Evie, though. She's a funny little girl. I feel sorry for her; I pray she's not in trouble."

"Kosher? What does that mean, Martha?"

"It means proper or correct. We have a new Jewish family in town. They're opening a shop for ladies' and men's apparel. They're a friendly lot, and by the look of the clothes in their window, they have good taste. I might buy a new dress for the races here in two weeks." Bert kissed Martha on the cheek.

"Why not love? You deserve it. And what do you reckon about the walls? Have I done a good job?"

"Well, they look better than they did, Bert."

Martha walked briskly to the hospital in the morning and at night. After five days, Jock regained coherence, slowly recalling what had happened. So as not to alarm Jock and perhaps send him reeling backward, the police stayed away and allowed Martha to report her findings. It made her feel even more vital than in her twenty years of connecting people through the telephone exchange. Martha had donned the detective cap and took it seriously. She wrote every scrap of information she'd squeezed gently out of Jock on a notepad, then relayed it professionally to Lyal Armstrong, the Police Sergeant in charge. Eventually and reluctantly, Martha relinquished her investigation when Jock appeared well enough to talk to the police. Sadly, she returned her imaginary Detective badge to Lyal after ten days.

"All I can remember, Sergeant," said Jock, "is two blokes bursting into my home when Flossy and I were having tea. That must have been a while ago." Jock stared at the calendar on the wall, "Christ, I feel like I've been asleep for a year. I remember they had heavy Italian accents. They demanded to know where Cathy and Evie were. I said I didn't know. So they started roughing me up. Flossy tried to stop them, and Matey attacked them as best he could until they laid a boot into him. I think they broke his leg. I begged them not to hurt Flossy. She has dementia and didn't understand what was happening. I told them I didn't know where Cathy went. She left on a bus, that's all I know. But that wasn't good enough. One gave me an uppercut and dragged me into my bedroom. They tied me up and slapped me around, saying they'd burn the house down with Flossy and me in it. So I had to tell them that Cathy took Evie to Melbourne, and I suspected they were on a ship back to Ireland." Jock brushed a tear from his eye, "and I bloody well hope they are."

"Can you describe the men, Jock?"

Jock described the same man Mrs. Hopkins had when he'd knocked on her door before assaulting her. After confirming this with the Melbourne crime squad, Sergeant Armstrong decided not to tell Jock about Cathy's assumed abduction. It would only upset him further.

Martha had also informed Lyal about the phone call she thought was Evie, "It triggered me to go and tell Jock, seeing he didn't answer his phone. And, of course, I found him, and thank God I did."

**

Evie had remained hidden in the Carlton house, too frightened to go outside lest someone tell the evil men who'd taken her mother away. *Why else would Ma leave me alone? Somebody musta knocked Mrs. Hopkins out and dragged Ma away. Should I go t'd' police? Ma said never trust 'em.* A knock on the door disturbed Evie's thoughts. She crept to her room and hid under her bed, holding her breath.

"Evie, Evie, are you there? It's Tilly Thompson from down the street."

Should I open the door? She's not so bad. But, Ma said she's a busybody, and I should never talk t'her. Evie remained hidden until the knocking stopped, and she heard Tilly say, "She must have gone. I'll get Fred to break the door open and take a look around later."

The sound of the front gate clicking confirmed Tilly Thompson had left.

Evie climbed out from her hiding place and went to inspect the kitchen cupboards, which now looked almost bare.

"Two tins of baked beans. One can of Campie. And powdered milk. Not much left." She pushed her hand deep into her pocket and came out with five shillings and two pennies. *I can't spend it around here. Somebody'll see me. I'll wait till dark, go t' d'phone box, and try Jock again.*

He'll be inside at night.

Night fell, and Evie inched out the back door, sticking close to the alleyway fence, only minutes before a drunken Fred broke the lock on the front door. He, his mate, and Tilly searched the house. They found no sign of anyone living there. A cunning Evie knew how to cover her tracks. Evie reached the telephone booth and saw the light globe smashed on the floor; she stepped over the glass. The numbers were difficult to see in the dark, but she managed to dial the Woolumbindi exchange thanks to the streetlights.

"Hello, Martha speaking. What number, please?"

Evie lowered her voice, "Two, two, five, six."

"Oh, that's Jock's number. I'm sorry, but he's in the hospital, and his daughter's coming to take him to Adelaide to live with her. Unfortunately, she's going to sell Jock's property. It's such a shame because he loves that place. It's been in the family for the past four generations."

Evie hung up the receiver.

"Hello, hello. Oh, where did you go? Bloody hell, that may have been Evie."

'Why do I have to talk so much? What sort of detective am I?'

Evie had nowhere to go or no one to turn to. Her last two pennies had disappeared down the telephone slot, and now all she had was five shillings.

Shadows loomed tall and eerie as she ducked behind fences and ran up laneways, trying to be invisible. Finally, she arrived home and noticed that the back door was open. Creeping inside, Evie felt a strong breeze coming from the hallway where the front door was ajar. She froze until she was sure the place was empty, then she hurried to close the door. Unfortunately, the lock had been broken, so she secured a chair under the door handle.

One more night here, and I'll hitchhike t'Adelaide.

Evie ate her last can of beans under the filtered light from a street lamp and pondered her choices. *If I go to d'police and tell em who I am and what happened, Da will be in trouble, and so will I for snitchin on him. Or I can hitchhike t'Adelaide t'see Jock. He's d'only one I trust.*

But I don't know how far Adelaide is from here.

Before she ate another mouthful, Evie prayed. "Please, God, keep Ma safe." *If that man wanted t'hurt Ma, he would have done it at Mrs. Hopkins'.* Evie thought harder about the situation before saying aloud,

"He probably just wanted t'take her t'Da. He would've taken me too, but I wasn't dere."

After finishing the beans, Evie washed up and then placed the empty tin in the next-door garbage bin. She rinsed her face and hands, then climbed into bed, cuddling the teddy bear Cathy had left behind on the night they'd left in a hurry. "I had Matey in me arms. So I couldn't carry yer, Teddy. I'm sorry."

Then she remembered the paper on which the Captain had written his address. It was still in her pocket. *D'Capatain lives far away, and I don't know if I got enough money t'send a letter.* Evie brightened when she remembered the sewing kit Ma had left behind. She slid out of bed, sewed the paper into the bear for safekeeping, and then fell asleep.

CHAPTER 25
DAVINA'S STAR BOARDER

Over dinner, Sven regaled us with humorous stories, including tales from his childhood and his aspirations.

"Travelling to Australia was my first wish apart from finishing Veterinary Science," Said Sven, grinning.

I'd noticed Felix giving Sven subtle looks of disdain. He appeared a tad jealous, whereas I only held respect for Sven, nothing else. He seemed a genuine young man full of life and adventure. I had no agenda with Sven besides his helping me with my horses. And to think I had a vet on instant call gratified me more than anything. But, of course, I never intended for Felix to feel jealous. Therefore, I would endeavour to keep my relationship with Sven professional. Despite all the drama and living with Hilda for the past month, Felix had shown me in so many ways how his love for me was still strong. And I would prove to him that I could never love another. But, of course, in my eyes, Felix was perfect. I'd never met anyone who disagreed with me, including Father, who, as I said, was a leading judge of character. *But is anyone perfect?*

Charlotte and Jacques seemed enthralled by Sven's stories that night, but they also added a few of their own, making it a memorable evening. And without Hilda there to dampen the ambiance, my happiness reigned and my anxiety dissolved. Felix and I could now live in peace.

I sensed it was the right time to begin our family. Being wealthy, I could afford to pay a Nanny, leaving me to ride and compete whenever I chose. It would be fun teaching my children to ride horses. Perhaps we would have a girl who'd follow my path, and then a boy who would trail after Felix.

Later that same evening, as Felix and I lay in each other's arms, with all grievances forgotten and forgiven, I said, "I don't know about you, Felix, but I'm ready to start a family." I laughed as he jumped on me. Oh, how I loved this man. We would be the happiest family that ever existed.

And we were, especially three and a half months later, when I could safely say I was expecting our first baby. Hence, Felix strutted about, the proud father-to-be, while Mother and Betty began knitting booties and cardigans for our future heir. Jacques carved a rocking horse, and Charlotte used her artistic flair to paint its eyes, mouth, hooves, and other features. She also made a small leather saddle and stole a hunk of mane from an unassuming horse.

The finished horse? Perfection!

At the same time, I made an appointment with a well-respected gynaecologist in Melbourne. I listened to what he had to say and left, determined to follow his advice on giving birth to a healthy baby. However, I didn't tell the doctor I intended to keep riding horses. And so I lied to Felix, "The doctor said, riding horses will be okay until I feel uncomfortable." I smiled with fingers crossed.

Within that time, Sven took return flights to New Zealand, ensuring he could stay in Australia for another three months. He'd spent two weeks in NZ and returned with many humorous tales. Sven was a delight to have around, plus an accomplished, talented veterinarian. For example, he'd saved the life of Carlina Grace's yearling filly, Sally, after she'd taken fright and attempted to jump a five-foot fence. Unfortunately, she landed on a rock, shattering a sesamoid bone. Sven operated with great precision, using screws to attach the fragmented bones. A senior Swedish veterinarian explained a new procedure to Sven over the phone to achieve the best result.

After six months of being locked in a stable post-operation, Sally could then run around her small paddock free of pain. Whether she'd be able to compete, only time would tell.

Sven was also excited to learn that Felix and I were expecting our first child, and like Jacques, he enjoyed working with timber (it must be a Swedish trait), so a child-size wheelbarrow came to life under Sven's talented hands.

"I think this will be good, Davina. When your children are old enough to walk, they can muck out the stables!" Sven said, bending down to hold the handles. He made me laugh, as did a retired Tommy Law, who'd pop in from time to time for a cup of tea and a chat. "I hope I'm still alive to see your little one take a six-foot jump," Tom would say every time he waved goodbye.

After living with us for nine months, Sven seemed in no hurry to leave, especially after meeting Florence, Bill's sister, and my makeover Queen. I invited Florence to a barbecue in March to celebrate Felix's birthday. The weather was unusually warm, so we all took a dip in the pool. When Florence appeared in her bikini, I couldn't help but be amused when I noticed Sven's jaw drop, as did his beer glass. At least the crashing noise broke his trance.

Florence glided towards us, looking like Miss Universe. Poor Sven approached her like a love-sick idiot. Florence, familiar with this kind of reaction, took it all in good humour. I love Florence for her down-to-earth acceptance of her beauty and for never taking on board endless compliments. Florence had become one of Australia's top models but refused to take her talent seriously. She once told me, "Most times, I hate being beautiful, Davina. It blinds people to who I truly am."

I understood because being wealthy blinds most people to who I really am.

My advice to Sven? "Try to get to know Florence. Look beyond her beauty. Florence is an intelligent and compassionate young woman who wants to lead a normal life. She uses her beauty only to earn money for her future. Did you know she's studying to be a doctor? Florence said her looks wouldn't last forever, so she's making hay while the sun shines."

Sven laughed nervously, but from then on, he approached Florence in a more considerate manner. His sincere interest in her thoughts and her future struck a mutual chord, eventually leading to romance. I couldn't be happier for them. Although Sven had intended to leave and travel around Australia, he deferred —little wonder.

Florence, of course, was Irene's future sister-in-law and her intended bridesmaid. Irene and Bill's wedding took place that June, when I was six months pregnant and reluctant to serve as Irene's maid of honour because of my condition. Bill and Irene had finally decided to tie the knot after many disagreements. As Irene had said, "Our relationship is on and off like a bride's nightie."

Although Irene initially refused, she ultimately accepted my offer to hold the wedding reception in our ballroom. Their special day arrived, warm and sunlit. Therefore, hosting a winter lunchtime reception rather than a dinner worked well for their guests. I'd loaned Irene my wedding gown, and she emerged as my image. As I've said, we could be sisters. I loved her to bits, and whether my pregnancy had something to do with it, I cried happy tears all day, except when I glanced at Florence and Sven, who seemed to croon to each other. And then I'd wipe my tears away and laugh, thinking they could be movie stars playing a romantic role. A huge part of me hoped they would marry and live not too far away, as I'd never met a more caring and astute vet than Sven. *A bit selfish, but not really.*

Finally, after a divine wedding reception, we stood to wave Bill and Irene farewell. Their car rattled with tin objects attached to the bumper bar, plus a sign on the rear window that read: 'JUST MARRIED.' I watched my dearest friend disappear and prayed for their happiness. *And safety,* as Bill remained a speed demon. They would stay in Melbourne overnight and fly to Hawaii the following morning. Irene had said, "I wish you and Felix were coming with us, I smiled and vowed, "We will holiday together in Hawaii in the not-too-distant future. I promise you, Irene."

Meanwhile, riding my horses —primarily in show jumping and cross-country events —provided me with the adrenaline rush I thought I needed to survive. It's hard to explain unless you depend on drugs, I suppose. I knew all the risks without being told by Jacques, *often*, that I should be caring for my unborn child and not putting us both in danger.

His warnings finally hit home when I was seven months pregnant, and I felt my baby trying to escape through my belly button when landing after jumping a five-foot fence. I simply changed tack and returned to dressage. At least I could still ride at seven months pregnant. *Pretty good, I thought.*

Felix was powerless to stop me. Like an ostrich, he hid his head in the sand and worked seven days a week. Although I'm sure he took time off on Sunday to pray for our safety. How selfish and arrogant to think I was invincible.

Felix never complained. But one night after a dressage event, he said, "I knew the woman I married. I will never try to control you, Davina. But please remember, you will only have yourself to blame if you take unnecessary risks with our baby's life. And you lose."

When thinking about his final rousing words the following morning, my water broke. I reached the hospital just in time to give birth to a four-pound baby boy, premature by seven weeks. We named him Jock.

He was an angel kept alive by a new state-of-the-art incubator. I sat by his side every hour, listening to the sound of machines created to keep tiny souls alive. Felix and I alternated between spending precious little time with Jock every twelve hours, ensuring he had at least one of us with him every moment. Unfortunately, Felix would have spent all his time with Jock, but he needed to finish a project on a high-rise apartment block or risk losing face with his company. I'd pleaded with him to leave and set up his own firm.

"No, Davina. Not until it is with my own money that I have earned."

Felix, like everyone else, refused my charity.

My fingers were never tired of stroking baby Jock's blond fluff, which I thought would be like his father's hair one day. While studying this tiny miracle, my heart soared and ached simultaneously; his fingers and toes were perfect, but so minuscule. I couldn't take my eyes off him; it was the only time I could have gladly given up my horses if they were to save our baby's life.

Tragically, Jock died only four weeks after he was born. The doctors said he suffered from a weak heart. They'd hoped Jock would have survived another month so *they* could safely operate. Of course, they had informed us of the prognosis at his birth. I refused to listen to any negativity. Jock would live. He had to because I knew it would be my fault if he didn't, given my disregard for the warnings not to ride horses.

I tried to console myself with the knowledge that hundreds of women rode while pregnant. And mares raced when in foal. I kept telling myself that Jock's death was meant to be. It was not my fault. Especially with Mother standing by, ready to pounce when she thought me strong enough to cope with her accusing attitude. I stayed away from her and everyone else until months later, when I regained the strength to face life again.

Sympathy cards had flooded in, and my dearest friends gathered to comfort Felix and me as we mourned our baby, who was supposed to live and grow into a fine young man like his father. I thought the pain would never end. But eventually, time heals —not completely, just enough to cope and carry on with life.

We never spoke of having another child at first, though every so often, when we made love, I would pray that Felix had planted his seed. He never once mentioned my riding horses while I'd been pregnant. I knew in my heart what he'd once said was true. The responsibility of carrying our child was mine. All I could do was hope for another chance at motherhood; this time, I would not ride horses. I'd lie in bed for nine months if need be.

I cannot say that losing baby Jock did not put strain on our marriage, but we both tried hard to regain normality, and it came. Although slightly subdued.

**

Twelve months had passed when Felix arrived home midweek, which was unusual as he stayed in South Yarra on work days.

"Davina, he said with a huge grin, like a little boy with a new toy, "I have finally saved enough money to open my own company." I must have appeared shocked as he asked, wrinkling his brow, "Are you not happy for me?"

I rose from my chair, ran into his arms, tears dampening his shoulder, and snivelled. "I couldn't be happier for you, Felix. I'm so proud of you. I could burst!" Then I laughed, "My father used to say that to *me.*"

"I am proud of myself, Davina." Felix held me apart and looked deep into my eyes. "You don't know how many times I have been going to ask you for money. But I'd say NO! I will do this myself."

Felix held me close again before lifting my face to his, "I love you, Davina, and I promise we will have more children. I can only hope that our child will become an architect. I want to leave something for them. The same as your father left for you."

He kissed me like he did when we were younger, when our lovemaking knew no boundaries. I'm sure we were blessed that evening, and I prayed *this* baby would grow strong and happy.

CHAPTER 26
EVIE'S SAVIOUR

Evie knew she'd slept too long when her eyes blinked into the bright sunlight. She'd intended to be on the road before daylight. Now, her chances of being seen by the neighbours would be unavoidable. Nevertheless, Evie stuffed her blanket with whatever food she could find, a water bottle, and her teddy bear.

A part of her felt happy she'd slept in, as she felt refreshed and ready to meet the day. She had a good feeling in her soul—or, as her ma said, a powerful intuition—it told her she'd soon be safe. She went out the back door with the bundle slung over her shoulder and grinned, thinking, *I must look like one of d'swaggy's Ma and me'd see on d'country roads. It's a big adventure, but I can do it. I'll Find Jock. He'll help me find Ma.*

With those words turning into a mantra, Evie trundled towards Lygon Street, where she intended to ask for directions to Adelaide. She walked through the back lane until she turned left onto the footpath. She almost walked headfirst into Tilly Thompson, who smartly grabbed Evie's arm.

"Where on earth are you going with that knapsack, Evie? And where's your mother?"

Evie kicked her on the shin and ran. Tilly went for the chase and caught Evie without effort. Tilly whispered, "Evie, I don't want to hurt you. I just want to help. Please tell me why you're living alone in that house?" Tilly caught her breath, then pulled Evie by the wrist. Evie grimaced, holding back tears; she attempted to kick Tilly again, but Tilly was too quick and shuffled backward.

"Alright, young lady. I've known for a long time what goes on in that house and how crooks stay there. So I'll give you two choices. Tell me the whole story, or I'll phone the police!"

Evie screamed, "NO!"

Tilly's heart softened. Her father had been on the wrong side of the law on numerous occasions. She felt Evie's fear. *Her parents must be in big trouble for Evie to be living alone.* Tilly had heard on the radio about a woman being kidnapped in Port Phillip two weeks ago, about the same time Evie came alone to Carlton. But she'd taken no notice. Tilly never did. The news was too depressing.

"Okay, now you're speaking, Evie. Was your mother kidnapped a couple of weeks ago?"

Evie nodded.

"Were you there when it happened, Evie? Did you see the men who took her?"

Evie shook her head, no.

"I think we should go to the police. After all, they're still trying to find your mother." Tilly paused. *I wish I could keep Evie safe, but it's not possible.* "The police will find nice people who'll look after you until your mother's found. Alright?"

Evie speared hate at Tilly.

"Don't look at me like that, Evie; it's just that I don't know what to do with you. I understand that you don't want to go to the police. And I suppose you can't help them. Not if you didn't see who took your ma." Tilly then gazed into the distance before she said. "I'm sure your father's part of a crime gang. They say his gang is untouchable because of their high connections. So I don't want to get involved with that tricky business. It's not safe for my family or me. *Such as it is.*" Tilly sighed deeply before giving Evie a loving look, and Evie's shoulders relaxed. "Come with me, Evie. I think I know what to do. I've heard about a place in the country called 'Buchanan House.' It's part of a horse farm." She smiled with a snort, "I know you like horses because I've seen you in the back alley riding a broomstick, pretending it was a pony."

Evie nodded.

"Do you understand I can't have you livin with us because my old man's a drunk?" Tilly shook her head, disheartened. "And the kids are always in trouble. Plus, I don't know anyone else who'd feed you until they find your mum." Tilly hugged Evie. "I'm not such a bad person, Evie. It's just that things haven't gone my way in life. Wrong choices, I suppose." Tilly said with a shrug, and Evie began walking with Tilly toward her home, listening. "I wanted to be a Physical Education Teacher, but my parents couldn't afford to send me to Teachers College. So instead, they sent me to work." She laughed, "After work, I'd run around the park to get fit, instructing my *invisible* students until people said I was mad. *Maybe I am.* Never mind. Enough about me. I need to phone Buchanan House and tell them your story. I'm sure they'll be kind to you, Evie. I've heard only good things about that place. The story about the lady who gifted the home to a charity for homeless children is a sad one. It was many years ago, of course. But still it's a tragic story." Tilly hung her head and sighed, and Evie joined her.

The mention of horses lightened Evie's worry; *maybe Mrs. Thompson's right. They'll help me find Ma. Anyone who loves horses must be good. But first, I'll have t' see if I can trust em, just like Ma said. 'Don't talk to anyone, and never trust em until you're sure. Always trust your instincts. You have a powerful instinct, just like yer Gran.'* Those words had taken root and grown to become part of Evie. She knew a wrong word to a stranger could be fatal for her ma. And maybe herself.

They reached the red telephone booth, where Tilly inserted her penny and was soon speaking to someone at Buchanan House. She came out smiling.

"They said yes, Evie. They'll be here this afternoon to pick you up."

**

Sean lay back in his deck chair overlooking the Adriatic Sea.

Cathy sat dreamily on the wall separating the garden from the sea cliff, admiring Sean's tanned chest against his white linen shirt. He'd worked in the gym daily. *His abs would match Mr. Universe.* Cathy thought, slightly amused. She turned to admire the Azure sea sparkling like diamonds under the hot Italian sun. The allure of living an almost carefree existence appealed to her *momentarily*, but Cathy struggled every waking hour. Even her dreams were filled with Evie crying and calling out her name. Cathy was trapped, with bodyguards preventing her escape, and with no money, her attempts would be useless. She'd have to wait for a chance to run to the police. That's one thing she'd promised herself.

Sean had become untouchable since the massive bank heist in Sydney.

An Italian Mafia mob had approached him hours before that lucrative job, promising he would become one of them, flying in and out of countries where significant heists would occur—guaranteed if he shared the Melbourne Bank money and got rid of his accomplices.

The Mafia had heard about Sean's exceptional criminal intelligence and cunning. Eventually, it reached the Melbourne branch. Sean was then '*in like Flynn,*' as the saying goes. Now, murder was another talent added to his list.

His plan to kidnap Cathy without Evie had worked better than he'd hoped. Cathy later told Sean that when she'd been abducted, Evie had gone to the shops to buy her aspirin. He couldn't have planned it better. Sean laughed so loud that Cathy smacked his face before she felt his painful hold on her wrist, his blue eyes angry. He said through clenched teeth, "Don't ever do dat again, Cathy." his demeanor suddenly changed, and he let her wrist go. "Don't yer understand! We have everythin and anythin we've ever wanted here. We're rich, Cathy." Sean extended an arm, "Look at dis place. It's a palace. Look at d'magnificent view. We got a private beach. You don't have t'cook or clean. We have maids t'do all d'dirty work."

Sean shook his head, running his fingers through his thick, dark hair, which he'd grown longer. Cathy had to admit he was the most handsome man she had ever seen. His good looks and charisma had matured positively, helping Sean rise to the top of the criminal world. But did Cathy want any part of his world? *No, I don't want t'be here. I wanta be back on d'farm with Evie and Matey, welcomin Jock into d'kitchen for a cup of tea and waving him and Evie goodbye as they ride away on d'horses.* The memory made her smile, knowing Jock was Evie's surrogate grandfather. Sean mistook Cathy's smile and embraced her, "I knew you'd be happy here." He whispered into her neck, and Cathy thought of the two candles flickering under a brass crucifix in her bedroom. She hoped it did not offend the God of love and forgiveness by having murderers living in the same house where she worshiped. *I only hope He listens when I pray.*

Cathy knew never to cry about Evie to Sean because his massive ego stood in the way of her loving Evie more than him. Sean had never wanted children, "They'll only get in da way of me' plans," he'd said to Cathy.

Now Sean was a prominent member of an Italian Mafia Clan, taken into the family by the Godfather, who'd lost his only son in a shoot-out. Sean strongly resembled his son, so the Godfather embraced Sean after admiring his extraordinary savvy. Unfortunately, there was no escape from the mafia for Sean. But Cathy prayed the good Lord would find a way for her to escape.

✷✷

Evie sat in Tilly's kitchen, hugging her teddy bear while Tilly ducked outside to empty the rubbish after she'd tidied the house. She soon returned, "I don't want these nice people from Buchanan House to think I'm slovenly, do I, Evie? I'm not; it's just having three young boys and a drunken husband to look after; well, it all gets too much sometimes." Tilly smiled as she removed half a glass of milk that sat in front of Evie. "If'n you don't want it, love, I'll tip it back in the bottle. I'd offer you a biscuit, but the boys took the last to school for their play lunch. I hope you liked the Vegemite sandwich. Oh, that's silly. You've eaten every crumb!" Tilly giggled and scooped up the plate.

Evie thought about and understood what Tilly had said about her husband. *I'll never get married and have children. It's too hard bowin and scrapin t'husbands who tink they're d'boss. No matter how lovely d'wife is. I'll live alone with me' horse and dog.*

Tilly handed Evie a comic book. She swung her feet under the table until she'd finished looking at the cartoons. Evie then placed the books on the shelf, her thoughts roaming; *I could say I wanted t'use d'bathroom and run away t'find Jock in Adelaide, but Tilly said day have horses at Buchanan House and Adelaide's so far* away.

"You're lucky I'm home today, Evie." Tilly broke Evie's pondering, "I work four days a week, and today's my only day off, except on the weekends." Tilly grinned at Evie as she wiped the table. "I wish I had a girl; they're much easier than boys. Still, we can't afford to feed another mouth."

Tilly then guided Evie into the lounge room, showing her where to sit, before picking up her sewing basket and beginning to mend socks. "Crikey, I've lost count of how many times I've patched these bloomin' socks. Wish I could afford to buy new ones for the boys."

Evie sat, focusing on Tilly Thompson. *Ma said, Tilly's a busybody, but she seems nice and cares about what happens t'me.* Evie's tears welled. She sniffed them back and listened to the Blue Hills serial playing on the radio.

When it finished, Tilly rose from her chair and placed her sewing in the basket. "Time to do the vegies for tea, Evie. Do you want to help me?"

Evie nodded and followed Tilly into the kitchen, where she handed Evie four potatoes to peel while Tilly sat opposite, shelling peas.

Later, a knock came on the front door, and Tilly jumped, "Oh goodness, that must be them! Evie, come with me."

Tilly opened the door, and Evie stood rigid, squeezing Tilly's hand. A tall, handsome young man with a mop of sun-streaked hair and a short red-headed woman scanned a smile over Tilly, then Evie.

"Please come in. Can I offer you a cup of tea? It must have been a long drive," said Tilly, brushing her dress down.

Evie studied their friendly faces. *Dey look nice.*

"Yes, please, Mrs. Thompson, that would be lovely. Me' name's Kathleen Brock, and dis is Anthony Green. We woulda come quicka, but Anthony, *d'children's teacher*, needed t'finish his lessons."

Kathleen smiled at Evie, "So yer name's Evie. How do yer do, Evie?" Evie proffered her hand without a word. "I hear y'Irish like me!" Still no reply.

They followed Tilly into the kitchen, where she cleared the table and put the kettle on the hob. Then, she placed the cups, saucers, milk, and sugar on the table. Evie's eyes sprang open when Tilly produced a vanilla tea cake from the cupboard.

"I made this last night. Just as well, as I didn't know you'd be comin." Tilly wrinkled her brow and said, *"Funny that."*

Evie eyed the cake longingly. Unfortunately, the Vegemite sandwich hadn't filled the spot. Finally, her wish came true. A slice of golden cake with vanilla icing came her way. Miss Brock then asked Evie questions, which she refused to answer. Tilly responded as best she could without mentioning the criminal aspect of Sean's life. Fortunately for Evie, Tilly didn't reveal that Cathy had been kidnapped over two weeks ago. Instead, she said in a hushed fashion, "I think Evie's been traumatized about something that happened to her because she won't speak. Not a word."

Evie listened carefully before deciding, *Tilly's me friend.*

As they were about to leave, Tilly told Kathleen, "I'd like to say goodbye to Evie alone. If you don't mind." Kathleen nodded before they withdrew to the front porch and waited.

Tilly bent down to Evie's height. "You heard me, Evie. I didn't tell them anything bad about your parents. It's up to you when you're ready to tell what happened, and I'm sure they'll help you." She hugged Evie, "I hope your mother finds you, Evie. Stay brave and never give up hope. Goodbye, and good luck."

They walked hand in hand to the front porch, and for the first time that day, Evie looked up at Tilly and smiled. Tilly waited until the car drifted out of sight before her tears flowed.

CHAPTER 27
DAVINA'S HAWAIIAN HOLIDAY

(Five years before Evie arrived)

I watched Felix's little yellow Volkswagen zip up the driveway. He loved that funny little car with a back-to-front engine. I knew he'd go straight into the kitchen for a coffee and Betty's chocolate chip biscuits. I was so excited, I couldn't wait to tell him the good news, so I hurried from my office, waving the airline tickets, calling out, "We're finally going to Hawaii, Felix! I've got the tickets! And I have other wonderful news. Both Irene and I are three months pregnant!"

Felix ran from the kitchen, and we almost collided in the dining room; laughing, he lifted me off the ground. "I am so happy, Davina," and teasingly said, "I have always wanted to go to Hawaii."

I slapped him on the shoulder as Betty walked in, holding a chilled bottle of champagne with a huge grin on her wrinkled face.

"I'll go tell your mother, shall I? Then you can all celebrate?"

I embraced Betty, "You too, my dearest Betty. And please go and tell Freddy." Suzie barked, wagging her tail, and I leaned down to pat her,

"I'm sorry," I said, "but I don't think you should drink champagne, Suzie," to which she barked again.

I looked up to study Felix. *I'm sure you wondered why I haven't been riding over jumps lately.* Felix broke my gaze and hugged me, "I am so looking forward to our baby, Davina," he said, "plus our holiday with Irene and Billy. We will make it a holiday to remember. And I must admit, I had a sneaky suspicion you were pregnant when you were not jumping your horses. But I didn't dare to ask just in case I was wrong."

"I knew you were Felix. I could see it when you swallowed your words after I'd cancelled my last competition." I held his beautiful face in my hands. "I promise you, Felix. I will not ride horses anymore. *Well, not in this pregnancy*. Our baby comes first."

He stood me apart before patting my tummy, "Did you hear that, little one?"

My only concern was who I could trust to organise jobs on the property and ensure my horses were well cared for while we were away. *Of course, Sven!*

Sven had remained in Australia, using Carlina as his base, but he would occasionally travel to different states. He'd then take his needed sabbatical to New Zealand, from where he'd just returned.

When I told him we were having a baby, Sven seemed as happy as we were, so he shared his news. "I, too, wish to marry Florence and start a family. But she told me she needed time to think about it. That is why I have travelled lately. It has given Florence time to consider. And now I have just spoken to her. Florence said she loved me and could see how our future would work. Maybe our time together would be sparse, but we understand the commitment we made to our chosen professions." Sven paused. I assumed he had to think about his next sentence. "Florence thought if she married a *nine-to-five worker*, is that how you Aussies put it?" He laughed before saying, "A man like that would never understand her absence. I think that is how she put it." Sven's chest puffed up like a proud peacock. "Florence will become a top surgeon in the future. Her grades and practical work have been outstanding."

With hugs shared, Sven had no hesitation in volunteering to look after Carlina and my horses. With the help of our reliable staff, of course.

"Thank you, Sven. It's a shame my brother, Joseph, never offers to take the reins, though I suppose he lives in a different world. Consequently, I can never rely on him." I was reluctant to ask; however, the question burned. "Have you heard anything about Hilda? I know Norman attends the same horse shows as Hilda."

Sven gave a worried sigh, shaking his head, "I have, Davina, and apparently, Hilda has not changed. She has been warned; if she is ever seen punishing a horse at an official show, she will be banned from competing. Norman told me this about a month ago."

"Oh my God, what is wrong with that woman? She should see a shrink and stay away from horses until she's able to control her anger."

"I agree. But please don't think about Hilda. She lives a long way away. Go on your holiday, Davina, and have a wonderful, relaxing time. I promise to look after everything, including your beloved horses. I would never let anything happen to them."

I walked away, content with Sven's promise. I then organised a million things, including a three-month supply of Mother's happy pills.

Felix and I drove away in his little yellow Volkswagen the following week. As I waved farewell to everyone, I noticed Mother looking complacent, with a faraway gleam in her eyes; it sent a shiver down my spine. I had a suspicion I would never see her again. Nevertheless, I shook it off and smiled, thinking about our holiday. I couldn't wait to don a bikini and show off my baby bump. I laughed at the mental picture of Irene and me looking like twins, as she'd unintentionally chosen the same swimsuit. What a hoot!

"What are you giggling at, Davina?"

"You'll see when we get there." But I relented, "Irene and I bought identical swimsuits, or I should say bikinis."

"Bikinis, really, Davina. Do you think you should wear bikinis when you're pregnant?"

I laughed hysterically; I think it was a mixture of relief that we were finally on our way to a much-longed-for holiday, plus my pregnancy and Felix's old-fashioned morals. I took a deep breath and rubbed his arm, admiring his perfect profile. It grounded me. My love for Felix was so intense that I needed two hearts to hold it.

We arrived at Essendon airport and handed our car keys to a parking attendant, who drove Felix's VW to the long-term parking lot. Felix grabbed a trolley and loaded our cases just as Irene and Bill arrived.

I ran into Irene's arms, screaming. "We're finally here, Irene!"

"Well, not yet, Davina. I'd like to get to Hawaii," Irene said dryly.

She always made me laugh. Then, arm in arm, we descended toward the ticket counter while the men followed, chatting about how bizarre it was that their wives were pregnant at the same time and how excited they were at us giving birth. I smiled. I, for one, wasn't looking forward to the pain of childbirth, and this time, I would demand that Felix remain throughout the entire business. Not that he deserved it, but I'm sure it would deepen his understanding and respect for the immense pain women endure.

We enjoyed a relaxing flight. I sat with Irene, and Felix sat beside Bill, who was over the aisle from us. Had we not been married, the time spent chatting and laughing with my dearest friend could have appeared as if we were two young schoolgirls giggling our way through life. On the other hand, Felix and Bill eventually put on their earmuffs and drifted off to sleep.

This scene repeated itself over the first week; we suspected the men were exhausted and needed rest. Throughout the second week, however, we joined them in snorkelling, swimming in the ocean, and enjoying the enormous saltwater pool, which featured a cocktail bar at its centre. The boys loved that!

Irene and I refrained from an overdose of alcohol due to our conditions. However, one or two margaritas went down well on occasion.

Our rooms overlooked the pool and the ocean. Both waterways had their advantages. I loved saltwater and wondered why Father had never purchased a holiday house by the beach. Instead, he always rented a cottage when we took our seaside vacations. I promised myself I'd buy a small house by the sea. Perhaps the furthest south of Melbourne, along the Mornington Peninsula – specifically Sorrento - it was my favourite place, besides Carlina. My father always said, *"The ocean breeze blows away the cobwebs, and swimming in the sea gives me peace of mind."*

I believe this to be true. As a young girl, I noticed how Father relaxed and became happy during the summer weeks by the sea. In contrast, Mother hated her hair becoming stiff from salt water or feeling the sand between her toes. I felt sorry for her. I'm sure relaxing occasionally and letting go of your anxieties must be beneficial to the soul. In my opinion, those summer holidays provided a much-needed cleansing of body and soul.

The following morning, I lay in our hotel bed, feeling a little sad that our Hawaiian holiday would soon come to an end, but happy, thinking we had three days left to enjoy all the decadent pleasures, when the phone rang.

Felix grumbled about getting out of bed, pulled his undies on, and answered it. I noticed after a minute, he appeared deeply concerned.

"What's wrong, Felix?" He placed his hand over the receiver. "I will tell you later, Davina. It is nothing to worry about."

I sighed and lay back down, watching Felix fumble with the telephone cord, twisting his body about while speaking cryptic words.

Eventually, he hung up and smiled briefly before dipping his eyes.

"It was nothing, Davina, only work. Unfortunately, the new architect I left in charge has taken ill." Felix walked to the window and stood, seemingly entranced by the waves crashing to the shore, before he said, "I am sorry, Davina, but I must leave immediately. The job is far too important."

I jumped up, "I'll pack my bags too, Felix."

I saw panic in his eyes when he faced me.

"No, definitely not, Davina!" He took a deep, calming breath. "Please stay here with Irene. Enjoy every minute. Stay longer if you wish. Remember, we need to look after our baby." He kissed me, then held me at arm's length with a smile full of love. "I know this is what you Aussies say: a bugger! But I must go alone and fix the problem."

I agreed. *Reluctantly.* And while it wasn't quite the same, Irene and I bonded more than we thought possible in those few days until the final day when she dropped a bombshell.

"Davina, I have to tell you something." She held my hand and took a deep breath before continuing. "An Italian race car manager spotted Bill when he showed remarkable aptitude in his first car race. As you know, Bill ran a close second in the Grand Prix around Como Park. And the manager said they needed courageous young drivers. The wealthiest man in Italy sponsors the team. Their star driver has aged beyond his winning reflexes, *he said.* So he coaxed Billy, sorry, Bill, into the team." Irene sighed deeply, then said, "Their offer was too good to refuse." She waited for my reaction, and when she saw my tears building, she said, "I'm sorry, Davina; I knew it would upset you. That's why I waited until our last day," Irene clasped my hand tightly. "I didn't want it to spoil our holiday." She then embraced me, rocking me like a baby while I cried.

To lose my dearest friend, especially when I was looking forward to spending more time together during our pregnancies, completely overwhelmed me.

I sniffed away tears after what seemed like forever and said, "I don't care what the doctors say. This baby of mine is going to get a soaking. I think champagne is in order, don't you, Irene? I mustn't be sad or selfish. I know you're living in Italy, and travelling the world will be a wonderful opportunity for you both. And I will come to visit you often!"

"Oh, thank heavens. I knew you'd be upset, Davina, but on the other hand, I knew you'd understand. Nothing will pull us apart. We'll be friends forever!" Her hazel eyes welled with tears. She stood and wrapped her arm around my shoulder, "I'll drink to that," I said. "Let's go to the bar, shall we?" I wrapped my arm around Irene's thickening waist, and together we walked to the bar.

Bill had gone surfing, and by the time he found us, we were giggling, tipsy with champagne, sitting by the open doors of the bar, admiring beautiful young tanned men and women swaying to and from the beach.

He froze.

"You're not drinking alcohol, are you, ladies?"

"Of course not. It's only champagne, Sergeant Major!" Irene said in a mock salute with her flute.

"Well, in that case, I'll join you." Bill sat down, and Irene poured him a drink. He gave an appreciative smile before we clinked glasses.

"Here's to your brilliant success in becoming the number one racing car driver worldwide, Bill," I said. "And to our babies. May we all be blessed with good fortune and happiness!"

It was our final night together before I flew home, and Irene and Bill would fly to Capri, where he was to sign a contract and meet his team. It was a bittersweet memory knowing I was about to lose my best friend, but at the same time, I could visualise Irene's future filled with excitement and travel. Irene had told me when we were younger that she'd never wanted to travel. All she wanted was to be a physical education teacher. But her aspirations changed when she met Bill, and even more so after she'd competed in the Helsinki Olympics.

At the airport, we said our sad farewell, promising to phone once a week and to follow up with letters. It was some compensation, I supposed. I also promised Irene that I would contact her parents regularly and include them in our events at Carlina.

Her parents had slowly changed their minds about our ongoing friendship. My mother had also become more relaxed and welcoming, without flaunting her wealth, which helped. My promise to include her parents pleased Irene more than anything. She squeezed me so tight before disappearing down the boarding lane that I found it hard to breathe.

And now I remember her embrace as if it were yesterday.

Soon after, Irene and Bill settled in Monte Carlo, only fourteen kilometres from the Italian coastline. Monte-Carlo hosted the most prestigious motor race in the world, 'The Circuit de Monaco,' and Bill would have the best chance of winning if he lived nearby; he could familiarise himself with the circuit.

I understood this, but the distance between Irene and me would feel like a wedge coming between us, and it hurt.

CHAPTER 28
EVIES'S WELCOME TO BUCHANAN HOUSE

(Five years after Davina's tragedy)

Evie sat transfixed in the back seat, breathing in the scent of leather, reminding her of old Pa when he taught her the art of tanning the hide of a cow who'd sadly passed away. "Gerty won't mind. She'll know I put her hide t'good use. Besides, it'll remind me of Gerty when I take comfort in seein her hide spread before the fireplace." So Pa had said to Evie with a wink.

Evie brushed away a tear before turning her thoughts to finding a friend at the home for abandoned children, assuring herself, *Dere'll be girls like me who've lost dere ma.* She tried to remember which way they'd come. *I reckon we've gone anudda direction from Jock's farm. But he's not dere anymore.* Evie's hopes plummeted whenever she thought about the people she'd lost. So she tried to purge her sadness, although one thing kept her hopeful: *they got horses at Buchanan House. Maybe they'll give me a pony.*

The miles drifted by in a moving picture of brown grass scattered with gum trees, cattle, and sheep grazing under a vivid blue sky, with white clouds drifting by. Evie's sadness momentarily eased with the vision of her ma's face smiling out from every shadow. *Ma's safe, I can feel it. She'll find me soon.* Evie sat determined. *Never give up hope. Dat's what Ma said. And Tilly.*

Finally, Mr. Green turned the car onto a long, narrow road. Large trees loomed on both sides, *d'not gum trees.* They looked like the trees Evie had seen in Ireland, with thick, grey trunks and branches growing out to meet the opposite limbs, their leaves like broad hands with fingers stretching out. Evie felt dwarfed in the face of such giants until Kathleen spoke.

"Here we are, Evie. Your new home."

A wave of anger surged, and Evie wanted to scream, *"It's not me, home! It's a place t'stay til Ma comes t'get me!"* But the words remained mute.

The two-story mansion appeared like a vision with its spacious verandahs encompassing the entire building. Evie had never seen such grandeur, especially framed within a spectacular garden of trees, shrubs, and colourful flowers, their delicate petals waving in the breeze. It took Evie's breath away. Jumbled feelings ensued when she spotted a swimming pool and smiling children running to greet her. *Should I be happy t'be here or sad dat Ma's not here too?* Evie had heard Kathleen talking to Anthony on their journey about a mother and son who had just arrived to take shelter from a violent husband the day before. *So if Ma came here, we could stay.*

Anthony drove the car around the circular driveway, with children chasing after it. He stopped and wound down the window.

"Please, children, give us space. You'll meet Evie soon enough." He opened his door as the group stepped back. Anthony walked around and opened Evie's door while Kathleen ushered the children into a group.

A tiny girl wearing a pink dress, her blond hair tied back with a blue bow and dimples deep enough to hide in, pushed her way to the front. She smiled and presented Evie with a rose: "I cut the thorns off. It's yours. It won't spike you."

Then, a taller girl said from behind. "Welcome to Buchanan House, Evie."

For the first time since her mother's warning, 'never speak t'strangers,' Evie struggled not to say 'thank you.' The words remained deep; despite feeling safe, she might unintentionally reveal secrets that would hurt her mother.

Evie nodded and accepted the rose with a Mona Lisa smile. Anthony Green noticed. His broad smile revealed pleasure at seeing a glimmer of hope from Evie.

After being shown her room, which she shared with Carole and the twins, Evie kept her teddy bear close, in case someone stole it, but more importantly, to access the vital information.

"You can leave your teddy bear here, Evie. No one will pinch him. They'd be in trouble if they did," said Carole in a baby voice.

Evie immediately liked Carole; *she must be around four years old. I wonder what happened to her, ma?*

In a single file, tiptoeing so as not to make a noise —another rule they had to follow —they made their way to the dining room, where tea was served at five-thirty. Evie sat beside Carole, and although she was younger, Carole seemed intelligent and happy to follow the rules. Evie studied her blond ringlets, bright blue eyes, button nose, and perfect cupid lips. *She looks like a doll. I'd like t'talk t'her. Maybe later.*

Kathleen Brock, the primary carer at Buchanan House, led everyone in prayers. Once finished, they crossed their chests and filed to the long tables to be served what Carole called *'meat and three vegs.'* "Every night it's the same except on Fridays. We have fish and chips. I can't wait for Friday." Carole giggled.

Evie's plate was loaded with mashed potatoes, pumpkin, garden peas, and a lamb chop. Her eyes widened. *I haven't eaten like dis since livin on d'farm.* They sat, and Carole smiled at Evie as she shovelled her food into her mouth.

"You can have my chop if you want, Evie. I don't like meat." With her mouth full, Evie nodded, so Carole forked the chop onto her plate.

Sweets followed after they'd scraped their plates and taken them to be washed. Evie noticed a list of names on the wall next to the sink, indicating whose turn it was to wash and dry the dishes after each meal. Her name wasn't there. *Maybe tomorrow?*

Once seated, the mothers and carers wheeled in an enormous trolley and passed around dishes of cantaloupe and ice cream.

"Tomorrow, we get stewed peaches and ice cream. It's a different fruit every day, except on Friday. We just get ice cream in a cone. After fish and chips, that is." Carole said with a knowing grin.

Evie's compassion went out to Carole; *I reckon she'll be a friend, somebody I can trust t'keep a secret.*

The following morning, after a breakfast of porridge and toast with marmalade, too bad if you didn't like either, as it was the main fare every morning, Evie followed the girls into the classroom.

"This used to be the Ballroom," Carole said.

Evie imagined women in beautiful gowns gliding across the polished floor, led by handsome men in tuxedos. Little did she know that a young Davina Buchanan and her brother Joseph had used the room primarily for roller skating. And many years later, Davina's wedding breakfast. But now, rows of desks lined the interior, and a giant blackboard stood front and centre. Mr. Anthony Green had placed the children aged four to eight on one side and the older children on the opposite side. A walkway separated them, allowing Mr. Green to inspect their work.

After her first day of learning arithmetic, spelling, and social studies, Evie felt left behind. Even Carole knew her alphabet. She saw the defeated look on Evie's face and whispered. "I'll teach you later, Evie." Carole smiled and patted Evie's hand like a consoling mother. Evie almost giggled at the thought that this small, delicate child would care about her. Instead, Evie nodded with a smile of thanks.

Everyone followed the daily routine, except on Friday, when the children played different games outside before swimming in the pool if the weather was hot enough. But first, Mr. Green gave swimming lessons.

'He could swim the English Channel,' everyone said. However, Evie wondered *why anyone would want to swim across the English Channel.*

Evie longed to ask Mr. Green about the horses she saw grazing in the connecting paddocks. Who owned them, and to whom could she ask about riding them? But the fear of talking to anyone remained as strong as ever. *Maybe I could sneak over t d'horses when everyone's asleep.*

The thought overwhelmed her until one moonlit night, she found the courage. Evie padded her bed with pillows, and with her teddy's head poking out, it looked like she was asleep. Feeling confident, she crept down the staircase and into the kitchen, grabbing two handfuls of carrots for the horses. Fortunately, the front door was unlocked, but the office light was on. *Someone's still up, probably Mr. Green.*

The night air dampened Evie's face, and with her hands chilled, she placed them in her pockets, which were full of carrots. She then climbed through the fence separating the garden from the horse paddocks. Once well away from the house, Evie scurried to reach the first paddock she knew held two horses. The bigger horse spotted her climbing through the fence and galloped off. The other, a pony who looked much older, regarded Evie quizzically. Evie proffered a carrot and spoke softly, coaxing the pony to come closer. Instead, the pony whickered, throwing her head in the air. Finally, Evie had the good sense to sit on the ground. Eventually, curiosity got the better of the old pony, and she came to Evie with her nostrils flared. The pony sniffed and then nuzzled Evie's hair, making her laugh. "Oh, ya beautiful. I wonder what ya name is, me, darlin. I tink I'll call y'Beauty."

The pony whinnied, bringing the other horse near. Then, tentatively, he nudged close. Evie held a carrot out to him, and he took it with a snort.

That night was the only time Evie had forgotten her heartache and fear of the unknown since her ma had disappeared. She remained with the horses that night until her pockets were empty and her blood chilled. Then, reluctantly, she left and returned to her room.

"Where have you been, Evie?" Carole whispered, "I was worried you'd run away. But then I saw your teddy and knew you'd come back. So where did you go?"

Evie spoke for the first time. "I went t'see d'horses." That was all she said. *Maybe tomorrow I'll tell her me story.*

"Oh, okay, but don't get caught, Evie. Goodnight."

Carole rolled over, feeling happy that Evie had finally spoken. *She's Irish.* Carole remembered her mum saying her grandparents lived in Ireland. Before she died, that was.

Evie soon drifted into a dream. *I can't find Pa; where is he? Oh, dere, he is mendin the fences. And dere's Daisy! I'm comin t'help yer Pa!* The dream was so pure it gave Evie hope. But when morning came, the regular Army-like routine awaited. Not that Evie didn't feel safe or well-fed; moreover, she had a friend in Carole whom she trusted.

After breakfast, Evie walked with chatty Carole to the classroom when Kathleen Brock appeared. "Good mornin, Carole," Kathleen beamed, "I want yer' t'come with me. I have someone who wants t'meet yer."

She took Carole by the hand and led her away. Evie stood watching as Carole walked down the hallway with Kathleen to what Evie knew to be *'the office,'* the room where people came to take children away. Instinctively, Evie knew she'd lost her friend. And she was right; Evie wasn't even allowed to say goodbye to Carole.

Evie sat beside an empty seat for the rest of the day, hoping Carole would return. *Carole talks a lot, and maybe dey won't like dat. And then she'll come back smiling at me when she sits at our desk.* But Evie's wish never eventuated.

Consequently, she refused to look at her school books. *I'll never get close to anyone again. I just want to be with d'horses. They understand me troubles. I hate Kathleen for taking Carole away.*

Anthony Green felt Evie's sorrow. Her lack of concentration had been evident since Carole left. He strongly disagreed with Kathleen's assumption that children would make a scene if allowed to say goodbye to their friends. A few days later, Anthony approached Evie after lessons.

"I know you're sad, Evie," said Anthony with his hand on her shoulder. "I can understand how terrible it must be for a child to have their mother taken away and not know where she is." He surmised that Evie's mother was the woman abducted at Port Phillip. Neither Tilly Thompson nor Evie would give anything away. A loyal Tilly had told Anthony stoically, "Evie will tell her story when she's ready. But, you must understand, there wasn't anything Evie could do. And the police would only give her to God knows who. So she's better off with you at Buchanan House."

"Would you like to take a walk to the nearest paddock? I've noticed the gleam in your eyes when you see the horses." Evie smiled and nodded.

They walked to the paddock, hoping the horses would come near. And they did. While Evie rubbed old Polly's nose, Anthony told Evie about Davina Buchanan and how she'd become a recluse after a tragedy.

"Miss Buchanan doesn't want anyone to enter the paddocks, I'm afraid, Evie. But I'm sure she wouldn't mind you patting the horses over the fence." Anthony's smile was full of understanding and kindness. Even at her young age, Evie felt warmed by the gesture.

From that day on, Evie ran to meet the two horses. If no one followed her, she would jump the fence and chat with them, and they seemed to listen, especially the old one, who Evie now knew was Polly. That was until somebody spotted her and took her back to the house. So, with no friends left to talk to and no one else seeming to care, Evie became even more introverted. *If I find another friend, they'll go too.*

Then, one day, Kathleen lost her temper when Evie refused to answer an important question. She grabbed her arm, dragged Evie to her room, and slammed the door. After that, Evie closed up even more. However, she'd warmed to Mr. Green, who always tried to cheer her up when he was not too busy; he and Polly were her only friends.

Most nights, Evie lay awake, praying, 'Please, Ma, find me.' Finally, on one stormy night, unable to sleep, Evie climbed down the fire escape that sat outside her room, intending to spend the night with Old Polly.

No one else had come to fill Carole's bed, so leaving the twins sound asleep became easy.

Evie found Old Polly snug in her open shelter every night. Finally, the scent of horses mixed with the earthiness of straw and Polly's prone, warm body against Evie lulled her to sleep. Although Evie had previously managed her adventure many times, Evelyn, the Nighttime Carer, found her bed empty that fateful night. Evelyn panicked and immediately roused everyone to search for Evie.

No one thought of the fire escape; instead, they checked all the doors and windows, trying to find Evie's escape route. A wise Evie had shut her bedroom window when leaving. And so, on this particular night, Evie met Davina Buchanan.

CHAPTER 29
DAVINA'S WORLD CHANGES

(Five years before meeting Evie)

My flight home from Hawaii held no delays, mishaps, or anyone to talk to except a stranger sitting opposite. I flew first class—one of the many compensations for being wealthy. I spent my time reading while envisioning our lives with a baby girl or a boy. I didn't care which, as long as they were healthy, I was determined to be the best mother I could be. Then I remembered the day I floated down the river, listening to different bird calls and promising to love and cherish my children, no matter what. They would learn right from wrong, be Good Samaritans, think of others before themselves, and be strong enough to follow their dreams. I knew Felix felt the same. We would have no problems raising our children in a harmonious environment. With that thought, I drifted off to sleep but soon woke from a dreadful dream. My mother ran screaming from the house, engulfed by flames. The nightmare was so untainted it shook me, so I broke the pregnancy rule, ordered a whisky, and hyperventilated until the warm, numbing fluid soothed me enough to cast the vision off.

My subsequent calm came while reading a Non-Fiction book, 'The Feminine Mystique,' by Betty Friedan, which I'd purchased at the airport after debating whether to buy it or 'To Kill a Mockingbird.'

I smiled as I read, mainly because I could have written it. I'd been lucky enough to have had a free-thinking father who'd tirelessly defended women's rights and accomplishments, especially during the Second World War. I loved that he was brave enough to speak against the men who appeared threatened by *the modern woman's* newfound power. Still, I enjoyed Betty Friedan's short stories, highlighting many amazing women. I felt a sense of inferiority when reading about some of their incredible achievements.

The plane landed safely at Essendon Airport, where I expected to see Felix waiting with open arms. Instead, Freddy, our chauffeur, stood white-faced and shaking. I then noticed two police officers, a woman and a man, standing alongside Freddy. I could see their expression, which said, 'We're so very sorry.' I hurried toward Freddy, who burst into tears. "What's wrong, Freddy?" I tried to stay calm, thinking *it must be Mother. My nightmare had come true.*

Freddy struggled to speak. That's when the policewoman approached. She held my hand and ushered me from the tarmac and into the security room. I began hyperventilating; she drew a glass of water from the tap and handed it to me. I gulped it down. Finally, I took a deep breath, "I'm ready. Please tell me what happened. It's Mother, isn't it?" I looked the policewoman in the eye.

"Firstly, my name is Jane." Her eyes glistened, and her voice trembled. I thought then that Jane was about to rescind her duty when the male officer stepped forward and held her arm. She turned to look him in the eye. "I'm alright, thank you, Jim." She took a deep breath and focused her attention on me.

"Mrs. Lohmann, I'm a junior officer trained in grief counselling. I am sorry to inform you that a tragedy has occurred at your property. A fire began in your horse barn. We don't know how it started yet. But in the early hours of this morning, at approximately one am, your husband went to…"

I screamed, "NO, NO, NO!" My hands flung over my ears to prevent hearing another word. Jane waited patiently. I could feel her hand lying gently on my back.

Finally, she spoke loud enough so I could hear, "Mrs. Lohmann, would you like a sedative before I tell you the rest?" She waited for my answer. "Perhaps you would like to go to the hospital, where they'll care for you until you get over the shock of losing your husband?"

I went into shutdown and must have passed out, as I remember lying in a dark room when I awoke. The only light came from the nurse in white sitting beside me. My eyes blinked open until I focused on her smile. "Where am I?" I asked groggily.

"You're in the hospital, Mrs. Lohmann. We discovered you were pregnant, and the shock may have caused a miscarriage." She held my hand, "I'm very sorry."

"I still don't know what happened to my …" Then, with a pleading look, I sat up and said, "Can you please tell me?"

"I'm sorry. I'm not qualified. I'll call the psychotherapist when you're ready."

I read the name on her badge.

"Thank you, Mary. Could you please say I'm ready?"

I wasn't ready. How could I ever be prepared to hear about the death of Felix?

Mary squeezed my hand, "I'll go and phone her right away. She said to call her anytime, night or day, and she'd come immediately." Mary walked to the door and then turned, smiling. "Miss Roberts only lives around the corner. Her Christian name is Tina."

With Mary's departure came a feeling of loss so profound I wanted to die. I knew intuitively my darling Felix had perished in the fire. What an agonising death. Try as I might, I couldn't release the image I had seen in my dream. Only this time, it was Felix and not Mother. What would I do without his love? Felix was my everything. I'd never find another Felix. So I prayed to God to take me, too. *But what about our baby?*

Mary entered and said, "I rang Miss Roberts, and she's on her way. Is there anything I can do for you, Mrs. Lohmann?"

It took every ounce of strength to answer, "No, thank you." I was about to say, '*Call me Davina*,' but I thought, 'No, I'm still Mrs. Lohmann.'

"Would you like a cup of tea and a sandwich?"

"No, thank you. Just sweet black tea."

Mary soon returned with the tea and said, "I saw Miss Roberts talking to another doctor in the hallway. She won't be long."

Mary placed the hot tea down, and I sipped slowly, trying to clear my mind and find the strength to hear about what had happened. The door opened, and a tall, elegant young woman dressed in jeans and a grey sweatshirt stood before me, her blond hair tied up in a messy bun. She wore a dazzling smile that lit up the darkened room. She proffered her hand. "I'm Tina Roberts, and I must apologise for my appearance. I grabbed the first thing nearest my bed." *Was this all about her? Who cares what she's wearing?*

"I have no idea of the time," I said, blankly looking toward the window, thinking how inappropriate her smile was.

"It's three-thirty a.m., Mrs. Lohmann, *Davina*. Do you feel well enough to talk?" Tina waited until I gave the nod. "That's good. Maybe we could start by you telling me about yourself. Perhaps begin with your childhood. It always helps to speak of the past before the present." At least she wasn't patronising. She was more business-like. Mary left, and Tina dragged the chair to face me.

As much as I didn't want to know, I asked, "How many horses were bur…" *Why am I even asking?*

"None of your horses have died."

"*Have* died? Do you mean they still could?"

"No, they're okay. Your vet is treating them."

I sighed and relaxed a little before Tina gently persuaded me, with more empathy than she'd shown on arrival, "It would be better for your healing process to talk about yourself first, Davina."

And I must admit, as challenging as it was — almost impossible — a certain peace slowly came over the days ahead as I recollected some of my childhood dreams and aspirations with Tina. I thought lapsing into the past would be like blotting Felix out. Instead, it gave me the power to be in the present with the truth.

We continued down this path for days, eventually turning into weeks. During our sessions, Tina sat silent, listening to my memories so intensely that I felt she could have repeated every word I'd said. Ultimately, I felt safe and comfortable in her presence. Although my heart had shattered and I didn't know how I'd cope, Father had raised me to be strong and face up to whatever came my way. Plus, I'm sure intestinal fortitude is in the Buchanan DNA. My past relatives were robust and persistent. It's how they survived and thrived in Australia's extreme and sometimes harsh conditions, but the deepest part of me wanted to curl up and die. I had nothing to live for. My future had disappeared as quickly as day into night. *But what about our baby?* I kept hearing that voice again, urging me to hang on and think about the innocent life I nurtured inside.

After what seemed to be an eternity in the hospital, I finally came to tell Tina about the day Felix left me in Hawaii. Tina said, "You've led a fascinating life, Davina."

"Yes, I have. So now tell me exactly what happened?" I hung my head, taking deep breaths, which helped slightly, before looking into Tina's ocean-blue eyes with all the courage I could muster. I then listened as she spoke about the bravery of many friends who loved my horses as much as I did. Then the knife came sharp and excruciating, "I must tell you, Davina, your sister-in-law Hilda was arrested. The police suspect she started the fire.”

Unfortunately, I gave Tina the hate-filled stare I'd intended for Hilda. Tina quickened her following sentence. “Luckily, your brother phoned your vet. He immediately came to treat the horses suffering from severe burns. He assured your brother they would recover. Regrettably, Sven, that is his name?” I nodded. “Sven was at his Fiancée's home that night, so he was not there when the fire broke out.”

I screamed with rage, holding my head and shaking it back and forth. “NO, NO, NO!” I sobbed, “I told them I didn't trust Hilda! She's evil! I hate her. I hate her!” I felt a sharp jab in my arm while Tina held my hand.

“Hello, Davina,” a smiling Mary whispered when I finally woke from the effects of the injection. At least she was a cheerful soul, and I felt grateful. “I'll call Tina, shall I?” Mary asked while I was still groggy.

I nodded, although I felt strange and not in the mood to hear about what Hilda had done. I had hoped Felix's death had been just a bad dream. Then, my stomach gave a peculiar twinge, followed by another. Perhaps I needed to eat.

“Mary, after you call Tina, could you please bring me a sandwich and tea?”

I thought of our unborn baby; that's the only reason I could eat. My wanting food seemed to please Mary. She smiled and left.

Tina walked in with an expression of calm mixed with fear, “Hi, Davina. I hope you feel more settled after your long sleep.” She said, holding my hand.

“Drugging, you mean.” I turned on my side and felt another spasm or cramp, only more painful this time. I cringed. Meanwhile, Tina had walked to the window and stood to take in the view. “It's a lovely day, Davina. Perhaps you would like to walk outside with me.”

“No. I'm waiting for my tea and sandwich.” I said, angry at her flippancy and the world. How dare it keep turning? *The pain in my stomach didn't help.*

Tina turned to face me. “Of course, you must be hungry.” She sat beside me and sighed. “However, I need to put closure on what I was about to tell you, Davina.” Before I had a chance to say NO, Tina said. “Felix lasted only an hour after attempting to save your horses, Davina.” She paused, giving me time to comprehend his death. “The nurse closest to Felix heard him say before he passed over, “Davina. I love you. I'm sorry." Tina squeezed my hand, and an involuntary smile escaped despite the pain. *'No, Felix, I'm sorry.'* I whispered before the pain hit harder, and fluid ran between my legs.

"Something's happening, Tina. Please help me!" I cried.

Tina darted to the corridor and called Mary, who came in and hurriedly placed the tea tray on the table. Then, seeing a pool of blood on the sheet, she looked at Tina, "I think Davina's having a miscarriage."

I screamed and cried until my lungs gasped for air. My only lifeline to Felix had gone. I wanted to die so I'd be with Felix and our babies in heaven. Instead, I thought I'd gone to hell. The entire scenario was unbearable.

I remained in the hospital for over eight weeks, receiving counselling and controlled sedation. I wished they'd given me a lethal dose, but with the persistent and compassionate Tina assuring me I had *many* reasons to live, I slowly healed *just* enough to face life without Felix.

Tina had offered to take me home and stay as long as I needed her. I thought that was a bit over the top, "I will be fine, Tina. My mother needs me, and so do my horses." I kissed her cheek, "But please come see me when you can. You have been a lifesaver. And I mean that. I would have killed myself if it weren't for you." *And I still might, I thought*; I held her hand and managed a wavering smile, "I know I have a long way to go before I can forgive Hi…" I couldn't say her name, "But Felix will send me the strength to carry on. Thank you."

It seemed such a trivial thing to say, *thank you*, after the past eight weeks with Tina sitting with me, walking alongside me in the hospital gardens, and encouraging me to speak of my anger, anguish, and a feeling of complete loss after losing not only my husband but also our two babies.

Tina repeated her mantra over those eight weeks, "It would help greatly if you wrote about your past life, Davina. Writing your memoir will help you discover who you truly are and what you still have to give. I promise. You will be able to move on then, never the same as before," She said wistfully, "but a purpose for living will appear in time. Plus, love comes again when we least expect it," she said, smiling.

I had to believe Tina. I had nothing else. And I must admit there were many times later when I was on the brink of ending my life.

When Freddy came to collect me from the hospital, his speech faltered. He did not know what to say or do, so I embraced him, "It's alright, Freddy, just take me home." *It wasn't alright, but what could I say?*

Betty and Sven greeted me warmly before we sat around the kitchen table, drinking tea and chatting about positive things that had happened on Carlina, until it dawned on me, "Where's Mother?"

I'd been in a type of dream, one that saved me from reality. Perhaps the pills prescribed had that effect. *I'd have to wean myself off them - eventually.* Betty dipped her head, "Your mother hasn't been well since..."

"Where is she?" I asked, anxious.

"The doctor said she should go to a sanatorium. Somewhere nice, away from here, so she can get over the shock," said Betty kindly. "We found her a lovely place in the Dandenong Ranges. Your mother always loved it there. Do you remember the picnic lunches I'd pack for your day in the mountains?" I nodded despondently, and Betty brightened, "Freddy took me to see your mother a few days ago. It's a really nice place, it is." Freddy nodded, and Betty stood, wrapped her arms around me, and whispered, "Your mother is the least of your worries, Davina. She's safe and well cared for, my pet. You need to concentrate on yourself." She kissed my cheek before wiping away her tears.

Betty was right, but I'd promised Father I would never place Mother in one of those homes. The guilt hit me hard, adding more pain to my load. I found little consolation as I thought about arranging Felix's funeral. Plus, the police were waiting to question me about Hilda and my brother Joseph. *Surely Joseph didn't or couldn't have anything to do with the fire?"* Although visions returned of my terror as a young girl when I saw his experiments explode. It horrified me, but Joseph would laugh, yelling, "It worked, sis, see!" Had Joseph unintentionally supplied Hilda with explosives? She indeed held him captivated. Everyone could see that. Joseph had never taken time for women; they had to make the first move, and I'm sure those who did would leave disillusioned by his one-track scientific mind.

Hilda had gathered Joseph as easy prey. If she couldn't get close to Felix and achieve her goal, she'd use Joseph. And he fell for it! Hilda was jealous of Felix's love and devotion to me. She wanted him in every way she could. It made me sick. I knew hate would destroy me, but I'd undoubtedly hold enough to see Hilda behind bars forever. I shook my thoughts away.

"As you say, Betty, Mother's safe and cared for. I'll visit her soon."

"Davina, would you like to see your horses?" Sven broke into my gloom. "Old Polly was lucky I left her outside. She never eats well if she is locked up. And, of course, Molly, we also left her in her paddock. The ambulance men said she kept running the fence, whinnying. I can only assume Molly was crying for help." Sven shook his head, and I felt his sorrow before he brightened.

"The injured horses are coming along fine. Jacques suggested we take them to the beach, bathe them in salt water, and apply seaweed to their wounds. I phoned many horse properties and found a place to stable them on the Mornington Peninsula. Jacques, Charlotte, and I alternated daily trips to follow the procedure for six weeks. It has worked so well that we brought them home for you to see."

"I cannot thank you enough, Sven." I held his hand, and we locked eyes. "If it weren't for you, my horses might have died." Sven teared up.

"I am so very sorry, Davina." He took a moment to blink his tears away, "But Felix insisted I stay with Florence for the night. He needed to talk to Hilda and Joseph alone and…"

"Felix also asked Freddy to drive us to Geelong and stay with my sister." Betty had jumped in, "I felt trouble brewing, so I encouraged your mother to join us."

Sven shifted in his seat and coughed before saying, "When Joseph phoned Félix in Hawaii, Joseph insisted you stay there Davina, because he knew Hilda had come to cause trouble. Hilda was finally banned from European horse competitions due to her temper. And she'd left university because she said everyone hated her. She was in a terrible way, drinking and perhaps taking drugs. Felix tried his best to calm her down. I don't know what he had in mind, but he didn't want anyone around." Sven hung his head and almost whispered, "I'm so sorry, Davina. When Felix told me to leave, I should have said no. I *knew* he needed me."

"Please don't, Sven. You're not responsible for what happened."

He sighed. "I understand, Davina, but I feel I am." He smiled shakily, "Would you like to see your horses now?"

"Yes, please."

On that cloudy, calm afternoon, as we walked together, I felt locked in time, as if the world had stopped trying to decide whether to turn the clock back and dissolve what had happened, preventing what had caused the death of one of God's Angels, my darling Felix. I wished for my feelings to be confirmed, but sadly, they were not; I was in the present.

We walked to the horse paddocks, where Carlina Jimmy, my best jumping horse, and Carlina Florence, whom I'd named because of her beauty, grazed peacefully. Florence was my favourite dressage horse. Next, I spotted Carlina Star standing away from the others. I named him due to the massive white star on his black forehead. Then, Carlina Volee was an all-around filly with a heart bigger than herself. She could jump the highest obstacles, win point-to-point races, and perform a brilliant dressage test. An Olympic prospect, for sure! And, of course, Sampson, the gentle giant who adored Miss Molly. He was spared from the fire because Molly would fret if he weren't with her in the outside shelter.

The injured horses were covered from head to toe with soft, almost see-through cotton rugs. Sven explained, "Charlotte designed the rugs to keep the sun and flies off. In addition, I covered their wounds with an ointment I mixed from Carlina thistle, seaweed, and a touch of fish oil." Sven smiled, "It is working so well that I might market it."

I wrapped my arm around his shoulder. "Thank you, Sven. I'm sorry, but *thank you* is all I can say. My emotions often get the better of me. I really don't know how I'm going to survive."

"We will all help you, Davina," Sven said, embracing me.

I managed to smile before patting each of my beautiful horses, still alive due to Felix's bravery. And my devoted friends. I spoke to each horse, saying they would have a home at Carlina forever.

I didn't want to see the charred remains of the barn. I'd have it bulldozed. Never again would I lock a horse up. Instead, I'd build more open shelters so all my horses could take refuge from bad weather. But, as much as I wanted to sit forever, just admiring my beloved horses, I knew I had to deal with the unavoidable: Felix's funeral. So we walked silently back to the homestead.

So many letters and phone calls from friends and family had gone unanswered. I could not handle it before. But now I had to.

I'd been informed while in the hospital that Felix's body lay frozen until I felt strong enough to handle his funeral. But first, I needed to call his parents and inform them as to where and when I chose the funeral. Regrettably, I initially laid some of the blame on them. After all, they had adopted Hilda, and being infatuated with their sweet, pretty little girl, they had failed to see the evil beneath.

I don't want to write about Felix's funeral, only to say my dear friend, Irene, who was six months pregnant, flew from Monaco to attend the funeral. Bill sent his apologies. It seemed his manager had no empathy, only a desire to win races, which Bill was expected to do on the same day I buried Felix. I genuinely feared for their future, as Bill was bound tight by a contract that only the manager could break. Irene told me she felt like the Racing Team Manager, Antonio, employed her merely to keep Bill happy.

The hardest part was consoling Felix's parents. They'd lost both children. My inner voice told me, *you lost your daughter to the devil long ago!*

I don't know how, but I managed to maintain my dignity as I recalled another of Father's lessons. I felt hollow but sad when the doctor advised me that my Mother was too fragile to attend Felix's funeral.

Jacques and Charlotte could not have been more helpful and compassionate. I could always count on them, though I remained determined never to overuse their support and friendship.

After the Wake, when most had left, Irene and I walked outside in the cold night air. Wrapped warmly in our overcoats, we gazed at the stars, their sparkling points set against a black velvet sky. I imagined Felix was one of those stars shining down on me while Irene desperately wanted to discuss their prisoner's life in Monaco. Whenever she began, I stopped her. I could not comfort Irene. I had nothing to give. Not that day or in the years to come, when issues got much worse within Bill's team: rivalry, blackmail, and life threats. It all came from the manager's involvement with the Mafia.

I must stay on track, as Tina keeps telling me, "Don't rush it, Davina. Re-live every moment as it comes."

Hilda's trial came two weeks after Felix's funeral. I needed every ounce of grit to be on the witness stand. The prosecutor questioned me about my *first* impression when meeting Hilda and our relationship until the death of my husband, *caused by her hatred of me.* It was agonising until a certain peace came when I finally heard Hilda being sentenced to prison without parole for twenty years.

The Judge acquitted Joseph of the charge of being an accomplice. He was heavily inebriated and slept through the drama of Hilda pouring gasoline around the timber barn and lighting a match. Joseph left the courtroom without looking me in the eye. One month later, he accepted an offer to be a science professor at Cambridge University in England. There he has remained.

The Court case seems a blur now, but I remember telling the jury that, in my opinion, Felix would have been unable to sleep after his heated confrontation with Hilda and Joseph. He'd asked Hilda, a year before, to leave Carlina and never return. I knew my husband well enough to say he detested hostilities. On the other hand, Felix would remain calm, seeking a peaceful solution to every problem. Hilda must have shown her true colours and brought Felix to breaking point the night of the fire. Her behaviour unnerved Felix, leaving him unable to sleep. At approximately one a.m., he would have been sitting in our office with a full view of the barn through the enormous bay windows. I know this because that is where Felix always sat when restless. I, too, found it a calming room. Perhaps my father's spirit remained there.

Felix had surmised when he took the phone call in Hawaii that a full-on brawl with Hilda would be imminent. So he'd asked Freddy and Betty to take Mother with them and go away for the weekend. And, of course, he told me a white lie about having to return home due to a work matter. And knowing I was pregnant with our second child, Felix didn't want to upset me about Hilda's return. I wish he'd told me; I would have phoned the police and had her taken away because I had evidence that Hilda had evil intentions toward my horses and me. Besides, I knew Paul, the local Police Sergeant. We attended primary school together and held a mutual respect. But, instead, my statement was claimed as an assumption!

Hilda more or less confirmed *my assumptions* when she later cried in the courtroom, "I didn't mean it. I didn't mean to kill Felix! I loved him. I just hate Davina!"

At least she'd returned to the scene when she realised Felix was attempting to save the horses. Hilda then doused Felix with buckets of water before waking Joseph, who called the ambulance and fire brigade.

The horrific scenario almost killed Felix's parents, as it did me. I loved and forgave them, especially when they fought to transfer Hilda to a prison in Helsinki. Far away from me. Finally, Hilda's transfer was granted after a long period of debate on both sides of the ocean. I breathed a sigh of relief, as I might have snuck into the Melbourne Women's Prison and killed Hilda if the transfer hadn't happened sooner.

I knew my life after that final blow would never be the same, particularly when living in the Carlina Homestead and the debilitating silence after always hearing Felix's laughter throughout the house. Listening to Mother and Betty chatting about the charity they cooked for—happy times with our friends, who came regularly for drinks and a barbeque by the pool. The memories began to haunt me to the point I needed to play music day and night to fill the emptiness. The melodies helped, but I'd burst into tears whenever I heard one of Felix's favourite songs.

**

After twelve months of agonising loneliness, with only moments of happy reflection while writing my life story, I asked Betty and Freddy to join me in our favourite room, the kitchen. I held their hands, gazing from one to the other, and said, "I love you both like family. I would never do anything to hurt you. But, unfortunately, I think I'm doing just that. Unintentionally. So I want you to think about retiring, with a significant sum of money from me, or Father's company, as it were." Betty tried to talk, "Please hear me out, Betty.

I can no longer live in this house. It provides too many sad memories. So I've been thinking of doing something I've wanted all my life." A smile escaped, "To donate money and provide opportunities to those in need. I'll become a philanthropist!" They sat back, shocked, and I chuckled at the look on their faces. "I've decided to turn this mansion into a home for abused mothers and their children, or abandoned children. They can play in the three-acre garden and receive private schooling in the Ballroom." I saw their worried expressions and caught on, "Of course, I will have lawyers draw up a contract. It must be returned to me if they choose not to continue. It will be a free leasehold."

Betty and Freddy stood instantaneously, hugging me like Moma and Poppa Bear. Then, Betty cried, "We've been talking about our future, Davina, and I, for one," she paused to glance at Freddy, "think it's a wonderful idea." Freddy nodded his approval, and Betty's expression turned serious.

"But where would you live, pet?"

"Please sit down. No. Before you do, Betty, would you put the kettle on and give us some of your famous chocolate chip biscuits?"

I felt happy telling them what I planned to do, finishing with, "I know you both love going to Geelong, and your sister gets lonely living in that big old rambling house. Do you think living with her would be a good idea, Betty?"

Betty's eyes welled, and she sniffed before saying, "I can't believe you've been thinking what we were thinking. The last time Freddy and I

216

stayed there, my sister asked if we would come live with her." Betty's face never hid her feelings. I held her hand, "I know, Betty, you'll be worried about me. Well, please don't. If I've survived all that has happened, I can survive anything. Besides, it will keep me occupied, organising the handover of Buchanan House to a reputable charity, or maybe I'll create my own charity. I won't live far away. I've chosen Freddy's cottage, as it's nearest to the homestead. So I can keep an eye on things. And if I can help them in any way, I will. That will be my stipulation in the contract."

**

And so it was that Betty and Freddy, with their belongings, including a substantial amount of money, left Carlina to live with Betty's sister in Geelong. A seaside escape, one might say.

I visited Mother in her care home in the Dandenong Ranges two days later. I drove Felix's little yellow Volkswagen. I would never part with it, as I sensed him sitting beside me. The feeling soothed me, and I spoke to Felix, pointing out places of interest, and I told him what was happening to Carlina. I knew he'd agree with everything I'd done. Of course, it was only a cover-up of how I truly felt. *Brokenhearted*. Though I tried hard to *soldier on*, as Father would say.

Finally, I arrived at the home, relieved to see happy, compassionate staff surrounding Mother, who had lapsed into her own world. Thankfully, it was a cheery one. She thought I was a child. Only this time, she loved me more than anything. She told me so at least twenty times that day. And I prayed to Father for his forgiveness in breaking my promise.

I knew I could never care for Mother during my prolonged grief.

CHAPTER 30
CATHY'S ESCAPE

Irene stood close to the barrier at La Rascasse Corner, alongside hundreds of spectators watching the Monaco Grand Prix, thinking, *Why am I still here? I should be home in Australia with Mum.*

Her world had undergone dramatic changes in the past four years. Irene's father had died from a stroke, but his death freed her mother to live life to the fullest. Especially when Irene sent her mother money to travel and buy whatever she wished. '*You deserve it, Mum,*' Irene said each time she wired money home. However, she'd sway her mother from coming to Monaco, as she would become another coin on the roulette wheel of their life. Money was no problem for Irene and Bill, but their freedom was. Constantly under surveillance, Bill desperately wanted to break his contract with Antonio. He'd tried to throw races, tell Antonio he'd lost his passion and, more importantly, his reflexes to be a top driver. It hadn't worked. Antonio saw through the facade and threatened Bill.

"You will win when I tell you. You will lose when I say so. I have a lot of money riding on you. Do you understand, Bill?" Antonio slapped Bill on the back with a deceptive smile. "I will tell you when I'm finished with you. In the meantime, do as you are told. And by the way, how are your wife and daughter?"

Irene was worn out with her life in Monarco and tired of waiting for Bill to speed his car around bends into the home straight. She was shuffling from one foot to the other when a stranger broke her train of thought, asking for directions. Irene gave directions loudly in her Aussie drawl. When the stranger moved on, Irene felt a tap on her shoulder and turned to see a young woman, tears trickling down her flushed face. "I need y'help," the woman whispered, "I heard yer Australian accent. I'm hidin, tryin t'escape me' husband. Can y'help me, please?" Irene's brow creased, searching for the truth in Cathy's eyes. "He beats me and threatens t'kill me." Cathy pleaded, "I must go home t' Australia t'find me daughter. He abducted me and left her there without a soul t'care f'her."

Irene placed her hand on her heart, thinking about how Antonio had sent a stern older woman who spoke little English to care for her daughter, Davina May. From that day on, Irene was barely given an hour to spend with her daughter. Irene held Cathy's hand. "What's your name?" Irene whispered.

"Cathy, Cathy Calan."

"As soon as my husband's car passes, Cathy, cheer loudly with me, then follow me. I won't let go of your hand. Okay?"

"Oh, Dear Lord. You're my saviour. Thank yer!"

"Shoosh. Not yet, I'm not. I'm trapped here, too. I also want to take my daughter home to Australia.

It had been the first time Cathy Calan had left their guarded home on the cliff in over a year. Sean's love of car racing and Cathy's good behaviour had convinced him to take her to Monaco. He'd bought her a collection of high-fashion couture and paraded his beautiful wife around the Casino's roulette tables. Cathy hated every minute but was clever enough not to show it. So, instead, she played the game of life or death until she found a chance to escape, which proved complicated, as Sean's bodyguards followed her everywhere. They even waited outside the bathroom while she used it. Cathy's advantage came while attending the Grand Prix. Her opportunity to flee had finally arrived, with hundreds of people crushing together. She'd told Sean she needed to go to the Ladies' Room and conveniently lost the bodyguard.

Life works in mysterious ways. On that same day, Cathy unexpectedly found a friend in Irene, Captain Teddy, whose ship had docked at Fontvielle Pier, close to the Grand Prix circuit, and *literally* bumped into the two women as they hurried to catch a cab. Cathy went weak in the knees when she looked into the eyes of Captain Teddy, and for a moment, he thought he'd injured the young woman. He apologised as he attempted to steady her.

"Captain Teddy?" Cathy said, her eyes wide in shock.

"Yes, some people call me that. May I ask who…" Then, looking closer at the woman he held in his grasp, he exclaimed, "Cathy…Cathy Calan! What on earth are you doing here? I mean, I'm sorry, I would never have thought…" He felt her body shaking, "Are you in some sort of trouble, Cathy?"

Meanwhile, Irene recced the scene, hoping Antonio or a team member hadn't spotted her.

"Yes, Sean's holdin me captive. He had me abducted, and they left Evie in Australia t'fend f'herself. Please help me!"

"Who's your friend?" Teddy looked at Irene, still scanning the crowd. Then, without looking at him, she said, "I'm Irene. I've only just met Cathy. She asked for my help after hearing my Aussie accent. I was taking her to our home. My husband's the famous driver, Bill Peterson." Irene turned to see the surprise on Teddy's face and continued, "We have our own problems. Nothing you can help with, Captain," Irene said, studying his uniform. "Can we go to your ship and talk?"

"Yes, of course, follow me. I have a driver waiting." Teddy's smile traversed both women, "I'm not as young as I used to be, and this is my final sail. I've always wanted to see the Monaco Grand Prix. So, I put my hand up to be a Canadian cruise ship captain. My ship is docked at Fontvielle. I didn't want to walk the twenty minutes here and back."

Nudging their way through the crowd, under the wing of Teddy's arms, they reached a little red Fiat car and scrambled in without delay.

"To the ship, please, Giuseppe," Teddy ordered.

Irene was about to speak until Cathy touched her lips, shaking her head. Captain Teddy also remained silent during the drive to the ship.

Once inside his cabin, Teddy poured three whiskies before offering them out, "I think we all need a drink. Now, please tell me about your troubles. And I'll see if I can help."

Cathy turned to Irene, "I'm sorry I shushed yer, Irene. But y'don't know who has allegiance with d'Mafia here."

"Exactly!" Said Teddy. "Now you go first, Cathy. Please tell me your story from when you left the Fair Sea in Port Phillip Bay."

And so Cathy's and then Irene's stories unfolded slowly, leaving Teddy's head spinning. Finally, he took a deep, meaningful breath before suggesting, "As I told you, ladies, this is my final sail. So if any problems arise in taking you both aboard the ship, I won't give two hoots!"

Resting her head in her hands, Cathy sobbed with relief while Irene stroked her back, "It's alright now, Cathy. Everything is going to be okay. You're going home with Captain Teddy." Irene smiled at Teddy, "Thank you so much, Captain. I'll remain in Monaco. There are too many issues to resolve before I leave with my husband and daughter."

"I understand. But I want you to keep in touch, Irene, because I can and will help you leave Monaco. *Lovely as it is.*" Captain Teddy smiled sadly. *I was not destined to see the Monaco Grand Prix. Still, I knew fate had played a hand when I first met Cathy and Evie. I've been destined to help them. Now, all I need to do is ensure Cathy finds Evie. And if it's the last thing I do, I'll succeed!*

Irene pushed a wad of money into Cathy's hand. "Please take this. You'll need it to find your daughter. I wish you luck, Cathy." Irene then wrote her address down and handed it to Cathy. "Please write to me, let me know where you are. Don't phone because our phone's tapped. And don't worry about me. I know God's on my side, as He is with you." Irene embraced Cathy, "My time to escape will come."

Irene stood and shook the Captain's hand, "I can only thank you, Captain. I'm sure the Good Lord sent you."

He hadn't let go of her hand, his eyes moist, "I must agree, Irene." He then ushered her off the ship. "Good luck, Irene, and please keep in touch." He said, kissing her cheek before opening the door to Giuseppe's little red Fiat. "Back to the circuit, Giuseppe, and then I will no longer need you. Thank you."

He handed Giuseppe more money than he'd make in a month.

"But what about the other…"

"The other lady is a passenger. Goodbye, Giuseppe."

Irene hurried home and wrote to Davina about how she'd just helped a Damsel in distress and the kind and lovely Captain Teddy, who'd saved Cathy Calan's life.

CHAPTER 31
DAVINA FINDS HER PURPOSE

I rarely look forward to the mail, as I feel compelled to respond to my friends, sharing with them the details of my mundane life. I'd have nothing interesting to say.

In a lazy mood, I shuffled the envelopes on this fine, warm day and smiled as I held one from Irene in Monaco, another from Phyllis in England, and a third from Norman in Helsinki. *Which to open first?* I decided on Norman. His letter would bring horsey news, particularly about Carlina River.

Before I opened Norman's letter, I felt the urge to lean back on my chair under the shade of the peppercorn tree Father had planted and reflect on the past five years of my life. Why? I don't know.

My horses came first to mind, as they usually do. I'd only ridden once in the past five years in a jumping event on Sampson, and we'd won. I thought winning would inspire me to get back into the game. But no, I was happy to keep myself and my horses fit by riding around Carlina and schooling them for three-day events. I could never entirely give up the dream of competing in an Olympic Three-Day Event. Then, the thought amused me: if I didn't get a move on, age would prevent it. I knew my passion for horses would never die, although competing had somewhat died down.

I continued to find solace in my horses, and the river remained my sounding block. I walked there most days to find solitude and open my heart to its ever-flowing current. It seemed to wash away my fears.

I smiled, thinking how my life had become bearable since Evie entered it. Sometimes, she'd stay overnight, and we'd ride around the paddocks the following day — Evie on old Polly, who still had a spring in her step at age twenty-three, and me on Florence.

I wanted to adopt Evie, raise her as my own, and teach her to be a top equestrian. But sadly, I knew this could never happen, not until we found Evie's mother, with the hope that she was still alive and fit to care for Evie. Unfortunately, her mother's disappearance remained a mystery.

Evie had begun opening up to me almost a year ago when I found her snuggled up with Polly during a storm. '*I don't trust anyone*,' she'd said, although little by little, I'd won her faith. It was then that Evie told me about her troubled journey until she came to Carlina. I'd promised Evie I'd not tell anyone, including my closest friend Irene.

However, I did entrust Tina with our patient-doctor agreement. I needed her help to inquire about Evie's mother. Tina suggested I hire a private detective. And that I did. After that, I kept thinking, "*C'est sera, c'est sera*, "what will be, will be." Although I felt guilty not caring as much as I should about finding Evie's mother.

I've grown to love Evie and only want the best for her. Besides, her parents' connection with crime sounded dangerous—especially Sean, Evie's father. And from what I could gather, he was a criminal at the highest level. Cathy had been abducted without a trace, and no one knew where she was. Although Evie's instincts told her Sean had arranged it. "Da didn't like me. Yer just gets in d'way. He'd say dat all d'time." Evie told me, and before I could stop the words, I said, "What a bastard!"

I sighed reflectively and opened Norman's letter. He only ever wrote good news. And this time, he'd written about the modern training techniques he'd learned at The Royal School for Andalusians in Jerez-De-La-Frontera, Spain. "Wow," I said aloud. Old Suzie, lying at my feet, woofed; no doubt she agreed. She likes me to read to her, even though her hearing's almost defunct. She wags her tail, which stops when I stop talking.

Norman's letter mentioned River and how he'd advanced supremely under the new techniques. *Bless Norman*, I thought, especially since he'd encouraged Sven to come live with us.

Sven and Florence eventually married and have been godsends, always visiting, constantly phoning, and including me in all they do. Most times, I decline. I suppose I'm what most people call me – *a recluse*. Another wave of guilt washed over me when I remembered I hadn't even attended their wedding.

They understood at the time.

I placed Norman's letter on the small table and sipped the delicious lemonade for which the cook in Buchanan House is renowned, while looking at Phyllis's lovely handwriting.

"Phyllis, how are you, my dear friend?" I spoke aloud, and Suzie woofed again. I ripped open the envelope and was completely surprised when I read about Phyllis and her long-time gentleman friend, Tom Forrester, finally announcing their engagement. *'You'll receive an invitation when we set a wedding date, Davina.'* Hmm, would I go or not?

Then I read about Phyllis becoming the Principal Dressage Instructor to the British Royal children. Therefore, she was invited to royal galas and other auspicious occasions. Again, I sat in awe of my friends' achievements. Did it make me feel jealous? No, it did not! Oh dear, was I becoming an old lady at the tender age of twenty-eight? I then decided to attend Phyllis's wedding, where I might meet Royalty. It would be something to tell Evie. *Maybe she could come with me?*

"Now you, my dearest Irene." I said aloud, "I hope things have improved over there. I feel so helpless sitting here, although I'm sure there's little anyone can do until they throw Bill on the scrap heap along with the wrecked cars. Then you'll come home. I can't wait."

I wondered if I was slightly mad, talking aloud to myself, and then Suzie barked, and I smiled.

Father's Peppercorn tree stood to the left of the cottage, and from where I sat, I could see the big house, *as Evie calls it*, and when she scrambles over the fence into the paddock adjoining. I'd told her to use the gate into the lane leading to my cottage. She wouldn't listen, and I couldn't help but smile at Evie's eagerness when she gave Polly a carrot, encouraging her to follow as she ran toward me, calling. *"Look, Davina! Polly follows me everywhere!"*

It's what Evie would say most days, when the weather was fine, like today. I looked at my watch. Yes, I'd soon see the same act from Evie and Polly. So I placed Irene's letter on top of the others and stood to stretch and yawn.

I needed to prepare for Evie's theatrical entrance and her riding lesson.

Then, like footsteps on my grave, a shiver urged me to open Irene's letter.

It's important!

I sat back down and read about Irene's chance meeting with an

Irish woman, Cathy Calan, who'd approached her at the Monaco Grand Prix asking for help. As I read further, I knew precisely who Cathy was— *Evie's mother.* It was confirmed when Irene mentioned Cathy's husband, Sean.

I wanted to rip the letter to pieces and pretend I hadn't read the words that would take Evie from me. But instead, I choked back tears and took many deep breaths. "It may not be her," I said, trying to convince myself before gazing up, focusing on the white cotton clouds drifting overhead. My thoughts went to Felix, and I wondered how he would react to this life-changing news *yet again.* I then had little trouble gaining the strength to tell Evie about her mother.

Felix was still my Guardian Angel.

As predicted, Evie came running through the paddock five minutes later, with Polly trotting behind. She then hurdled the laneway fence, then the garden fence, and stood breathless before me, panting and smiling until her expression changed. I remained silent, entranced by how beautiful Evie was, with her blue eyes and golden hair, not to mention her quick wit and courage. *Who could not love her?*

"Are y'alright, Davina? Y'look like y'seen a wee Gho... a... Leprechaun."

I smiled at Evie's tact. *She'd thought of Felix.*

"Yes, I'm alright, Evie." I held her hand, "Please sit down while I tell you some wonderful news." Evie tilted her head, puppy-dog fashion, and sat cross-legged at my feet alongside Suzie.

I took a deep breath and slowly released it before reading Irene's letter aloud.

I thought Evie would jump with joy, but she sat dumbfounded. It took a while for her to speak, "Cathy. You mean my ma? Is she truly my ma?" I nodded.

"I never gave up hope," said Evie in a sad refrain, "And I pray every night f'God t'find her." I wondered what was going through Evie's mind as she stroked Suzie's coat for a long time. Then, finally, Evie jumped up and hugged me tight, "Thank y', Davina, f'findin me' ma." She kissed my cheek, and I felt the wetness of her tears.

"I didn't find her, Evie. God knows I tried. I even hired a private detective. But he kept running into dead ends. So, I need to call and tell him we've found your mother. I'll then write to Irene about her remarkable, almost unbelievable news." I thought about what I'd said. "I think God simply answered your prayers, Evie. He found your mother."

"Why don't y'telephone y'friend, Davina?" Evie said, her expression puzzled.

I thought we'd had enough intrigue for the day, so I said, "It's a long story, Evie. I'm sorry, but writing a letter or sending a telegram is the only way." Then I recalled, "Do you remember Captain Teddy, whose ship brought you to Melbourne from Ireland?"

"I'll always remember Captain Teddy. His address is hidden in me' teddy bear. I call him Captain, too." I belly laughed for the first time in five years.

It felt so good.

"This story, indeed, is unbelievable," I laughed again. I'm sure Evie thought me mad until she caught on and joined me.

Of course, we didn't ride that afternoon. Instead, we walked to the big house to share the good news with everyone. I cannot remember being so torn between doing the right thing and knowing that being reunited with her mother would make Evie the happiest child in the universe. And me, the saddest person.

I had fallen so in love with this funny, courageous, talented little girl. I held visions of Evie and me competing at horse shows together. I'd be proud to watch her rise to the top of the equestrian world. Was I living my dream through Evie? I don't know. All I knew was that my life would soon lack the love and hope I'd found in her. Could I possibly survive another loss?

Again, I didn't know, and I didn't care anymore. A person can only take so much heartbreak before their heart withers and dies. Still, I wished I had enough courage to see this through. And love enough to find happiness in Evie's joy. Then what?

CHAPTER 32
CATHY'S HOME COMING

Cathy's escape from Monaco had not been without danger. First, the police were informed about the disappearance of Cathy Calan by her distraught husband, Sean, who suspected she'd been abducted. And so he'd pleaded with the authorities to find her. Therefore, the police searched the ship when Sean discovered Cathy had been seen in a car with Captain Teddy. Luckily for them, his boat was still in the dock.

Coincidentally, Teddy suspected the authorities would be coming, so he disguised Cathy as a young engineer working in the boiler room. With her face smothered in black grease and her hair tied up under a cap, the police gave her no thought. They'd come looking for a pretty young blond woman in a pink dress with matching shoes. Fortunately, Cathy, in her greasy overalls, did not paint the picture.

Later, when the ship left port, and Cathy felt safe under the Captain's care, she laughed, "Abducted from Sean! I'd say I've been *saved* from Sean. I was terrified all d'time. D'only ting keeping me from killin' him was seeing Evie again. I had t'stay strong. Strong enough to report my abduction to d'Commissioner of Police in Melbourne! After dat, I don't care what happens t'Sean or his Mafia Gang! I hope dey rot in hell!"

"The Mafia has tentacles all around the world, Cathy." Teddy said, placing his hands on her shoulders, "Please think about your safety and Evie's when *we* find her. It may be wise not to say anything. I think we should go to ground."

Cathy's heart soared. She clasped her hands in prayer, "WE? Yer mean you'll help me find Evie when we get t'Melbourne, Teddy?"

"Yes. However, I must first hand over the ship in Canada. And then I'm free to do as I please for the rest of my life, Cathy."

Cathy embraced Teddy, "I don't know how t'thank y'Captain. It's like d'Good Lord sent y'to us." He laughed, then held her apart, "I know,

I've been told that so often, I'm starting to believe it. The universe operates in mysterious ways, Cathy." His blue eyes creased, holding back emotion. "All I could think of when watching little Evie struggle up the Fair Sea's boarding ramp with Sean yanking her arm, yelling '*hurry up!*' was that I'd carry her in my arms and console her if that were my child. Besides, Evie looked so much like my daughter, Rosie. God rest her soul. My heart cried out for Evie." Teddy sighed and wiped his eyes before he brightened. "Tonight, Cathy, we'll enjoy a delicious dinner with champagne to celebrate—no more hiding in your cabin. None of the other passengers knows who you are. I'm sure." Then, with a quizzical look, "On second thoughts, would you mind if our hairdresser cut and dyed your hair?" Teddy touched her chin, "And we'll change your name, just to be safe."

Cathy agreed. So later that evening, Vera Evans walked arm-in-arm to the dining table with Captain Teddy. With her short black hair and an elegant satin dress, nobody who knew Cathy would recognise her, especially when she dropped her Irish accent under the Captain's advice and spoke with an upper-class English brogue. *It's fun, like bein an actress in a movie.* Cathy mused.

From then on, Cathy exuded happiness, and her beauty shone as she cruised the Mediterranean Sea, exploring exotic places like Cairo and Istanbul, feeling safe and carefree. Sadly, her adventure ended when Teddy docked the ship in Canada. However, she was revived by the crew's excitement about celebrating Captain Teddy's past forty years at sea.

He'd captained warships during the Second World War, and when the war ended, he married a younger woman. Shortly after, he took up a Captain's role, mainly on cruise ships. His good fortune turned when his young wife and only daughter were killed in an automobile accident while Captain Teddy was sailing around the Pacific Ocean.

But today was a day of celebration, and so Cathy accompanied Teddy to the Gala evening, which appeared fit for a king; such was the widespread respect and gratitude for the Captain. But then, whispers around the dinner table about their relationship made Cathy blush. *Captain Teddy's old enough to be me, da. What nonsense.* Nevertheless, Teddy protected Cathy by never letting her out of sight. And most days, they discussed what was needed to find Evie and how they would later disappear without a trace. Of course, the threat of Sean locating her and Evie and then abducting Cathy again, or worse, would always be a worry. Then, to Cathy's surprise, an exciting and informative letter from Irene arrived at the Canadian port the morning after the Gala.

✢✢

At the same time, Cathy sailed away with Captain Teddy; Sean prepared to fly to Australia in search of her. '*The kid's of no consequence. I couldn't give a shit about her.*' He'd told fellow gang members, laughing.

The Godfather was informed of Sean's misdemeanor and observed another side of Sean that he hadn't witnessed before. *How could a man care less about his daughter?* The thought had upset the Godfather so much that he called Sean to his office. Sean appeared there the morning before he planned to fly to Melbourne. The office and adjoining rooms were an expansive part of the vintage hotel the boss's family had owned for generations. Leather-bound books lined the walls, cloaking escape routes and hidden treasures.

Sean knocked on the heavy mahogany door before it opened, revealing a huge bodyguard who stood aside to allow Sean to enter. With a broad smile, he strolled forward and proffered his hand to the Godfather, who sat behind his impressive desk, "So, Boss, have you got a job f'me t'do while I'm in Australia?" The Godfather leaned back in his chair, ignoring Sean's hand. Instead, he scrutinised the man he'd always admired but now thought differently. He tapped his cigar slowly into an ashtray. "You're not going to Australia, Sean." The Godfather said with the arrogance of one who held total power.

"But Boss, I need t'bring me wife back. She was abducted and…"

"Now, listen to me, Sean, because I will only tell you once!" The Godfather's temper rarely rose, but it burned when family members were threatened.

"My son's death is why I gave you a job. I trusted your loyalty." The Godfather puffed on his cigar, pain etched on his face, "You look so much like him, Sean." Then, with sudden aggression. "But I'm telling you, you're nothing like him. My son would never have left his daughter behind—if he'd lived to have one. On the contrary, he'd do everything he could to protect her."

The Godfather stood and walked toward Sean, his expression mean, his eyes boring into Sean's. He shoved him in the chest, and Sean raised his hands, "But Boss, you don't understand!"

"I understand, *Sean*. You think you can say what you like in front of my men, and they will not tell me? So, who do you think you are, *heh*? Tell me. Are you the boss now? You go without my permission and call

229

the fuckin police to search for your wife! Nobody does anything without my say-so. You got it?" He pushed Sean in the chest hard, then, with a pointed finger, he said, "You will stay here. You will do as I say. You will never see your wife again. From what I've heard, she never wanted to be here. Certainly not without her daughter. And I don't blame her." The Godfather sighed, returned to his desk, and sat facing Sean. "If you disobey me, Sean, it's a long way to the bottom of the Asiatic Sea! But it'll be quick wearing concrete shoes! Now get out of here!"

**

Cathy dreaded flying after being kidnapped by the Mafia. She'd flown to many countries on their small private plane before reaching Italy. The sudden surge upward, with no safety net below, and the rapid descent onto the tarmac made her stomach feel like it would hit the ground before the plane did. Unfortunately, it was the quickest way to reach Australia.

The letter she'd received in Canada from Irene informed her, '*Evie is living with my dearest friend, Davina Buchanan.*' It went on in detail until ending with '*you must understand that for Davina to lose Evie entirely after her past tragedy could break her completely. Please consider this, Cathy.*'

Cathy clenched her fist and screwed the letter into a ball.

CHAPTER 33
DAVINA PEACE AT LAST

I'd come to know Anthony Green platonically over the past five years of his teaching at Buchanan House. I'd noted his compassion for the children and his love of fun when attempting to cheer the lost souls in his care. His gentle demeanor reminded me of Felix, which made me want to get to know Anthony better, especially since he was also fond of Evie. We held a common denominator.

My struggle while waiting for Evie's mother to collect her brought back the pain of losing Felix, and I'd grown tired of Tina's consultations. Although she'd become a good friend, she failed to understand my feelings for Evie. Tina constantly warned me against getting too close. And when I took a long look at Tina, I realised she held no one near and dear, only clients like me. I began to pity her.

One evening at dusk, I decided to confide in Anthony. That morning, I'd walked along the river, which helped me figure things out. As I have said, the river speaks. And it said, *talk to Anthony.* Well, that's my excuse. Mad as it may sound. So I walked down the lane towards the big house, admiring the sunset washing the sky with pink, mauve, orange, and deep purple. It was so beautiful that it took my breath away. I felt at peace, so I stopped to take it all in. Then, with my eyes raised, I watched the last grey cloud drift away and heard Felix say, *'Go to him, Davina.'* I'm sure I'll reflect on these moments when I'm old and grey and call myself a delusional old fool. When I lowered my eyes from the sky to look ahead, Anthony appeared as if by magic—his expression kind and understanding.

"It's a beautiful evening, Davina."

"Yes, it is Anthony. I was just coming..."

"To see me about Evie?"

"Yes." I smiled. "It appears we're on the same wavelength."

I cannot explain why I hadn't formed a friendship with Anthony. Maybe the timing? However, tonight seemed to bring a magic that allowed me to see my future in a flash. I was holding a newborn baby, with Anthony smiling alongside me. He touched my shoulder, bringing me into the moment, "Are you okay, Davina? You look pale. Come sit with me on your garden seat."

From the moment our bodies touched as we watched twilight turn to night, I knew I was where I was meant to be.

EPILOGUE

Evie's ma, Cathy, arrived two weeks after I'd finally bonded with Anthony.

The distinguished, grey-haired gentleman, Captain Teddy, who accompanied Cathy, reminded me of my father, so we established an immediate rapport. I could see their situation as if a veil had lifted, and my heart sang unselfishly for Evie's happiness.

The three united with happy tears and hugs before Cathy decided to stay a while after I'd offered them a three-bedroom cottage.

Evie beamed with delight as she guided Cathy and Teddy around, introduced them to the horses, and showed her riding prowess, while I thought, what a shame to lose such a promising young pupil. More so - my soul mate.

I needed to assure myself that we would remain friends no matter what.

After ten days, when we were all together in my kitchen, Cathy said, "It's time for us t'leave, Davina. "

Her words hit like a bullet. Still, I gathered composure.

"And where will you go, Cathy?" I asked with a catch in my throat.

"Captain Teddy's offered us a home in England." She smiled and wrapped her arms tightly around Evie, "Sadly, me da died over a year ago, but he left me some money. Money enough t'send Evie t'boardin school while I cook and keep house for Captain Teddy." Cathy threw Teddy a beaming smile.

Suddenly, I remembered all the letters I'd sent to Evie's grandad, which came back with the notice *'return to sender.'*

Evie escaped Cathy's grip and hurried into my embrace, her gaze fixed on Cathy. "What are yer sayin', Ma? Y'never told me about Old Pa's money! I don't want t'be leavin Davina, Polly, or Mr. Green. I'm stayin here!"

My eyes moistened as Evie sobbed in my arms.

"Yer t'be doin what y'told Evie! And dats dat!"

Teddy rubbed Cathy's back. "Perhaps you should have spoken to Evie before you told Davina, Cathy."

"I'm her mother, and I've been to hell and back, Teddy."

"I know you have Cathy, but so has Evie. Imagine what it was like for her when you were abducted. A small child left to fend for herself. Too frightened to trust anyone because you told her not to." Teddy embraced Cathy, and she appeared to melt in his arms. He looked over her head, expanding a warm smile to Evie and me.

"I think it's best I go back to England. And Evie, you stay here with your mother if Davina agrees." He held Cathy at arm's length and looked at her squarely, "Give yourself more time to work things out before you decide, Cathy."

Two days later, Teddy accepted a ride to the airport from Jaques and waved goodbye while Evie leaned against me, throwing him kisses.

**

Twelve months have passed since that day, and in that time, Bill was involved in a horrific accident in Italy. I shouldn't say it, but it was inevitable. I'm only grateful it was not fatal. Overjoyed to be finally free, Irene, along with their six-year-old daughter, Davina May, returned to Australia, where Bill had spent many months undergoing rehabilitation at the Melbourne Hospital. And Irene resumed her Physical Education Degree, *much to my delight*.

The human threads of Evie's past were pieced together with the help of my private investigator. Mr. Frith. First, Evie needed to know if old Jock was okay living with his daughter in Adelaide. He was. However, he and Matey would much prefer to live with Evie and Cathy. I arranged for them to arrive the following month. At this pace, I thought I'd need Buchanan House to house the gathering clan. Plus, another Jock? Although I later learned that Jock's real name is Arthur Smith. They said the two cottages I provided for them were perfect.

Cathy has replaced the retiring cook in Buchanan House, a position she loves.

Evie sent a letter of thanks to Tilly, Evie's friend and, as it turned out, her saviour. After being delighted to hear of their reunion, Tilly arrived on a bus two days later and stayed happily with us for three days.

While driving Tilly back to her home in Carlton, I listened to her lifelong struggles and smiled when she promised to return and stay longer. I could only imagine that escaping the drudgery of Tilly's day-to-day life would be a godsend.

There was a steady stream of letters from Captain Teddy, asking whether Cathy had made a decision. Evie finally responded in a loving yet diplomatic manner.

> *Thank you for everything you have*
> *done for us, Captain Teddy,*
> *but Ma and I are very happy living*
> *here with Davina and Anthony.*
> *Love, Evie and Cathy xx.*
> *P.S./You can come live with us, too,*
> *if you'd like. xx*

Anthony and I are finally a couple, and although I will never totally heal from my heartbreak, Anthony is the best medicine I could have found.

My mother slipped into the embrace of Alzheimer's and passed away six months ago. My brother Joseph returned home for Mother's funeral and made peace with me before returning to England and his wife, Madeline, a fellow science professor. Joseph left happy because I was happy, and I'd forgiven him.

Hilda remains in the Helsinki jail. I struggle to forgive her, even though she has a mental illness. What takes my mind off my personal struggle is that Felix's parents have suffered terribly, so I speak with them constantly and recently told them about Anthony. "No one could ever replace Felix," I said, "but I have finally found peace of mind and heart."

"We are truly happy for you, Davina. We wish you every happiness in your life with Anthony," said Hans and Nina.

The day I told Anthony about my once-in-a-lifetime relationship with Felix and the heartbreak of losing him, Anthony held my hand and looked deeply into my eyes, "I only have to imagine myself in your position, Davina. I don't know if I'd be strong enough to cope as you have. But I'll be happy if you love me half as much. And I hope to always be here for you."

And I hoped so, too, as I'd grown to love Anthony very much.

My nearest and dearest friends, Irene, Jacques, Charlotte, Sven, and Florence, remain ever faithful, and without their love and understanding, I would not have survived my tidal wave of grief.

I now laugh at Jacques when I asked him to give Evie riding

lessons, and he said, "Yes, of course. After all, Davina. I am *still* the best riding instructor money can buy. As your father so aptly put it." *Bless him.*

After proofreading my memoir, Anthony asked me to marry him. I said yes. Yes, to our future happiness. And yes, to giving all we can to those less fortunate so they can live life to its fullest.

Before putting my pen down, a rather spiffy-looking Italian fellow arrived unannounced two days ago and asked to speak with Cathy. After her initial shock, Cathy's fears now lay at rest. His message was simple.

"I have been sent to tell you, Mrs. Calan. Sean will no longer bother you. The boss wishes you to have a happy life with your daughter." He tipped his hat, smiled, and left in a black Lamborghini sports car.

I trust I will never need to write another memoir.

Well, not for therapy reasons.